Also by Linda Broday

Bachelors of Battle Creek
Texas Mail Order Bride
Twice a Texas Bride
Forever His Texas Bride

Men of Legend
To Love a Texas Ranger
The Heart of a Texas Cowboy
To Marry a Texas Outlaw

Texas Heroes
Knight on the Texas Plains
The Cowboy Who Came Calling
To Catch a Texas Star

Outlaw Mail Order Brides
The Outlaw's Mail Order Bride
Saving the Mail Order Bride
The Mail Order Bride's Secret
Once Upon a Mail Order Bride

Texas Redemption
Christmas in a Cowboy's Arms anthology
Longing for a Cowboy Christmas anthology

Once Upon a
MAIL ORDER
Bride

LINDA
BRODAY

sourcebooks
casablanca

Published by Sourcebooks Casablanca, an imprint of Sourcebooks
P.O. Box 4410, Naperville, Illinois 60567-4410
(630) 961-3900
sourcebooks.com

Printed and bound in the United States of America.
OPM 10 9 8 7 6 5 4 3 2 1

Author's Note

Dear Reader,

We've come to the end of Outlaw Mail Order Brides and I'm sad to say goodbye to Hope's Crossing. The people there are my friends and I hope they've become yours too. When I first began this series, I had no idea of the heart these men and women possessed. They're the kind of folk you want beside you when trouble comes. They don't run. They stand and fight until they defeat the threat. These are my kind of people.

Through the books, the town has flourished and grown, and businesses have flooded in. Hope's Crossing is a place where hope lives, memories are made, and friendships are forged. Oh man, I would love to live there.

I hope that I've given you a different way to view outlaws. The good ones are just like us and want the same things—families, love, and a place where they can grow old in peace. They lived in a very interesting time, when a man could be an outlaw one day and a lawman the next, or vice versa. It depended on the circumstances and where a man happened to be. Men like Wyatt Earp, Doc Holliday, Wild Bill Hickok, and so many others found themselves labeled both outlaw and lawman during their lifetimes. The line often blurred. But what these men all shared, right alongside my characters in this series, is that they burned for justice and to right wrongs, no matter how they had to do it. Most of the time it wasn't pretty.

I've saved the best of the series for last. You'll finally get to know the kind of man Ridge Steele is, and I think you'll like his honor and courage. The strength of Adeline Jancy staggers me. She's just the sort of woman to give him the love he yearns for. So put your feet in the stirrups and hold on tight. It's going to be quite a ride.

Happy Reading!

Linda Broday

One

THE SUDDEN BANG OF A HEAVY PRISON DOOR ECHOED LIKE A rifle shot down a long, dimly lit hallway. Adeline Jancy flinched as though struck, her hand clenching tighter around the letters from Ridge Steele, the man she'd agreed to marry upon release. In her other hand, she gripped a pitiful burlap bag that contained all her earthly possessions.

A nearby door opened, and she blinked at the unaccustomed light, her eyes watering from the glare.

For three long and dismal years, she'd lived in solitary confinement below the prison, in silence so complete that she could hear the twitch of a rat's whiskers a yard away. She'd thought of this moment, dreamed about it for so long. Freedom. A chance to start over. But now that it was here, was she truly ready? Her knees buckled.

The squeak of shoes met her ears, and a heavyset woman appeared.

"Jancy, it's me—Nettie Mae."

Now, the door to her cell no longer between them, Addie finally saw the face of the woman who'd brought her food each day. Middle-aged and gray-haired, Nettie had kind eyes. Tears gathered in her own eyes as she hugged her sole friend.

Nettie kept talking, the first time Addie'd heard her speak louder than a whisper. "You gotta listen and listen good. Two men are waitin' at the front gate to grab you when you leave the prison. I 'spect you know what they want."

Yes, she knew.

Addie'd expected her release to be difficult and Nettie confirmed it. During the night, she'd played the scenarios over in her mind countless times. She might get shot, she might die.

She might meet a fate even worse than death. But if so, she would face it with her head held high. Not cowering in fear.

Gas lamps held in brackets lining the walls every few yards emitted loud sizzles that sounded like thousands of flying insects. An unpleasant odor permeated the air.

"Mr. Luke overheard those men. He's going to catch you before you reach the door and take you out the back way. You're gonna be fine. I can tell Mr. Luke's a right good man."

Addie's heart pounded. Gonna be fine—if the warden didn't stop Luke on his way in. If the ones waiting for her didn't get wind of a change in procedure. If she and Luke weren't spotted and followed. Her release involved too many ifs.

She braced herself, determined. Now was not the time to panic. After all these years, she had to finally take control of her life. Sweat lined her palms. Her welcoming committee wanted what she knew—and she'd take that to her grave first. Ezekiel Jancy be damned! She'd defied him before and paid dearly. Everything she'd suffered was worth it if it meant that a small innocent stayed safe from Ezekiel's iron will.

Her pulse throbbed in her neck and she wet her lips. She took Nettie's hands and wished with all her might to find words to express her gratitude. She forced air up to make herself speak, but not a peep emerged. Prison, trauma, and solitude combined with her rusty, weak throat stole her ability to speak. Before her stood the one person in the world she longed to thank, and she couldn't utter a sound. She blinked hard and stuffed the letters into her burlap.

"I know, child." Nettie patted her shoulder awkwardly with one misshapen hand. "Save your strength. I'm glad I could help." Nettie turned to walk away, and Addie reached for her.

"You go on now and marry that handsome outlaw. Leave your memories at the door and have a good life far away from this hell." Nettie sniffled. "I'll die in here, but you're getting out. Make every second you have left count for something good." She gave Addie a little push. "Go. Mr. Luke's waitin'."

Her heart bursting with conflicting emotion, Addie took

a deep breath. She walked down the hallway toward free-dom—or death, if this didn't go right.

At every noise, she jumped, her nerves like fine glass ready to shatter. A few feet from the door, a tall man appeared quietly from a side room. Dressed as a cowboy, he had the coloring of a Spaniard and wore a soft, dove-gray hat. Long dark hair hung to his shoulders.

"Miss Jancy, I'm Luke Legend. Trust me to get you out of here. I won't let anyone harm you." He relieved her of the pitiful burlap bag.

Without waiting for her to nod, he took her arm and led her a different way, down a maze of corridors. Doubts jumped into her head like circus fleas on a dog—where was he taking her? But instinct and Nettie's soft assurance urged her to trust him, and she really had little choice.

Finally, they reached a door and emerged into blinding sun-light. She threw her hands over her eyes to block the bright pain.

"Un momento. I prepared for something like this."

She heard a rustling sound, and a second later he draped a soft, clean cloth around her head. Ahhh, blessed relief. She could've wept at the kindness of this man who'd thought of everything.

"There. You can open your eyes now."

She peered through her fingers and saw she wore a black veil. Again, she tried to speak, to thank him, but nothing came.

"Hurry. When you don't show up at the front door, those men will be onto us. They look desperate." Though Luke's voice held an urgent tone, the comforting hand on her back imparted trust that he knew the safest way out of this.

She had to trot to keep up with his long strides and was out of breath by the time they reached a horse and buggy waiting in the shade of a tree. He helped her in and went around to his side, strapping on a gun belt and holster.

Moments later, as they careened from the prison, shots rang out behind them.

"Get down as low as you can." Luke drew his revolver, leaned out, and returned fire.

Hoofbeats pounded on the hard-packed road, and she could scarcely tell the sound apart from her frantic heartbeat. Each time they made a curve, the buggy came near to overturning. Addie hung on for her very life, praying to see the town of Austin coming up ahead. They should be close. If memory served, the prison had only been a mile or so out of town. But it had been so long since she'd been brought to the prison, and the years could have blurred the details in her mind.

Though she didn't rise to look, the pursuers mounts sounded upon them, and a flurry of shots kept her head lowered. One round barely missed her, splintering the wood just above. Luke yelled for his poor horse to go faster. The ground sped past until finally the sound of the men behind began to fade.

They pulled into Austin at long last, but Luke slowed little. He wove their buggy in and around the other wagons and horses before pulling to a head-jerking stop.

"Come on." Luke lifted her from the overworked buggy and set her down. Taking her hand, he pulled her into a mercantile. They raced through the store and went out the back.

Addie struggled to keep up, while dozens of curious pairs of eyes stared, probably wondering about the woman in the black veil. They must think she was late to a funeral. Luke paused outside to glance around. Wrinkles between his eyes deepened in thought, and he muttered something in Spanish that sounded dire.

Two men entered the other end of the alley. Even from the distance, she knew neither was her father. They must be on Ezekiel's payroll instead.

Or… Her throat caught. Maybe one was the dead girl's father. He could be after Addie as well, seeking revenge and his grandson.

Gunshots splintered the wood of the back door, and hard pieces of metal and wood landed around her as the men gave chase.

Luke grabbed her hand again, and they ran back onto the street, dodging passersby on the boardwalk.

She gasped for air, and her lungs burned. Her weak muscles and too-large shoes added to the struggle of keeping up. Plus, being short made for a whole lot of discomfort when the man pulling you had long legs.

"I'm sorry," Luke panted. "Keep going. I've got to get you safe."

The busy street helped a great deal in losing the two men. They wove over, around, and through tight places, running until Luke finally spied the Houston & Texas Central Railroad depot ahead with a train sitting on the tracks.

"There! We've got to make that train. With any luck, it's going to Fort Worth."

Hope sprang up inside her, and her heart leaped. Maybe this would be their escape.

White smoke billowed up around the steam engine, and the monstrous hunk of metal began to inch down the tracks, picking up speed. *Oh no!*

"We can make it if we run," Luke shouted.

She gathered some breath and put wings to her feet. She sprinted along beside him, her very life depending on her ability to keep running. They arrived as the last four cars were pulling past the platform.

Gunshots sounded somewhere close, and Luke ducked behind a wall. "I don't know how they found us, but here's the plan. Both of us can't make it, so I'm putting you on. If I'm right, this train's going to Fort Worth. I'll wire my wife, Josie, and she'll meet you there. I'll follow when I can."

Beads of sweat rose on her face and trickled down her back. Her hands trembled as fear set in at the thought of being on her own again. Trains terrified her, especially without Luke to help. She'd never done it before, nor been in a strange city alone.

The caboose was about to pass them. Oh Lord, she'd have to jump!

What if she missed and landed under those big wheels?

Luke pressed some bills into her palm. "This'll pay for your ticket and anything else you might need. Ask anyone if you have questions. I'll stop those bastards from getting on."

Oh Lord, oh Lord, oh Lord! She couldn't do this.

She barely had a second before he took her hand, and they bolted alongside the train, now moving at a pretty good clip.

Run faster!

A bullet slammed into the wood at her feet, and others plinked against the side of the iron car.

Please don't let them hit me. Please don't let them hit me.

Her hammering heart leaped into her throat, and her mouth—as parched as a piece of sun-dried bread—wouldn't let her swallow.

One second before the caboose cleared the platform, Luke yelled, "Jump!"

As she did, he pushed from behind. The heel of one shoe caught on the edge of the metal landing of the caboose. The ground underneath passed in a blur as she used all her strength to pull herself upright.

She raised her gaze in time to see one of their pursuers holding Luke's arms behind him while the other thug drove a fist into his stomach. She sagged against the metal railing.

Luke Legend had been shot at, chased across the countryside, and was taking a beating—all for a woman he'd never laid eyes on before today. Gratitude burst inside her for the gift she'd been given. But at such cost.

They sped down the tracks. She was on a train going who knew where, with everything she owned in the world left behind in Luke Legend's buggy, the most cherished of which were Ridge's letters. It didn't matter though. She'd read them so often, she could recite them. They'd found a place in her heart.

Addie glanced around. For now, she was safe and on her way to finally meet him.

❧

Ridge Steele walked down a dark street near Fort Worth's Hell's Half Acre long past dark. The week's ride from Hope's Crossing had worn him out. But he'd arrived in time to collect the books the schoolmaster, Todd Denver, had desperately needed for the school term to begin. If they didn't arrive,

Denver would have to move on and the school year would have to be canceled. No parent wanted that.

With the freighters on strike and no end in sight, they'd had no way of getting the books there, and as the mayor, it had fallen to Ridge to make the trip after them. The telegram from Luke had said that Ridge's bride wouldn't arrive for another week or so, due to needing some recovery time, so he'd had nothing holding him back from making the trip.

Ridge paused and leaned against the gaslight outside the Sundance Saloon and debated going inside. From the raucous yells, it sounded a little rougher than he liked. He gazed up at the stars and found he was grateful for the extra time Luke had given him. The idea of marrying a woman he'd never met could be daunting. Who knew what sort of disposition Adeline Jancy would have? His friends had all gotten lucky with their mail-order brides, but there could always be that one to spoil the string.

The lights from his hotel beckoned at the far end of the street. He tugged his worn Stetson lower over his brow, pushed away from the gaslight, and strolled toward his bed. Tomorrow, he'd start for home.

The thumbnail moon didn't hold back the darkness, the night offering more than a dozen places to hide. This wasn't the safest part of town, and he regretted taking the shortcut. As usual, when away from the protection of the outlaw town of Hope's Crossing, a heightened sense of awareness tingled beneath his skin. Blame that on the price on his head and too many narrow escapes.

Two figures drew his attention, moving erratically about twenty yards ahead. At first, he thought they were drunks holding each other up. But upon taking a harder look, he noticed one was a man, dragging a woman by one arm toward a dark alley.

Before he could wrestle her into the space, the woman managed to get to her feet. She walloped the man about the head and shoulders with a shoe until he turned her loose. The varmint tried to reach for her again only to have her sidestep his grasp. She lunged, grabbing his shirt, then before he could blink, slapped him across the face with the shoe. The sharp sound ricocheted up and down the row of dark buildings.

"You little slut!" the man shouted, backhanding her. "I oughta kill you!"

Without a word, the petite woman kept hitting him. Her hefty companion, or accoster, whichever he might turn out to be, cowered on the ground. Ridge chuckled. She had more grit, more fight in her than ten women.

But when she faltered, the man leaped up and grabbed her again. "I'll show you what happens to someone with your temper, you bitch." He put a hand around her throat and lifted her high in the air, her feet dangling above the ground.

Ridge pulled one of his twin Colts and rushed forward. He jammed the barrel of the gun to the back of the man's head and snarled, "Turn her loose and let her down easy."

The man's shoulders tensed. The piece of horse dung released her and slowly turned. "This ain't none of your affair."

"I'm making it mine." Ridge held the pistol on the man and made a half turn. "Are you all right, ma'am?"

Anger filled the scrappy woman's eyes. She nodded and jerked her shoe from the ground, holding on to the side of the building for balance while sliding her foot into it. Though her bottom lip trembled, she didn't cry. She didn't appear to be a working girl, her clothes far too simple and plain for someone who sold her body. She looked young, and too soft to have been part of that life. Although he couldn't tell what color her eyes were, he was struck by the shape and size and the fringe of black lashes framing them like expensive Spanish lace.

Some women were only pretty in the dark, and he'd seen plenty of those, but he got the feeling she'd also be pretty in daylight.

He softened his voice. "Are you lost, ma'am?"

Another pert nod. He got the impression that if she'd had something more than a shoe to fight with, she might not have needed his help at all.

"Keep going west on this street, and you'll get out of this

neighborhood. Or tell me where you're headed, and I'll take you myself."

"I saw her first!" the man yelled. "Me an' her was gonna get acquainted."

"There isn't a 'you and her,' you imbecile. Got that?" Ridge twisted the man's arm behind his back and returned his Colt to the holster. "Bother her, or any other woman, again, and there won't even be a 'you' anymore." He shoved the man against the side of the building and was rewarded with a loud grunt.

The poor excuse of humanity shook his head to clear it of drunken cobwebs then stumbled off, cursing the woman, Ridge, and himself. But by the time Ridge swung around, the lady with gumption had disappeared. After looking up and down the street for her, he had little choice but to pray she reached her destination without further incident.

The hotel beckoned again and he set off, his thoughts remaining on the silent angel who'd lost her way.

Two

THE GOOD BOOK TOUTED THAT THE TRUTH WOULD SET A MAN free.

Ridge Steele snorted. Not when lies served people better. Most believed whatever they wanted. The truth hadn't aided him any when he'd desperately needed a good helping.

The swift fall from preacher to outlaw had rocked him to his core and turned his life into one he didn't recognize. He winced at the memories of the unjust accusation, the crime that had driven him from his faith. He couldn't bring himself even to say the ugly words.

Memories swarmed like a hive of bees inside his head. The dead man lying with his head on a rock. The mob's angry yells, the girl's ripped dress, the rope whirring out of the darkness, the tree. No questions asked. No thought to his innocence.

No ears to hear the truth.

The late August sun beat down, but the sweat wasn't entirely the summer's blame. He raised a trembling hand and shook away the images. It did no good to dig up old bones. His bride would arrive at some point today, and he had too much to do that didn't include combating old nerves. New nerves took priority. He knew even less about how to be a husband than he now knew about giving sermons.

What kind of woman was Adeline Jancy? Would she, too, be quick to judge, quick to anger, quick to believe the worst? Her letters seemed sweet and caring, but he hadn't spoken of his past and didn't intend to ever talk about it. He'd only told her he was an outlaw, a wanted man. Maybe she was hiding things as well. What did he know about her? Only that she'd been released from prison two weeks ago and that Luke

Legend, the bride procurer, had picked her up and would bring her to Hope's Crossing.

What crime had she committed? He couldn't imagine anything that would have been bad enough to land her behind bars for three years, but she'd only said they'd talk about it when she arrived.

Ridge batted a pesky fly away from his face and stared toward the town's entrance between the high cliffs.

"She'll be here." The quiet statement came from Clay Colby, his best friend and the founder of Hope's Crossing. Clay's dream had brought an outlaw hideout up from ashes to a thriving community, complete with a telegraph office, hotel, and stage line service—among most anything else you could want.

"I suppose. Just nervous, I guess." He pounded a nail into a board on the new bank they were building.

"Ridge, unless you want to tell her, she doesn't need to know. I certainly won't breathe a word, and no one else is aware of what happened five years ago."

"You know, I still dream about that night and wake up in a cold sweat." Ridge glanced at his friend. "If you hadn't come along when you did and freed me of that lynch mob, I wouldn't be here. I can't remember if I ever thanked you."

Clay grinned. "Sure you did—many times over. I couldn't have built this town without you. We've fought bad-to-the-bone seeds and trouble together for a long time."

"Yep, we have." Ridge squinted at the town's opening again beneath his dusty Stetson. "What did you and Tally talk about in the early days of your marriage?" Tally Shannon had also been a mail-order bride, and he remembered how rocky those first months had been. Clay had moved out for a while to give her time to adjust.

Somehow, he'd make this work with Adeline. He only hoped it wouldn't require moving out of his own house.

"Who said we talked?" Clay grinned then grew serious. "Just relax and don't bark at her. Be gentle and listen to what she says—and what she doesn't. You'll be fine."

"I hope so." Ridge pounded the board extra hard. "I haven't been with too many women, none that I didn't have to pay. They scare me. I'm afraid I'll accidentally say something wrong and she'll run off in tears."

Clay chuckled. "They're not as delicate as you think. In fact, women are pretty damn tough."

"I can't help but wonder what her crime was."

"Her situation might be similar to yours."

"Maybe." True, she *could've* been accused of something she hadn't done. It seemed to happen often enough.

A wagon came through the entrance into town, drawing Ridge's attention. For a moment, his heart thudded hard against his ribs and his mouth turned to cotton. But it was only Sid and Martha Truman. If he made it through this day, it would be a miracle.

But then he'd have the night to sweat over. What did a man say to a stranger who expected conversation—and certain other things? How did a man sleep beside someone he'd never laid eyes on before today? He groaned. Why in the hell had he ever let Luke Legend talk him into this?

Or rather, Luke's pretty wife. Lord, Josie could wear down an iron steam engine.

Ridge let out a worried breath and picked up another board. One answer that he couldn't argue with was the deep loneliness that gnawed at him until he felt like screaming. There came a day in most men's lives, he supposed, when a fellow got tired of listening to his own heartbeat in the dead of night and longed for companionship. A gentle touch.

And a chance to keep his name alive, to pass it down.

That was him. Two months ago, he'd looked around at all his friends, married with a passel of kids between them and happier than he'd ever seen. He'd envied that.

"Tally was held in an asylum for a while—I recall she had a lot of damage from that. Do you think prison would be part and parcel about the same?"

Clay kept his attention on the tobacco he tapped in a line on the thin paper. "I suppose the two places would bear similarity. No doubt Miss Jancy will need a lot of patience and care."

"Yeah."

Tait Trinity rode by on his blue roan and waved. He was another man who'd listened to Luke. He'd taken a mail-order bride last fall while he still had a five-thousand-dollar bounty on his head, and from all appearances, he and Melanie Dunbar had made it work. But then, he'd later gotten a pardon from the governor. Ridge had no hope for that unless the girl who'd lied, a woman now, came forward and told the truth.

Besides, since then, he had killed others in self-defense. He had to answer for those, one way or another.

Ridge picked up another board. "Tell me again why we're building this bank and don't yet have a banker."

"One's coming next month." Clay held a nail to a plank and slammed it into place with one powerful strike of the hammer. "My understanding is it's a father and daughter, and they're traveling by stage from San Francisco."

"A bank is a sure sign of progress. I wouldn't have given you two cents for our chances when you first got the idea to build a town here. Now look at it. We've expanded homes outside of the canyon and have almost every kind of business imaginable." Ridge pushed back his hat. "Tell me—are you satisfied now, or do you yearn for more?"

Clay licked the edge of his cigarette paper to seal it and patted his pocket for a match. "There are a few things I wish we had. A library would be nice, and an opera house, but I'm satisfied." A match found, he lit the cigarette. "Still, fire terrifies me. This could all turn to ash in a matter of hours."

Just like Ridge's life. One minute, a man could have everything he needed, and the next, it could be stripped away in a flash like it was never there.

"Are you happy being mayor?" Smoke curled around Clay's head.

"No. I wish we'd elect a new one. It's time to give up the job." Ridge lifted another board and placed it against the frame.

"And do what? Go back to the ministry?"

Ridge sucked a sharp breath between his teeth. "I'll never preach again. God doesn't listen to a man like me. Besides, the church already has Brother Paul."

From the corner of his eye, he noticed a slow-moving wagon coming into town. A second quick look told him that a man and two women occupied it, and they were heading directly for him. The spit dried in Ridge's mouth. His hand trembled around the hammer he gripped.

He stared as it kept coming, unable to look away. Damn. This was it.

"Nice day, amigos." Luke Legend set the brake and jumped down from the wagon. "What are you building?"

Ridge glanced at the woman sitting next to Josie. A black lace scarf covered her head and obscured most of her face. She seemed to huddle deeper into the folds, as though wishing to escape his notice.

"It'll be a bank," Ridge muttered, and reached to shake Luke's hand. "Good to see you. Miss Josie, how's life treating you?"

Josie gave a shake of her blond hair and replied with an infectious smile. "Real good except for being homesick. We left little Elena Rose at the ranch with Stoker this time, so I'm missing her something fierce."

Ridge started around the wagon to help his bride down and introduce himself when Luke steered him away from the others.

Luke kept his voice low. "There's something you need to know before you meet Adeline."

His chest tightened. Was she disfigured? Was that the reason for the veil? "What's that?"

"She can't speak."

Three

SHOCK JOLTED RIDGE. "WHAT DO YOU MEAN SHE CAN'T TALK? Can't for a medical reason? Did someone cut out her tongue?"

He'd heard how bad prison was and had once met a convict who shook and jerked all the time. Someone had used him as a test subject for a new device, rigged up with paper soaked in salt water and something to do with zinc and copper.

Ridge searched his memory to recall if Adeline had said anything in the few letters they'd exchanged. But no, there'd been no mention of this.

"Nothing like that," Luke assured him. "It's more like she won't try. The doctor at the prison said they kept her in isolation for the whole three years as part of her punishment. With no one to talk to, she seems to have forgotten how. Anyway, she's going to require a lot of understanding." Luke shifted, and the silver conchas running up the sides of his black pant legs flashed in the sunlight. "There's more."

Good Lord, what else? What did that prison do to her?

"Someone's hunting her."

A wave of fury crashed over Ridge. His voice held a sharp edge. "Who? Why?"

"Don't know, but Adeline does. I was waiting for her at the prison and overheard two men talking about her. One said the best time to grab her was when she came out and that the money for the job would keep them well off." Luke grinned. "I took her out the back way."

"Dammit!" Ridge studied the faint bruises on his friend's jaw that said he'd had to fight to keep Adeline safe. Anger rose. Ridge clenched his fist. Whoever wanted to harm her would now have to deal with him.

"When they realized what we'd done, they chased us. I

was barely able to get her onto a train to Fort Worth." Luke paused. "Wish I knew more."

"Makes two of us."

"The question is...do you still want to marry a hunted woman? One who might never talk to you?"

Here was an excuse if he wanted to take it. It was unlikely that anyone would fault him for it. Only one thing wrong with that—he wasn't happy the way he was. He needed more from life than merely existing from one day to the next. And what about Adeline? His rejection might finish the process of destroying her. Plus, she needed protection—and that was something he at least knew how to give.

"Yes, I'll marry her—if she'll have me."

Luke slapped his back. "Then I'll introduce you, and we'll plan a wedding."

Ridge took some nervous breaths and matched Luke's stride as they moved toward the wagon. Josie reached for Adeline's hand and squeezed, then Luke helped her down. She didn't lift her head. Ridge, well over six feet, towered above the slim, petite woman.

Adeline wore a simple dress of blue calico that hugged in all the right places. Ridge grew warm thinking about running his hands over those curves. The strands of blond hair poking from the heavy black scarf were golden in color, deeper and richer than Josie's lighter shade.

Luke put an arm around her. "Miss Jancy, meet your bridegroom, Ridge Steele. I personally vouch for his character. I've fought by his side and know he's a good man to have around. He'll fight for you until you're strong enough to do it yourself."

She stood rooted in silence. Ridge wished he could see her face.

"That's a promise, Miss Adeline." Ridge cursed his suddenly raspy voice. She struck him as a wounded, exhausted, little wren, battered by heavy storms. "Thank you for coming. I'm only an outlaw, a wanted man with little to my name. But everything I have is yours—if you want it."

She lifted her head and removed the black scarf. Kissed by the sunshine, her hair curled around her shoulders and flowed down her back. Emerald eyes stared up at him, framed by thick, dark lashes, and a jolt raced through him.

The brave, determined woman he'd seen under a Fort Worth night.

Ridge sucked in a breath. He'd been right in thinking she'd be pretty in the daylight. By God, she was beautiful. Although Luke, Clay, and Josie stood right there, they'd somehow melted away. Adeline was the only person he could see. Shoulders squared, her determined gaze bored into him, and her chin raised a notch. Despite everything, she had fight left in her. He'd probably find out how much if he didn't watch it.

Did she recognize him as well? Her expression didn't indicate if she did. But then it'd been dark that night, and his Stetson had shielded most of his face.

He brought her hand to his lips and cleared his throat. "Miss Adeline, I'd be honored if you'd be my wife. Will you accept my proposal?"

One jerk of her head confirmed her answer.

"Is tomorrow too soon? Or would you rather wait a few days?"

Panic crossed her face. Josie calmly handed her paper and pencil, and Adeline wrote, *"Tomorrow."*

"Good. I have a room for you at the Diamond Bessie Hotel. Let's get you settled, then we'll nail down the details." Ridge and Luke moved to the back of the wagon and lifted out two trunks. The small one was brand-new and would hold far too much for someone who'd just obtained freedom.

When Ridge lifted an eyebrow, Luke explained, "The ladies did some shopping."

Adeline would've needed everything, he imagined, since people didn't usually come out of prison with much more than the clothes on their backs.

As he lifted her small trunk on his shoulder, thoughts ran through his head. Ridge now had a purpose and someone who needed him. That was reason enough to marry Adeline Jancy.

~~~

Adeline stood with Josie, her gaze following the men as they headed to the hotel next door. Ridge hadn't disappointed her—at least not yet. Like his letters, he truly seemed to care what she thought. He'd already given her choices. Three years ago, the law had stripped her of the ability to make choices even about the smallest things. She'd lived in a world of silence that was so loud in her head, she often thought she'd go mad. Maybe she had, to some degree. In an instant, and for three long years, she'd become a mere number instead of a person.

One bang of a gavel had left her utterly alone. Unloved. Terrified.

The family she would never again claim became strangers who stared with questioning eyes and muttered words of hate.

But then, even before prison, she'd never had much freedom to make her own choices. Her father had seen to that. "Pray without ceasing" had been drilled into her from age five.

At first, Ridge's former occupation as a preacher had given her much worry. She didn't want another aloof, rigid lord and master like Ezekiel Jancy. But through Ridge's letters, she'd found him refreshingly different. He'd written at length about his distaste for those who enslaved others.

As your husband, I vow to never force you to my will. I don't hold with those tactics, he'd written.

She blinked at the bright sunlight, the sensation still making her eyes water even after a little more than two weeks. Ridge cut quite an intriguing figure. He walked with ease, his long legs encased in denim, twin Colts hanging low from his hips. Dark brown hair touched his shoulders, a bit unkempt as one might expect of an outlaw. But his sensitive amber eyes had told her the most.

They spoke of deep hurt, of long, endless nights of the soul, and of biting disappointment and frustration. Maybe at his circumstances. At this point, she had no way of knowing.

He'd never revealed in his letters what'd happened to change him into an outlaw. Adeline only got the impression he hadn't left his ministry willingly. Something or someone had forced him out. From the start, he'd been quite honest about his current life as an outlaw and spoke of being hunted, of waiting for the agony of the bullet that would end his life.

She knew about such a wait. Only hers had been for her body and soul to be set free. She was halfway there.

Luke and Josie had visited the prison after hearing of her plight from Nettie Mae, and after being denied access to Addie, they'd sent messages again through her kindly friend. They'd assured her that only an outlaw like Ridge Steele could provide the safety she needed. Thus, she began her correspondence with the wanted man. Addie glanced at him through the hotel window. It appeared they might be correct. He had the bearing and manner of a man who, based on that critical first impression, had the strength and courage to stand up to anyone.

"Shall we?" Josie linked her arm through Adeline's, and they strolled up the hotel steps. "Ridge is a kind man with a caring heart, and he certainly is handsome. Oh my goodness! I get tongue-tied when I'm around him, and my brain doesn't want to work right. I'm scared Luke will find out and be upset, so I try to avoid the man." Josie laughed, paused a moment, and changed the subject. "My dear, we'll stay a few days to make sure you're all right."

Adeline wished she could speak. She'd tell Josie that she'd chosen to marry Ridge because she liked what he'd said in his letters, not because of how handsome he was.

> *Life is 10 percent made up of what happens to you. Everything else is how well you cope with the events. Don't waste time being bitter. A mistake is not a life sentence. We learn, we grow, and we move on—hopefully as better people.*

Those words had spoken to her. She would try each day to make Ridge proud of her and make sure he had no regrets for marrying a convict. As for her, she had no qualms about tying herself to an outlaw. No one else could keep her safer than someone who lived free of rigid rules and social norms.

He'd spoken of his own principles and rules he'd set down for
himself, complete with lines drawn in the sand that he'd never
cross. She shared her personal conviction with him that those
were much more important than the dictates of others.

Before going inside, Adeline stood on the hotel porch for
a moment and gazed out at Hope's Crossing. The town sat
in a canyon rimmed with high rock walls and only one way
in or out. Luke said it had once been an outlaw hideout and
very easily defended. Now businesses lined one side of the
wide town square like staunch soldiers, with dwellings on
the other.

A group of children played chase, and two dogs barked
alongside them. Two women walked together, talking and
laughing, while another hung wash out on a line. A tall windmill rose next to a church, which was surrounded by a white
picket fence.

The calm and peace floating in the air seeped deep down
into her bones.

Here she would rest and heal. Then she'd make sure no one
found the stolen child. The motherless boy would be three
years old now, still vulnerable. She'd die before she gave him
away. And she very nearly had landed in a grave. She shivered
as fragments of the nightmare passed through her mind. If she
did nothing else in life, she would keep him safe.

Adeline pulled her thoughts back to the view. One thing
seemed curiously missing—the public whipping post. Maybe,
hopefully, these people were more civilized than where she'd
come from. She allowed herself a snort. Funny the differences
in people's perceptions of a civilized society.

These simple people in Hope's Crossing seemed content
with what little they had. Josie said they were kind and welcoming, not closed off and ruled by suspicion and fear. Time
would tell the truth.

Painful memories swirled and twisted the picture in front of
her into horrible scenes of suffering and despair.

Adeline shuddered and took the images inward into her
hiding place. Ridge had assured her that the people of Hope's

Crossing would open welcoming arms, for each person here had a checkered past and now focused only on the future. But how much could she believe? It would take actions to convince her.

Her whole life had been built on terror—where the only way to survive was not seeing, not hearing, not feeling one single blessed thing.

Only when it had come down to her moment of truth, she hadn't been able to keep her head buried in the sand.

The days and months ahead would decide what kind of future she had. Yet how could she get acquainted with the women when she couldn't speak? A frisson of worry rose and knotted in her stomach.

"Coming?" Josie asked.

Adeline nodded and went inside. The hotel was nice, but then according to Luke, it had been built only three years prior. She liked the bright, airy feel, the high tin ceiling and pretty wallpaper.

Ridge collected a key from the clerk and strode toward her. "You're on the second floor. Lead the way, and I'll carry your trunk."

With a nod, she turned to the stairs, and he followed. At the landing, he told her to turn right to Room 205. A few moments later, she stood inside, glancing around. The room was inviting, a handful of wild red roses set in a vase on a small table. A pretty quilt of pink and yellow covered the bed, and it looked very comfortable, a nice change from the hard ground she'd slept on during the journey and the cold slab she'd called a bed for the last three years.

She moved to the flowers and lifted a rose to her nose. A long-forgotten memory flooded over her. A cool arbor. Wild summer roses that shielded her hiding place—the refuge she'd often escaped to when things became unbearable. She bit her trembling lip and fought to swallow past the lump.

Ridge set down her trunk and took a wide stance. He seemed a bit uncomfortable in her presence, jerking off his hat and holding it in his hands. She watched him from beneath lowered lashes. "I picked the flowers. I hope you like them."

Surprised by his thoughtfulness, Adeline smiled and reached for her paper and pencil. *"Wild roses are my favorite. Thank you."*

"You're welcome. I thought you might need some cheer." Ridge glanced around the room as though checking to make sure it was suitable before turning his attention back to her. "It's not home, but it'll do for one night. Luke and Josie are just down the hall."

She nodded, walked to the french doors that opened onto a small balcony, and stepped out. After her dank underground cell, she couldn't get enough fresh air. A large overhang shaded her from the sun.

Ridge followed, crushing the hat he still held. His large presence frightened her, at least a little. He could knock her across the room, break bones if he chose. It would take time to trust, time to heal, time to know his heart. Though he'd gently courted her through his letters, his tender words were just words in the end. Ezekiel was most adept at using words to wound.

But something in this outlaw reminded her of a tall oak with thick branches stretching out, shielding her from harm.

Tense muscles in her neck and shoulders relaxed. This path felt right and good.

At least for now. Time would tell for sure.

"I have no idea what you're thinking, but it has to be very difficult to marry someone you've never met. I'll give you all the time you need." His voice was low, deep. "I've never forced any woman to my will, and I won't start with you."

Adeline swung around and met his gaze. The lines in his face had deepened, and she wished she could smooth away the worry, to say that she'd find a way somehow to be a real wife. Only she had no idea what that looked like. She'd never seen a marriage worth modeling hers after, with the possible exception of Luke and Josie's. They seemed to have the right idea, but she'd known them only a short time. People often projected misconceptions.

Maybe Ridge did too, and would make her a fool for trusting so quickly. Yet believing in something seemed better than this yawning, lifeless hole inside that tried to swallow her.

After several beats of silence, Ridge cleared his throat. Shadows filled his eyes. "I don't know what you expect of me. Hell, I don't even know what to expect myself. But I vow never to raise my hand to you in anger. Our marriage will be one based on respect, not fear."

She nodded but wished with all her heart she could unlock her words and tell him that she could take anything, as long as he didn't hurt her.

But of course, she just stood there like some mute.

"I'm sure you have a lot of questions. I built a house for you just outside of town. I hope I thought of everything, but if you need something else, I'll get it. I'd like to take you there after you've rested and we've discussed the wedding plans. Would you like that?"

Her nod brought a gentle smile to his face that revealed a flash of white teeth. Josie was right—he was handsome. She'd be tongue-tied too, if she could remember how to form words in the first place.

Ridge sauntered toward the door, his gait loose and easy. "You don't seem to recall, but we've met once before—in Fort Worth. It was dark, though, and you were having quite a tussle with a drunk bent on spending time with you." He swung around with a teasing grin. "I'd like some advice about where to best wallop a person with a shoe for maximum damage."

Surprise swept through her. She studied him, wracking her brain. The mention of the shoe jogged her memory. When she'd gotten off the train, she'd gone the wrong direction and wound up on that dark street in the clutches of that disgusting drunk.

So Ridge had been her savior. He'd handled the inebriated fool with ease.

She covered the space between them and reached for the paper and pencil on the table. She wrote: *Thank you for coming along and freeing me from that wretch's hands. He terrified me.*

"You certainly didn't look scared. Just mad as a soaked cat."

"Looks are often deceiving. What were you doing in Fort Worth?"

"Picking up schoolbooks for the teacher. The freight haulers are on strike and we had no other way to get them here."

Images of her old one-room school crossed her mind. She'd loved being a teacher. Until...

She grabbed hold of the table, her legs wobbly.

Ridge steadied her. "Anything wrong?"

"I'm just a little tired."

"Then I'll leave you to rest. Josie will come get you soon." He gently kissed her cheek and left.

Adeline stood rooted to the spot, her hand covering the place his lips had lightly pressed. Tears gathered in her eyes. Twenty years old and no one had ever kissed her before—not on the cheek, or hand, or lips.

The sensation of his warm mouth on her skin would be enough for a whole new type of dream.

Ridge Steele had made a contract with her, and he seemed a man committed to keeping his word. Still, she'd watch him carefully. Some men lied. Tomorrow she would stand at his side and become his wife, and she'd brave every bit of adversity thereafter planted next to him—come rain, come shine, or come the hereafter.

Because that's what a good woman did. God so help her, she wouldn't let others ever define her again. Despite being locked away, she was decent and *good*.

❧

Midafternoon, Ridge sat with Adeline in the hotel lobby. Luke and Josie joined their conversation, and he was grateful for their help because he didn't know beans about weddings. Or, more importantly, silent brides.

Adeline sat with eyes lowered, hands clutched in her lap. He admired the curve of her delicate jaw, the sweep of her dark lashes, and a determined tilt to her chin. Despite her silence, *timid* was not a word he'd use to describe her. Adeline Jancy had strength.

After a little small talk with Josie and Luke, Ridge turned to his prospective bride. "This is your wedding, Adeline. What do you want? Would you like it in the church?"

Panic crossed her green eyes. She gave him a definite shake of her head. *No.*

"All right. The church is out, and frankly I'm relieved. We're not formal people."

"Ridge, how about up on the bluff overlooking the town?" Luke suggested. "Quite a few marriages have happened up there, and it's a beautiful spot."

Hope formed on Adeline's pretty features, and she nodded.

"All right, the bluff it is. Noon tomorrow?"

Adeline agreed.

So far so good. A list formed in Ridge's head. Find a wedding ring. Dig out his best suit. Polish his boots. "I'll make arrangements with Brother Paul."

Another question—this one quite delicate—would require some stealth. When they rose, Ridge pulled Josie aside. "Does Adeline have a dress? The small trunk I carried up to her room wasn't large enough to hold much more than a few changes of clothes."

"Relax. This isn't our first wedding to see to." Her furious whisper told Ridge she was offended at the notion that she and Luke would let Adeline be embarrassed. "Luke and I bought her a dress. It's in our room."

"How was I to know that?"

"We've overseen how many marriages in this town?"

"Quite a few I suppose."

"And how many brides appeared without a dress?"

Ridge frowned, a little perturbed by her tone. "None."

Josie's eyes narrowed. "I rest my case."

"I apologize, Miss Josie. Now if you'll excuse me, I have a date with my bride." He hurried to put Luke between them. *Josie should've been the outlaw,* he thought sourly.

Soon he and Adeline were in a borrowed buggy and riding between the cliffs out to where three homes dotted the prairie beyond. They were spaced wide, room for more between them in the future. "Town was getting overcrowded, so some of us built out here. I predict more will come."

During the short drive, he told her about the twenty acres of land he'd staked out around their place.

"It's not much to look at right now, but next year I plan to plant fruit trees. Peaches grow pretty well here, and we can have a garden. I dug a well on our property, and the water is sweet." He glanced at her and found her green eyes dancing, a smile on her lips. Happiness filled him that she was satisfied with such pitiful offerings.

Adeline grabbed her paper and pencil lying on the seat and scribbled. *"Can I have a cow and some chickens?"*

He stopped the buggy and took her hand. "Adeline, you don't have to ask for anything. Just let me know whatever you want, and I'll get it. Your wants, needs, and even whims are as important as mine. We're equals. Understand?"

She swallowed and gave a slight jerk of her head. The breeze lifted a tendril of gold and laid it across her eyes. Ridge brushed back the strand and found the texture like fine silk. Adeline flinched, pulled her hand away, and scooted as far from him as she could get on the bench seat. They weren't even married yet, and already he'd made a mistake. Dammit! Luke had told him to be patient, that this would take a while. She'd reacted like he was going to hit her.

For sure someone had. A muscle worked in his jaw.

"I'm sorry. I wasn't trying…" He picked up the reins and set the horse in motion. Best if he kept quiet, so they rode the rest of the way in silence.

Once at the two-story frame house, he set the brake and helped her down. He tried to look at the place they'd be call-ing home through her eyes and saw little to commend it. A ton of work still needed doing, but he was glad he'd added colorful flower boxes under the front windows. Tally Colby and some of her friends had filled the planters with pretty marigolds and daisies, and frilly curtains framed the wide windows. Ridge hadn't liked them much, but the women said Adeline would.

As he got time and money, he'd whitewash the place and

pray the wind and sand wouldn't strip the paint off too soon. And plant some trees. They did have one—a lone elm at the right corner, outside the kitchen. A weary soldier, it leaned until its branches nearly touched the ground. Ridge felt like that tree at times, especially after a night drinking with Clay and Jack.

Adeline handed him a piece of paper. *I like it.*

"Glad to hear that. Let's go inside." He prayed he'd remembered to straighten things up. He'd lived here on his own for the past month and sometimes forgot that ladies liked stuff neat and tidy.

"Our nearest neighbors are Travis and Rebel Lassiter, and their three young ones. You'll like them." He opened the door and gave her the grand tour. She paused for a long time in the parlor, sadness darkening in her eyes. There wasn't a mess there, so she must have been thinking about something else. She'd said almost nothing about her former life in her letters, instead talking about books she'd once read and asking questions about him and the town.

Maybe one day when she was stronger, he'd get her to talk about family. He didn't even know if she had any. But his curiosity would have to wait. They were on her schedule. He wished she could speak. Written communication was fine if that's all there was. But a person said so much more when actually speaking the words. Cadence, rhythm, tone all revealed the state of mind of the speaker. If being safe helped, he'd do all he could to reassure her.

Moving on, she inspected the kitchen, opening cabinets and checking on dishes and pans. Her note simply read, *"Good."*

Upstairs, she ran her fingers approvingly across the quilt on the bed. The golds, browns, and greens added a bright splash of color to the bland room, even he could see that. And he was glad he'd hung a picture—a sweeping landscape of the Hill Country that reminded him of a home he could never go back to.

"The women in town gave us the quilt as a marriage gift," he explained. "They said it's the wedding ring design, whatever the hell that is."

The happy glimmer in her emerald eyes seemed to indicate she must know what that meant. Or maybe she was laughing at him.

She nodded at the small, round table tucked into a corner with two chairs, and slid her hand across the smooth wood of the tall chest of drawers.

"I emptied two drawers for you, Addie. But I can empty more if that's not enough for your things."

She raised her eyes to his and he wasn't sure what he saw there. Acceptance? Disinterest? What? Before he could figure it out, she returned to the hallway.

Next, she glanced inside at the spare bedroom that they might one day use as a nursery. Ridge grew warm and unbuttoned the top of his collarless shirt. A baby was another subject they'd avoided in their letters. Maybe she didn't want kids. He hadn't let himself think about it much. Wanted men usually didn't dream too far into the future—it was a hazard of the profession.

Maybe if he got rid of this dark cloud hanging over him…

He couldn't tell anything by Adeline's expression—whether she liked the room or not. Joy did, however, leap to her face when he showed her the bathing room.

"You only have to turn this knob, and you have hot water." He leaned over to demonstrate. "And there's no lugging the water outside when you finish. Just lift this stopper, and it drains right out into the yard."

There was no mistaking her happiness and he was glad he could put that smile on her lips. She turned for the stairs, and he followed her down. At the bottom, she opened a small door to a little enclosed space under the stairwell. Her eyes lit up as though she'd found buried treasure.

Ridge ducked through the door. "This is just empty space. Not sure what to do with it."

Adeline fiercely scribbled the word *"Mine"* on a piece of paper.

"Sure, whatever you want. I can put a bench in here, but I don't think it's large enough for a bed." He frowned. Did she mean to sleep under the stairs? He wasn't sure how much he'd like that.

But for someone who'd been living in a tiny cell for three years, maybe a room this size felt normal. It's possible she was more damaged than he'd thought. And if she wanted a bed in there, he'd damn sure make one fit. Somehow.

She took the piece of paper from him and wrote *"Safe,"* then shoved it to his chest again.

Her forceful claim of the space rattled what little calm he'd managed to gather. The wounded bird had found her nest. God help him, he and this airless room would keep her safe until she gathered strength to fly.

Four

A SUMMER STORM ROLLED IN WHILE ADDIE AND RIDGE ATE supper in the Blue Goose Café. The sky opened and in came a gully washer amid rumbling thunder that sounded like apples falling from a wagon. Lord knew they needed all the water they could get this time of year. While they ate, Ridge watched his bride. She seemed ill at ease when folks stopped by their table to congratulate them, so he did all the talking as though it were perfectly normal and invited each to the wedding.

He could almost see her ticking off the minutes in her head until she could escape to the privacy of her hotel room. But he was too. He itched to get this wedding over. Only after that could they settle into some semblance of a routine. He'd be occupied enough keeping her safe from the men who hunted her. He prayed they'd show up here. The corner of his mouth tightened. They wouldn't much like their reception. He ground his back teeth so hard, he thought he cracked one. His preacher's softness had long vanished. He'd learned from his outlaw friends how to make someone sorry they'd been born.

Also, he had his land office to run, and it seemed like new folks were arriving every day. He meant to speak to Clay about clearing the rubble from the back entrance to town. A few years ago, as a matter of defense, they'd blown the rocks and collapsed the passage, but it was past time now to clear it and make the main street a thoroughfare. That would eliminate the clogs that often occurred at the single entrance and exit.

Adeline picked at her food and jumped at every loud noise.

"It's all right." Ridge started to touch her hand but didn't want to risk making another mistake, so he stopped and just spoke softly. "Nothing to worry about, but we'll hurry and get out of here."

The flicker of a smile on her lips revealed her relief. He held her chair, and they moved to the door. Rain was coming down in sheets. He didn't waste a second in removing his frock coat and putting it over her head. Thank goodness it wasn't that far to the hotel. Once they reached the protection of the overhang in front of the businesses, they'd be fine.

"Ready?" he asked.

Her green eyes sparkled under the café's lamplight, and he decided then and there that she was the prettiest woman he'd ever seen. She nodded, and a bit of a smile formed.

Even though they walked fast, he was soaked by the time they reached the overhang and she handed him back his coat. She scowled at the way his wet shirt plastered to his skin and tried to pluck it loose.

"I'm fine." His voice was quiet as he studied the worry lining her face. "I won't melt."

She gave her customary nod then lowered her gaze. The next second, she jumped at a peal of thunder and clutched him. He put an arm around her, just enough pressure to reassure her. "Let's get you inside." A light touch on her back guided her to the hotel doors and into the lobby.

Outside her room, Adeline turned to him like she wanted to say something. When no words came, she lowered her gaze.

"Did you leave a light on so it won't be dark?" he asked.

She provided a yes answer the only way she could.

"Okay. I'll see you in the morning." He waited for her to slip inside then went downstairs. The ride out to his house in the rain wasn't appealing, so he sat in the hotel lobby to wait out the storm.

The chair offered far too much comfort, and he leaned his head back to rest his eyes. Sometime later, a gigantic boom shook the hotel, followed by piercing screams. He jumped to his feet, roused by the chaos. Lightning had struck! He took the stairs two at a time and banged on Adeline's door.

The smell of smoke filled the hall. Ridge tried the knob. Locked. He kicked the door in and rushed inside the dim room. The smell of seared wood met his nose, and through the french doors could see the balcony smoking from what appeared to have been a direct lightning strike.

He covered his face with an arm to block the smoke. "Adeline, it's Ridge! Where are you?"

The scuffle of shoes against the floor led him to a corner where her trunk sat open. Adeline was stuffing her belongings into it, her face pale.

"Leave that. This smoke's getting thick, and we have to get out of here. I don't want to scare you, but I'm going to pick you up now."

Although visibly nervous, she reached for him. He lifted her up, and she slid an arm around his neck. She was still fully dressed, even down to shoes, which told him she'd probably been lying atop the covers instead of crawling into bed. Maybe she'd intended to sleep as she had in prison.

Out in the hallway, he glanced down at her small form, her face buried against his chest. A flood of tender feelings washed over him, filling a portion of his dark, empty places with light.

An angel with a broken halo. That perfectly described her.

It was too soon to know if he loved her, however, he intended to try. But Adeline—she didn't know what a rotten deal she'd gotten in him. Who knew if he could ever learn how to be a proper husband?

"Where's the smoke coming from?" A large man puffed, out of breath from hurrying up the stairs. Five more were behind him in various stages of undress or nightwear. All carried buckets of water.

"Inside this room on the balcony. So far just smoldering." He tightened his hold around his soon-to-be wife.

Luke and Josie were waiting in the lobby and rushed up when they saw him. Ridge set Adeline on her feet, but she clung to his hand. "She's all right. Lightning struck her room, but I didn't see any damage other than smoke yet. They're dousing it now."

"Thank goodness." Josie put an arm around Adeline.

"I'll go check to see if they can move her to another room." Luke strode to the desk and rang the bell. The clerk appeared from the back.

It didn't matter if they had another room or not. Ridge had already decided to take Adeline out to their home, where he could watch over her. Besides, she didn't seem inclined to turn his hand loose anytime soon.

They moved to a sofa, and he told her his idea. Her nod of agreement was all he needed.

When Luke returned with news that there were no other accommodations, Ridge told him the plan.

"But it's raining," Josie objected. "And you can't get to her things until the men up there finish."

He hadn't given that any thought. "Adeline, is there anything you can't live without until daylight?"

A headshake settled it.

"Sounds like the rain is letting up, and my place isn't far." Ridge removed his coat and buttoned Adeline up inside it, then grabbed an umbrella from the stand in the lobby. Soon they were headed beyond the lights of town.

Within twenty minutes, he parked the buggy in front of their home. The rain had slowed to a mere sprinkle, but puddles stood between them and the door. He swung her up and carried her over the water, depositing her in the dark entry.

"Wait here while I light the lamps."

When he returned, Adeline was still standing there. She stared up at him with those shimmering green eyes. In the flickering light, they looked like bottomless pools. His heart skittered sideways like a frightened stallion, and he worked to speak. "Would you like something hot to drink?"

She indicated no, then turned and went to the little space she'd claimed beneath the stairs.

Ridge hurried to get a blanket and pillow. He found her inside sitting against the wall, her legs pulled beneath her. "If you're determined to sleep here, take these. Anytime you want to come out, you're welcome. All of this house is yours, not just this space."

When he set down the lamp he carried, Adeline shook her head vehemently and tried to push it away.

"No, ma'am." Ridge set his jaw. "I've given in to you on

everything else, but you *will* have a little light in here. I insist. Just to banish the ghosts."

He didn't know if the sound she made was a huff or a resigned sigh. Maybe a little of both. At any rate, she scowled, taking the pillow and blanket.

"I have to go see to the horse. You know where the kitchen is if you'd like some water or anything." He turned and left, leaving the door open.

In short order, he had the horse fed and warm in the barn, then returned to check on Adeline. The door of her little safe room was still open, surprising him. He'd have bet money she would've shut it, not trusting anyone. She was stretched out on the blanket, asleep. And wonder of wonders, the lamp still burned, casting a soft glow over the sleeping form on the floor.

Ridge went for the quilt off the bed and covered her. Then he kissed her forehead. He didn't know what this new life of his would look like, but he'd try to give Adeline a happy home. A place where she mattered and was wanted. And maybe somehow in all this, he'd find his way through the darkness that lived inside him, shadows where no lamplight could reach.

Alone and dog-weary, he turned toward the parlor and the sofa where he would sleep.

⁂

Their wedding day dawned, plenty of warm sunshine to mark the occasion. Ridge drove his bride back to town and dropped her off at Tally's house, since her hotel room was still scorched. Then he went to check on the condition of the bluff. As expected, it was muddy. He and the men went to work, covering the ground with hay.

"How did Miss Adeline do at the house?" Luke asked.

"Real good after we got a few things straight. She was in the kitchen cooking breakfast when I got up." Ridge didn't mention the tiny room under the stairs.

"Good. She'll fatten you up."

"What are you saying, Luke?"

His friend grinned. "That it's damn good to have a wife. You need someone to take care of your bony rear."

Clay and Jack Bowdre each pulled out a bottle and passed them around, along with a lot of good-natured ribbing. Ridge took one swallow, done for the day. He wouldn't start off his marriage to Adeline on the wrong foot.

Figuring her out was going to take keeping his wits about him.

❧

Adeline was a bundle of nerves about a great many things, but not where Ridge was concerned. It was herself she worried about. What man would want to stay with a mute wife? Conversing in written form was a terrible way to begin a life together. Before long, this silence would start to grate on him. It would on anyone. Then what?

Her gaze went to the white box on the table, her wedding dress inside. Josie had tried to talk her into a fancy dress of white satin, but Adeline had insisted on practicality and chosen this simple, spring-green frock, void of lace, frills, or a train. She'd relented on the short, lacy veil though.

After all, it seemed to be a rule for brides to cover their faces. Maybe it kept the groom from running as hard as he could until the woman had him caught good and proper in her snare.

Laughter bubbled up in her chest but stopped at her mouth, and the thought hit her that she'd made a joke. A smile curved her lips. It had been a very long time since she'd had a reason to be lighthearted, even for a second, and it felt darn good.

Her thoughts turned to Ridge, and memories of the previous night whirled in her mind. How strong and tender he'd been when he'd picked her up and carried her from the smoldering hotel room, and again at the house, across the mud puddles. The rain-scented land—fresh, clean—had clung to his clothes. It had been so very long since she'd smelled rain hitting the baked earth, the air giving off a hint of gingerbread. Yes, that was the fragrance she'd been trying to think of.

Memories stirred again of home, of her classroom, the

students she'd taught. And of that fateful night when everything had gone horribly wrong.

So much blood.

Frantic cries for help. Pounding on her door.

Rough hands grabbing her afterward, horrible accusations—the judge's sentence of three years in solitary confinement.

Her life stripped away. Everything gone, replaced with cold concrete.

The door rattled. She jumped, but relaxed when she saw it was only Josie coming in with a few of the women from town. As Josie made the introductions, Adeline watched their eyes, but never once saw them glance down or look away in discomfort. Each took her hand and welcomed her.

She especially liked Tally and Nora. They didn't seem to notice her silence, and she thought maybe there could be some friendship budding there. Maybe that's what Ridge meant when he'd written that everyone in Hope's Crossing had a past and no one acted better than anyone else. She was going to like it here very much.

A section of one of Ridge's letters popped into her head.

> *I have great plans for us, my dear Adeline. We can be a part of something lasting here that will stand for generations. Texas is changing, this land is changing, and I want to change with it. My way of life is fast disappearing, and that scares me, but we can have a bright future if we learn to adapt and grow. Take this journey with me, and maybe we can find what we both seek.*

She loved the hope and courage of his dream. That was what had sold her on this crazy idea.

Now, in Tally's home, everyone was talking and laughing. Josie put an arm around Tally and spoke of old times. Oh, how Adeline wished to join in. To be normal. But she wasn't. Maybe she would be eventually. It frightened her to think that this paralysis might last the remainder of her life. She didn't want to live this way.

"Oh my goodness, look at the time! We've got to get you ready." Josie pulled Nora over to Adeline. "You fix hair so beautifully. Do you mind arranging her hair while we get the dress out?"

"I think you have me confused with Rebel." Nora laughed. "That woman is the best I've ever seen. But since she's not here, I'll try my hand."

"You're a dear. Where is Rebel?" Josie picked up the white box and moved it to the bed.

Tally tucked a strand of her red hair back into the low knot on her neck. "That's right, you don't know. Rebel and Travis had a baby boy a while back, and he's not feeling well."

Josie's smile stretched. "That's wonderful news. I know how much she wanted another child. What did they name him?"

"Rafe."

"I love that." Josie pulled the wedding dress from the box.

Adeline felt as though she stood in the middle of a swirling tornado with chaos all around. The small room couldn't hold all the ladies and the talk both. They meant well, though, and despite the noise, she was truly grateful for the help.

Two hours later, she stood before a mirror and did not recognize the woman staring back. The spring-green dress was gorgeous in its simplicity. Someone—Tally, she thought—called it "understated elegance." The scooped neckline wasn't low, yet it showed off the long curve of her neck. Nora had brushed her blond tresses until they shone and worked magic in arranging them in loose curls that cascaded like a waterfall from the crown of her head.

Never had she considered herself anything but homely. Yet she found the word fetching coming to mind now.

She turned to her new friends, blinking back tears, and took their hands. No words were needed. They understood and hugged her.

"Now go and marry that handsome man of yours." Josie wiped her eyes. "In no time, he'll be the love of your life."

Adeline didn't know about that. She didn't know if love

existed for her, or even what it would look like if it did. If it was what her mother and father had, she didn't want it. They lived bitter, rigid, judgmental lives. She'd do without that and live in silence before turning into them.

Although fear tried to take root, she pushed it away. An inner voice told her to take heart and trust that this marriage would work out. Until she had reason to think otherwise.

~

The sun was welcome on Adeline's face and helped melt the ice inside her as she stood on the bluff next to Ridge. Panic set her heart pounding. Whether this decision was right or wrong, it was too late to change her mind. All that remained now was to make the best of it.

Her groom looked resplendent in a white shirt and dark frock coat. He'd left his twin Colts off. He'd told her a gun was necessary here, but he hoped with the coming changes, he would have to wear it less and less. She prayed for that. Guns terrified her, and she wanted to throw them all into a fire and melt them.

Ridge shifted and glanced down at her. "You're a beautiful angel, Adeline. Green looks real good on you." His voice was low and rough, and he winked. "Don't worry. I'll watch over you, trust me on that."

Trust. There was that word again. She trusted few people.

She stared at him for a moment before sliding her palm into his hand, and warmth flowed into her. Her fingers curled as though they'd found a refuge. Slowly, she relaxed and focused on the minister's words. The Lord's Prayer—the devotion that had seen her through the darkest days and given her hope— faded into the background. For now, she was safe in her new home and she gave thanks.

As Brother Paul moved into the wedding vows, she nodded in all the appropriate places. Ridge spoke his clear answers in a ringing voice, as only men trained in preaching the Good Word were wont to do. Maybe in time, he could find his way back. If that's what he wanted.

She'd learned a long time ago that a church was only a building. It was the spirit inside that either made it a holy place or a rigid prison. Hers had been the latter.

The ring Ridge pulled from a pocket surprised her. Where she came from, no one was allowed to wear jewelry of any kind. It was a simple silver band, and though she knew better than most how fleeting happiness was, she felt cherished when he slipped it on her finger.

If he could show her kindness, she'd not ask for anything else.

"This is a forever marriage, pretty lady. You and I," he whispered.

The solemn words startled her. All her life she'd yearned to belong to someone kind who wanted her. Someone who would stand with her to watch each sunrise and sunset, who listened to her wants. Ridge Steele did appear to be this kind of person. The tenderness he'd shown her so far brought tears to her eyes. But had she been locked away too long to recall how deceitful men could be? If Ridge Steele kept the promises he'd made, she'd not ask for anything more from him except time to heal and mend her broken spirit.

"You may now kiss the bride." Brother Paul closed his Bible.

Ridge lowered his head and lightly pressed his lips to hers, sealing the vows. Adeline let her eyes drift shut and soaked up the new sensations. If Ridge never kissed her again, she'd have this one to remember.

Her mother's admonishment sounded in her head. *Once you're married, your husband owns you. Remember that, girl.*

Ridge released her and she studied his amber eyes. Vows or no vows, if he turned out to be cruel, she'd leave and never look back.

She was done with being owned.

Five

A CELEBRATION COMMENCED DIRECTLY FOLLOWING THE NOON
wedding, complete with music, dancing, and tables laden with
food. Ridge kept an eye on Adeline, making sure she wasn't
alone for too long. The womenfolk had included her in their
circle with lots of laughter and talking, but when he saw her
looking around for him, he pushed away from the post where
the men had gathered and went to her.

He offered his hand. "Mrs. Steele, I believe you owe me
a dance."

She glanced up with relief and stood. Then before she could
take a step, panic darkened her eyes, and she shook her head.

"It'll be fine," he replied. "Hell, I don't know how either,
but I'll bet we figure it out."

Tally lent gentle support. "Give it a try, dear. None of us
are experts. It's the custom to dance with your new husband."

Finally, Adeline forced a smile and gamely took his hand.
Her body had the tension of someone walking the gallows'
steps. "Relax. I won't bite. Listen to the music."

She stared up at him and came into his arms, her body
warm against him. Slowly she began to relax.

The waltz was a beautiful dance and his favorite, but he
wanted to put her more at ease. "We'll just stand here and
sway to the music if it's okay with you. My knee's been acting
up."

The suggestion seemed to take the pressure off. She relaxed
and moved in his arms to the sweet strains of the fiddle. The
fragrance of wild roses and sage drifted on the breeze as the
musicians filled the air with song.

Ridge lowered his head, resting his cheek against her soft
blond hair. "We won't stay long, just enough to keep from
being rude. These people are our friends, and they're happy

we found each other. I've been a bachelor for a long time."
He chuckled. "The ladies think I need a woman to take me
firmly in hand. Don't know where they got that notion. The
least I can do is show my appreciation for the midnight oil they
must've wasted on putting this shindig together."

His pretty wife leaned back, staring up into his eyes, a
solemn expression on her face. She stopped moving and pulled
her hand from his, placed her palm over his heart.

"You saying I have a good heart?"

She nodded and gave him a brilliant smile that took his
breath.

"We might just work out a sign language before you know
it." Suddenly, he knew they'd be okay even if she never spoke
aloud again. Clay had been right in suggesting the best communication didn't involve words.

The feel of her lips under his would forever remain in his
head.

They waltzed twice more, and the third time, Adeline
caught the hang of the wide, sweeping circles. Her eyes
sparkled, and her face glowed with happiness. He'd wager that
this was probably the most fun she'd ever had. But she was
getting tired, and her feet began to drag.

"Let's go home." He rested a hand lightly on the small of
her back and led her to the horses. Well-wishers followed the
couple, laughing and pelting them with rice.

Ridge took the long way, pointing out some things, showing her the parcels of land he was selling at the land office.
Heeding Clay's advice, he spoke in a soft tone so she could
get used to his voice. He talked about what he hoped to
accomplish—and a little of his fears.

Not enough to frighten her. Shielding her from those was
foremost in his mind.

"I have dreams, Adeline, but whether or not I achieve them
depends on things I cannot control." He reached for her small
hand. "The law tends to leave us alone for the most part, but
occasionally they ride in with warrants. How long I'll escape
their notice is anyone's guess."

She tried to reply but the words wouldn't form. He kicked himself that he forgot to bring some paper and a pencil, because her thoughts were important.

"It's okay, I have plenty of time." He kissed her fingers. "I'm just glad you came."

Her nod came first, followed by the kind of smile that made him happy to be alive.

Finally, he turned the buggy toward their home and helped her down at the front door as the sunset provided quite a show of purple and orange streaks across the wide prairie sky.

"Go on inside. I'll take care of the horses and get them bedded down. I'll bring your trunk in when I'm done."

Adeline nodded and turned. Still silent, still haunted by whatever had happened to her. But she had smiled several times today, and that huge improvement gave him hope.

When he returned with the trunk, the aroma of coffee filled the air. The welcome surprise nearly knocked him down. He saw no sign of her and didn't know where else to set her things except at the place she'd chosen under the stairs, so he left the trunk there. The door was closed, but he imagined that was where she'd gone. Sadness pushed out his earlier optimism. Was this to be permanent, her drifting through the rooms like a ghost? Were they doomed to live separately in the same house? He didn't know if he could take that.

Upstairs, the bedroom showed no sign she'd been there. He followed the aroma tickling his nose back down, pausing to put his ear to the door of her little space. No sounds came from inside. Maybe she'd gone to sleep.

As he filled his cup from the coffeepot in the kitchen, he heard the faint meows of a cat. Curious, he opened the door that led onto the back stoop and found Adeline sitting on the top step, holding a small kitten. A yellow mama cat sat in front of her, calmly grooming herself. Adeline startled and glanced up at him, pure joy lining her face. You'd think someone had given her a fortune in gold dust, not a scrap of yellow fur.

Maybe they had.

Careful not to slosh his coffee, he stepped out and settled

beside her. "Thank you for making this. I love the stuff any time of day. You did a great job too."

Adeline put her fingers flat to her lips, then brought them out toward him.

"What are you saying?"

She did it again and then once more, clearly frustrated.

"Hold on a second." He went in the house and came back a moment later with paper and pencil.

She wrote: *"I was saying thank you for the compliment. I'm glad it tastes all right. I haven't made it in a long while."*

"It's the best I've had." Ridge took another sip. "I'm happy you're making yourself at home."

Addie bent over her paper then handed it to him. *"I want to know your rules."*

Shock rippled through him. He set his coffee down and stared into the distance, an ache in his chest. The question, as well as her look of defiance, rattled his calm. "I have none," he answered quietly. "I'm not your keeper. Feel free to do whatever you want here—all of this is yours. Do as you wish, come and go as you please."

It was her turn to look surprised. She wrote: *"You will never own me."*

"No one owns you! Not me. Not anyone. Don't you get it? You're free." Anger rose and sharpened his tone, which he instantly regretted. He'd already broken one of his vows to never raise his voice to her. Dammit! But just the thought that someone had planted that notion in her head made him see red.

It would take time to sink in that she was a free woman. Maybe if he repeated it each day, she'd come to believe.

Silence grew thick between them as Ridge worked hard to rein in his temper. Adeline focused on the kitten, holding it against her cheek. When at last she met his gaze, her pretty green eyes were large, but at least he couldn't see any fear in them.

"I apologize for that outburst, but I don't hold with the thought of anyone owning another. Why would you say that? Who put that drivel in your head?"

She lowered the kitten and picked up the pencil. *"My father. He owned all of us."*

Everything inside Ridge stilled. What had she gone through—even before prison? And what in God's name had they accused her of?

"My mother says a husband owns his wife."

The mama cat brushed against his pant leg, her tail curling around it. He stared down at the new scribbles, heartsick. "Adeline, I don't know how you lived before, but here you'll always be free. Your voice is as loud as mine."

She hugged the kitten, gazing out at the barren landscape. He could feel the war going on inside her. Would they be able to come to a point where she could trust him and believe what he said?

"Where did you live before prison? Do you still have family?"

Her face froze. She wrote *"NO"* in bold letters, breaking the pencil lead with the force of her press, and jumped to her feet. Clutching the kitten to her breast, she opened the door to the kitchen.

"Adeline, those are…" She vanished inside before he finished lamely, "…outside cats."

The mama cat barely made it in after her before the door slammed, leaving Ridge alone in silence.

Hell!

He'd asked too much, too soon. Judging from her reaction, her life must've been a nightmare. Thick anger choked him. If she wanted to turn the house into a wild animal sanctuary, if she needed life around her, he wouldn't object.

Ridge stood and walked to the barn. Physical labor was what *he* needed—the harder the better. Maybe dig another well, much deeper this time. Or perhaps build a new barn he didn't need. Anything to keep himself from thinking about Adeline's past.

∾

Adeline found a box in the kitchen and lined it with a tattered, old blanket she'd found lying in a corner, then she took it to her little space. The cats would sleep with her.

She was sorry for being rude to Ridge, but she wasn't ready to answer any questions. Her life before was dead to her, and she'd already said far too much. No one would ever believe the kind of oppression she'd lived under—always watched, everything scrutinized, the tiniest things criticized, the punishment.

Why hadn't she left? She should've just run.

The answer was the children. She had been trying to save them, to be their voice. Instead, she'd condemned them to even more cruelty and pain. Everything seemed so hopeless.

Pain cut into her like a dagger. The hated sound of her father's sharp voice sounded in her head. "You're willful and rebellious, Adeline. Public whippings fail to rein you in. I'm using my influence to have you sent where there will be nothing for you to do except reflect on your sins and get your soul right. But I can make all this go away if you tell me where to find my son."

She'd faced him defiantly and spat, "I didn't kill Jane Ann. You know I didn't. You pound the message into people's heads to tell the truth while you lie over and over."

A chilling grin had curved Ezekiel's mouth, and his brown goatee twitched. "The judge believes what I tell him. I'm a holy man of God."

Sarcastic laughter bubbled up inside her at the memory. She sat on the floor and rocked the kitten, taking comfort in the small, warm body.

Not long after, she heard the back door open and some banging. She put the kitten in its box and went to the kitchen to see Ridge struggling to wrestle a wooden bench inside; only the door wouldn't stay open. She hurried to hold it for him.

He set the bench down on the floor and wiped his brow. "Thanks for the help. This is all I can find at present for your space, but I'll do better. At least you won't have to sit or lie on the floor. I can fix it up for you."

Adeline swallowed hard, guilty at making extra trouble. He was trying to please her, and she kept begging for more and more patience. She couldn't speak, couldn't dance, couldn't talk of family. Heavy sadness dropped around her.

She couldn't sleep in his bed.

Ridge took her hand. "Do you mind if I call you Addie? It seems to fit you."

Adeline curled her fingers against his palm. She liked the shortened version of her name—especially the way Ridge's husky voice made it sound.

"I'm sorry for pushing you," he went on. "I am curious about you, where you come from, and your family, that's all. But we can talk whenever you're ready."

He paused, and when he spoke again, the hardness layered beneath his words revealed some new things about this outlaw she'd married. "This man hunting you had best not show his face. I will kill him with no regrets. No one hurts my wife."

She blinked in surprise and clutched her chest, her fingers fanning across her breastbone, and stared. That he could voice this violent threat in such a calm manner stunned her. But at the same time, she knew in her heart he wouldn't enjoy killing. His letters had already told her that much. Ridge seemed to have a code he lived by, and she suspected that set of rules figured in all he did.

I vow never to raise my hand or my voice in anger. Our marriage will be one of respect. He'd spoken that vow that day, and she'd found the words comforting.

The outlaw Ridge Steele had become her champion, and still she didn't really know how to feel about him.

But maybe if she'd had him by her side three years ago, the outcome might've been far different.

❦

Ridge stared up at the ceiling in the dim bedroom and listened to the house settling. It had come as no surprise that Adeline had decided to sleep in her space beneath the stairs with the kitten and its mama for company, but at least she had the bench to lie on. From what Luke had said, it was an improvement over what she'd had.

What the hell had happened to her? Something in prison or something before? Or both? Since she'd called an immediate halt to his questions about family, he suspected they played a big part. If he could find out, he'd try to fix the problem— either by talk or with a bullet. For her not to speak seemed to suggest something very sinister had taken place.

He could protect her better if she'd tell him the nature of the threat that followed her. All he knew was that men were hunting her. He had no descriptions, no names, nothing.

Moonlight through the window shone on the clock on the wall. It was just past midnight. He threw back the covers and reached for his trousers, then padded quietly to the stairs in his bare feet.

The door to Addie's space was shut, but the knob turned when he tried it. She had the lamp lit but the wick turned low, and the weak light revealed her asleep on the bench, the kitten in the crook of her arm. Mama cat stirred in her box and blinked up at him. They eyed each other for a full moment before the feline gave him a look of disdain, stood, and promptly turned her back on him.

For a long moment, he stood staring down at Addie, admiring the dark lashes resting on her high cheekbones like black fringe on a shawl. At times she seemed shy and afraid, but he knew that was simply a smokescreen, for he'd glimpsed passion inside her and more than a little anger when she'd beaten the drunk with her shoe.

And despite the strange new surroundings, she'd made him coffee without being asked. Just figured it out. Yes, Adeline Jancy would turn out to be a good wife. He'd stake his life on it. Tucking the quilt around her, he touched her cheek with the pad of a finger. "Sleep, my lady. You're safe from harm."

Six

ADELINE WASN'T SURPRISED THAT LUKE AND JOSIE DECIDED TO leave for their home on the Lone Star Ranch the day following the wedding. They'd missed their small daughter terribly in the two weeks they'd been away.

Luke turned to Ridge before climbing into the wagon with Josie. "Be careful, amigo, and keep your guard up at all times. Those men will track Adeline here eventually. I guarantee it."

Ridge clasped Luke's hand. "They'll have to go through me to get to her."

Addie listened to the two men and watched their interaction, her heart swelling to see the admiration they had for each other. She curled a hand around Ridge's elbow, giving the couple a send-off. Although she hadn't known them long, she hated to see them go. They were her closest friends. But life had to go on. Nothing stood still—not time, problems, or the stars.

Josie had said something very profound that morning. *Rise above the dark clouds and you'll find golden sunshine. It's there. You just have to look for it. And remember, life must be lived fully—no matter the trouble that comes, the season, or condition of the trail.*

At the moment, Addie's roads were washed out and littered with holes. Still, in spite of everything, hope lived inside her.

As they struggled to adapt to marriage and each other over the next three weeks, Addie soon learned Ridge's likes and dislikes, his moods and the things he valued. He loved meat but picked at vegetables. Blessed with a strong sweet tooth, he wanted dessert at every meal if possible. He tried never to curse around her, but she often saw the strain it took on his face. Sometimes she smelled whiskey on him after he'd spent time with the men, but never saw him drunk or wobbly.

Of all his qualities, she loved the way he made her feel, like she was the most cherished woman ever born, always seeing to her needs. He'd tabled questions about her family and previous home, for which she was glad. She still wasn't ready to tell her story, but she knew she would have to do it soon.

He deserved to know the kind of woman he'd gotten.

All in all, Addie was happy with the new life she'd chosen. Ridge was gone much of the day, which left her on her own to do housework—or nothing at all, if she so desired. She always kept the doors locked in case of intruders, made a habit to check the windows, and listened for anything that signaled danger.

Each time she thought about the men hunting her, pain throbbed in her chest and took her breath. She knew who they were and who had sent them, and that was the most terrifying part. Often during the day, she had to stop and remind herself that she was safe, her hiding place near.

But nights were spent with Ridge in the parlor, her in the rocker, and he in his comfortable chair. Their first time together like that, he'd pulled a book titled *Oliver Twist* from the shelf, a riveting story about a poor child born in a workhouse. She loved the sound of his voice as he read to her. Ever since then, it had become a nightly ritual. Sometimes, she studied his face as he concentrated on the page—especially his nicely shaped mouth—and remembered their wedding kiss.

A part of her wished she was the bride he wanted out of all the other women in the world. Only he hadn't truly chosen her, not in that way. Nor she him. They hadn't met and fallen in love like most couples, hadn't been neighbors or childhood friends. He'd known nothing and still knew very little about her, other than the fact that she was being hunted. She prayed he would never come to regret making her part of his life.

Even so, she knew her silence had to drag on him and she hated that.

He was a good man. A kind man. She often found herself studying him from under lowered lashes and admired his ability to keep occasional irritation in check and his voice calm even when he probably wanted to yell.

His hands and long fingers also fascinated her. They, too, seemed perfectly formed. Luke and Josie had told her that he had a lightning-fast draw, rarely missing his target, assuring that he would be her secret weapon. Yet at the same time, he was gentle and never complained when Miss Kitty or the wee one jumped into his lap. The first time it happened, he'd sloshed coffee on his shirt, and she'd braced herself, waiting for an explosion. But none came. After that, he seemed to enjoy running his long fingers across the kitten's soft fur.

Maybe the cats calmed him as much as they did her.

Midafternoon one day, a knock sounded on the front door. Fear raced through Addie, and she instinctively bolted for her safe room. A baby's cry halted her before she could close herself in, and she moved to the window to look out. A pretty, black-haired woman stood on the porch, a baby in her arms, a wagon nearby. But what shocked Addie more than the unexpected visitor were the denim trousers the visitor wore that showed off her hips and legs.

The woman didn't seem to pose much of a threat, so Addie opened the door.

"Hi, I'm Rebel Lassiter, your neighbor." The woman, somewhere around her late twenties, smiled and held out her hand. "Pleased to meet you. I'm sorry I missed your wedding. Little Rafe was puny, and Travis was in Tascosa on business."

Oh! This was the woman Josie had talked about who could fix hair. Adeline returned the smile and waved Rebel inside. How she wished she could speak, but all she could do was stand there like a stupid stump.

Rebel seemed unfazed by her silence and thrust the child into her arms. "Please hold him for a moment. I have a hot peach cobbler waiting in the wagon." Then she was gone in a flash.

Rafe, no more than one year old, judging by the two tiny bottom teeth, stared at Adeline with a look of complete shock. He puckered up to cry.

The boy wasn't alone in his state of confusion. Adeline blinked and tried to think of what to do. Although she hadn't held a child this small in years, she jiggled him up and down and made silly faces at him. He switched gears and laughed—then promptly tried to stick a finger up her nose. That part was familiar. Her littlest sister used to do the same.

A shadow darkened the open doorway, and Rebel rushed in. "I'm back." She carried a luscious-smelling cobbler straight to the kitchen and set it down on the table. Adeline followed with Rafe, her gaze on those practical denim trousers.

How she'd love to own a pair! But whatever would Ridge think?

A wide smile graced Rebel's face and made her dark eyes sparkle. "This is just my way of saying welcome to Hope's Crossing. I hope you'll be as happy here as I am." Rafe reached for his mother, and she took him from Addie. "My husband, Travis, and I have two older children besides this one. I'm sure you'll see a lot of us."

Without a doubt. Adeline nodded, a smile still glued to her face. She reached for her paper and pencil and wrote, *"I'm happy to meet you, Rebel. Thank you for the nice welcome—and the dessert."*

Rebel accepted the paper, read it, then took Adeline's hand. "Please don't feel embarrassed. I know about your situation. In hindsight, I probably should've held off before descending on you, but I couldn't wait to meet you. Out here, we women have to stick together."

"Stay for tea? I can make some."

"Oh, no, I must hurry back—I have a birthday cake to make. Ely, my oldest, is eleven today. I want to have it ready when he and Jenny get out of school." Rebel wiped Rafe's nose. "We're losing the schoolmaster soon, and I don't know what we'll do. I hope they find a good teacher before too long."

A wave of longing for one part of Adeline's old life came roaring back. She'd loved teaching and had grown so fond of her students. If only she could speak, she'd apply for the job. But at present, that was out of the question.

She accompanied Rebel and the baby to their wagon and

waved as they pulled away. In parting, Rebel called out, "You'll make Ridge very happy. I just know it. If ever anyone needed a wife, it was that man. He's salt of the earth."

Adeline went inside, closed and locked the door. Leaning against the heavy wood, she thought of all Rebel had said. Could she make Ridge happy? In her observation, people had to make themselves happy and not depend on others.

Some, like her parents, chose to stay locked in a cheerless, dismal existence. They embraced bitter words and judgmental attitudes as though pain and grief were to be welcomed. Ezekiel Jancy had been cursed with all girls and never hesitated to let everyone know his disappointment. His quest for the boy he'd so desperately wanted, an heir to carry on his life's work, had been fruitless.

A familiar yearning to jot down her thoughts grew strong inside her and drew her to her pencil and little stack of paper. She'd kept a journal most of her life, and that had proven disastrous when, at her trial, they'd used her words against her, cementing her fate. Yet it seemed safe enough now, so she sat at the table and began to write her thoughts, scattered though they were.

I suppose an outlaw seems like a poor choice for a woman like me, but no one else is strong enough to protect me and stand up to my powerful father. Ezekiel wants to force me to reveal where the boy is, but I'll never tell, because once I do, he'll kill me. Only someone like Ridge, who lives outside the law, can protect me. I'll always be grateful to Nettie Mae. I learned about Luke Legend's private bride service through her, and through Nettie, I corresponded with Ridge. If not for that, I would've fallen back into my father's clutches upon my release.

I was six the first time I really saw my father for what he was. Even at that age, I saw his fake caring, his obsession with control, his rigid thinking—none of it was normal. I was older than my three sisters, and each time another of us was born, my father's displeasure became louder. I yearned to live free of his horrifying rages and find a place where laughter and light could erase the darkness. I'm beginning a new life here, where there are endless possibilities, and I'm excited. I have companions in Miss Kitty and her baby, Squeakers. I love them dearly.

The sound of hoofbeats and jangling tack came from behind the house. Fear stiffened her. Adeline dropped the pencil. Her safe room beckoned, but she wanted to be sure. She rose and crept to the door, moved the curtain aside just a fraction, then relaxed when she saw Ridge and Clay riding in. Her gaze shifted to the two horses they herded—a spotted pony and a buckskin.

The beautiful buckskin aroused an old yearning inside her. How she'd wanted her own horse. She'd asked only once. Ezekiel had delivered an instant rebuke in a cutting voice, said she was unworthy, that horses were reserved for boys. That had stung to the quick, and she'd never asked again. Addie blinked hard and shook her head to rid herself of the memory.

The men dismounted, and Ridge strode toward the back door. She unlocked it as he got there, then stepped back.

He poked his head in. "Can you come out for a minute, Addie?"

She nodded and went outside.

"Nice to see you again, Miss Adeline," Clay called, touching the brim of his hat.

She waved and smiled. Clay was such a good friend to Ridge and seemed very nice.

Her hand got lost in Ridge's big, calloused palm as he led her to the horses. "Take your pick, Addie. Whichever one you like. A wedding gift from me."

Sudden thickness clogged her throat. She tugged free of Ridge and ran to the tan buckskin with a black mane and tail, laying her face against the animal's neck. Tears filled her eyes. The buckskin belonged to her. Only her. She hugged the powerful animal, and his muscles quivered against her chest.

Ridge touched her shoulder, his voice soft. "I thought you'd like that gelding. He's a beauty and has already been gentled. He'll make a faithful companion."

She turned and flung her arms around his neck, clinging to this man who'd seen her value when no one else ever had.

As the overwhelming emotion started to fade, Ridge's heartbeat, steady and true, pulsed in the corded tendons of his neck. His breath was uneven and ragged, and the fragrant scent of the land that clung to his clothes rose to fill her senses. He folded his arms around her.

Embarrassed, she released her hold and stepped back. His somber amber gaze, his expression held something she'd never seen before. He didn't exactly smile, but this man she'd married seemed happy in some strange way. If only she wasn't so ignorant about things. Her tongue worked but no sound came out. She flattened her hand to her mouth and gave the sign they had worked out to mean "thank you."

"You're welcome. I'm glad I can make you happy." He cleared his throat. "You are very special to me. Always."

A warm glow swept over her. She turned to the buckskin and caressed the space between the animal's eyes, vowing silently to love him. The buckskin stared into her eyes, seeming to feel the hurt inside her. The deep connection moved her and she marveled at the love that came through her fingertips. That such a beautiful horse could love her was amazing to consider, but she felt the same way about the gelding.

Adeline prayed she would come to love Ridge as she did this buckskin. What had Rebel said? Salt of the earth. Yes, that was it. He did have that fundamental goodness that made him rise above all others.

By pointing to Clay and Ridge, then pretending to drink from a cup, she told them she'd make coffee.

"That'll hit the spot," Ridge answered. "We'll take the horses to the barn. Won't be long."

Inside the kitchen, she quickly grabbed the paper she'd written on and took it to her safe room. Then she got coffee on to boil. Soon, the two men filled the space with their large bodies. They sat at the table, talking, and Adeline listened quietly.

Clay took a sip of coffee. "You'll soon have this place set up the way you want."

"I suppose, but it's not moving fast enough to suit me. I'll pick up our cow and chickens tomorrow, and the peach trees should arrive in the spring." Ridge turned to Adeline. "We still have time to put in a small garden—some fast-growing things like onions, turnips, beets, and squash. I'll help you." He grinned. "Between the buckskin and the garden, you won't have time to get bored."

"What are you going to name that buckskin?" Clay asked.

She shrugged. The matter of a name hadn't even occurred to her.

"We'll think of something tonight." Ridge brought the cup to his mouth and took a swig. "I've always been partial to Soldier or Ranger. My red sorrel is Cob. But you'll find the perfect name."

Pondering the subject, Adeline rose and, with the cats following, went out to the barn to spend some time with her new friend. A name needed to mean something special.

≈

Ridge's gaze followed his wife as she went out the door, glad he'd made her happy. Adeline needed more reasons to smile. He dragged his attention back to Clay and the news that his friend was buying five hogs to raise. "They'll provide a lot of food," Ridge agreed.

"I'll get plenty of scraps from the café to feed them." Clay drained his cup and reached for his hat. "I need to be going or Tally will shoot me. I'm supposed to help Violet with her schoolwork. Say, did you hear that the schoolmaster is leaving?"

"News to me. What's Todd going to do?"

"He met a young woman back East, and they're going to marry, but she refuses to come here." Clay chuckled. "You know how that is."

No, not really. Ridge resented Clay talking like all women were the same. If Addie objected to something, she usually had a reason. "How soon is he leaving?"

"End of next month."

"Guess we'd best look for another teacher, then." He filed that away and turned to an issue that had been on his mind. "Before you go, we need to discuss opening up the back entrance to town. It's time, and the sooner the better. Hope's Crossing is suffering growing pains."

Clay nodded. "Call a meeting, and we'll hash it out with the citizens. It'll mean a lot of backbreaking work, hauling off those huge boulders."

"Worth it, though. The stagecoach won't have to turn around and go back out the same way, which means less congestion. I think it'll help sell more lots," Ridge pointed out.

"I agree." Clay stood and moved to the door. "See you later."

Ridge finished his coffee and took the cups to the dishpan. Addie had enough to do without picking up after him. He glanced out the window toward the barn, the sun still high in the sky. Plenty of time for a ride.

She had the buckskin out of his stall and had found the brush to groom him with, her strokes long and smooth. Watching from the lid of the grain bin were Miss Kitty and Squeakers, taking it all in. Addie must've heard his boots striking the ground and turned.

"I thought I'd find you here. From the looks of things, you're about to put your poor horse to sleep. His eyes are getting awfully heavy. How about we ride instead, and wake him up?"

Panic washed over her face, and through the flurry of gestures that followed, he figured out she'd never ridden a horse.

"Don't worry. I'll teach you."

Addie's smile almost blinded him as she signed a thank-you.

"It's easy, and you'll soon get the hang of it. I'll start with saddling him."

Ridge explained every step of tacking up. She listened to every word and sometimes leaned closer to see. When she wanted to try her hand, he let her.

Finishing with hers, he saddled the spotted pony for himself. "I need to see how well behaved he is," he explained. "Okay, let's get you on the buckskin."

He made a step with his hands and boosted her up with a palm on her backside. Heat crawled up his neck to touch her in such a familiar way, but she seemed too enthralled with the horse for it to register. That was a relief.

But when he stood up, he was confronted by a very exposed and very shapely leg, reminding him of the unsuitable nature of riding astride in a dress. Very casually, as though he did so every single day, he rearranged the fabric over her bare skin.

Hopefully, one day he'd be more at ease with these things.

After a quick lesson in how to steer and stop, they meandered out, with Ridge riding next to her. "We'll take it slow until you feel more comfortable."

Gradually, she relaxed her grip on the reins, and they moved to a trot. The buckskin was a pro and required very little direction. The horse seemed to have a sixth sense when it came to his rider, which relieved Ridge's mind.

"Having fun?" he asked.

Addie nodded and wiped her eyes. She seemed overcome with emotion, and he imagined she'd yearned to ride a horse for a very long time. Her father, the one who ruled everyone, probably kept her from it. Maybe it was on his rule list. She must've lived in pure hell.

And then gone to prison—for something. His lips tightened, and a muscle in his jaw worked. Clearly, the woman wouldn't harm a flea—unless it was trying to hurt her. That night in Fort Worth, when he'd run across her beating her assailant with her shoe, popped into his mind, and he chuckled at the memory. For all her quiet thoughts, she was certainly no daylily.

But until she could speak or decide that she was ready to write down answers to his questions, everything else would remain a mystery.

Seven

A SENSE OF UNBELIEVABLE FREEDOM ENVELOPED ADDIE AS SHE rode across the uneven ground, the breeze on her face and sun on her back. And it was all due to Ridge.

The buckskin was an amazing animal and responded to the lightest touch. An odd feeling had come over her the moment she'd rested a hand on his neck—a deep connection she couldn't explain. A sense of sadness and pain had passed through her, but had it been hers or the horse's? Maybe he could read her also. She didn't understand but knew she would always treasure him.

The horse wasn't the only one who seemed to be able to sense her feelings. Both Miss Kitty and Squeakers reacted to her moods. Maybe all animals had this ability and she'd never noticed.

In some strange way, upon pledging her troth to Ridge, her world had opened up like an unfurling rose to all sorts of new ideas and sensations.

He rode a length ahead, allowing an unhindered look at the man she'd married. Ridge sat tall in the saddle, alert, scanning the land ahead. Muscles played across his broad shoulders with the slightest movement, his arms stretching the fabric of his shirt taut. He breathed in the fresh outdoor air as though he took it all the way down to the bottom of his lungs.

This man who lived outside the law seemed to care for her and had seen to her comfort. Ridge treated her as an equal, as someone of worth. Her stomach quickened.

Be careful, she scolded herself. *You don't know him. His kindness could be a trap to get you to let down your guard. He could be just as ruthless, and trusting him could bring more pain.*

Addie tried to keep herself focused on her buckskin and the amazing ride but soon found herself studying her husband again. Ridge was a part of this land, at home in the barren vastness, rocky ravines, and craggy mountains in a way she might never grow to appreciate. She missed trees and lush greenery, but she wouldn't trade what peace she'd already found for anything.

Ridge dropped back beside her. Shadowed by his worn black Stetson, his face seemed carved by the wind and sun—or maybe it had simply been chiseled by hardship. "A little creek lies just ahead. We'll stop there for a spell. Our northern-most boundary is a half mile beyond that point."

Adeline nodded. She loved how he included her as owner of this parcel. She hadn't just gotten a husband; she'd become a landowner too. Something—and someone—that was hers to keep. She finally had a place to be. Despite her need for caution, a thread of happiness curled along her spine.

She was still contemplating that when Ridge stopped. Alarm knotted in her stomach as he slid one of his guns from the holster. Two figures stood near some horses about fifty yards ahead. No, it was three people, counting the one sitting on the ground.

Ridge's whole demeanor changed. He stiffened and stared at the intruders through narrowed eyes, his grip tight, back rigid. A cold and frightening chill went through her. Whatever was wrong, she had to be ready to react.

"Wait here and stay in the saddle. I need to find out what they're doing on our land. If they shoot, ride to town as fast as you can." He pulled the other gun from his holster and handed it to her. "If they get past me, shoot to kill."

Addie swallowed hard, taking the weapon. The unexpected weight pulled her hand down and she almost dropped it. She'd never shot a gun, much less killed a person. But if the strangers harmed Ridge or came at her, she'd try her best to send them to eternity.

Her gaze followed him as he trotted away, and fear tightened in her chest until she could scarcely breathe. Two of the men raised their weapons at his approach. Addie sucked in her breath and held it.

Would this be the day when her world collapsed yet again?

∽

"Howdy." The hair on the back of Ridge's neck stood as he stared at the two heavily armed strangers and the three horses tied to the branches of a scrub oak. Then his gaze shifted to the wounded man on the ground. He was young, barely looked old enough to shave. "I'd like to ask what you're doing on my land. And you can lower those weapons anytime."

"Didn't realize we'd left open range, mister, and we needed water." Dirt and blood caked the speaker's trousers. The interloper, his long hair tied back with a narrow leather strip, hesitated for a moment before pointing his rifle at the ground. The other rough-looking cowboy followed suit.

To show good faith, Ridge returned his pistol to his holster, although he eyed the pair's every move. "I don't begrudge anyone water. Who's the boy?"

"Prisoner. Taking him to Mobeetie for trial," snapped the second trespasser. He spat a stream of tobacco juice on the kid, drops beading on his unkempt beard, and laughed when the boy cowered. The coltish kid had a gag in his mouth, and his dull eyes wore a look of defeat.

Bounty hunters. Ice filled Ridge's veins. *Dirty, stinkin' bounty hunters.*

"What's his charge, if I may ask?"

The tobacco-chewer cut his sharp eyes to Ridge. "Nosey people are apt to get shot."

The man's long-haired friend moved closer, squinting at Ridge. "I think I know you, mister."

"I doubt that," Ridge answered evenly. He stole a quick look to check if Addie had kept her distance, relieved to find she had.

Long Hair slid his hand into an inside vest pocket and yanked out several crumpled wanted posters. He handed them to his partner. "Hiram, look through there for this fellow. I know I saw that face."

Ridge measured his opponents. Two against one wasn't bad odds, but definitely raised the stakes. He could take down one, no problem. He wasn't sure about the second. "Look, get your water and go about your business and we'll all leave here alive."

Just then Hiram froze in mid-chew, clutching Ridge's wanted poster. He jerked his rifle up. "Ridge damned Steele. Drop your weapon!"

Ridge went for his Colt, but Hiram's bullet tore through the fleshy part of his upper arm before he could draw. Dammit! Pain burst inside him and ricocheted through his body. He ignored what he could, jerked out his Colt, and took aim at Long Hair.

A look of surprise froze on the man's face as he collapsed in the dirt, clutching his bloody chest.

A flurry of sudden shots came from behind Ridge. He turned to see Addie riding toward him, firing wildly. He assumed she was aiming at the second bounty hunter, but it was impossible to tell. The bounty hunters' horses skittered nervously at the sudden burst of noise.

At the moment, he had no time to worry about that. He bent low and swiveled, turning his weapon on the man who'd shot him. Orange fire leaped from Hiram's rifle as he fired at Ridge again.

The projectile missed by a hair. Ridge returned fire and caught the bounty hunter in the upper thigh. The man ran to his horse and leaped into the saddle. Teetering over, hanging half off, he raced away in a cloud of dust. Hell! Ridge emptied his Colt at the fleeing man without stopping him.

Ridge bent over Long Hair and found him already dead.

The boy had thrown himself flat on the ground when the shooting started and sat up slowly. Ridge cut his ropes and took the gag from his mouth. "You all right, son?"

"Need water." The kid was scrawny and looked to be all legs. If he ever grew into them, he'd be a man to reckon with. His straight, sandy hair hadn't seen a comb in a month of Sundays, and his face was bruised, his lip bloody.

"Sure." Ridge removed his hat and filled it from the creek, then brought it back. The boy took long gulps.

A shadow appeared on the ground behind him. Ridge

jerked around to find Addie, the Colt at her side. Concern filled her green eyes.

"Addie, I told you to ride when shooting started. And what was the deal with you firing that weapon? You shot everywhere but at the damn bounty hunter." Lashing out was the wrong thing to do, but his drumming heart hadn't yet settled. Blood still surged through his veins like a runaway train.

Anger tightened the delicate lines of her face. She sidestepped his reach and touched his blood-soaked shirt.

Ridge forced a calmer tone into his voice. "I'm all right. It's not bad."

Her temper showed in the way she jerked up her dress, tore a strip from her petticoat, then went to the creek to wet it. She wrapped it around his arm. Though her dander was still up, it didn't reflect in her gentle touch. He'd not felt the like since he was a boy.

In the loud silence, he met her stony glare with one of his own. After a moment, he spoke. "Appreciate the caring, but next time I tell you to ride when there's trouble, I expect you to do just that." He hated the bite of his sharp words, but she had to understand.

Anger darkening her eyes, she frowned, threw back her shoulders until her spine was ramrod straight, then pointed toward their home and shook her head as though to say "not hardly." She kept shaking her head and waving her arms wildly to drive home her opinion of the matter. She'd march off a few steps then march back and continue her heated gestures, obviously too riled to settle.

Damn, but she knew how to argue without uttering a word!

"Stop it. My job is to keep you safe, and I can't do that if you won't follow instructions," he barked.

Her eyes narrowed to mere slits. She jabbed a finger into his chest, then into hers, and crossed her index and middle finger.

"I get that you think a wife has to be by her husband's side, but I—"

She whirled and plopped down beside the boy, folding her

arms and turning her head away, evidently dismissing what he was saying.

"What's wrong with her, mister?" the kid asked.

"Not a damn thing except she can't talk, although as you can see, she can speak her mind as good as any man. And then some." Grumbling under his breath, Ridge stomped to the bounty hunters' two remaining horses for one to tote the dead man. The angry clank of his spurs reflected the rage burning in him as he loaded the bounty hunter on a mangy brown gelding.

This had come far too close to working out for the other side, so close, it scared the bejesus out of him. Any of those flying bullets could've hit Addie, the possibility buckling his knees. And on top of that, he had another death on his tarnished soul.

Dammit to hell!

Footsteps alerted him, and he whirled to find Addie behind him again. Rage at his hopeless situation and what he'd just been forced to do brought scathing words spilling that he couldn't stop. "This is why I can never preach again! I have blood on my hands, not just this man's, and I'm wondering why the hell I burdened you with marrying me!" He stalked to his horse and rested a hand on the saddle, taking several deep breaths, thinking it would help cool his temper. It didn't. He spun. "I'm a wanted man, and those bounty hunters would've taken me alive or killed me, then I shudder to think what they'd have done to you. I've only put you in danger, drawn to you the same damn thing I'm forced to live with. Truth is, I'll only get you killed."

Not waiting for her response, he strode angrily to the creek and stared into the clear, fresh stream. The minute he stepped in, it'd stir up the mud and turn brown.

That was his life. Brown and dirty and ugly.

"I'm not good or decent or kind!" he continued. Shame kept him from looking at her, because if he did, he couldn't say what he had to. "I've done things you wouldn't believe. Ride as far as you can get while you have the chance. Find someone who'll treat you right. I'm too far gone."

She placed a light palm on his back. Unclenching his jaw, he swung around. Her anger had cooled, but she stood there as though waiting for something—an apology? He owed her one for sure.

Releasing a sigh, he studied her for a long moment, then pulled her against him and buried his face in her golden hair. "I'm sorry. I'm so sorry. For all of it." Most of all for the lie that started everything and led him straight to the outlaw trail.

Movement behind them loosened his hold. The young man was attempting to stand, only to drop back to the ground. "I need to help the boy, Addie. I think he's hurt."

She stepped back, dried her eyes, and was all business again. Matching his stride, they went to the kid.

"What's wrong? Is your leg broken?" Ridge squatted down beside him.

The kid sniffled. "I don't think so, but those bounty hunters tried. They kept hitting me, said they'd make sure I didn't run."

Typical. "What's your name, son, and how old are you?"

Addie untied a dirty bandana from around the young man's neck and went to wet it in the creek.

"Bodie. Bodie Nix. I'm fifteen."

"Nice to meet you, Bodie. I'm Ridge Steele, and this is my wife, Addie. There's a town called Hope's Crossing not too far from here. I'm going to take you to the doctor there, and then if you're not opposed to it, I'll offer you a place to stay with us."

"Don't you want to know what I did to get brought in?"

"Can't have been too bad. Want to tell me?"

"I stole some food and a hog to feed the kids at the orphanage. They were starving." Bodie glanced toward the creek, his Adam's apple bobbing when he swallowed.

Thickness lodged in Ridge's chest. The bastards! The kid did nothing to warrant the bounty hunters' treatment. He looked away, taking a deep breath.

"Are you really an outlaw like Hiram claimed?" Bodie asked.

"Yep."

Addie returned and wiped the boy's face with the damp cloth. Her mouth tightened into a rigid line when she saw the severity of Bodie's bruises. Her light, gentle strokes appeared to have touched something inside the boy. He closed his eyes, a soft sigh escaping his mouth.

His spurs rattling, Ridge stooped to pick up his wanted poster. The headline screamed, WANTED DEAD OR ALIVE—$3,000!

Damn, the price for his capture had risen. He tried to fold it and put it away before Addie saw it, but he wasn't fast enough. She caught a glimpse before he stuffed it in his pocket. Dammit! Surprising him, she placed her palm against his chest over his heart and drew a circle.

"Addie girl, I still doubt the wisdom of marrying you, but I can no more send you away than stop breathing, and I hate myself for my weakness." He wrapped her in his arms, and she snuggled into the folds of his shirt.

When they broke apart, she helped him get Bodie onto the gray mare belonging to the bounty hunters, then accepted a boost onto her buckskin. Wordlessly, Addie had made her feelings plain. For better or worse, they were in this together—for however long they lived.

Worry niggled in Ridge's brain.

The bounty hunter knew where he was, and he'd be back. Logic said he probably wouldn't come alone.

❧

Dr. Mary was the first to see them ride into Hope's Crossing and came running, followed by Clay and Jack. Careful of his wound, Ridge dismounted, then lifted Addie down. He scanned the size of the growing crowd of curious onlookers. "The boy needs to be seen to, Doc. I'll be by later."

The petite woman of medicine wore her customary bullet necklace, made from slugs she'd removed from patients. They clinked together with each movement. "Let's go, kid. I'll patch you up."

"His name's Bodie Nix," Ridge called after them.

"I expect to see you at the hospital too, when you finish talking," the doc shot back.

Hell!

"What happened?" Jack asked, the tin sheriff's badge pinned to his shirt reflecting the sunlight.

"Addie and I went for a ride over our property to try out new mounts." Ridge gave them a quick rundown of the encounter with the bounty hunters. "The dead man there recognized me, and they started shooting. I killed this one, but the other got to his horse and hightailed it. I put a bullet in his thigh but don't think I hit him anywhere else."

Clay took a drag from his cigarette. "Dammit to hell!"

"I know. Just when we start to get comfortable, lawmen or bounty hunters find one of us," Ridge agreed.

Jack shot a gaze to the sole entrance to town, and Ridge could easily imagine the string of cusswords running through Jack's head. They were in his too.

"That's the problem," Jack grated out. "We've gotten too damn comfortable. Counting you, we still have at least half a dozen wanted men here, and that's only the ones I know. Others don't talk about their pasts, so we might never know until it's too late."

"This changes things." Clay threw his cigarette to the dirt and ground it out with the toe of his boot. "We need to call a town meeting—tonight. We have matters to discuss that affect us all."

"I agree. Until then, Addie and I need to get something to eat and check on the kid." Ridge gathered the horses' reins.

"What are we going to do with the boy?" Clay asked.

"I found him. I'll take him in." Ridge glanced toward the small hospital awash in the afternoon sunlight. "Besides, I have to hire someone to stay on the property with Addie now anyway. I'm generally gone in the daytime, and I won't leave her alone. Not with that bounty hunter around." And the men likely still scouring the countryside for her. They'd find her sooner or later.

The urge to ride out in search of them was hard to suppress. He needed time.

Addie's small palm slid inside Ridge's hand, and surprise rippled through him that she'd evidently put his angry outburst behind her. He wished with all his heart that she hadn't witnessed his rage, wished that his soul wasn't stained beyond redemption. She should be scared spitless of him now, so why was she so calm? A delayed reaction? He sighed. Someone should've given him a book on women. It would sure help to know what she thought about things.

Hell!

"I'll bury the dead man where no one will find him." Jack took the reins of the horse from Ridge. "I saw the boy's bruises. How bad are his injuries?"

"His leg took the brunt. Bodie said they hit him over and over, so he couldn't run. He has trouble even walking now. Probably have a limp for a while." Ridge's anger flared up again.

"I'm glad you shot this bastard, and the other too. Hope his wound is painful." Clay spat.

Ridge glanced down into Addie's pretty green eyes. Her pert nod said she agreed with Clay. She was a funny combination of frightened and fierce. If she ever got the hang of shooting straight, she'd be a force to reckon with.

If she had the time for them to find out. There was no way to know just yet how bad this would go, and what kind of trouble he'd brought the people of Hope's Crossing.

Eight

UNBUCKLING HIS SPURS, RIDGE STEPPED INTO THE DOCTOR'S three-bed hospital with Addie at his side. Though he tried to be quiet, his bootheels made the racket of a dozen hammers on the wooden floor. Bodie lay on one of two beds, battered and bruised, his eyes closed. The kid didn't stir at the noise.

Dr. Mary appeared through a curtained doorway. "Now let's take a look at you." She motioned him toward a table. "Hop up."

He glared. "I'm not a trained dog."

"You can all stand to be trained, Ridge Steele, don't think you can't," snapped the doctor. "I'm tired of patching you men up and sending you back out there, only to see my good work undone. I've had to start a new bullet necklace thanks to you all." She removed his shirt and prodded the wound.

"Ow! Gives you something to do besides complain," he shot back. "Where did you learn your bedside manner? Embalming school?"

"Shush! I know how to hurt you."

Addie put a hand over her mouth, her eyes dancing, evidently enjoying the sparring. Ridge winked at her.

"How's the kid?" he asked Dr. Mary.

"Poor thing's exhausted, and his leg will need rest. It's badly bruised and may have a small fracture but should be okay if he keeps off of it until it heals." She narrowed her eyes at him and puffed on the cigar tucked in the corner of her mouth. "I hope that dead man you toted in was the one who did it."

"He was one of them. I also shot the second one but not sure how bad. He got away."

"Hmph! Maybe he'll show up in town, and I'll get a shot at him myself. I'd like to make him pay for what he did to that poor, half-grown boy. I'm keeping Bodie overnight, and you can pick him up tomorrow."

"Thanks." Ridge glanced at Addie sitting beside him. "I'm going to hire him to stay with my wife during the day while I work. He seems like a decent kid. Just needs a break." If Ridge's hunch was right, Bodie would fit right in with the folks in Hope's Crossing. Every one of them could use a good helping of luck. And a hand up.

∾

Addie and Ridge took supper that evening at the Blue Goose Café. Ridge was quiet and in a strange mood during the meal. He still seemed furious with himself over the shoot-out with the bounty hunters. They'd given him no choice, but even so, having to kill one of them had obviously affected him deeply. She'd seen his anguish, heard his angry words, and didn't stand in judgment. She couldn't find it in herself to be angry at the words he'd flung at her. From all appearances, Ridge seemed to be living life as best he could in an impossible situation—even when trouble found him.

Once they'd eaten, they walked to the church where folks had gathered for the town meeting. Addie took a seat near the back, wondering what decisions they'd make. The setting sun required the lighting of lamps, and they flickered along the walls like a hundred fireflies.

Unlike New Zion, no one had forced them to attend. Odd that it was standing room only.

Ridge, looking every bit a man of authority, strode to the pulpit. "Thank you all for coming. A situation has developed that you should all be made aware of, and we have some decisions to make." He told them about the bounty hunters and the exchange of gunfire. "One got away. I don't know how bad off he is, but my gut says he'll be back."

Loud murmurs rose among the crowd. One man jumped to his feet and shook a fist. "If he comes back here, he'll find more of the same! We want to be left in peace to make a living and raise our families."

"That's what we all want," Ridge agreed. "But this land is changing, and lawmen are becoming more and more plentiful. It's a dangerous time for men like us. We've talked before about opening the back entrance to town, and now we need to hear your thoughts on the matter. More and more people are coming to settle, good people who want to make a difference here. We can't grow if we stay closed off."

"We might not have a town to grow if the law has its way!" shouted a man several rows up.

These people were scared of losing everything they had. Addie's heart went out to them. Their determination and strength to keep their life here impressed her. An unkempt woman with short, wild hair crept into the church, scanning the crowd, looking for a seat. Addie scooted over to make room, and the newcomer sat beside her.

Clay walked to Ridge and whispered something.

The assembly had gotten loud. Ridge tried to speak over the noise and finally had to bang on the pulpit with his fist for attention. "Clay's just reminded me that we'll soon have a bank, and the banker's set to arrive next month. The gentleman could pull out if he finds the town closed. This might play a part in your decision, so think about that."

The woman next to Addie muttered under her breath, "You'll regret opening up the back entrance, mark my words."

Jack came forward, his badge winking under the lights. "I'd like to say something." He turned to face them. "Folks, we've been real lucky so far. Those with the most to lose should have the loudest voice, not me and others who've obtained pardons for our crimes. But I bought in to Clay's crazy idea to build a town here because I sought a better life than being on the run. We've fought tooth and toenail for that dream, fought for all of you. Sooner or later, it'll be time to lay down our guns. That time might be now."

"What are you talking about?" The speaker was the big fiddle player, Dallas Hawk. Gray streaked his dark beard, and red mottled his puffy cheeks.

"I'm saying that it might not be good to act like we're

hiding something. Bounty hunters and lawmen will start breathing down our necks more than ever. If we open up the town and go about our business, show them we're law-abiding, they might stop sniffing around and leave us alone."

Except that Ridge had a price on his head that would appeal to a lot of desperate men, law-abiding now or not. Addie picked at the edge of her shawl.

A man wearing red suspenders got to his feet and drawled, "Jack, I seem to recall a time when you dyed your hair blond to throw a posse off your scent."

Everyone chuckled.

"That's true, Horace, I did," Jack admitted.

"Trouble is, that bounty hunter has already seen Ridge," Red Suspenders continued. "He knows to come here, and no hair dye's going to throw him off the scent this time. I vote we keep the back entrance closed, just the way it is."

"Damn right," the woman beside her murmured. "We don't want bounty hunters here."

"I'll turn this meeting back over to Ridge." Jack sat.

Ridge took Jack's place. "Okay, folks. I think it's time to vote. Raise your hand if you want to keep the back entrance to town closed." Almost every single person raised their hand.

"It's unanimous. We'll leave it closed." Ridge nodded to Clay. "Now, one more order of business. Do we post a guard at the entrance to town as we've had to do in the past?" Again, almost every hand went up. Addie smiled. She liked how democratic these people were. It was so very different from her community, where one crazed man made all the decisions.

"I think we have a majority. I'll get with Clay and Jack to make up a list of days and times for each man's slot, and we'll post it tomorrow." Ridge moved through the crowd toward Addie but kept getting stopped by folks who needed a word.

The woman next to her rose. "Mrs. Steele, welcome to Hope's Crossing. My name is Eleanor Crump. I've heard about you and know you can't speak, so don't you worry. I'd like to come visit sometime just to sit, if that's all right."

Addie nodded and squeezed Eleanor's hand before the woman turned and slipped out into the twilight.

Rebel Lassiter approached Addie next, with a tall, blue-eyed man by her side. "I'm happy to see you, Addie. This is my husband, Travis."

The cleft in Travis's chin deepened with his smile, and his eyes sparkled. "Mrs. Steele, you've got a good man in Ridge. I don't know what this town would do without him. If you ever need anything, don't hesitate. Rebel and I will help you, day or night."

Addie immediately liked Travis, who seemed to be cut from the same cloth as Ridge. She returned his smile and nodded. He appeared to know about her inability to speak, probably from Rebel, so she didn't feel as uncomfortable as usual.

Rebel glanced at the door, her eyes sad. "I was happy to see Eleanor Crump talking to you. We all need each other here in order to survive. The poor recluse kept herself separate from us until last Christmas. Since then, she seems to be making an effort to fit in more. Maybe she feels a kinship with you."

Perhaps. But why? Addie didn't know anything else to do but nod as the heat of embarrassment rose over not being able to utter a word. Ridge finally made it to her side, saving her from feeling like a dunce. He took her arm. "Let's go home."

The cool August breeze was welcome on her face as she rode horseback beside her husband. Dr. Mary had bandaged his upper arm and sent him away with instructions to keep it clean and wrapped. The bullet had passed through the soft tissue and would cause no harm as long as Ridge let her keep the ointment and clean gauze on it. But he was a stubborn one and Addie knew she had her work cut out for her.

Several times that day, it had crossed her mind to wonder what she'd do if Ridge died. Truth was, she didn't have any good ideas beyond continuing to live in Hope's Crossing. But despite the kindnesses she'd been offered so far, she couldn't be sure that anyone would lend a hand when trouble came.

And it would.

Ezekiel Jancy's reach was long. He would find her eventually.

And then? An icy shudder raced the length of her body. He'd first haul her back for a whipping in front of the town. To save face and keep control over his followers, he really could do no less. Then…

Oh God! The spit in her mouth dried. She was on a collision course with a madman.

Her mother would be no help. She was weak and shrank further inside herself with each passing year. If Ezekiel got his hands on Addie and dragged her from the town, she'd have no hope for survival.

They arrived at the house, silent and still, and rode around to the barn where Ridge dismounted and lit a lantern. He placed his hands around her waist and lifted her down as though she weighed nothing.

"Here we are."

Addie glanced up. His collarless shirt hung open at his throat, exposing the thick muscles of his neck. A single bead of sweat poised on his skin, then trickled down to pool in the hollow space between his collarbones. She yearned to brush it away but couldn't, yearned to kiss him, yearned to be whole, but she hadn't decided fully if he was the kind of man she could bank her life on. Their fight stood between them, and she still felt his anger, even though most of it had been directed at himself. Next time, God forbid, she'd try to follow his instructions.

His deep voice came thick and quiet. "Addie, I'm sorry for yelling at you at the creek. Not my finest hour."

Ridge's large frame, his strength, made her feel small against him. She rested a palm on his chest. Oh, to be able to speak and say she forgave him and understood far more than he thought.

"I wish you could holler and give me the tongue-lashing I deserve. Maybe one day." Sadness in his amber eyes broke her heart. "Let's get you into the house. I'll light the lamps and check the shadows before I unsaddle the horses."

As they walked toward the back door, Ridge put an arm around her as though it was the most normal thing in the world. But it was too soon to think that way.

Ridge's voice was raspy when he spoke again. "I meant to tell you...I have an account at the mercantile. Get whatever you want and charge it. I pay the bill at the end of each month."

She nodded and went in the house. While he lit the lamps in the kitchen, she grabbed her paper and scribbled, *"Do we have money?"*

He laughed. "I make a good living selling land. I'm not rich, but I do okay."

"You don't rob, like some outlaws?" She cringed at the way that had shot out onto paper. Too bold and nosy. But she was supposed to be sharing his life, wasn't she?

"No. I've done a lot of things, but I don't steal."

Miss Kitty and Squeakers strolled imperiously into the kitchen. Addie picked up the furry baby while the mama swished against Ridge's pant leg.

"What are you wanted for?" She kicked herself for not looking closer at the wanted poster when she'd had the chance... or maybe she hadn't really wanted to know.

The lines of Ridge's face hardened, and his voice turned cold. "I'll be back in a bit."

The door closed behind him, and she was left standing in silence, cursing her curiosity. Ridge had a right to hold back, just as she did at this point in their relationship. It was too soon to probe each other's deep, festering wounds. Once they got on solid ground, there'd be time enough for that.

Her gaze caught on the cobbler that Rebel Lassiter had brought that morning, sitting untouched on the table. She hadn't even told Ridge about it. Getting a kitchen towel from a drawer, she covered it, then moved to the parlor to wait for his return.

As with the habit of writing down her thoughts and the comfort that brought, she missed her knitting. The repetitive motion had always helped pass the time and soothed a ragged spirit. Tomorrow she'd go to the mercantile for yarn and needles and look for fabric to make herself a riding skirt. She'd need one if she intended to ride her buckskin, which she did.

She couldn't wait to get back on her horse. Riding with the wind in her face was the freedom she'd imagined.

Ridge was supposed to help her with a name. Fine. She'd think of one herself. For the next hour, she mulled over every name she'd ever heard, but none seemed right. She rose and paced the length of the parlor then back at least a dozen times.

The same as she'd done with every dilemma, she sat with paper and pencil, making a list of the ones that had come to mind.

One name drew her. *King*. She circled it and tapped the pencil. Yes!

King said everything about the horse and how truly thankful she was.

Excited, she went to the kitchen to look out the window for Ridge, but the pitch-black night failed to yield his tall figure. Dejected, she went back to the parlor and sat with Miss Kitty and Squeakers.

Reading didn't interest her without Ridge's voice saying the words. She took out her paper and pencil instead and wrote a short letter to her friend Zelda Law, the midwife who'd fled New Zion that horrible night with the newborn. As prearranged, Zelda would need to know how to find her in order to bring the child. The arrangement was never supposed to be anything but temporary. Though Addie longed to ask about the boy, she refrained from mentioning him, worried that the letter might fall into the wrong hands.

Finally, she rose and turned out all but one lamp as she retreated to her safe space.

While she braided her hair into one long rope down her back, Addie thought about her life and everything that had led her to Hope's Crossing. She missed her sisters, Thea, Tola, and Remy. She preferred those nicknames to the long, cumbersome given names her parents had bestowed. No doubt their father had thoroughly poisoned their minds against her—something he did best. Maybe one day she might try to see them again.

Pushing those thoughts away, she secured her braid with a worn ribbon and went to bed.

Sometime after midnight, Addie woke. Had Ridge ever returned? She crept up the stairs barefoot, careful not to step on the creaky fourth board. The bedroom door was open, and light from the moon revealed Ridge's sleeping form. And the empty whiskey bottle clutched in his hand.

The room reeked of alcohol.

He lay atop the coverlet, fully dressed except for his boots. His holster hung on a post at the foot of the bed. Relieved that he was back, she started to leave, then stopped. Utter loneliness hung thick in the air, stifling her. Ridge Steele's fight with his demons had not ended well.

An urge that was part curiosity and part the need to touch him compelled her to move closer. She slid onto the bed beside her husband and lay there for a while, listening to his soft breathing. When he didn't wake, she boldly curled her hand around his long, tanned fingers, her head barely touching his sleeve. Sadness oozed from her heart. This was her place to take.

And she yearned to.

So why not? She had no idea of how to go about it. She didn't know how all this worked. Even before prison, she'd been clueless about marriage.

Maybe he drank because of the situation she'd insisted upon. Guilt washed over her. He'd given her an amazing horse, a comfortable home, an account at the mercantile for whatever her heart desired, for God's sake.

She deserved none of that. Her selfishness and fear had forced this separation.

And what about her?

Tears slipped from the corner of her eye, wetting his arm. There was something terribly broken inside her. The same horrible loneliness that he must feel enveloped her. What good was it to marry if not to claim all the advantages of having someone to face life's trials with? Someone to help ease the heavy burdens. She desperately wanted to fill that aching void that had gotten larger than ever. She yearned for strong arms around her, for someone to lean on when she grew weary— for someone to help fight her father's power.

Tomorrow, she'd go see Dr. Mary and get her opinion about her condition.

Yes, that's what she'd do.

Ridge mumbled something in his sleep and rolled to face her, the whiskey bottle clattering to the floor. He threw his arm across her hip, trapping her. Addie lay very still, afraid to breathe. His scent enveloped her and seeped into every pore, and for the next few moments, she felt something wonderful and new. Ridge was hers to claim, and she'd find some way to keep him. If she could only unlock her brain and find her words.

Afraid he'd awaken, she lifted his arm and tried to slip away, but he reached out and drew her against him, wrapping his arm around her. Now she was truly held fast, and there was nothing she could do but wait—and pray he didn't wake up.

He would mistake what she was doing in his bed and expect…

What exactly?

Somewhere past her panic, she was reasonably sure he'd never use force against her. The time she'd been here had shown her that.

Lulled by his strong heartbeat, she began to feel safer than she had in a long time. Slowly, Addie drifted off to sleep.

"Why are you lying girl?" Ridge shouted. "You know the truth. Tell them I didn't touch you!"

Addie jerked awake, her stomach knotted. What was he saying? Who had lied about him? It sounded like someone had accused him of attacking her. This was something more than a simple lie—this went much, much deeper.

While she pondered her next move, Ridge suddenly rolled the other way, freeing her. Addie eased away from his side and hurried down to her little dismal room that had first seemed perfect for her needs. Now it had become empty, airless, and sad.

She had to find a way to fix herself, then maybe she could help rid him of his demons.

Daylight would come in a few hours, and she couldn't wait to implement her plan. It was long past time. She wanted to talk. She had things to say.

Nine

RIDGE WOKE TO A DREAM TEASING THE EDGES OF HIS MIND. He'd dreamed that Addie had shared his bed and woke to her scent, the warmth of her body next to him. He sat up abruptly, the room empty, her fragrance curling about him like cigar smoke. An indention in the pillow on the other side of the bed caught his eye, as though someone had lain there.

Could Addie…?

Impossible. Best to get his day started and stop thinking about figments of his imagination. He finger-combed his hair, which was plenty good enough, pulled on his boots, and buckled on his holster. When he went to spread up the covers, he froze. Lying there on the sheet was a faded yellow ribbon that had not been there yesterday. He lifted the pillow to his face. The scent of wild roses lingered like a sweet melody.

His little bird had come to his side. Hope sprang in his heart, where there hadn't been much to go around. If he could stay patient, keep his temper, give her time, and earn her trust, maybe she'd soon get over this fear that had her hiding in the shadows.

Guilt swept over him. He shouldn't have avoided her last night, but the questions about his crimes poked him hard. Shame had risen up in him, too strong to ignore. Time was supposed to heal all wounds, but being accused of rape and murder wasn't something that he'd been able to erase from his name…or memory. And it was a story he couldn't bring himself to tell Addie.

The thought hit him for the hundredth time that maybe he could make a trip to that small town and try to talk some sense into the young woman, get her to speak the truth. But like always, logic took hold. Going back wouldn't change one thing. Besides the danger of such a move was too great. He'd barely escaped with his life before.

What made him think this time would be different? This time they'd hang him for sure.

No, he couldn't go back. Even if the lady recanted, Tom Calder, the powerful rancher, would see that he swung for killing his boys. Ridge was safe here, and this was where he'd stay.

Pots and pans rattling in the kitchen told him she was up. At the bottom of the stairs, he leaned into her little room and placed her ribbon on the bench. Best to pretend he hadn't found it.

She turned at the sound of his boots, a cup of coffee in her hand. No smile for him, but no frown either. Miss Kitty groomed herself by the warmth of the stove while Squeakers tried its hardest to grab dust motes. His heart thudded, surprising him. Home wasn't just the place where a man laid his head. It was a feeling. It was where his heart found heaven. *This* was home. The only place he wanted to be.

Ridge took the coffee. "Thanks. I hope you slept well." He pulled out a chair. "Bacon sure smells good."

Addie handed him a piece of paper, then went back to watching the skillet.

The note read: *"I can't stand being this way. I want to talk to the doctor about my problem. Will you come?"*

Happiness surged in his chest. This was the first outward sign he'd had that she wanted to make changes.

"Yes, of course. I need to collect Bodie anyway."

When she didn't turn around, he rose and stood behind her, putting his hands on her shoulders. "Together we can whip any problem. If anyone can help you get a handle on this, it's Dr. Mary. She's one of the wisest people I know." Not only about medicine but life in general. The doctor mended both body and soul. "I haven't said this before, but I'm proud of you, Addie."

She turned and studied him, her mouth moving. He could see her trying to form words, then her face betraying her disgust when she couldn't.

"It's all right. We'll get there," he said softly.

80   LINDA BRODAY

Impulsively, before she could turn or back away, Ridge covered her lips with his as though he did it each morning.

Addie stiffened for a heartbeat then relaxed. Though he sensed she wanted to run, she stood in place and rested a light palm on his chest. That was a start.

The kiss was light, yet full of tender yearning. Very slowly, she curved her lips and returned the token of affection. The heady taste of her overloaded his senses and made him happy to be alive. One day, he'd make her glad she'd tied her lot to his. For now, though, light and easy was best.

He released her, and instead of hurrying away, she gave him a trembly smile and cupped the side of his face for a long moment, staring into his eyes.

He didn't move, didn't breathe, didn't dare blink. Time ceased until the smell of burning bacon broke the spell. She snatched the skillet from the heat and grabbed a plate. Ridge chuckled and sat, feeling as though he'd found a lucky four-leaf clover hidden among the thistle. Burned bacon didn't bother him.

Then, as she puttered around the kitchen gathering the rest of the breakfast, Addie delivered the second surprise of the morning—she began to hum. Sweet sound filled the kitchen. Miss Kitty stopped washing herself and stared.

∼∽∾

Once they arrived in town that morning, Addie went straight to the mercantile and mailed her letter to Zelda Law. Then, taking Ridge's arm, they went together to Dr. Mary's office. She settled herself next to him in a chair and glanced around at the cabinets full of medicines, instruments, and medical books. Addie's nose twitched at the strange smells, and her hands trembled. Maybe she was too broken. Maybe the trauma of her father and prison had done too much damage, and she would never go back to the way she was before.

"Mrs. Steele, what can I help you with?"

Prepared, Addie handed Dr. Mary a note she'd written back at home. The thirtyish doctor, her brown hair in a tidy topknot, studied it then turned her gaze on Addie. "I don't know if I can help you, but I'll try. First, I want to examine your throat. Ridge, can you hold the lamp up?"

For the next few moments, Dr. Mary held Addie's tongue down with a depressor and peered into her mouth, then asked her to move her tongue around, with more peering. "As I suspected," the doctor announced, sitting back. "I see no physical impairment. To get to the root of the problem will require a lot of questions."

Addie automatically tensed. Questions meant answers, and those meant delving into painful things that she'd buried…and Ridge would find out exactly the kind of wife he'd gotten. Maybe he wouldn't want her anymore.

Dr. Mary's unusual necklace clanked as she laid the tongue depressor down. "How far are you willing to go, Mrs. Steele?"

Addie's mouth went dry. Decision time. She met the concern in Ridge's amber eyes and reached for her paper. *All the way. I want to be able to say all the things I want. And call me Addie.*

"I suppose that settles it." Dr. Mary rested a gentle hand on Addie's knee. "We'll do this in small increments. It may take weeks, or months, but we won't give up. Can you make any sound at all?"

"*Yes,*" she wrote. "*I can hum.*"

Ridge squeezed her hand. "She just discovered she could this very morning. It surprised us both."

"That's wonderful. Addie, tell me about your home, your family." At Addie's frown, Dr. Mary added, "Take your time."

Where to begin? So much had happened. Addie gripped her pencil and pressed so hard on the paper the lead broke. Tears bubbled in her eyes.

Ridge lifted her up from the chair and pulled her against him, rubbing her back. "It's all right. No one here wants to hurt you. You're safe."

Physically, yes, but she wasn't safe from the ugly memories that clawed and clawed, trying to steal her very soul.

"I think we're moving too fast," Dr. Mary said softly. "If

you'll sit down, I'm going to sing. Ridge, you can join in, and Addie, try to hum along. If you can't, that's fine. Just do what's comfortable."

Addie wiped her eyes and took her seat as the doctor and Ridge began to sing. The first song was an old hymn, and although the sound brought comfort, she didn't hum. It was when they moved onto faster songs, ones she didn't know and of the sort that were probably sung in saloons, that the catchy tunes grabbed her. Carefully, she forced the sound out. The more she hummed, the lighter, and happier she felt and the stronger the sound came from her lips. The doctor seemed to be on the right track.

The kid, Bodie Nix, left his bed and hobbled into the office on a crutch. He paused in the doorway for a while, listening, then he, too, started to sing along. Bodie's and Ridge's voices amazed her, combining in beautiful harmony.

After four songs, Dr. Mary stopped. "I think we made progress. Addie, come back tomorrow morning, and we'll do nothing but sing. If you feel up to writing something down, go ahead, but it's fine if you don't. We have no rules for this."

No rules. Addie found that freeing. No rules meant she couldn't mess up.

Ridge stood, beaming. "I'm so proud of you, Addie. One day you'll talk as well as anyone." He squeezed her palm.

A warm feeling blossomed from deep inside, bringing a smile to her lips. She threaded her fingers through his, happier than she'd been in a very long time.

He swung to the kid. "Bodie, I'd like to hire you on as my number-one hand. That is, unless you have other plans."

Bodie's eyes widened. "I'd like that just fine, Mr. Steele."

"I have one rule—you have to call me Ridge."

The young man grinned like a fool donkey eating briars. "Okay—Ridge."

"I'll have you a place to sleep, so don't worry about that." Ridge squeezed Bodie's shoulder. "Addie and I are heading to the mercantile now, so we'll all go and get you what you need in the way of clothing and other items."

The grin disappeared from Bodie's face, replaced by an obstinate frown. "Only if you take the cost out of my wages."

Dr. Mary chuckled. "That boy drives a hard bargain."

"That he does," Ridge agreed.

"Addie, in case you're interested, a dressmaker has come to town," Dr. Mary said. "I hear she's very good. It won't be long until she has more business than she can handle, so if you want to order something, best do it soon."

Addie nodded cautiously. Her own sewing was only passable, and she'd love to have something made by a professional, but there was the cost to consider. Though Ridge hadn't yet limited her, she didn't want to put him on hard times.

"What's the woman's name, Doctor?" Ridge asked. "It slipped my mind."

"Tara Quinn. A very friendly woman, from what I hear."

They were on their way to the mercantile with Addie leading the buckskin when she remembered she hadn't told Ridge the name she'd chosen for her horse. She pulled some paper from her pocket and jotted *King,* then handed it to Ridge, who'd stopped to wait for them. She pointed to the horse and grinned.

"That's a fine name, Addie. I like that, and it fits him well." His warm gaze brought heat to her face.

Bodie stopped to pick up a rock. He rubbed it on his shirt and studied it, then stuck it into his trouser pocket. "I had a black roan named Prince a long time ago. Then my ma and pa died, and a man took Prince away."

Addie wanted to ask him why he was keeping the stone, but it didn't seem like the time. She just listened to his sad story instead.

"Where did you live after they passed?" Ridge asked.

"First one relative then another, but nobody really wanted me. They said I was a bad seed and nothing but trouble. I don't know, maybe I was. They claimed it so much, I decided to make it true." The kid wiped his nose on his sleeve and his crutch clattered to the ground. "I just wanted someone to care whether I lived or died."

A deep ache settled in Addie's heart. She'd known such a feeling. She retrieved his crutch and handed it back, then put an arm around him. Bodie needed her and Ridge more than she'd realized at first, and she figured she needed them both just as much.

They browsed through the mercantile, and Ridge helped Bodie with clothes, while Addie picked up yarn and needles, a notebook, and enough heavy broadcloth in navy blue to make a riding skirt.

"Nice to see you, Mrs. Steele."

She'd been in deep concentration, her attention on the bolts of fabric, and almost didn't hear the soft voice at her side. A glance revealed the woman who'd sat beside her in church. No name came to her mind, though Addie remembered the older woman's disheveled appearance.

Ridge evidently noticed Addie's predicament and came over. "Good morning, Eleanor. I trust you're doing well."

"I am, Mr. Mayor. And you?"

He met Addie's gaze, and she felt her cheeks warm again. "It's been an unbelievable morning." His smile warmed his eyes, and Addie could see how happy her teetering steps had made him. He seemed very different from the somber man she'd married.

Eleanor set a bag of sugar on the counter. "Mrs. Steele, I'll visit soon."

Addie nodded and gave Eleanor a smile. Ridge provided the words, "Come anytime, ma'am. You'll be welcome."

After Eleanor paid and left, Ridge spoke quietly in Addie's ear. "I don't know her full story, but I think she would like a friend."

Addie could be that. Everyone needed someone, and doing what she could for the woman would ease the quiet of the long days. Addie laid her knitting supplies and fabric on the pile Ridge had started and turned to go outside with Bodie. But as she walked toward the door, she spied exactly what she truly wanted—a pair of denim trousers like the ones Rebel had worn. They would be perfect for working in the garden or riding King.

Ridge lifted an eyebrow and grinned when Addie laid them on their pile of purchases. Warmth stole up her neck at his reaction, but instead of snatching them back, she gave him a stubborn tilt of her head and stood her ground.

He chuckled. "These too, Owen."

"You know, folks are snapping up those new Levi's right and left. I can't keep 'em in stock," Owen Vaughn said. "It's impossible to wear them out."

Addie wandered to the ladies' boots as the men kept chatting. Part of her still worried about the cost, but the temptation to browse was too much. The boots looked to be very well made and the leather stitching quite remarkable. She glanced down at her ill-fitting shoes.

"Hold on a minute, Owen, we may not be through." Ridge came over to her. "What size do you wear?"

Addie shook her head and tried to walk away, but Ridge would have none of it. "Oh no you don't. What size?"

She shrugged.

"Sit down."

When she did, he pulled off her shoe, studied it for a moment, then reached for one of the boots and placed them sole to sole. He put that boot back and got another and did the same. "I think this might fit. Clay makes these, and you'll find none better in all of Texas." He knelt, and with his warm hands around her foot, slipped it into the buttery soft boot. "Stand up please."

She'd never worn anything so comfortable. The fine leather molded around her foot like it had been made especially for her. He pressed on the toe of the boot, and she wiggled her toes at him.

"I think it's a perfect fit. Let's put the other on."

When he slipped the second one on, Addie sighed with delight. Her feet felt as though she walked on a cloud. She caught the question in Ridge's eyes and nodded.

"We'll take these boots, Owen, and the lady will wear them." Ridge picked up her pitiful shoes and, with what seemed like sheer glee, threw them into the trash barrel. Guilt took hold in Addie's gut. Ridge had spent far too much money on her, and all at once. Her father's voice grated in her ear. *You're not worth a new pair of shoes. These old worn ones of your mother's are plenty good enough. Complain and you'll go barefoot. If you'd been a boy—*

But she'd had the audacity to be a girl. She'd held her tongue and stuffed paper inside the toes of her mother's old shoes. Over and over through the years, she'd held her tongue, itching to scream out how much she hated him. Held her tongue when he ordered her whipped. Chose to live in darkness to protect the child from him.

"Do you see something else you like?" Ridge asked, startling her from her thoughts.

She shook her head, guilt-wracked for even implying she might want more and hurried outside where Bodie waited. The kid rose from a bench and stuck the crutch under his arm.

A wagon pulled up with some chickens in the bed and a cow tied on behind. The driver called out, "What do you want me to do with these, Steele?"

"Can you follow me to my place? It's not far."

"Lead the way."

Ridge helped Bodie into the back of the wagon and handed him their purchases, then handed Addie up into King's saddle. Addie rode slowly around the cart, looking the cow over with a critical eye. It appeared to be a fine animal.

Her gaze swept to Bodie, her real-life Oliver Twist. Then she shifted attention to Ridge, and her heart had an odd reaction she couldn't describe. Such a high price on his head. Her throat tightened. One day, the law would come for him.

How could he be bad when he did so much good? He rescued Bodie and gave him a place to live, made sure he had what he needed. And her. She glanced down at her shiny new boots and patted King's neck. Then there was Ridge's kiss at breakfast and going with her to Dr. Mary's. He truly seemed to care that she regained her voice.

The words he'd cried out in his sleep crossed her mind. He hadn't done whatever they accused him of. Some girl had lied.

Addie knew too much about lies and evil, false accusations and rotted souls.

Addie turned her thoughts back to Bodie and Ridge and wouldn't trade either one. They were her family now, and better in every way than the one that had thrown her onto the trash heap.

It was time to cast aside her doubts. She needed no more proof.

This was the only place she wanted to be. Next to Ridge. Watching his back. Sharing his life. Finding some way to be his wife.

The day had yielded so many surprises, she could scarce recall them all. But the best of them was the visit to Dr. Mary's and rising hope that she would find her voice.

The minute her words returned, she'd thank Ridge for marrying her and giving her a new start.

Ten

RIDGE GOT BODIE SETTLED INTO A ROOM IN THE BARN THAT he'd built for a hired hand. The kid never stopped grinning, calling the place the best he'd ever had. How pitiful his life must've been to think the small room with bare boards and a menagerie of livestock on the other side of the wall was heaven.

Then, eager to start earning his keep, Bodie began to hobble around and build a sturdy chicken coop.

"I'm riding out for a bit. Keep an eye on things and don't let anything happen to Addie." Ridge laid a Winchester beside the kid's chair. "For strangers if they come nosing around."

Bodie shook a long strand of hair from his face. "You can count on me, Mr...I mean, Ridge. I have a good aim and a steady finger."

Satisfied that Bodie could, and would, guard Addie, Ridge stuck his foot in the stirrup and swung his leg over. He rode to the creek where he'd encountered the bounty hunters.

Jack had buried the man Ridge killed in an unmarked grave and scattered brush over it. But Ridge didn't like the gnawing in his gut. He was being watched—the bounty hunter that Bodie called Hiram had to be lurking somewhere close.

Faint tracks were still visible in the dirt, and Ridge followed a set that led away. In a ravine, he found signs that Hiram had stopped there to bind up his wound. Ridge picked up the tracks leading out the other side.

Why hadn't he looked for this earlier? Hiram might have stopped long enough that Ridge could have caught up with him. Ridge called himself every name he could think of. He'd missed a chance to end this. However, in his defense, he'd had Bodie to get medical treatment for, not to mention protecting Addie. In the end, he decided he couldn't have done anything differently. Best to let it go or it would eat at him.

Hiram had traveled north, then doubled back, which told Ridge the bounty hunter's wound hadn't been that severe. Ridge lost the tracks outside the entrance to Hope's Crossing. The road leading into town was little more than a wide path between the two walls of the canyon where the town sat. There was no other way in or out of town. Dammit! Had Hiram managed to sneak into town before they'd put a guard in place? Cussing a blue streak, Ridge dismounted and scoured the ground. Hundreds of tracks from people coming and going over the last day had obscured Hiram's.

A whinny reached Ridge and he glanced up to see his neighbor, Travis Lassiter, looking down on him from the back of his horse. He rested his arm on the pommel of his saddle. "Need some help, Ridge?"

"I could at that." Ridge explained quickly. "It's important to find out where this two-bit bastard went from here—and if he's still hanging around."

Travis swung from the horse. "Two pairs of eyes are better than one. I'll help. Show me what the track looks like, and we'll widen the circle until we pick it up again."

They searched painstakingly for over an hour, and Ridge was on the verge of giving up when he finally saw the tracks he was looking for. He and Travis followed the trail—a trail that led onto Ridge's property and right up to the house.

Ridge's blood froze. The sign was unmistakable. Someone had hunkered down on the ground underneath the parlor window.

Brown globs of tobacco spit revealed that the watcher had stayed there for some time.

Dark foreboding crawled up Ridge's neck. The man could've been watching Addie, here all alone. He'd have seen Ridge leave when Addie's questions had become too hard to answer. Maybe the watcher had witnessed the kiss they'd shared that morning.

Ridge struggled to breathe inside his tightening chest, his mouth drying.

Even now, the bastard could have his silent wife in his sights.

And she wouldn't be able to scream.

～✦～

Later that evening, a long, full day behind them, Ridge, Addie, and Bodie sat around the supper table. It felt comfortable, like they'd done it a million times before. Ridge's gaze lingered on Addie. She'd made big strides that day toward regaining not only her voice, but her independence.

"You fixed a mighty fine meal, Addie. Can't beat fried potatoes, greens, and ham."

Her cheeks colored a nice rosy pink, and she gave him a wide smile.

"I was thinking that after we finish, we might sing in the parlor. Would you be willing?"

She nodded and manipulated her fingers to mimic knitting. Then she opened her hands like a book and pointed to him.

"Yes, after we sing, I'll read. I'm anxious myself to get back to the story." He explained the book to Bodie. "Maybe I'll take a break and let you read."

Bodie ducked his head and mumbled, "I never learned my letters."

"What grade did you get to in school?"

"Never been." The kid stared off into space. "All my relations said I was too dumb for learning, and the only choice left for someone like me was working." His face tightened. "But they didn't fool me. They took all my money—for room and board, they said. And if I didn't work, they got nothing."

A muscle in Ridge's jaw tightened. "You're not dumb, Bodie. What do you think about going to school now?"

"Too old. I'd be a laughingstock."

Yeah, he was probably right.

Ridge scooted his plate back and propped his elbows on the table. "What if I teach you here in private?"

"I'd like that. It's downright embarrassing not to be able to sign my own name."

Addie scribbled something on her paper and handed it to Ridge. *"I taught school for a few years. I could help."*

Ridge reached for her hand and squeezed her fingers gratefully. Finally, she was starting to open up about her life. "I didn't know that. You'll be a huge benefit. My knowledge is somewhat limited, and the boy needs to learn more than to read and write. He needs to be able to count and cipher and all that other stuff."

He helped Addie with the dishes, loving the quiet closeness of being with her. Their hands touched frequently as they passed the dishes back and forth, each brush sending a jolt of awareness through him. He liked it so much, he started doing it on purpose.

Little by little, he was learning his wife. Quite a few things surprised him, especially her willingness to try Dr. Mary's suggestions. She truly wanted to speak again. It brought hope to see her put her fighting spirit towards recovering her voice. He could see in her eyes how much she yearned to rejoin life. Going to see the doctor today could be the best thing they'd done so far, and it had all been Addie's idea.

The pair of denims she'd chosen at the last minute at the mercantile crossed his mind, and heat climbed up his neck. When she put those on, he didn't know if he'd be able to keep what sense he had about him. Rebel Lassiter wore them and he'd never felt a thing, but there again, she was only a friend.

Once they finished with the dishes, Addie tended to the wound on his upper arm, cleaning, and dabbing on a salve the doctor had given them. He closed his eyes and soaked in her caring touch, pretending she wasn't afraid to come to their bed. For a second, he imagined her fingertips running the length of his naked body. To be touched like that would be heaven. He'd been with painted women some, but lying with a wife would be very different.

Very different in so many ways. Heat built in his stomach.

After Addie wrapped his wound, they went to the parlor and sang two songs. He was happy to hear Addie hum along. Then he reached for *Oliver Twist* and read while she pulled out her yarn, the needles clicking away. She and Bodie rolled the hanks of wool into three balls—brown, gold, and green. He didn't know what she had in mind to make, but the colors were pretty.

The kitten grabbed the colorful spun wool and managed to wrap itself up in a tangled mess. Miss Kitty swatted at her baby as though trying to make it behave and quit acting like a complete nincompoop. Ridge paused to watch and chuckled at their antics. He'd never known a peace like this and wasn't giving it up. If the bounty hunter found him again, the man would have to kill him. Ridge would never leave this little family, their home, willingly.

"Read some more," Bodie urged. "I want to see what happens."

"You like the book?"

"Shoot, yeah! It's a lot more interesting than all the begettin' in the Bible." The kid grinned. "Never could understand why they didn't talk in plain English."

"To make kids like you wonder about it." Ridge read a little more and closed the book. "That's enough for tonight. It's bedtime, and we have lots of work to do tomorrow."

"Yes, sir. I reckon we do." Bodie pulled himself to his feet. "Good night."

Addie rose and kissed Bodie's cheek, then pushed back a curl that had fallen onto the kid's forehead, just like a mother would. Her tender caring brought a hitch to Ridge's breath, and he worked to get air past the ache in his chest.

After Bodie left, Addie turned toward her small space.

"Wait a minute," Ridge called, striding to her. "I want to ask you something."

Arms full of yarn and mending, she lifted her eyebrows in question.

"I'd like to kiss you good night—that is, if you're agreeable. As husbands and wives do."

She smiled and moved toward him until she stood very close. The gold flecks in her green eyes sparkled, and the smell of the peach cobbler they'd had for dessert filled each breath.

She didn't seem afraid. Maybe she wanted this as much as he did. She lowered her lids and seemed to hold her breath.

Ridge anchored her with his hands, spreading his fingers behind each ear, and slowly moved his mouth over hers. Very gently, he kissed her, devouring her softness. The kiss was more deliberate than the one that morning. A lot more. He slid an arm around her, splaying his large hand across her back.

Warmth rushed through him and pooled in his belly. Her breath melded with his, and her lips parted slightly as she leaned into him for the space of several heartbeats. Not wanting to press his luck, he ended the kiss and took a half step back, not sure what to expect. He prayed he'd done nothing to upset her. He thought he was heeding Luke's advice to go slow, but any slower, and they'd come to a complete stop.

"Would you like to do this each night—as our private ritual?" He smiled at her nod, finding the promise of more kissing bursting inside his chest like a roman candle. "Good night, Addie. Sleep well."

He turned down the lamps, made sure she didn't need anything, and went up to bed. Maybe tonight he wouldn't need whiskey to silence his demons. Addie would be his medicine. The question of whether she would pay him a midnight visit again rolled through his head as he undressed and crawled between the sheets. Just in case, he left the bedroom door wide open in invitation.

Maybe that was the trick to having a successful marriage— never closing a door, any door, between a husband and wife. An unbidden smile brightened his thoughts along with the hope burning inside him.

∼≫

Addie sat on her bench and listened to Ridge moving about upstairs, his kiss tingling on her lips. The fat Miss Kitty curled beside her while Squeakers leaped into her lap and settled with a happy meow. A feeling of contentment stole over her. She'd found a place where she was supposed to be, somewhere she mattered.

The lamp burned low but provided enough light to see by. She braided her hair, then reached for her writing notebook to voice some of the thoughts running through her head.

> *I don't know what love is, or if I'll ever know. Maybe it's nothing more than being immensely grateful for what someone has given you, gratitude that bursts inside your chest and spreads through you like a flame. Tonight, Ridge made me feel this way. Around him, I matter for the first time in my life. I feel his deep caring down to the soles of my feet, and I know beyond a doubt that if it came to it, he'd willingly die for me. Although I'd never want that. Never. I love his kisses, the taste of his mouth, and his warm hands on me. If this isn't love, I think I'll surely die when love does come.*

A smile crossed her lips as she thought about lying next to him on the bed. If he'd noticed she'd been there, he hadn't said anything. Yet...her faded ribbon had been lying there in plain view on the bench after she'd looked all over for it.

What would he do if she announced she wanted to sleep with him all the time? A rush of flutters spread through her and settled in her stomach. Yet she needed to purge herself of all the hurt, anguish, and despair in order to hopefully one day claim her rightful place. Dr. Mary was right. She had to start facing her past in order to reach for that bright future glimmering within sight. She turned to a new page of the notebook and continued.

> *I've come to realize that there are some people whose brains can't be manipulated by others. I'm one of them. I always had this knowing deep inside, about how wrong Ezekiel's and his follower's beliefs were. No matter how long they held me captive to that life, I wouldn't, couldn't, accept any of it as the truth. My brain simply wouldn't allow me. I suspect my mother can't buy into their thinking either, although she pretends well. Still, she'll never get a chance to break free. She's not strong enough. My father has her too beaten down.*

There may be some hope for my younger sisters if I can get to them in time. But failure would mean the public whipping post that Ezekiel is so fond of using.

A shudder rippled through her body. Addie sat there a moment before turning the page to write more. Now that she'd started, all the words she'd held inside for so long spilled out almost faster than she could get them down.

My father, Ezekiel Jancy, calls himself the New Messiah and heads up a religious order of his own in the town of New Zion, in the rolling hills of central Texas. He became so obsessed with having a son to carry on his work that he turned into a monster and destroyed a young girl's promising life. I had to do something to stop him, and it cost me dearly.

Memories so thick she could taste them almost choked her. Her hand shook, and she laid down the pencil, unable to go on. After a few moments, she tore out the last two pages and set them aside until morning. But she left her musings about love in the notebook. No one would ever see those. She put everything away and curled up on the bench under her quilt. But sleep refused to come, her mind dwelling on the sweetness of Ridge's lips on hers. The promise of more beat in her heart like a drum.

She was Ridge Steele's wife, and she wanted to stay where she was safe—in his arms.

❧

The next morning, Ridge woke before dawn. Disappointment flared to find no evidence that Addie had come to their bed. He dressed and went out to milk the cow and feed the horses. He'd no sooner started his chores than the kitchen door opened and Addie joined him in the yard to gather the eggs. To anyone who saw them, he and Addie would look like a normal couple.

One step forward and two back. He'd have to learn to

rejoice in the small steps and take heart in the backward progress, even if it killed him.

The sky lightened to a nice shade of apricot as the sun readied itself to make an appearance. He loved this time of day and the mysteries it held. He never knew what events would unfold before nightfall. The air was crisp, the fragrant scent of sage whispering against his skin.

Ridge let his gaze sweep over his and Addie's property. The kitchen opened into a sizeable back area, the barn sitting about a hundred yards to the right. A small corral hugged the front of the barn where he let the horses exercise. He was proud of what he'd already built.

Just then, the sun broke low on the horizon, the morning rays bouncing off the red rock of the canyon and flashing along its walls like pure gold. His chest tightened with the beauty.

Addie stepped from the chicken coop with her basket and into the golden light. The sight stole his breath. Real peace softened her features, and he liked to think she looked happy. Maybe caring for the chickens and cow were familiar chores that she'd missed while in prison.

She caught his glance and smiled, and his heart tumbled end over end. He stared at her, mesmerized for a long moment, thankfulness tightening his chest before he sighed and lifted the pail of fresh milk. Time to get moving.

After a hearty breakfast, Ridge took his plate to the dishpan. "Bodie, I'll put you to work repairing some harnesses and other barn chores you can do sitting down. Stay off that leg."

The fifteen-year-old shook back his long hair and frowned. "I don't need to be coddled. I came to work."

"I know that, but for now, you have to go easy. I'm not going to have Dr. Mary coming after me when your leg doesn't heal." Ridge nudged Miss Kitty lightly out of the way with the toe of his boot. "Addie and I have to go see the doctor this morning. I'll leave you armed, Bodie. If anyone comes sneaking around, shoot him."

"Yes, sir."

The boy stood, nearly as tall as Ridge when he wasn't

stooping over the crutch. As the boy maneuvered through the door and outside, Addie removed her apron and hurried into the next room.

"I'll saddle the horses," Ridge called after her, but before he could move to the door, she was back. She handed him two pieces of notepaper, her hand shaking.

"What's this?" Ridge took them from her and read her neat angled handwriting. The first one told about her father. New Messiah his hind foot! He'd heard of those kinds of radical beliefs. Ridge struggled to tamp down his anger. This wasn't the time for him to indulge in personal feelings on the matter. This was about Addie and the way she was trusting him with buried secrets.

He moved to the second torn sheet of paper, and fury grew in his stunned silence. He couldn't believe the depths to which Ezekiel Jancy's obsession had seemingly gone, the degradation he'd inflicted. A horrible picture emerged, one that twisted and turned inside him. *A public whipping post.* For a long moment, he fought to erase the image of Addie being punished for rebellion against such injustice.

What had she done to help the young girl in her letter?

Whatever it was, it had landed her in prison. He realized she was waiting for his reaction. He knew beyond a doubt that the happiness of their marriage hinged on what he said next.

Ridge laid the papers on the table and took her hands. "Thank you for feeling comfortable enough to share those things with me. If you truly care for someone, you let them into your life—as you've done. I'm very proud of you and what you've overcome." His voice turned raspy with emotion. He kissed her forehead. "You're my hero. My angel."

Addie stepped back and made wild gestures with her arms, then grabbed the paper and wrote: *"No! I'm not brave, not strong enough. Don't put me on a pedestal."*

"We can argue this point all day, so I'll drop it, but whatever you did to help that girl was the right thing. Thank God you didn't listen to that crazy talk and let your father tell you what to think. I've heard of zealots like him before." He pinched the bridge of his nose and let out a loud sigh, wishing he could find the right words to say what he wanted, but they escaped him. Finally, he broke the silence. "Will you show these to Dr. Mary?"

She pointed to the first one, about her father and nodded. The other had evidently been meant only for Ridge. Baby steps.

He smiled. "Ready to go hum to some songs?"

A mischievous grin spread across her face and she scribbled the words *"Old Joe Clark."*

The song had long been a favorite of his, sung in Hope's Crossing whenever they gathered at the large outdoor community fire, a tradition the men had started three years ago when they'd first decided to build the old outlaw hideout into a real town.

Ridge laughed heartily and tweaked her nose. "You do have a sense of humor, my love. If that's what you want to hum along to, then I'll move mountains to make it happen." They strolled arm in arm to the horses, all thoughts of the New Messiah momentarily forgotten.

Eleven

ADDIE EMERGED FROM DR. MARY'S OFFICE FEELING LIGHTER than she had for years. She could only imagine that it was the songs—they seemed to be unlocking every pent-up thought inside her. She'd shown the doctor the short paragraph she'd written about her father, and Dr. Mary's reaction had been grim, although she'd tried to hide it.

"I understand more of what we're dealing with now," Dr. Mary had said, patting Addie's shoulder. "This is good, very good. Write more when you feel like it. It all has to come out and you'll feel better for it."

Probably so, but Addie still resisted delving too deeply into her pain-riddled past and reliving all those horrible days, months, and years.

The town bustled around her as she stood next to Ridge, warm sunlight on her face banishing the darkness. She pushed aside the unwelcome thoughts and smiled up at him, determined to think of happier things. Like the way his hair hugged the collar of his frock coat, and the muscle that bunched in his jaw when he was deep in thought.

"You did good today, Addie. I wish you knew how happy you make me." He put on his hat and adjusted it low over his eyes to block the sun. "I have to go meet a couple at the land office and take them to look at a few pieces of property. Why don't you stay in town and get acquainted with some of the women?" He paused to watch some riders passing through the town entrance, his gaze narrowed. "It's a lot safer here than out at the house, and I'd feel better about leaving you on your own."

She thought about that for a moment. Yes, she supposed it was time. At her nod, Ridge kissed her cheek and asked her to meet him at the café for lunch. He strode toward his office, whistling as he crossed the square. Addie admired his backside and the handsome figure he made, glad such a man belonged to her. She stood in thought for several minutes, considering her options, then went to ask directions to Eleanor Crump's place.

The older woman looked startled to open the door and find her standing there, but she quickly recovered from her shock and stood aside. "Come in, Mrs. Steele."

Addie removed the paper and pencil she'd stuck into her pocket in case she needed to *talk* to someone and wrote: *"Please call me Addie."*

"In that case, please come in, Addie."

She entered the tiny house that was little more than a lean-to and found it wonderfully clean. Being poor hadn't kept Eleanor from taking pride in her home.

"Can I get you something? Maybe a cup of tea?"

Addie nodded and sat in one of the two chairs at the small table, her paper in front of her.

"I'm glad you came by." Eleanor filled the kettle and put it on to boil. "You and me have something in common, which I'll tell you about after we've gotten better acquainted. It's not a story to tell today or in one sitting."

Curiosity rose. What could she and Eleanor have in common? What had she heard, for heaven's sake?

Eleanor pulled out the other chair and pushed back her reddish-brown hair, strands of silver woven through it. The woman had tried to take some pains with her appearance today and it showed, her hair tidy.

"Don't worry, dear, no one has been talking behind your back."

Surprise swept over Addie. Could Eleanor read her thoughts? She'd heard of people way back in the hills who had such a gift.

"I can see the questions in your eyes," Eleanor explained. "The eyes give everything away. I know you can't speak, but that's the extent of what I've heard. I once lost my voice too. But, as I said, that's a story for another day."

That hint of something more intrigued Addie no end. She wanted to ask a million questions, but she let the older woman set the pace.

Eleanor put her chair facing Addie and took her hands. "Let's just sit quietly. There is no place to be or nothing to say. It's simply us and the here and now. For the next few minutes, just *be*."

A lot could be said for simply "being." Addie closed her eyes and let her mind drift, listening to the sounds around her—the bird chirping outside the window, the buzzing of bees, the faint laughter of playing children.

Her heartbeat was steady, and she felt totally at peace.

The fire crackled inside the stove, and a piece of wood dropped. Contentment settled about Addie like a warm shawl. She had everything she needed, at least for now, and was with a new friend who understood her.

Somewhere in the quiet, from some unknown place, she saw the truth. Withdrawing so completely had been her way of coping with everything she had no control over. Not speaking had been what she'd needed for a while to help her heal from the horrible things she'd seen and endured.

But silence had no place in her life now. She wanted to step back into life. The overwhelming desire to talk descended on her.

Everything became crystal clear. But how could she coax the words back? That was the big question.

When the kettle whistled, Eleanor made the tea and filled their cups—all without saying a word.

Other than sitting with Ridge and Bodie the previous night, it was the best hour Addie had spent in a long time. At the end of her visit, she reached for her paper and wrote: *"Thank you, Eleanor. I loved the quiet."*

"Me too, dear. Don't worry. Your condition is temporary and will change in time. Please come to see me again whenever you want."

Addie returned to the center of town, steeped in indecision. It was still too early to meet Ridge, and she wouldn't go home

without him. While she contemplated her next step, Tally
Colby saw her and waved. She was carrying a small boy in her
arms, and a beautiful woman accompanied her.

"Adeline, meet Melanie. She's Tait Trinity's wife, and a
mail-order bride like us."

So Melanie had been a sent-for bride too. Addie wondered
how many women in the town had been. Melanie was clearly
in the family way, and her warm smile brought out twin
dimples. "Adeline, I'm so happy to meet you. I missed your
wedding due to our nephew Jesse coming down with a fever,
but I heard it was lovely."

Addie's nod and smile seemed sufficient. She studied
Melanie, wondering about her story. One glimpse of those
dimples, and Tait had probably been smitten.

"Come with me and Melanie. We're going over to Nora's
to plan our September dance." Tally's smile widened, and a
far-off look filled her blue eyes. "My Clay is quite fond of
dancing, and when I first came here, Dallas Hawk would pull
out his fiddle every night after supper and we'd dance up a
storm. Now it's only once a month. I miss the old days." Tally
scanned the town, and when her gaze landed on Clay, her
face softened.

When Addie nodded that she'd come along, Tally shifted
the toddler to her other hip. "I don't think you've met my son,
Dillon. He's two and unruly at times." Tally whispered, "He
takes after his father."

Addie didn't know how to react to that, so remained
noncommittal.

Melanie slipped an arm through Addie's. "I don't get to
meet with the ladies often. Tait and I are raising his twin
nephews and small niece. They came to live with us after their
parents were killed last year."

"I have to say that after a rough patch, they've adjusted
quite well," Tally said.

"They have." Melanie laughed and showed her dimples
again. "There was a time I wanted to strangle them, but I
adore those boys and little Becky."

Tally wiped Dillon's nose. "I'm glad you and Tait weathered the storm. They're sweet kids, and they needed you."

It didn't matter that Addie couldn't speak, because the women kept up a running chatter all the way to the Bowdre house. Nora met them at the door and led them inside. She was a pretty woman, with generous curves and an infectious laugh that put Addie at ease. She learned a lot about these women by listening and remembering what Ridge had told her. Tally had once been held against her will in an asylum, and that brought a common bond. And all the women, mail-order brides themselves through Luke Legend's service, had endured more than their share of trials.

Nora, Tally, and Melanie were as different as daylight and dark from the women of New Zion. Despite her initial comfort around them, part of Addie wondered what their motives might be for befriending her. Everyone had a motive, some way they tried to protect what was theirs. She'd had to watch every word she said around the women of New Zion lest they report her for an infraction. What did these women of Hope's Crossing feed off? They seemed truly genuine; still, looks often deceived.

The cost of trusting could be steep. She had to be careful until she knew them better.

Once they got Tally's and Nora's children settled, out came tea and a plate of cookies.

Addie envied the glow lighting up Nora's face. The woman had found her bliss, the one place in all the world where she fit.

What about Addie's place? She liked to believe she'd found that with Ridge, but would she be able to hold onto it? How soon would her father find her, drag her back to face what could be her final days? Pray God she was strong enough.

Nora's happy laughter at something Tally said sent the dark thoughts fleeing. "Adeline, I'm very happy you could join us."

Tally patted her hand. "Me too. We should've done this before now."

Addie took out her paper. *"You're both so welcoming. Everyone in the town has made me feel like I belong."*

"That's because you do." Warmth in Nora's voice erased most of Addie's reservations. These happy women seemed to have no ulterior motivation. They were real.

They talked some about their children, then Nora changed the conversation. "I have an exciting announcement."

"You're in the family way again." Tally reached for a cookie.

"Tally Colby!" Melanie exclaimed, her mouth full. "Just because I am doesn't mean Nora has to be."

"Well—" Tally gave an innocent shrug.

"Good heavens, no!" Nora chuckled. "I have my hands much too full right now."

Tally bit into a raisin cookie. "Just stop with the suspense and tell us."

"For the last six months, Jack has been studying law. He's now an apprentice under attorney Bernard Taggart in Canadian. When his apprenticeship is up, he'll make the trip to Austin to take the bar exam." Nora beamed. "I'm so proud of him."

Addie scribbled *"congratulations"* on her paper. She might have need for a good attorney. Yes, this was great news—for her and the town. She hoped Ridge hadn't yet heard so she could tell him at lunch. Her stomach quickened.

Tally placed her cookie on a small plate in front of her and clapped. "That's excellent, Nora! How did you manage to keep the secret? I'd have been bursting to tell someone."

"That's the thing, you'll never guess what went through my mind when he kept mysteriously disappearing for hours at a time and missing meals. He became very absentminded, and I imagined the worst."

"You thought he didn't love you anymore."

"Exactly. I thought he was sneaking around and seeing another woman right under my nose. I was furious and ready to pack the kids up and leave." Nora laughed. "So I decided to follow him, and he caught me."

Addie's heart stopped, and she looked closer for bruises but saw none. Mistrust and trailing a husband would surely earn a beating, but Nora seemed unharmed. Even happy.

"Let me guess. He came clean, and you made love." Tally grinned.

Nora's laughter bubbled over. "I declare, Tally, you must be able to read minds."

"Nope, I just know how you two lovebirds are. But Melanie and Tait are far worse. They can't keep their hands off each other."

"Hey, we can't help it," Melanie protested.

"Wasn't Jack angry that you misjudged him?" Addie wrote.

"Maybe a little at first, but I have my ways of putting him in a good humor." Nora's eyes twinkled at what was surely the memory.

Tally lifted her teacup. "I'll just bet you do, my friend."

The differences between these two and the pinched faces of the women of New Zion again became glaring.

Addie relaxed and let the warmth in the room fill her.

The women compared notes on their children before taking pity on Addie and changing the subject.

"I need to go check on Willow and Dillon. They're too quiet. I'll just be a moment." Nora came back laughing, holding two string-wrapped children by the hands. "Sawyer and his friends were making kites and left their supplies out."

"Oh dear Lord!" Tally jumped up to help untangle the sheepish pair.

When they came back to the table, Nora refilled their cups. "We need to get started on the plans for the dance."

"Let's set it for two weeks from today," Tally suggested.

Nora glanced at a calendar lying on the table. "The first Saturday in September would make it on the second."

"It could double as a harvest dance," Addie wrote. *"We could use all sorts of fall decorations, and it would be fun."*

Melanie grinned. "Thanks, Adeline. That's using your head, and I agree."

"Please call me Addie. Ridge does, and I like it."

"Indeed." Nora's brown eyes twinkled. "That Ridge is very quick on his feet."

Addie grinned and was relieved when the conversation returned to the dance.

They discussed who would be in charge of refreshments, and Tally took that. Addie volunteered to do the decorations, and Nora the hay bales for seating around the dance floor, which Addie learned was built by the bigger kids.

The time snuck up on Addie, and she was startled when she looked at the clock. *"I need to go,"* she scribbled and pushed her chair back.

Her pulse raced as she left the Bowdre house. Ridge would be surprised at all she had to tell him. And she'd sit there and stare at his kissable mouth and whiskey-colored eyes like some besotted schoolgirl.

⤕

Ridge digested the news that Jack was now a law apprentice, wondering why his friend had kept quiet. Jack had always been smart, though, especially about the law. They could use a man like that.

Addie sat across from him, looking prettier than a dew-kissed sunrise after a storm. Light flooded through the café windows, creating a circle around her, and cavorted in her golden hair. She seemed different somehow. Comfortable, confident, relaxed.

"I'm in charge of the decorations for the harvest dance, first Saturday of September. Any suggestions?"

That she would volunteer for anything floored him, but nothing made him happier than to see her getting involved in the town.

"As a matter of fact, I do." Ridge pushed back his plate. "I can get you all the corn cobs you want, stalks too. I think the pumpkins are ready, and I know where you can find oodles of gourds and rocks."

"I can sew some festive bunting to hang from the storefronts, paint the rocks real pretty in orange, yellow, and red. And maybe have lots of streamers everywhere. What do you think about hanging lanterns around for lighting?"

"Nothing to hang them on, since the dance will be out-doors. But you can set them on things." Ridge covered her hand with his. "Lady, you amaze me. You're in a strange place, a strange house, with people you don't know—a husband you're just learning—and you're flourishing."

"I'm nothing special."

He barked a laugh. "Addie, my love, you just don't realize. I wish you could see yourself as I do." Color rose to her cheeks. Discomfort apparent, he changed the subject. "What else did you do this morning? Paint the windmill, teach all the children Spanish, build a library while I was out trying to sell some measly land?"

"Stop teasing." She laid down her pencil and met his gaze.

"I'm sorry. I'm just happy to see you blossoming." He sobered and announced that he'd sold the property he'd shown that morning, and she saluted him like a soldier to a general. He reached for her hand and brought her fingertips to his lips, kissing them. Who needed words to carry on a conversation?

They shared a moment of comfortable silence, just like a normal married couple. Then she wrote: *"I went to visit Eleanor Crump."*

Of everything, this was possibly the most surprising piece of news. "Oh, you did. How did it go?"

"Eleanor said she was once like me but didn't explain how. But she understands me, Ridge. We just sat and held hands, and I felt an enormous peace come over me. I've never known anything like that. Eleanor seemed to sense what I went through."

"That's pretty incredible. I'm glad you went to see her—you could both use the friendship. She seems to be awfully lonely. Rebel had no luck trying to get her to socialize."

"You know nothing about her?"

"Only that she was once married to a notorious outlaw, and he was killed by a posse."

"Recently?"

"No, probably ten years ago or more. Way before my arrival."

Addie must have worried, or still did, that he'd meet a similar fate, and that was a grief he didn't want to saddle his wife with. At the same time, he couldn't do anything about his fate. He just prayed when the bullet came, Addie would be far, far away.

Other than that, he wouldn't pray for anything else. His prayers had dried up just like his soul.

Twelve

RIDGE SAW ADDIE HOME, THEN TOOK BODIE ASIDE. "STAY close and keep your eyes open. That bounty hunter is lurking around. I can smell him."

Bodie's gaze never wavered, the kid showing neither fear nor surprise. "Figured as much. I thought I saw something last night in the dark but couldn't be sure, so didn't say anything. By the time I got out to the yard, he was gone. He could've taken me at any time."

"You're not the one he wants. It's the three thousand dollars I can fetch him." And Hiram wouldn't leave without Ridge. For the first time, he regretted moving away from the safety of the town. Dammit! One bad decision could cost him everything.

"That's a lot of money, but you don't have to worry about me." Bodie stared toward the house.

"I know. Tell Addie to keep the doors locked. Hiram might try to get to me through her."

"I s'pect so, only she said something about spending time with King. She won't stand to be locked in the house. She loves that horse."

"Yep. If you can't talk her out of it, stay right with her and keep that rifle handy." Ridge released a low curse and strode to his sorrel, his spurs clinking with each step. He climbed into the saddle. "Don't let anything happen to her. Let's go, Cob. We got us a rabid wolf to find."

He checked ravines, gullies, and creeks within a five-mile radius around Hope's Crossing and found nothing. Maybe he was wrong, and Hiram had ridden on. Maybe his wound had gotten bad, and he'd gone to find a doctor.

Ridge was about to give up the search when he recalled an old adobe house ten miles away. A shepherd had lived there once, but the place had long since crumbled and fallen in. Maybe Hiram had taken refuge there.

The warm afternoon sun beat down, and Ridge kept wiping sweat from his face. A mile from the place, he slowed to a walk to keep the noise to a minimum. His senses sharpened to a fine edge. Every swish of the breeze in the tall grass whispered a warning. The beating wings of a fly that buzzed around his head sounded like a beehive. He jumped at the call of a nighthawk that nested on the ground somewhere ahead. Cob snorted and blinked as the pesky fly found a new target.

Ridge scanned the waving grass, tall enough to easily hide a man on his belly.

The hair rose on his neck. Someone was watching.

As he threw his leg over to dismount, a shot rang out. Ridge ducked and slapped Cob on the rear to send the gelding away from the gunfire, then fell onto his belly, jerking out his Colt on the way down. He lay motionless, his heart thudding against his ribs. His mouth dried until he could no more make spit than fly. Inch by agonizing inch, he slowly reached down and unbuckled his noisy spurs, then got rid of the hat that would give him away.

For a moment, he studied the situation, taking in the rocks and brush, then inched forward. A covey of startled quail rose from the tangled brush. Dammit! That gave away his location!

A second shot followed, the slug hitting the ground in front of him, spitting dirt in his face. This time, Ridge had seen the shooter—or at least the general vicinity of his hiding place. The bullet had come from a high ridge on the left, giving the man a distinct advantage. Still, the cowardly bastard was relying on a handgun, not the accuracy of a rifle.

Ridge didn't return fire. He wouldn't waste ammunition until he had a clear target. He gauged the distance to a stand of cedar trees, then stood and made a run for them. Bullets sprayed around him, but none hit. Once surrounded by the thick, leafy shield of the cedar, he breathed easier. He peered through the branches, saw movement, and squeezed the trigger.

A slew of cusswords broke the silence, telling Ridge he'd at least grazed the assailant. Good.

Ridge sprinted to a group of sandstone boulders, and from there to a stand of mesquite. Taking his time, eyes on every flutter of movement, he tightened the net until he finally reached the bottom of the rocky ridge. But as he began the climb to the man's perch, loose rocks showered down on him. A moment later, a rider emerged from thick growth and galloped away, lying flat against his mount's long neck.

Ridge took aim and fired a volley of shots, but the man kept riding. Ridge scrambled down to the floor of the ravine again, but by the time he found Cob, the rider had vanished. Ridge returned the Colt to his holster and swung into the saddle, continuing on to the adobe ruins.

The place stood silent in the waning afternoon light. An owl perched on what little was left of the roof. Ridge took note of the disturbed spiderwebs and went inside. The cold ashes of a campfire, bones of a small animal, and remains of a tobacco pouch and cigarettes told him someone had stayed there. Probably for more than one night. He couldn't be certain it had been Hiram, but it made sense that the squatter had been the bounty hunter.

Ridge had him on the run again, but he wouldn't be satisfied until he finished this fight.

His, Addie's, and Bodie's lives depended on it.

∾

Addie gathered her broom and dust cloths and went upstairs. It was time to tackle the part of the house she'd avoided, and it was clear Ridge didn't consider cleaning his priority. The dirt would probably be thick enough to grow turnips before he paid it any mind. Thank goodness he'd gone looking for a wife. In Addie's experience, wives were the only ones who kept husbands from falling into total dust disasters.

It took her a moment to throw off the feeling of trespassing into his sanctuary as she stepped into the bedroom. She didn't belong here where he undressed and slept, where he kept his private things. She called herself three kinds of crazy and reminded her feeble brain he was her husband. Addie jerked up the rug and took it outside to beat, then went to work on the dust that had gathered on the furniture other than the bed.

Intent on getting the work done as fast as possible, she lifted a small wooden box that sat on top of the tall chest of drawers, and a tintype dropped to the floor. She reached for the picture, her breath catching at the sight of the couple staring up at her.

It was Ridge and a pretty woman in a fancy dress and hat. Addie scowled at the way his arm was tight around the lady, who was practically sitting in his lap. They were smiling and happy, much too cozy for a mere acquaintance. She had to be a wife or a fiancée. Why hadn't Ridge mentioned her?

After staring at the couple as though she could force the tintype to give her some answers, she put it back exactly as it had been, under the small box, and hurried to finish and leave the room. But the picture haunted her.

How could she ask Ridge about it without making him think she'd been snooping? No answer came to mind.

Finally, she changed into the denim trousers she'd gotten at the mercantile. The legs were too long, and the waist swallowed hers, but she loved the freedom, the comfort. She wasn't sure if she'd wear them in town like Rebel did, doubted she had that much courage. Or even to wear them in front of Ridge! His warm chuckle when she'd laid them atop their purchases at the mercantile still brought heat to her face. Maybe she'd try them when he wasn't around.

She removed the trousers and set to work on alterations. Bodie kept coming in to check on her as she hemmed the trousers, and the third time she finally asked him what was going on.

"I don't think Ridge wants you to know." Bodie glanced down at his feet.

Wants? She didn't care two hoots what Ridge wanted. This was her life. She snatched up her paper. *Tell me. If there's danger, I have a right to know.*

"Probably so, ma'am." Bodie hesitated a second longer.

"He found tracks the other day. Ones that led right up to the house, where someone sat outside the window and watched."

Chills raced up her spine, and she gripped the arm of the chair, felt the color draining from her face. Whoever it was had watched her. Nothing unnerved her quite like having eyes following her every move. Just like in New Zion.

"Are you all right, ma'am?"

Slow anger built. *How long have you known about this?*

"Only since morning."

A strange kind of calm came over her. She laid aside her sewing. *Where is Ridge?*

"He rode out to search."

And he hadn't said a word. Not one. Other than Bodie telling her to keep the doors locked, she'd never had so much as a hint that danger had been right outside their windows. Bodie kept avoiding her eyes, and she felt guilty. It wasn't the boy's fault, and directing her anger onto him would be unfair.

She scribbled. *Thank you for telling me. You can go back to whatever you were doing.*

Bodie wore a look of relief. "Gladly, ma'am."

Addie went to cook supper, biding time, her anger simmering until the keeper of secrets rode in. She wrote out her note and waited.

At last she heard him and hurried out.

He was unsaddling Cob and glanced up when she joined him in the yard. "Addie, everything okay?"

She slapped her note to the middle of his broad chest with her question, *"Why didn't you tell me about the bounty hunter stalking us?"*

"Because I didn't want to worry you. All right? So shoot me. You have enough on your mind at the moment."

"I have a right to know if I'm in danger."

"Of course, you do, and I'll tell you when I have something solid."

"You're treating me like a child. Stop. I'm a grown woman, and I deserve to have your full consideration."

Ridge pushed back his hat, and a nearby lantern revealed

the anger creasing his face. "Look, I haven't actually seen the man, only evidence a trespasser left behind. I think it was the bounty hunter, but if so, he's after me, not you."

His spurs jangled each time he moved, seeming loud in the stillness.

"But it could be the men hunting me. Either way, you should've told me." She jabbed a pointed finger into his chest.

His irritation built, deepening the lines, and something else was there…hurt? He dragged the evening air into his lungs. "I vowed to protect you, and I mean to keep that promise. What would you have done differently if you'd've known? What?"

Good question. Likely nothing, but still!

"Let me decide for myself. Don't shelter me, tell me what to think, or how to feel."

"Believe me. From now on, I won't." He picked up the bridle from where it'd dropped and flung it over a stall rail.

Guilt rose at his anger. They had to find some way to coexist peacefully without these spats. She hated arguing, and it should have no place in their marriage—only love. Whatever elusive thing that might be.

What else was he not telling her? Did it have anything to do with the woman in the tintype that he kept near his bed? If only she had the courage to ask.

Maybe it was better not to know.

She went to the barn door and looked out at the growing shadows, dark and broad enough to hide a man intent on killing them. Her rigid shoulders and back relaxed, anger gone.

An arm slid around her waist, and she swiveled to meet Ridge's whiskey-colored gaze. "I'm sorry, my love. I should've warned you to be on your guard. Old habits die hard, but I'm trying. Don't give up on me."

She tenderly laid a hand against his stubble and nodded. The scent of leather blended with an abundance of sage, alive in the night mist, bringing hope and joy. She was home. This was her land, and she'd fight to the last breath to keep it.

A noise drew her attention, and Bodie limped from the

darkness, a rifle on his shoulder. He'd made himself scarce during their argument, forgetting his crutch, and shame filled Addie. She owed the kid better than bickering. He had nowhere else to go except to people who didn't want him. She didn't want to make his life more miserable.

"Anything out there?" Ridge asked.

"Nope. All's quiet."

"How far did you go?"

"To the big stand of mesquites." The kid propped the rifle next to the barn door.

That thicket was the best place for someone to hide near the house. Since no one was there, it meant they were safe. At least for now. Addie relaxed and shooed them toward the windmill to wash. Their argument forgotten, she ran into the kitchen and started dishing everything up and setting the table.

Her men were hungry, and she couldn't wait until bedtime to get her kiss and feel Ridge holding her, his heart beating next to hers—such a small thing, that had come to mean so much.

❧

With supper over, Ridge and Bodie made another turn around the property while Addie sewed in the parlor. The cats played chase, jumping first into her lap, then out. She stomped her foot and shook her finger, and they settled down.

The back door opened, and Ridge strolled in, carrying some books and a slate. "I went by the school today, and Denver loaned me these."

"I hope you don't think I'm too dumb to learn." Bodie scooped up the kitten and scratched it behind the ears, worry on his face and lining his voice.

"Is that wishful thinking, son?"

"I just want to make you proud is all." His voice lowered as though he was too timid to say the words. "No one 'cept my folks ever said they were proud of me."

Addie's heart stilled, and tears hung in her throat. She watched the interaction between the man and boy, saw their deep respect for each other. More importantly, heard what they didn't put into words.

"Stop right there." Ridge softened his voice, squeezing the kid's shoulder. "We don't have to open these books for me to tell you that I'm very proud of you. Some folks have book learning, and some have horse sense—which you have in spades. You know what needs doing, and you see to it without someone telling you when or how. That's worth a whole bunch, and it's something no one can teach. So, whatever you're thinking, you can quit."

Bodie eased into a chair. "I guess."

"I'm not blowing smoke. I mean it." Ridge pulled a chair next to the kid, and the lessons began.

Addie watched them, proud of both. Ridge never lost patience with Bodie's mistakes, slowly repeating the alphabet until Bodie caught on. She wasn't sure who was teaching whom.

Finally, Ridge closed the book, and Bodie moved to the floor. "My turn, Addie. I need help with multiplication and division."

She scooted beside him and taught him some of the harder math problems, their hands brushing and her awareness of him building. *"I think you used this as an excuse to sit beside the teacher,"* she scolded on paper.

"Me? That's a bold accusation, Mrs. Steele. But entirely true." He nibbled behind her ear.

"I'll have to keep you after school."

"Please do. I have an idea how to pass the time." His wide grin showed his white teeth.

After a little more serious study, they quit. He was a quick learner.

He handed Bodie the slate. "If you find time tomorrow, you can work on the alphabet by yourself." He stood and stretched, his gaze finding Addie. Her heart leaped. "Been a long day. I'm teaching you to shoot tomorrow, Addie. I want you to be able to defend yourself in case Bodie and I aren't around."

She nodded, happy that he'd listened to her.

"I'm going to bed." Bodie got to his feet. "Good night."

Addie set her sewing aside and went to give him a hug. He blushed when she kissed his cheek.

"Good night, son." Ridge went to check that the front door was locked, then did the same to the kitchen door behind Bodie. She liked this simple routine of securing the house and how safe it made her feel.

Ridge returned. "Before we go to bed, I want to tell you about my afternoon. No more keeping things from you. And while I talk, you can change my bandage."

Addie gathered the water, ointment, and bandages, happy that he was relenting and letting her doctor him. He removed his shirt, and she stared at the sinew of his broad chest and back. This husband of hers was strong and made her proud to be his wife. She loved how the lamplight softened the lines of his face and took the darkness from his eyes. His skin was warm under her hands, and if her father were here, he'd scream that she was sinning.

No matter. She jutted her chin. She had the right to her thoughts, and Ridge was her husband—even if it was in name only so far. She pushed the thought out of her head and went to work, enjoying this small wifely duty.

For the next half hour, Ridge spoke about his search and the gunfight. Addie realized how close he'd come to dying, and her blood froze. If the man had mortally wounded Ridge that far from home, he could've died before anyone found him. If he was ever found. She'd never have known what happened to him. What would she have done? How would she have managed alone?

She wanted to yell at him for taking such a chance, but she'd only have wasted her breath. Her outlaw husband already knew the high stakes. He lived with them each day.

New bandage in place, he put his shirt back on. Seated on the sofa next to him, her hand in his, she was caught again by the slight curl at the end of his long hair, and the thick muscles in his neck. There was more to Ridge Steele than a gun. So much more. Her stomach flipped upside down, their good-night kiss on her mind.

As though reading her thoughts, Ridge stood and pulled her up, folding his arms around her. "Now, it's time for us."

His amber eyes held desire as he slowly lowered his head to meet her. Addie held her breath, her heart beating faster, and closed her eyes. Their lips brushed, and heat rushed from her belly, a shooting star leaving a blazing trail.

Their breath mingled, and she took him inside her with each inhaled flutter. He teased and nibbled his way across the seam of her lips, and just when she thought she'd die from want, he pressed his mouth firmly to hers as though sealing them together with the strongest solder.

Emboldened, she slid an arm around his neck, her fingers tangling in his hair. Hunger for something more, something deeper, curled along her spine and up her back. *Ridge,* her heart silently cried out, *teach me, give me what I'm begging for.*

A strange sensation came over her, and she felt as though she were falling from a great height. She clutched his shirt, wondering at the wetness that formed at her center.

He suddenly released her and stepped back, his expression as dazed as she felt. "I should go check outside one more time. Good night, Addie."

Her gaze followed his tall figure, aching for his arms around her. If she lived to be a hundred, she'd never forget this moment and how alive he made her feel.

She went to her space and got out her notebook and pencil.

> *I think I'm in love. If Ridge had undressed me down to the bare skin tonight, I wouldn't have minded or said a word. In truth, I wanted him to. I wanted to feel his hands touching me. Everywhere. I wanted...him. All of him. I want to lie next to him and feel his strong body. I thought this space here under the stairs was what I wanted, but it isn't. Not anymore. Only now I've created a situation by sleeping apart and can't figure a way out. What can I do?*

She wanted normal...

A life.

A love.
A real marriage.
Was it really as simple as being brave enough to take it?

Thirteen

AFTER BREAKFAST THE NEXT MORNING, RIDGE SADDLED THE horses and tied them outside the kitchen door, then waited for Addie to change into riding clothes. His mind wasn't on shooting lessons. Not at all.

He sipped on a fresh cup of coffee, deep in thought about the kiss they'd shared the previous night. It had taken all his willpower not to carry her upstairs to bed, but that would've scared her out of six months of her life. She probably would've locked herself in her space beneath the stairs and never come out again.

Truth of the matter, the kiss had seared its way through him and rendered him unable to think clearly. And in a little while, he'd be inhaling the rose fragrance of her soap, touching her to adjust her aim, remembering the taste of her very kissable mouth.

"Patience, you fool," he muttered into his cup. Luke and Clay had warned him to take it slow, not to let his own needs override his common sense, but dammit! He had no common sense when Addie was anywhere near. If he didn't watch it at target practice, he'd probably shoot his damn foot off.

Light footsteps jarred him from his thoughts. He glanced up and swallowed a big gulp of hot coffee, scalding his mouth.

Every line, every curve of Addie's body was in plain view, outlined by the trousers they'd bought at the mercantile and a shirt that hugged her breasts. To further complicate matters, her hair was loose. The golden curls fell about her shoulders and spilled down the front, calling even more attention to her luscious bosom. Good Lord! How was he supposed to keep from losing his ever-loving mind? And that wasn't even considering the heat rushing to his core, a flare that had every nerve in his body standing at attention—especially the part that he didn't want her to notice.

Ridge slipped into his frock coat and buttoned it as though preparing for a blizzard. He smiled. "Ready?"

She glanced at his coat and frowned before giving him a nod and moving out the door. King whinnied and pawed the ground, seemingly happy to see her. She rushed to hug him and ran her hands over his sleek neck, looking for all the world like she was saying good morning. Ridge cleared his throat, not regretting for a second that he'd given her the buckskin but envying the horse the feel of her touch.

He pulled himself away from the sight and turned to adjust Cob's cinches.

Bodie hobbled from the barn, the kitten tumbling after him. "I'll hold down the fort, Ridge, and get to work on those repairs."

"We won't be gone too long." Ridge's spurs clinked as he moved to help Addie. Though she was gamely trying to propel her short frame onto King, she just couldn't make it by herself. He placed his hands on her shapely backside, intending only to help her up. Her flesh was firm under the denim, tight under his palms.

She glanced around with a frown, and he realized he was taking too much time savoring the feel. Hell! Heat flooded his face, and he tried to look anywhere but at that part of her... but found it impossible. Finally, he gave her a little shove, and after quite a bit of wiggling, she settled herself on King's back. With great effort to appear casual, he sauntered to his horse.

They rode out to the stand of mesquites that Ridge planned to remove in the near future to make room for his peach trees. The house looked small in the distance, framed by the blue sky overhead and the soft brown earth beneath. A slight breeze ruffled tendrils of Addie's hair that shone like gold dust and framed her face.

It took all he had to look away. He couldn't, wouldn't, lose her, or he'd shrivel and die.

Tying their horses where they could nibble on the grass, Ridge set up some cans on a dead mesquite. Addie watched it all in silence, biting her bottom lip. She seemed nervous.

Understandable. Failure did things to a person's self-esteem, and hers was still fragile. His job—if possible—was to see that she did good. Acting nonchalant, he walked back to her, trying his best to watch for trouble.

He drew a line in the dirt with his bootheel. "Okay, come over here and stand behind this line." When she did, he pulled one of his Colts from its holster. "First, you have to get used to the weight. A gun isn't as light as you might think."

She took the heavy weapon, and her arm dropped. His voice was gentle. "To start with, why don't you use both hands to hold it steady?"

At least she could raise it level. He moved behind her and held her gun arm out in front of her, his hand curling around hers, pressing so close that daylight couldn't shine between his chest and her back. Bad, bad idea. The breeze laid some strands of gold across his nose. Then came the light scent of wild roses, the brush of her body against his—the pressure of her tight butt rubbing against him that sent heat crawling from his belly.

Hell, he was roasting alive in the damn wool coat! His breathing ragged, he stepped away, turning his back to collect himself.

Breathe in. Breathe out. Slow and easy. He pinched the bridge of his nose and forced himself to think of planting turnips. Yes, that was something safe. Turn the fallow ground over, place the seeds in the freshly turned row, then cover them with soil.

Several long minutes passed before he swung around. She stared at him as though he'd lost his mind. She wouldn't be wrong. As bad as he hated to, he disposed of the coat, draping it across his horse. He drew a long breath of air and took his chances. A minute passed before Ridge resumed his place behind her. "Look down the barrel and line the tip up with one of the cans."

Ignore her softness and her scent curling around you. Pay no attention to her tight behind. Dammit, this is business! His voice came out raspy. "When you have them lined up, pull the trigger very gently. Don't jerk it. Just smooth and easy."

She followed his instructions to the letter. The bullet splintered the fallen tree, missing the cans.

"That's all right. It was close. Actually, that was very good. If that had been a man, you'd have hit his chest. Good job."

Addie whirled, grinning. Her lips were right there—plump and moist. So close. So perfectly shaped. So enticing. There was only so much a man could take. Awareness sizzled between them like ten thousand lightning strikes, and he had no damn sense.

Ridge put an arm around his tempting wife and claimed her as he had the previous night. Addie leaned into him, the Colt she still clutched crushed against his belly. He deepened the kiss, and she didn't pull away. The only thing he felt was her in his arms, her body fitting into every inch of his as though God had created her just for him. The kiss carried him to a place he'd never been—where everything was perfect and right and there was no need for guns. Where he wasn't a wanted man. And neither of them had to hide.

Deepening the kiss, he explored the soft lines of her back, waist, and hips. And when she slid an arm around his neck, he knew she welcomed his caresses.

Finally, he let her go—and that's when he saw her tears.

"What's wrong, Addie? Did I hurt you?" He didn't think he'd held her that tightly.

She shook her head.

"Are you sad?"

Her nod indicated yes.

"What are you sad about, my love?"

She pointed to her mouth.

"Because you can't speak?"

She nodded, and more silent tears fell.

He pulled out a handkerchief and wiped her eyes. "I'm sure there are things you want to say, and that must really frustrate you, but this isn't forever. You're making great progress. It's just going to take patience." She rested her head on his chest, and he rubbed her back. She had to be so tired of having things she couldn't voice. "We're going to get through this. You and me—together."

Several long moments passed, then Addie stepped back, angrily dashed away her tears, and resumed target practice, all business.

He shot her an admiring glance. "Good. I think you're a natural, but I don't understand why you shot so erratic when we had the fight with the bounty hunters."

Her smile wasn't all that wide, but she was trying. Addie motioned to the horses and made tracks down her face like tears.

Of course. "You were afraid you'd hit the horses."

Her eyes bright, she nodded and raised the Colt. Ridge stepped behind to hold her arm steady, and this time she hit the can. By the time they quit for the day, she'd hit the target fifty percent of the time, which was darn good in his opinion. Especially since the misses weren't that far off.

Relief swept over him. If the bounty hunter dared show his face, Addie would be ready.

※

Over the next few days, Addie sewed bunting and made enough streamers for the dance to decorate the entire town. Ridge complained of the fabric lying about everywhere, said he felt like he was living in a dance hall.

One morning she put it all aside and went to visit Eleanor Crump again. He was glad to see them becoming comfortable with each other. But Addie returned, fretting that Eleanor had been no more forthcoming than before. It seemed the two women had spoken about religion mostly, and both shared a certain opinion of a lot of preachers.

Ridge kissed Addie and told her not to give up. When she was ready, Eleanor would tell her secrets.

Life together moved from one day to the next as the opening petals of a flower. He lived in anticipation for what each morning would bring. He'd seen no more signs of the watcher, whoever he was, and could only pray he'd given up and moved on.

He looked forward to Addie's kisses and nightly embraces

more and more. He'd gotten bolder, let his hands roam a bit more than usual, and she hadn't seemed to mind. Touching her had become his new favorite pastime. He couldn't get enough of her velvet skin, her smiles, and her kisses. She was like a drug he craved. It was as if he spoke to her with his touch. A light brush of her cheek could say more than any words. She, in turn, found ample opportunity to take his arm, hold his hand, or melt against him when he kissed her.

And deep down, more than anything, he loved the interest she'd taken in Hope's Crossing and the upcoming dance.

Bodie's leg had almost healed, and the kid had gotten rid of the crutch, his limp barely noticeable. He, too, was becoming comfortable. In the time he'd been in town, he'd already struck up a friendship with Clay's daughter, Violet, who was three years younger.

Ridge sat the kid down for a talk. "Always be respectful of girls, son. Never force Violet to do anything against her will." He gave Bodie a stern look. "You hurt her in any way, I'd best not hear about it. I'll kick your rear end from here to the Rio Grande, and after I'm finished, Clay will take over."

"Yes, sir."

"Just think of Violet as your grandma."

Bodie shook the hair back from his face. "My grandma was as mean as a skunk-bit coyote."

"Good. Picture her face in your mind when you're talking to Violet." So much for the *man* talk. Ridge hoped Bodie listened.

A few days later, Ridge accompanied Addie to the doctor for her session, then headed to work, thinking about his wife. She accepted his kisses and caresses, eagerly in fact, yet chose the space under the stairs over his bed. That puzzled him. What else could he do to do to win her over?

Clay and Jack rode up and dismounted, tying their mounts to the hitching rail in front of the land office. Since the day Ridge had been shot at, they'd taken turns riding out and checking the abandoned house to see if Hiram had returned.

Jack entered ahead of Clay and pushed back his hat. "The

bounty hunter still hasn't shown. The place is as empty as a dead man's pockets."

Clay dusted off his clothes.

"Hey, stop that!" Ridge blew the dirt off a stack of papers. "Now I'm going to have to clean."

"Hell, you haven't cleaned in here since you moved in." Clay dropped into a chair.

"It boggles my mind how you'd be privy to the goings on in this office." Ridge moved the stack and went to look out the window at the peaceful town. "Where else could Hiram be holed up?"

Jack snorted. "There are caves all over this area. Take your pick. Could be in any."

"I feel safer with the guard at the entrance." Ridge went back to his desk and dropped into his squeaky chair. "At least he can't ride into Hope's Crossing without us knowing. But I'm wondering about those of us living outside the town. We're pretty much easy pickings."

"Maybe you should take a room at the hotel for a while," Clay suggested.

"It's a good idea," Jack threw in. "That would keep Miss Adeline safe. Bodie too."

Somehow, Ridge thought Addie would balk at the idea. She enjoyed the property and their animals—milking the cow, tending to the chickens, and the hours spent with King. Still, he should suggest it. Ever since their argument, he'd tried to give her more of a say in matters. It was hard, though. He automatically wanted to shield her from every worry. However, he'd learned his lesson and wouldn't dare make that mistake again. Somehow, he'd try to keep her abreast of the situation, even if it harelipped the damn governor.

"How is Miss Adeline?" Clay asked. "Any closer to getting her voice back?"

"Nope. Dr. Mary is helping a lot, though. She's optimistic that Addie's voice will return soon. She says all it'll take is one big scare to jar the words loose." Ridge leaned back and propped his feet on the desk, hoping Addie would find her way to sleep with him soon. His bed was lonely, and he didn't care if she spoke or not as long as she lay beside him.

"Fretting about it won't bring it any faster." The chair squeaked when Clay shifted, removed his hat, and hung it on his knee. "Violet's been talking a lot about Bodie," he said casually.

"Figured as much." Ridge managed to look nonchalant.

"Should I be worried?"

"Nope."

Clay drew himself up in the chair. "Don't you think it's time you had *the talk* with him?"

"Hell, I ain't his pa. I'm his employer."

Jack watched the back and forth, grinning, his arms folded.

"Well, someone has to be his pa, and the kid *is* living on your property."

Ridge glared. "For your information, I've already spoken with him. Relax."

Clay returned the glare. "Well, you could've said so in the first place! I'm still keeping my eye on that boy."

"He's not a boy. He's a man," Ridge clarified quietly.

"Hell, that's even worse!" Clay got to his feet and stomped out of the land office.

"You shouldn't tease him like that, Ridge." Jack pushed away from the wall. "Violet is his pride and joy. Always has been. Maybe it's because she was born blind. That would make anyone protective."

"I know, but he makes it so easy. There isn't one boy ever going to be good enough for his little girl, and I can understand that. I'd probably feel the same way." Ridge quickly scanned a document, rose, and filed it in a cabinet.

"Sawyer is pretty sweet on her too, but I don't think Clay knows, or else he'd have cornered me as well. I'm dreading the day."

"Good luck there." Many a friendship had been ruined by less. Ridge changed the subject. "Addie's been working on the decorations for the dance, and I've been thinking. Let's have it in the barn this year. It wouldn't take much to clean it out, then we wouldn't have to worry about the weather."

"Sounds good. It would save having to build a floor again." Jack stuck a match stem in his mouth. "Remember when we used to have a dance near every night on the bare ground?"

"Sure do. I think Clay would still do that if he had his way." Ridge chuckled. "I've never seen any man like to dance the way he does."

"Shoot, me neither."

A moment's silence filled the room, broken only by the noisy traffic of horses and wagons in the busy town beyond the door. Something else that had changed. "I might ride out to some of these nearby caves this afternoon. I've got to do something to flush Hiram out."

"I'd go with you, but I promised Sawyer I'd go hunting with him. I don't spend enough time with the boy as it is." Jack paused, then added quietly, "Hiram may have left to get reinforcements. There's always that possibility."

"Yeah. Hell, I hate that I brought him here." If only he'd taken Addie riding somewhere else that day. But if he had, they wouldn't have been there to free Bodie, so he guessed things turned out the way they were meant to.

"Not your fault, Ridge." Jack opened the door and left.

Ridge sat in thought a spell longer. Maybe Hiram had gone for reinforcements. The man would have his pick of help among the rough men hanging out in Tascosa. The outlaw Billy the Kid had called it home once, until Pat Garrett killed him last year. But there were plenty waiting to take a man's money and do the job. Until the threat was gone, they had to keep Hope's Crossing locked tight.

Silver Valley, the lying woman, Tom Calder, and the hangman's rope crossed his mind. Ridge shuddered and turned his thoughts to Addie. If he wanted their marriage to work, it was time to trust and bare the past—both his and hers.

Fourteen

ADDIE SAT IN ELEANOR'S HOME, SIPPING TEA AND NIBBLING ON a moist slice of applesauce cake. Slowly, the recluse was changing. She'd begun combing her hair and twisting it into a knot on the back of her neck, sprucing herself up more. Today Eleanor wore a black cameo on a ribbon. The change surprised Addie so much, she had to blink and look again.

"What a beautiful cameo," Addie wrote on a piece of paper.

Eleanor's smile held sadness. "My Charley gave it to me one Christmas. I dug it out of the ashes." She fingered the keepsake at her throat. "Addie, don't ever outlive those that love you."

"Yes, ma'am. Would you tell me about him?"

Silence hung like thick moss from tall cypress. Addie sat waiting while Eleanor finished her tea and cake. Finally, Eleanor pushed the small plate away. "I recollect telling you I would, and today seems as good as any."

The woman rose and collected the plates, dropping them in a dishpan of soapy water. "People wonder why I live on the fringe of town. The answer is because I have all this ugliness inside."

Addie picked up a flour sack drying towel and helped her friend.

"I was married to the outlaw Charley Caddell for twelve years."

Even though Addie had been sheltered from the world, she'd heard of the man. Caddell was hunted worse than anyone she'd known. He'd come to New Zion once, shot and in a bad way. Her mother had tended to his wound, after which her father had ridden him out of town.

"We lived outside of Springer, New Mexico Territory, on a farm. A few hours after he left to hunt one day, I was hanging wash on the line. My two little girls and their brother were in the house. Riders descended on us like a flock of buzzards with guns blazin'.' They pinned me down with gunfire and set fire to the house. I screamed that the children were inside and tried to get to them, but the men held me back." Eleanor put a trembling hand over her eyes and took a deep breath. "Charley came riding in full-bore, shooting in a panic. He raced right past the posse like they weren't there." Eleanor's voice broke. "They gunned him down in the yard, shooting him full of holes. Charley fell two steps from the flaming doorway. He fought with everything he had to get to our babies."

Addie drew a shocked breath, her heart breaking. She helped Eleanor back to the table. Part of her didn't want to hear the rest, but Eleanor wasn't finished.

"Folks claimed I came unhinged that day, and they weren't wrong. I screamed so loud and so long, I lost my voice, just like you have. I stayed locked in silence like that for a good long while."

Maybe it was the same, except Addie hadn't screamed. She'd just woken one morning to find her words had disappeared, erased from her brain.

"Changed my name to Crump to discourage questions. Now I'm trying to find my way back, but most everyone steers clear of me like I have something they might catch."

Addie hugged her and scribbled on her paper. *"Not everyone. You're a dear friend, and I feel fortunate to have met you. How did you get your voice back?"*

"I didn't do anything special. I think I had to heal on the inside first. And then one day, I found myself whispering the Lord's prayer."

"I try to speak but the words won't come."

"Just give them time, my dear. Time heals everything."

"Maybe you're right. I'm sorry for what happened to you. How horrible."

Eleanor looked out the small window. "I couldn't understand why God let me live." Tears streamed down her cheeks.

"In minutes, I lost all my family." She lifted her face and whispered, "Silence makes the most eerie sound."

Addie nodded in agreement, understanding completely. She lifted her pencil. *"You have friends in Hope's Crossing who won't judge. Open your heart, and you'll find them, and me, inside. Maybe it's time to step back into life."*

"I know, honey. Last Christmas I started trying to make my way back and actually took part in the Advent that involved the whole town. Rebel Lassiter was such a dear to me." Eleanor got a faraway look in her eyes. "She came near to dying that Christmas. Told me to start with baby steps, and that's pretty much what I've done." Eleanor poured them another cup of tea. "Addie dear, I don't know what happened to you, and I don't need to, but that man of yours does. He deserves to know what you're hiding."

Addie pondered her words. She did owe Ridge the truth.

"I've lived a lot of years and seen more trouble than two lifetimes. But one thing I've learned is that secrets don't do anyone any good. It's time to let them out before they destroy you."

She was right. Right about all of it.

"I loved my Charley and lost him. You still have Ridge; if the law has anything to do with it, you may not have him for long. Don't waste time."

Her pleading words hung in the air. Finally, Addie wrote: *"I'll tell him soon."*

Eleanor grabbed a woven basket and went out to the garden. She came back with squash, green beans, and onions, and handed the lot to Addie. "Fresh vegetables for your supper."

She accepted the gift, hugged her dear friend, and left, all the horror, heartbreak, and despair of Eleanor's story replaying in her head. Her blood stilled. Eleanor was right. Men could ride in at any time and kill Ridge, leaving her so lost and alone. A widow.

Would she have Eleanor's strength, enough to keep living? Her heart pounded. Or would she take a Colt one night and hold it to her head?

Whatever the future had in store, she had to grab every bit of happiness with Ridge before time ran out—make lasting memories to carry inside for dark and frightening days, remembrances that would never fade. And she had to start now.

✒

The late afternoon sun hung in the sky, the rays shining through the branches of a large cottonwood tree, creating silver filigree designs on the dirt path outside of Eleanor's tiny home. Addie's thoughts had moved to planning supper with the vegetables Eleanor had given her, when two men burst through the tangle of brush.

She screamed as they grabbed her with their rough hands, dropping the woven basket. The vegetables spilled to the ground.

One man clapped a hand over her mouth. "Shut up, Adeline."

The other assailant snarled and jerked her around. "We don't want to have to get mean, but we're tired of chasing you. Shoulda known you'd take up with a bunch of rotten, thieving outlaws."

Addie trembled and stared into their faces, recognizing them both from New Zion. Her father's men. The one she knew only as Tiny was anything but, towering over her, his muscles bulging. The other was Pickens. This man had mean eyes and a hard face. She'd long suspected her father of keeping the pair around simply to do his dirty work.

She jerked and kicked, trying to loosen their grips, to no avail.

Eleanor appeared in her door. "What are you doing there? Turn Addie loose!"

"Get back inside, old woman." Pickens pulled a pistol from his holster and pointed it at Eleanor. "This is none of your affair."

"Do you think I'm scared?" Eleanor glared, and her voice held firm. "I've faced jackasses far meaner than you, and I ain't afraid to die."

"Go on or I'll shoot you. You won't be the first woman I've killed."

She reached behind the door and pulled out a rifle. She ratcheted a bullet into the chamber and took aim at Pickens. "Let Addie go and do it now."

Addie's heart pounded. They'd kill Eleanor for sure. Addie knew Pickens didn't deliver idle threats.

Sometimes her father had let him wield the whip during someone's punishment, and she knew of at least twice Pickens had nearly killed the person on the receiving end. The sight of blood seemed to excite the man, and he didn't know when to stop.

"You shouldn't have raised that rifle, old woman." Tiny tightened his steely grip around Addie's arms. He could probably break Eleanor in half with his bare hands if he had a mind.

"Fire that weapon, mister, you'll bring every outlaw in this town running." A smile grew on Eleanor's face. "You don't have the sense to realize that you're boxed in. There's only one way out—how do you plan to get there? You're not too bright if you ask me."

Pickens's confidence slipped. His gaze swept the area, a crease appearing between his brows.

Tiny swallowed hard. "Don't we have another way out, Pick? You said this would be easy. Slip in, grab her, and leave. I think this old woman might shoot us."

"Shut up, moron. Adeline'll make a mighty good shield. They won't shoot." Pickens waved his gun at Addie. "We just want to ask her one question."

"Ask away, sonny," Eleanor snapped. "Only she can't talk. Maybe it was you who scared the words right out of her."

Pickens faced Addie, his eyes heavy lidded and cruel. "We just want to know where the kid is. Tell us where you hid him, and we'll leave."

Addie shook her head, her eyes flashing. Never.

The unmistakable click of the hammer of a pistol came from behind the pair. Pickens and Tiny froze, Tiny's grip loosening.

"I hope you said your prayers before you entered our town, boys." Ridge stepped from the brush on the side of the path, followed by Clay, Jack, and Travis. All had their guns drawn. Relief weakened Addie's knees. She'd never been so glad to see them.

Ridge shot her a quick glance. "Are you all right, Addie? Did they hurt you?"

She shook her head and took the chance to run from Tiny and stand beside Eleanor.

The men closed a circle around the two varmints. "I recognized your kind when you came into town." Ridge took their guns. "Let me make one thing perfectly clear. I will protect my wife to my last breath."

Tiny glanced from one face to the other and licked his dry lips. "We weren't gonna hurt her. I swear."

"We haven't had a hanging yet in Hope's Crossing." Jack poked Pickens in the back with his gun. "Might be time to change that."

Clay studied Tiny, looking him up and down. "Just because we haven't had one doesn't mean we don't know how a hanging's done. In fact, we know better than most."

"We don't even need a judge or a gallows, either," Travis added with a cold smile. "We can make it short and sweet."

"Hell, man, hold on there." Tiny's eyes bulged, a rivulet of sweat running down his face.

Pickens swung his stony gaze to Addie. "We ain't done nothing but talk. If she says different, she lies. No law against talkin'."

Ridge snorted. "It appears to me that we stopped you before you had a chance to carry out whatever it was you meant to do. We'll put you in our strap-iron jail until we decide what needs doing. Now march."

Once the others were gone, Ridge put his gun away and went to Addie. She snuggled against him, safe and warm in his arms.

And she rather liked it.

Fifteen

RIDGE UNDERSTOOD ADDIE'S QUIET MOOD ON THE WAY HOME. Pickens and Tiny had given her a big fright. He was just grateful that he'd seen them ride in earlier that day and realized who they were. Since the guard had only been on the lookout for Hiram, he'd let them pass. The two had hung around the saloon for a good bit, then Ridge had followed them to Eleanor's. He trembled to think how easily he could've lost Addie today if he hadn't been paying attention.

The light would've gone out of his world.

Ridge shot Addie a sideways glance. She stared straight ahead, her plump lips trembling, the breeze fluttering short tendrils of hair next to her ear. He needed to ask her what the men meant with their questions about a kid, but he wouldn't press her tonight. Still, he couldn't help but wonder. Who was the child, and why would Addie know? Was the child hers?

The silence was a little awkward. He didn't exactly know what to say to her. They'd moved onto unfamiliar ground, and he wasn't sure when or why.

He'd wanted a few private moments with the pair Addie's father had sent to get some answers, but Jack and Clay sent him to Addie. Ridge reckoned there was time enough for some justice later. Tiny and Pickens weren't going anywhere.

With a beautiful sky overhead and a few lazy clouds on the horizon, Cob and King snuffled softly as they entered their property and headed toward the house. As had been Ridge's custom, his nerves even more on edge now, he gave the place a wary scan, looking for anything out of the ordinary. Bodie came around to the front to wave, and Ridge relaxed. Everything was fine. For now.

"Your cats are waiting for you on the porch. They must've heard us and come running."

Addie craned her neck and smiled. The sight of her smile was a relief after seeing her so somber. Now if only she would find her voice again—there was lots he wanted to ask her. Things he wanted to say that were best spoken, and answers gotten directly from her own lips.

Tonight, though, he'd find a way to tell her—somehow— why he became an outlaw. No more putting that conversation off. He'd skirted that issue for too long. Not because of her speaking problem but due to his, and the fact he'd intended to keep that hidden from her. Yet he saw now that keeping secrets from a spouse kept a relationship from growing, and Addie had to feel it between them.

He sure as hell felt hers and hoped she would trust him enough to let it out soon.

Bodie walked beside them to the barn, grinning from ear to ear. "I got all my work done early, then started on my learning. I can recite the alphabet start to finish. Wanna hear?"

Clearly, he'd been itching for them to get home. Ridge chuckled at the kid's enthusiasm. "Sure."

With a deep breath, Bodie started. He stumbled a tad toward the end and had to correct himself but got it right by the time they reached the back of the house.

"That's great. I'm proud of you." Ridge dismounted and took the basket of vegetables, setting them aside to give Addie a hand down from King.

"Do you really think so? You're not just saying that?"

"I meant it, son." Ridge collected the reins of both horses. "Addie, I'll take care of King."

She nodded, then went to their young ranch hand. She patted his chest, then put her arms around him and gave the boy a hug, acting like a proud mama.

Bodie pulled away, happy but obviously also embarrassed at the show of affection. After Addie went into the kitchen with her basket, he faced Ridge. "I wanted to please you most of all, but I also want to learn. I want to be able to read and write and all that other stuff that will make my life easier. You know?"

"Yes, son, I know. I'm glad to help." Ridge walked the horses into the barn, and Bodie followed, talking away.

"I think my pa would be happy I'm trying to get smart. He always said a man never knows all of anything and keeps learning all his life."

Ridge removed the bridle from King and slipped a halter on. "Your pa must've been a good man." What had gotten into the kid? Ridge suspected he'd kept a lot inside, and now that Bodie was safe, it needed to come out.

"He was. He sure loved my mama. They used to kiss a lot." Bodie unsaddled Cob. "I can tell how much you love Addie," he added quietly.

The last part of the conversation struck Ridge like a bullet between the eyes. He stilled. "Why do you say that?"

"You know, it's not so much what you say but how you say it. When you talk to her, your voice gets all gentle and melty like my pa's used to." Bodie rested a hand on the horse's back, and a distant look filled the kid's eyes. "Pa's voice made me feel warm inside. Yours does too. Thank you for giving me a chance."

"I'm happy to do it. Everyone needs someone to care about them." Ridge's reply was hoarse and rough. He cleared his throat. "Anyone would do the same."

"You're wrong. They didn't. All my relatives treated me like I had cholera or the pox, and it would rub off on them. I heard one uncle say they would have to burn the bedding I slept on. They couldn't wait to pass me off to the next one."

Ridge turned to face him. "Don't waste another thought on those people. As far as I'm concerned, they're downright stupid. You have worth and never forget it. You have more to be proud of right now than your relatives will ever have in their whole pathetic lives. I'm glad you're here with us, and I know Addie feels that way too. You're family."

The kid coughed and turned away for a moment. When he spoke, his voice was rough. "I like that. I sure do. Can you read more in that book tonight about Oliver?"

Ridge put Cob in his stall. "Yeah, I'll read."

Bodie finally hushed and let Ridge think for a spell. Loving Addie? Sure, he cared for her and would take a bullet meant for her, but that was what a good man did. Sure, she made his life better, and he'd do anything to make sure she stayed happy, but it didn't mean he was in love. Nope. Love was something big and noisy, like Chinese fireworks. The kid had everything all wrong.

He finished up and fed the horses, then stood there a moment watching Miss Kitty and Squeakers play. Finally, he took a deep breath and went inside as the evening shadows fell. Delicious smells coming from the stove and Addie hunched over a notebook at the table, writing by the lantern light, were things he'd remember the rest of his life.

If he was right, he had just enough time for a talk before they ate.

She glanced up and offered a quivery smile, deep despair lining her face.

"What is it, love?" He moved a chair beside her and put an arm around her shoulders.

Addie turned the page of her notebook, writing: *"Eleanor convinced me that I need to tell you some things. I know you have questions. But it's hard."*

"Yes, it is." He kissed her cheek. "I only want to know one thing, and the rest can wait. Do you have a child somewhere that you need to see to?"

She shook her head. *"Not mine."*

"Is this kid in danger?"

"Safe for now."

"Okay. I need you to listen to something I have to say, and it might make it easier for you to speak your piece in return. We've both kept our pasts bottled up for too long, and I don't want any secrets standing between us. We can't move forward until we do." He removed his hat and laid it on the table. Curiosity sat in her pretty eyes. "First though, I'm sorry for letting those two hoodlums get so close to you. I should've taken care of them long before you stepped out of Eleanor's, but I took time to go for reinforcements."

She shook her head and scribbled: *"You couldn't stop them by yourself. Pickens is a cold-blooded killer. My father kept him and Tiny around as an added measure of control."*

"Still, I apologize that I put you in danger." A long inhale filled his lungs with air. "You asked me how I became an outlaw and why there's such a large bounty on my head. I hope you understand when I tell you the story.

"I once pastored a church in Silver Valley, and I was good at my job. One night I was riding home alone after visiting a parishioner's gravely ill child." He paused and stared at his open hand, his mind's eye seeing a large red stain covering his palm. "I heard yelling and a woman screaming, from a ways off the road. I pushed through some trees and found myself surrounded by a group of men. They had a woman with them, a young one, doubt she was more than seventeen. Her dress was ripped nearly off and she was crying."

Ridge got up and went to the window to look out, spreading his arms wide on the counter. "I asked the men what they were doing, although it was pretty clear. They snarled that it was none of my concern. Ride on, they ordered. I didn't wear a gun back then—didn't see any need for one. I made the mistake of dismounting to speak with the woman, and the men grabbed, slamming me to the ground.

"I remember them shouting and trying to figure out what to do with me. One hollered that I was the preacher and would talk. Another said it'd be a cold day in hell when he'd let me ruin them. I got back to my feet, but one of them—probably not even old enough to have been in long pants too many years—got in my face. I shoved him away." Ridge winced at the memory he couldn't shake. "He went down hard, striking his head on a rock. Died right then."

Addie gasped.

Ridge tried to keep his voice even, but the words came out rusty. "The law says I killed him. His pa refused to hear the truth."

A chair scooted away from the table, and Addie's footsteps came to him, and her warm hand was on his back. He turned

to see her tear-filled eyes. Wordlessly, he opened his arms, and
she walked into them.

❧

Addie glanced up and tenderly laid her palm against his jaw,
her heart aching for the man she'd married. Telling this story
was tearing him apart, yet he kept going—for her sake, because
he wanted no secrets between them. A twinge of guilt pricked
her. She rose on her tiptoes to press her lips to his. The kiss,
though brief, would let him know she admired and cared for
him.

"Let me finish while I can. I'll never speak of this again,"
he murmured.

She nodded, and he continued. "They dragged me and the
girl into town to the sheriff. One of the men, her own father,
forced her to say that I was the one who committed the crime
against her, and my worthless accusers heaped more lies on
top of that.

"I found out later that her bastard father had given her to
them for the night to pay off a debt. They threatened to put a
bullet in the man's head unless he got his daughter to lie and
save their hides. The sea of voices drowned me out. No one
listened to what I had to say."

Tears rolled down her cheeks. She held him tightly, her
arms around his waist, wishing she could take his pain from
him.

"A group of vigilantes grabbed a rope, and they took me to
a tree. I remember staring up at the stars, wondering why God
had let this happen. I had always lived an exemplary life and
done His work without complaint. How could my life end
because people who knew me chose to believe lies instead of
the truth?" Ridge shuddered. "They put the rope around my
neck, and I knew I'd seen my last sunset."

Addie held him tighter, pressing herself against his tall body.
It was all she could do to make him aware he wasn't alone.

"The next part was a bit fuzzy. As I waited to die, Clay
Colby galloped in, shot the rope in half. I didn't know him

before that moment, but he helped me escape. His only explanation was that he never liked a stacked deck." Ridge glanced down, his haunted eyes boring a hole into her. He tucked a lock of hair behind her ear.

Addie saw how these events had crushed his spirit and turned him into someone he'd never planned to be. She took a moment to look at her situation and found that Ezekiel, the punishment, prison had also changed her in countless ways. They were both different people.

They stood in silence for several moments, and she watched a muscle in his jaw work. His Adam's apple bobbed up and down when he swallowed. Finally, he spat in anguish, "I'm a killer, and a lie branded me a…despicable piece of humanity." He stepped away from her. "Me, a man of God, someone who preys on women! I vow to you that I've never done that. Ever!"

She reached for her paper. *"I know that."*

"That wasn't the end of it, though. The young man I killed was the favorite son of a wealthy rancher. Tom Calder and his older son gathered some men and came after me with a vengeance. I ended up shooting his namesake between the eyes. I took both his boys from him. Calder went home a broken man, vowing to see me in a grave before he dies." Ridge rubbed the day's stubble along his jaw. "Killing only leads to more killing. It never ends. I'm positive I'll meet up with Calder in the near future. He just has to find me first."

His voice had risen, but she wasn't afraid. Her own anger rose as she faced him and shook her head, writing, *"He's a fool. His younger son's death was an accident, and the other was due to his own stupidity. I can see that you're a decent man, a good man, someone I'm proud to be married to—and you know who and what you are. Nothing else matters."*

"Might I remind you that I have a price on my head? I can be arrested, hanged for it."

"We'll make sure you're not."

"How?" His eyes blazed with helpless fury. "How can we do that?"

She didn't know, but she'd do whatever she must in order to keep Ridge free—and that was a promise. She hadn't found the only decent man in her life only to lose him now.

Sixteen

RIDGE WORKED WITH BODIE'S LESSONS AFTER SUPPER, THEN read a chapter from *Oliver Twist* aloud while Addie darned socks and knitted. Anyone looking in at them would never have been able to imagine the undercurrent of danger hidden beneath their relaxation. They could be any happy family in Texas. Except they weren't just anyone's. Addie and Bodie were his—and they were all he had.

He thought of his four sisters, married with children, who cursed him to this day, refusing to utter his name. His parents long dead. Yes, Addie and Bodie made up his family.

Addie shifted in her chair, listening with rapt attention as Ridge got to the part in the book where the character Nancy developed a caring for the young orphan Oliver. Addie sniffled and wiped her eyes. Soft lamplight shone on the delicate curve of her cheek, the graceful column of her neck, the sensitive glimmer in her pretty eyes. That picture might give someone the impression she was meek. But brother, would they be wrong. She had fire and passion beneath that calm exterior, and he couldn't wait to awaken it fully.

Bodie lay on the floor, his chin propped on his hands, also riveted by the emotional story.

Reaching the end of the chapter, Ridge closed the book. "I need to take a walk around before I turn in."

"I'll come too." Bodie got to his feet.

"Addie, I'll be back in a little bit." Ridge waited for her nod, then reached for his rifle over the mantel and went out.

The moon shone brightly, lighting up the ground. Ridge stood for a moment, listening to the sounds of night creatures. Everything appeared normal, but sometimes that fooled a man. "Bodie, you go around the house to the front. I'll check farther up near the mesquite thicket."

"Yes, sir." The kid got his rifle from the barn and began his patrol, the darkness swallowing him.

Ridge moved away, his ears and eyes attuned to what belonged and what didn't. A night hawk flew silently overhead, and a coyote howled in the distance. Despite appearances, something was off. His gut warned him as the hair stood on the back of his neck. He crept through the darkness, entering a world he'd had to learn well—the ugly side of survival, kill or be killed.

With Tiny and Pickens locked up before they got word to Ezekiel Jancy, it had to be Hiram, he felt.

The bounty hunter was close. The man's evil greed reached, trying to burrow inside.

"Bodie, stay alert," Ridge whispered into the slight breeze. A backward glance at the house, now fifty yards away, revealed soft lamplight shining through the windows where Addie waited.

Then he saw it—a hunched figure of a man running from the barn. Ridge couldn't tell if it was Bodie or someone else. His gut screamed to hurry back to the house.

A flash of orange fire spat from a figure in the shadows, and the boom from a scattergun carried on the breeze.

Apparently drawn by the sound, Addie stepped out of the kitchen door. The light silhouetted her as she pulled her shawl closer around her. Oh dear God!

Ridge yelled a warning but couldn't stop the dark figure from hurling himself at her.

A blood-curdling scream split the air. His heart thundered in his ears as he bolted toward Addie. *Please, just get there in time*. She shouldn't suffer for his crimes. He ran as hard as he could, praying with every step.

Bodie reached Addie first. The kid grabbed the dark figure, slinging him away like a sack of grain. "Get in the house, Addie!" Bodie screamed.

"I'll kill you this time, boy!" the attacker shouted. "You're not worth spit anyway."

Dammit! Ridge was still too far away. He willed his feet to go faster. Panic and heavy breathing hurt his starved lungs. His body started to seize up from the exertion and lack of air. So engrossed was he in the scene, he stepped into what must've been a gopher hole and sprawled. Cursing, he rose and pain shot from his ankle all the way up his leg. Despair washed over him. Using the rifle to lean on, he limped on, keeping his eyes glued on his little family.

Addie made it to the door and halfway inside before the attacker caught her again, yanking her back out into the night. Bodie leaped onto his back, his arms around the man's throat until he turned Addie loose. Instead of running, she picked up a board and slammed it into the attacker's stomach. A loud grunt told Ridge the blow had hurt.

Bodie went flying off to the side again as the man turned his attention on Addie.

Thirty yards. Ridge tried to take a shot but found nothing clear. He blocked his pain and mustered everything inside him toward the fight.

Addie stood her ground and swung the board again. This time the attacker was ready and sidestepped the blow. He grabbed the weapon, snatching it from her with a mighty yell, and sent her sprawling onto the hard-packed soil.

Twenty yards. Ridge could do nothing but watch. *Dammit!* He raised his rifle, but Bodie blocked his shot. Ridge lowered the weapon and kept moving instead. The kid fought bravely, not giving an inch. Even so, Bodie was quickly running out of strength.

Fifteen yards. Ridge raised the rifle again to the same results. Ten.

Five. Bodie blocked his shot again.

Ridge sucked air into his body and launched himself onto the enemy, both going down hard. Ridge's rifle came loose and hit the ground the same time the dark figure's gun sailed from his hand. Ridge drew back a fist and delivered a powerful punch to the man's jaw.

They rolled into light from the kitchen window and he saw the man's face clearly—*Hiram*.

Hiram rose and shook his head to clear it, then went at Ridge, head-butting him in the midsection, knocking the wind out of him. Ridge could barely see as he doubled over, struggling to force air into his lungs. Hiram gave him little chance to gather his wits before he came at him hard again.

"Give up, Steele. You're whipped," Hiram snarled.

"I never give up against scum like you." Ridge wiped his mouth. "What are people going to say about you? You can't even whip a preacher."

Hiram let out a yell that they probably heard in Hope's Crossing and ran at him. Ridge hooked an arm around Hiram's thick neck and jabbed his face.

Squaring off, they threw punches left and right, some connecting, some not.

Seizing a slight advantage, Hiram raised his elbow and brought it down hard on the back of Ridge's neck. Stars circled Ridge's vision, and he collapsed in the dirt.

Everything moved in slow motion, his head swimming as he tried to force his legs underneath him. From the corner of Ridge's eye, he saw Bodie coming to help. Hiram was waiting and grabbed him, slamming a fist into the kid's jaw. Bodie crumpled to the ground, moaning.

No one was left to help Addie.

Ridge's stomach knotted, and he couldn't breathe. He tried to summon all his strength and struggle to his feet, but before he could, Hiram blinded him with a fistful of sand. The grit felt like boulders, and he couldn't see a blessed thing.

Dear God! Where was Addie? He couldn't let Hiram get her. Ridge finally made it to his feet, but he'd lost Hiram in the thick haze inside his head.

❧

Addie watched in horror as the bounty hunter made a dive for his gun, stood, and aimed.

Ridge can't see him.

Her heart tried to burst from her chest. If she didn't warn him in the next breath, he'd die.

She held his life in her hands, and a scream would tell him nothing.

Get the words out to tell him what to do. She wrung her hands.

The deadly click of the hammer sounded loud in her ears as Hiram pulled it back.

Addie worked her tongue. Oh God, she had to form the words. Oh God! Please.

Sweat formed on her palms and trickled down her spine. She opened her mouth, praying the warning came out. "Turn around, Ridge! Turn around! He's behind you!"

The words burst free, and her shout jarred Ridge to action. With a quick jerk, he slid his Colt from the holster while in motion. One squeeze of the trigger, and he shot point-blank into Hiram's chest.

The bounty hunter crumpled, blood soaking his shirt. Addie clapped a hand to her mouth, watching Ridge limp to the man's revolver and kick it away, then check to see if he was alive. Relief flooded her when he closed Hiram's open eyes.

She threw herself at Ridge, sobbing. He pulled her close. "It's all right. You're safe."

"Hold me. I'm so c-c-cold," she begged.

He placed a gentle kiss on her trembling lips, the warmth of him melting the icy layers of fear. Addie dissolved into his arms, clinging to him with all she was worth, returning his kiss. For a moment, it was only the two of them in the world.

She slid her arms around his neck and knew there was no other place on earth she wanted to be than here with him. She was an outlaw's wife and would stay by his side through life, death, and every trial.

Ridge broke the kiss, smiling. "You talked, Addie. Your voice is back."

Her first attempt to reply came out raspy and unsure. "I—I—"

"Don't rush. Just take your time, sweetheart."

She cleared her throat and tried again. "Y—You were about to die. I—I had to warn you. I just opened my mouth, and out the words came. My voice is pretty r-r-rusty, though."

"It'll get better with use. I'd be dead if you hadn't yelled."
He tightened his hold and kissed behind her ear.

A loud groan interrupted them, and Ridge limped with
Addie's support to help Bodie up. "How bad are you hurt?"
Ridge asked.

The kid was holding his jaw. "I'm not sure yet. Hiram
could sure pack a wallop, but I don't think it's broken. I was
trying to keep him away from Addie."

She pressed a kiss to Bodie's cheek. "You were amazing.
Thank you."

"You're talking!"

"The words were there all along. I just had to find them.
I knew it was up to me or that bounty hunter would kill
Ridge." Her eyes met her husband's. She slid an arm around
his waist, loving the solid muscle and bone and heart that made
up this man—one who had protected her with so little regard
for his own life.

Ridge tightened his hold. "I knew you would. Where
there's a will, there's a way. Why don't you go into the house
while Bodie and I take care of Hiram?"

"First, tell me why you're limping."

"I sort of stepped into a hole, running to get here in time
to help. I'll be fine."

"I hope so. You won't be long?"

"No. I'll put him where the animals can't get him and take
him into town in the morning." He brushed her cheek with
his lips.

The feel of his mouth on her skin sent tingles through
her. "I'll get what I need and clean both yours and Bodie's
wounds." She hurried into the kitchen and was greeted by the
cats, their backs up. Miss Kitty gave her a loud scolding, low-
pitched grumbles interspersed with long, drawn-out meows.
Just when the cat started to wind down, she started up again.

"I know, I know, and I'm sorry you got left inside. But it
was for your own good. You'd only have been in the way."
Addie scratched them behind their ears, then pumped water
into a large metal bowl.

Her whole body ached from being tossed around and slammed to the ground. She'd be sore for a while, with some bruises of her own, but otherwise fine. Ridge and Bodie were a different story. She gathered soap and plenty of clean bandages and sat to wait for her men.

While she waited, she had a moment to herself. Addie placed her fingertips to her lips and smiled. She'd *yelled*, not just a tiny peep. It seemed strange to use her voice after years of silence. Her throat didn't exactly hurt, but her voice was different—a little lower than she remembered. It sounded strange in her ears. Her smile widened. Now she could say whatever she wanted instead of having to write everything down. Dr. Mary would be astonished.

The door opened, and Ridge limped inside, Bodie following. Both had damp hair, which told her they'd washed up outside. Deep scratches and angry skin showed above the collarless neck of Ridge's shirt, a shirt now torn and bloody beyond anything she could repair. Her breath caught when his whiskey-colored gaze sought hers.

Bodie had a multitude of scrapes and bruises, and though he had an eye that would be swollen shut by morning, he was grinning like a donkey eating briars. "We did it, and we're all alive. And Addie can talk again. I'd say we did all right."

"You said a mouthful, son." Ridge wiped something off her cheek.

"Dirt?" she asked.

"A badge of honor. Sweetheart, you fought like a wildcat." A crooked grin curved Ridge's mouth. "Remind me to give you a wide berth when we're having a disagreement."

"Stop teasing and sit down. You're bleeding."

"Yes, ma'am." He removed his shirt and tossed it aside.

Addie didn't know where to begin, so she washed the blood away from the older gunshot wound on his arm, happy to see that it looked in fair shape, then set to work on the new scrapes. A deep bruise and knot on the back of his neck had risen about an inch, and he flinched when she washed it.

"Sorry," he mumbled. "It hurts."

"I'm trying to be careful."

"I know."

After tending to Ridge, she turned to Bodie. "You're next."

"You don't have to do anything special for me, Addie."

"Hush and be still." She patted his shoulder. "You fought like a man out there."

By the time she finished, his grin couldn't get any wider or his thanks any deeper. He reminded her of a pup who'd been kicked about but still wagged his tail with hope that someone might see his worth. Her heart went out to him.

"Now, go get to sleep," she said softly. "We have a long day ahead of us tomorrow."

Bodie ducked his head as though afraid to let her see how much her fussing meant. "Yes, ma'am."

Once the door closed behind him, Ridge, still shirtless, held out a hand. "Will you sleep in my bed tonight, Addie? I don't think I can let you go."

Seventeen

ADDIE PUT HER TREMBLING HAND IN RIDGE'S AND MET HIS eyes. Sleep in his bed? She swallowed hard. "I don't know how…" Her voice trailed off. The burning heat in his gaze made the rest of what she'd planned to say unimportant.

Water dripped from the pump's spout in the stillness of the kitchen, and Squeakers rubbed its head against her legs, but she didn't miss the soft pleading in Ridge's voice, see the hope in his eyes.

"We'll just sleep, but I'd like to hear you breathing softly next to me." He chuckled. "I'm too stove up right now to lift as much as an eyebrow. You're safe."

"I trust you, Ridge. Have from the first. I just had some things to work out inside myself before trying to become a wife that way." Warmth settled over her when he draped a casual arm around her neck, his hand hanging down the front, his fingers almost touching her breast.

She was conscious of his bare skin down to his waist—and a narrow strip of fine brown hair on his stomach that disappeared into his trousers.

"I'm not afraid, Ridge." Well, maybe the good Lord would forgive her for the little white lie. She was filled with trepidation and worry.

Would she disappoint him, or do something wrong? This was new territory.

The cats ran ahead of them as Addie and Ridge moved toward the stairs, turning down the lamps as they went. The felines stopped in what looked like amazement when she didn't turn in at her little room. Loud and insistent meowing came from the doorway before Miss Kitty reluctantly followed them up to the bedroom.

Ridge helped her turn back the covers. "I'll leave you to get undressed."

"No need. If you don't go ahead and fall onto the mattress, I'll find you on the floor." Addie let her hand rest on his bare back, feeling the muscle underneath. "I'll run downstairs for my gown and undress down there."

"Tomorrow you can move all your things up here." The suggestion seemed casual enough, but she saw the hope shining in his eyes as he hung his gun belt on the bedpost. "That is, if you want. There's plenty of room."

"I want," she said softly.

"Addie, I almost lost you twice today. I'll not let a third happen."

"You can't promise that, so quit it. None of that was your fault. If I'd stayed inside, the bounty hunter wouldn't have gotten me. I messed up. The gunshot scared me, and I was afraid he'd hit you or Bodie."

"I'm too tired to argue."

"Then don't. Ridge, I was thinking: What if you go back and face the woman again, get her to fix the lie? She could clear you."

"I've thought long and hard about that and weighed the danger. Darling, if she was going to set the record straight, she would've already. I'd just open myself up to be caught. Besides, even if she did change her mind, there's also the rancher, Tom Calder, to consider. He'd take great joy in watching me swing from a rope." He stared deeply into her eyes, a warm hand below her jaw. "No, it's just too dangerous. I'm safe here."

"I see your point. I don't want to lose you. I'll be right back." She hesitated a moment before adding, "Dear."

The cats curled up together on a rug, apparently too tired to chase after her. She hurried down the stairs, feeling her way in the dark, her memory of the layout not failing her.

She didn't take long, but by the time she returned, Ridge was already fast asleep, breathing softly with nothing but the sheet covering him. Bruises were starting to turn purple on his chest and arms.

Addie quickly braided her hair, then turned down the

lamp's wick and slid into bed. She leaned up on an elbow to press her lips to his. "Good night. I can't wait to see our life unfold."

He roused and opened his eyes. "Can you talk to me for a bit? I want to hear your beautiful voice."

"I suppose." She settled next to him and lay stiffly, talking about their animals, how much she loved taking care of them, and what she liked best about her life with him. Within minutes, he was snoring softly. He'd known she needed to become accustomed to the feel of the strange bed.

Addie smiled. She'd married a smart man. Sneaky, but smart.

She lay there beside him for a while, sleep not coming. The clock in the room seemed to measure each breath rather than the passage of time. Addie turned on her side to face Ridge, grateful she had this little time to become somewhat used to sharing a bed with him without the pressure of lovemaking. As a teacher, she'd read about a man's anatomy and knew the basics, and she imagined there would be pain. How would she handle that?

Yet, she was ready to be a wife.

Apprehensive, she slid her hand across the sheet and touched his shoulder. He didn't move. A new boldness came over her. She inched her leg ever so slowly forward until it touched his and discovered he wore nothing beneath the sheet. *Absolutely nothing.*

Shock raced along her body for second, mimicking her heartbeat. When her pulse steadied, she smiled and snuggled next to him, her palm resting on his broad, bare chest, trusting in her outlaw and his tender touch so gentle, she wanted him to never let her go.

From where Addie lay, she could see the tall chest of drawers and the box on top, hiding his secret, and all her old insecurities flooded over her. There had to be a reason why he'd never told her about the picture.

Maybe the fancy woman in the tintype was waiting to steal Ridge from her. She'd know all about men and how to please them. She'd be sure of herself and confident of her abilities. What did Addie know? Not much, but she'd fight for Ridge.

∽

Ridge woke sometime before dawn and rolled over. His head pounded, and through the haze, he tried to focus on the owner of the leg lying so intimately on top of his. Who was attached to the other end? He scowled, then his heart leaped. Addie?

For a moment, he couldn't recall why she'd be in his bed—then it all came roaring back. The bounty hunter. Their fight to survive. Addie's bravery.

Dark lashes feathered against her delicate skin, his beautiful angel. He lifted a gold curl and held it to his nose, whiffing the sweet fragrance of a mountain spring. His long wait had ended. Here she was beside him, and it wasn't a dream.

He let a finger drift down her throat to the satiny skin peeking from her gown. She slept so quietly, her bosom rising and falling with each breath. He yearned to kiss her, but he didn't wish to wake her. Not just yet. He wasn't finished watching her sleep. Every detail about her interested him, from the tiny mole above her top lip to her earlobes in the shape of small, perfect shells.

A meow came from the foot of the bed. Miss Kitty stretched and moved up between them, turning herself into a chaperone and forcing Ridge to remove his hand. He glared at the cat, and she arched her back. "So that's the way it's going to be, huh?" He kept his hiss in a whisper so it lost some of the impact. "Just see if I let you in here again. I'll haul you off so far you'll never find your way back."

Ha! That should fix the problem. He was bigger and had more power than a mere feline. Or so he better.

Addie opened her eyes, and his war with the cat was forgotten as he fell into the startled depths of her gaze. She jerked her leg away from his.

"Good morning, love." Ridge smiled at her sudden timidity in the thin morning light. She was clearly uncomfortable with the new arrangement. "It'll get easier."

Miss Kitty licked her face, and Squeakers snuck in between them as well to get its ears rubbed.

Addie bit her lip and met his eyes. "I hope I didn't crowd you. I tried to stay on my side and give you enough room."

"I had more than enough room, and you're welcome on my side anytime. We don't have a his and hers. Only an ours." Ridge gave her a light kiss and let a fingertip drift across her cheek. "You look like a beautiful princess. I don't think I deserve you."

"Are you always so eloquent this early in the morning?"

Her smile held no fear, which surprised him a little. He'd half expected to wake and find her back in her dreary little room under the stairs.

"I guess you'll have to find out." He tweaked her nose and started to rise. "Fair warning, sweetheart. I'm going to get up now and dress. I don't mind you watching, but if you'd rather not see, better hide your eyes."

"Thank you—dear." She rolled away from him and faced the other way.

He could have been offended, but her relief didn't give him any trouble. It'd take time to smooth these things out. Sleeping next to him was just the first step.

Ridge sat on the side of the bed, the sheet falling away, and reached for his trousers and boots, then padded to the chest of drawers for a clean shirt. He strapped on his gun belt. "I'll see you downstairs after I milk the cow."

"Okay."

The silent house seemed different as he strode through the rooms. It was as though killing Hiram had lightened the whole atmosphere. In the kitchen, he lit the stove for Addie and got coffee on to boil. Stepping onto the back porch, he inhaled a deep breath of clean air that finished purging the blackness inside him.

Bodie emerged from the barn, scratching under his arm, his face a mass of purple bruises. "Morning, boss. I hope you slept good."

"I never felt a thing once my head hit the pillow. You?" Ridge moved toward the kid.

"Had a lot of thinking to do before I went to bed, then I slept off and on. Mostly off." Bodie handed him the empty milk pail. "I reckon we'll tote Hiram into town this morning."

"Right after breakfast. Folks will be happy that we don't have to post guards anymore. How's your jaw?"

"Hurts."

"Probably have to give it a week or longer 'til that stops." Ridge went on to the cow and found peace in the milking. He'd always found that mundane chores helped settle a person, and this morning he needed that more than ever. Killing anyone stole a piece of a man's soul. Even so, he was glad Hiram was dead. He'd pull the trigger again in a heartbeat to rid the world of one more ruthless man.

Addie came out of the house, and he stopped to stare at the way the morning rays caressed her face and touched her hair, turning it a deeper shade of gold. She took his breath and made him happy to be alive. How had he gotten so lucky? His chest swelled.

After breakfast, Ridge loaded Hiram's body in the wagon, and the three of them drove into town. They rode past the outdoor jail cell, and Tiny and Pickens gripped the bars and craned their necks to watch them go by. Rascal that Ridge was, he drove past them real slow to give them a good look at the dead bounty hunter. Maybe seeing the body would be a deterrent, if they thought about trying to break out.

Which he was sure they did. All prisoners yearned to escape. Let them try.

Addie put her hand on Ridge's arm after he swung her down. "I want to go speak to Dr. Mary while you men take care of this."

"Bet she'll be tickled to hear you now," he predicted.

She pushed through the gathering crowd, and he turned to Clay and others who pressed him with questions about the dead man. But his thoughts were on Addie—and bedtime.

Tonight, he'd try holding her beneath the covers as they talked. One slow step at a time.

❧

Addie burst through the door of the small hospital. "I can talk! I finally have my voice back!"

Dr. Mary came running from the next room, drying her hands on a long apron. "Praise be! Sit down, girl, and tell me what happened."

For the next half hour, Addie sat and related the details of the previous night. "He was so addled…if I hadn't warned him, I'd be a widow today, and I couldn't bear that thought." She lowered her voice. "There's more."

"What else can you possibly have that's better than that?" Dr. Mary patted Addie's hand.

"I slept beside Ridge last night for the first time."

Dr. Mary's eyes twinkled. "How was it?"

"Good." Addie dropped to a shocked whisper. "He goes to bed *naked*."

"You don't say!" Dr. Mary laughed. "I think you're going to be all right. Your marriage is on the right track. No doubt you'll soon find yourself in the family way."

A long pause followed as Addie thought about all that might imply. "I'd like that, and I think Ridge might too. Sometimes the sight of that man makes this glorious heat rise up inside, and I feel like I'm just going to burst into flames.

"I don't know what love is. I certainly never saw it between my parents. They can barely tolerate each other. But Luke and Josie have this deep connection, and I think that must be love." Addie picked at a string on her skirt. "Can you tell me what love is, Doctor?"

The doctor's mouth tilted up in a smile, and she answered softly, "It's exactly what you're feeling. It's the heat, the quickening of the stomach, that acute awareness of everything Ridge is doing and automatically picking him out of a throng of people. It's getting through the difficult problems together. You're in love, my dear."

A quiver of excitement swept over Addie. She brought her fingertips to her mouth and remembered the tingle, Ridge's kisses, and the feel of his arms.

She was in love. This wonderful thing she felt was *love*.

After they returned from town, Addie moved her things upstairs into the bedroom and spent the afternoon outdoors with King. Now that the danger had passed, she could have ridden wherever she wanted, but she decided the creek was far enough. Bodie had wanted to come along to watch after her, but she'd insisted on going alone.

"Stop treating me like I'm bone china or something," she told both Bodie and Ridge. "I won't break. Sometimes a woman just needs to be alone to think, and I have lots on my mind."

The day was beautiful, with just enough breeze so it wasn't too hot. White, fluffy clouds dotted the sky, and red cliffs loomed nearby. King wandered over to a patch of grass to nibble contentedly. She took off her boots, sat down on the creek bank, and stuck her feet in the water. One of the worries on her mind was the lack of a reply to her letter. It had been a while since she'd written, and she should've heard from Zelda Law by now.

Had the old midwife died while Addie was in prison? She had to be in her seventies by now. Maybe Ridge could take her to Seven Mile Crossing to find out. However, the trip would take at least a full week. It could be worth the effort, though.

"We'll be safe at my brother's," Zelda had assured her three years ago. "No one will find the boy." That much was true, or Tiny and Pickens wouldn't have tried so hard to track Addie down.

She had to come clean and tell Ridge about Zelda, that night, and the boy very soon. The previous evening's events had kept her from baring her soul then, but Ridge deserved to know. He'd told her his secrets, after all, and it had taken a lot for him to trust her. Her heart had broken for him, and she was glad he'd made good friends like Jack and Clay and the others after going on the run. They'd go to the ends of the earth for one another. She envied that.

Zelda Law had been her only true friend, though Addie'd

grown close to several of her older students when she taught school. Jane Ann, for one. The thought of the pretty girl— now lying cold in a grave—made Addie's heart ache.

There was no justice in the world. Not against men like Ezekiel Jancy, who wielded power like a sharp-edged weapon.

She sighed and rose, putting her boots on, determined to banish sad thoughts from her head. Striding to King, she removed his bridle and pulled a long red streamer, like those she'd made for the dance, from her pocket, unfurling it. Caught by a wild impulse, Addie ran, holding the wide piece of ribbon aloft and laughing. This was her day, and she was in love. Throwing her head back in laughter, she weaved in and around the buckskin, making the ribbon dance in the air.

Soon, she noticed King following, trying to mimic her movements. She stopped and twirled and ran, and King matched each as best he could. "Come, King. Let's march to the castle."

The horse snorted and nodded his majestic head, falling in step behind her. This truly was an amazing animal. She threw her arms around his neck and hugged him. "I love you so much, King. Don't ever leave me."

He blinked his luminous brown eyes, nuzzling her face. She'd never had a friend like this.

The moment passed, and Addie put her colorful streamer away. "That's enough for today. Let's go slow and look for things to decorate the upcoming dance. I can't wait to waltz with Ridge again."

King stood still while she climbed into the saddle, and they meandered their way toward home. As they walked, Addie's thoughts turned to the previous night once more—but this time, on sleeping next to Ridge. It hadn't been as scary as she'd first thought, and it had been nice to lie there listening to his breathing and know she wasn't alone in the dark. Yet he would soon expect more—a lot more.

Her mouth went dry, and her stomach quickened. *He didn't wear anything to bed.*

Eighteen

"I HAD A GOOD DAY. HOW ABOUT YOU, DEAR?" FILLED WITH nervous anticipation, Addie helped Ridge turn down the covers. He seemed a little quieter than usual, and she wondered why.

"Any day I end alive is one to celebrate, I guess." He hung his gun belt on the post at the foot of the bed and sat in one of two straight-backed chairs in the room to pull off his boots.

Addie supposed burying a man would have an effect on him. She changed the subject to one less troubling. "On my ride today, I found out that King is an extraordinary horse."

"I suspected that. He has intelligent eyes."

Her stomach quickened at the sight of his bare chest. He unbuttoned his trousers and had them partway down before she could turn away. One glimpse of his flat stomach already made the room too warm, but then he turned, and his bare backside sent heat flaring inside her. Her hands trembling, Addie finished braiding her hair and quickly slid into bed. Her heart fluttering wildly, she faced the wall.

The cats meowed at the door, raising holy hell, but Ridge had made it clear that for now, they weren't allowed into the bedroom. She didn't know why this sudden change of heart. She'd thought he liked them.

He lowered the wick of the lamp and got into bed with a long sigh. With the room plunged into dim shadows, she turned onto her back, every nerve ending alive, conscious of the fact he slept in nothing. One thing she should've realized. This man who'd taken a chance on her filled the bed like he filled a room—fully and completely, leaving no space between their bodies. If she rolled, she'd be up against all that maleness. Unsure what it was she really wanted, she lay perfectly still.

Ridge lay on his side, propping himself up on an elbow. "Tell me about King."

She burned under his gaze that seemed to notice everything. In a desperate search for solid footing, she talked about her day and the surprising ease with which her buckskin mimicked her actions. Before long, she relaxed. "I wish you could've seen him. It was like he could read my mind."

"Maybe he can." His fingers drifted down her throat ever so slowly. "I'll try to make time to come with you tomorrow."

Silence fell over them. Addie shifted toward him in the dim light. "I don't know what to do," she whispered. "Last night we were exhausted and fell right to sleep. But now—"

"Relax, love. That's all you have to do. I'd like to touch you if you don't mind. You have the softest skin I've ever felt. I won't force you to do anything you feel uncomfortable with. That's not my style."

She barely breathed past the thunder of heartbeat and mounting anxiety.

Sliding a hand behind her ear, he lowered his mouth. His breath whispered along the seam of her lips and aroused every nerve ending. The kiss made her weak with hunger for everything he had to offer. She melted against him, desire burning like a strange fever along the edges of her mind.

Addie parted her lips, and he slipped his tongue inside to court hers, and she tasted the wild Texas land he loved.

"You're so beautiful, Addie." His quiet words brushed her face. "And you don't even know it. When I look at you, I wonder if I'll ever be the husband you deserve."

"You're everything I want, Ridge. I couldn't ask for more."

The barest tips of his fingers explored her face, throat, and across one shoulder. His gentle caresses set a flurry of butterfly wings whipping in her stomach and along her ribs.

"That feels so good. Will you touch me more?"

"Tell me where."

"Everywhere. I want to learn your touch."

"Simply wish, and I'll try to fulfill it." Very slowly and deliberately, Ridge's hand followed the curves of her body still clothed in a gown. His fingers aroused quivers every place he caressed, and Addie thought she'd die from sheer longing for more.

"I don't know where you learned such a tender caress, but I don't want you to stop."

He nuzzled behind her ear. "I never reveal my secrets."

"More's a pity." She placed her palm against his jaw, loving the strength, then left a dawdling path down his thick neck to his chest, savoring the different textures of his skin—some places smooth, some rougher with bone and muscle underneath.

"I've never felt a man before. Or had one touch me." Her soft words filled the quiet.

"I hope you like this, because I plan to do it a lot. If you're willing of course." The deepness of his voice vibrated beneath her fingertips. "Your satiny skin is addictive."

Feeling bolder, she slid her hand down to that narrow strip of fine hair that had intrigued her. The long, velvety patch reminded her of baby hair. How would it feel to have his naked body pressed to hers? A delicious shiver wove through her. If that was anything to go by, she'd want this feeling again and again. Not for procreation, but for enjoyment.

The sudden switch replacing his hand with his mouth brought a new and startling awareness. The flutter of his warm breath in the hollow of her throat, his hot kisses on her lips, stole her thoughts and sent a new kind of heat surging through her, this one threatening to drive her insane.

Her breasts ached, and wetness formed between her thighs. If she could stay right here—

But he moved his attention lower and flicked a fingertip across her straining nipple, and intense pleasure burst through her. She gasped. All that stood between them was the cotton of her nightgown, and she yearned to rip it off.

She slid her hand down the silky strip of hair, following the path south until she encountered crisp hair and a firm erection. She jerked her hand back.

"Touch me, Addie. Don't be afraid." He placed his moist mouth over her nipple, collecting the fabric of her gown in his lips along with the raised, hard nub.

She arched her back to give him greater access. "Ridge."

The sensations seemed to be drawing all her inhibitions out, and she knew she wouldn't be satisfied unless she went further—to whatever pleasures lay beyond this.

"Make love to me," she begged. "Make me your wife."

Ridge froze and raised his head. His eyes met hers in the dim light of the room. "Do you know what you're asking?"

Her gaze didn't waver. "Yes. I want you to fill me, claim me for your own. As it should be between a husband and wife."

Bold as could be, she reached down for the hem of her gown and pulled it up to her hips. They sat up together, and Ridge tugged it off, then ran his hands over her bare skin, across her upper chest and down to cup her naked breasts. Addie put her arms around him and pulled him closer until the hard plane of his chest was crushed against her.

Deep in the recesses of her love-drugged mind, she reminded herself to keep her back away from his touch. She had to hide that part of her body from prying eyes. Yet in the next second, she soared to new heights of gratification and almost forgot to care. The sudden friction when she rubbed against him was beyond anything she'd felt before in her life. She stilled and closed her eyes, soaking up the sensations that whirled and twisted through her like a herd of bucking, stampeding horses.

He groaned. "You make me crazy. I need to feel your skin, taste you, caress you." He buried his face in her hair. "You're like this wild land—a place a man could live on for the rest of his life and never fully know."

He kissed her with a fierce hunger and held her tight, pulling her close as though trying to draw her inside him. Then he laid her back on the bed, and with painstaking slowness that tested her patience, he moved down her body, caressing and kissing every last inch.

"You have beautiful legs, my love." He nibbled up and down each limb.

"Stop talking about my legs and come back up here."

She had second thoughts about that command, however,

when he parted the hair hiding her entrance and slid a gentle finger into her wet heat. He withdrew, hovered at the opening before plunging in again.

With each movement, she grew achier and hotter. Until this very moment, she hadn't known that pleasure like this existed. That anyone like Ridge existed. She pushed herself hard against his hand and let out a cry as waves of pleasure gripped and crashed over her. They dragged her out to deep waters, where wondrous shudders took hold of her body.

Ridge rose above her and positioned himself, slowly stretching her tight folds with his body. A sharp pain brought a gasp to her lips, but she didn't tell him to stop. She wanted this, and from what little she did know of her body, she knew the pain would go away.

Once he was all the way inside, he paused to let her absorb him, and her pain vanished. Taking a deep breath, she matched the rhythm he set, her arms around him, holding him tight. Somewhere amid the friction of their bodies, another engulfing wave began to build again, growing higher and stronger within her.

"Ridge!" She placed both hands on his buttocks and held tight.

A sheen of sweat covered her skin and pooled between her breasts. Addie gave a cry and shuddered, riding the wave until it crested in showering sparks around her. She was blinded by the magic and beauty and oh such wonderful, glorious heat.

Ridge stiffened and took his pleasure, throbbing inside her. Addie gripped him tight and held him until he relaxed. After a moment he rolled off and dropped to lie beside her, his raspy breathing matching hers. She curled against his side, smiling.

Something wonderful had changed inside her, something between her and Ridge; now maybe they could have a real marriage.

Once her frantic heartbeat slowed, Addie raised on an elbow and ran her fingers across his chest, tracing every rise and fall. "Thank you for giving me what I wanted."

Books had told her about the mechanics of procreating, and

she'd witnessed births, but nothing had ever prepared her for how lovemaking felt. There had been no mention of the thrill, the smashing heights and towering waves that held her suspended, or the thundering of her heart upon release. Perhaps lovemaking didn't affect all women equally. She wasn't naive enough to even imagine that all partners were the same. The depth of gratification probably depended on the connection between the woman and the man she loved, and without a doubt, Addie had married the best. Ridge seemed to sense exactly where to touch and how hard.

There was enough light still in the room to let her see the happiness in Ridge's eyes. He caressed her cheek with his cupped palm. "I didn't hurt you, did I?"

"Far from it." She pressed a kiss to the hollow of his throat. "I may have gotten a little carried away. I was afraid you'd stop."

"No chance of that. I doubt a team of horses could've had any effect."

That was kind of him to say, and certainly a lie. All it would've taken was a soft no from her, and he'd have quit immediately. He didn't fool her.

She lay facing him, her fingers creating lazy circles on his chest and stomach. Her gaze drifted to the chest of drawers and the big secret he was keeping from her. She took a deep breath. If she couldn't ask now, would there ever be another time? "Ridge, I was cleaning in here a day or two ago, and I found something of yours that puzzled me."

He pinched his brows together in thought. If he was pretending not to know what she meant, he was doing a good job. "What was it?"

"A tintype. Of you and a fancy woman. It was on your chest of drawers. Who is she? Were you married before?"

His expression closed off to her, and he rolled over to sit on the side of the bed, head in his hands. "I wish you hadn't found that."

Fear rose in her throat. "Were you trying to keep it hidden?"

"Not exactly. That picture was taken a long time ago." Ridge raked his fingers through his hair, still not looking at her. "I thought I'd left all that behind me."

Questions rose and barely came out through stiff lips. "Who was she? Your wife?"

"No. Suzanne and I...we were engaged once, but she broke it off. At first, she had thought the idea of being a preacher's wife exciting, a departure from a life she found dull and boring. But soon enough, she decided it would have taken too much work to make me into the kind of man she preferred."

"That's horrible. She must not've loved you at all."

"The sad truth is that her position in society meant a lot more to her than I did."

"But you must still love her. Else why keep the tintype?" She would've burned it long ago if it had been her. Addie rose and threw on her gown.

"I tossed it into a drawer when I unpacked here, and it must've gotten caught in the folds of one of my shirts. I found it on the floor a few weeks back and tossed it on top of the chest without giving it a second thought."

"Yet you kept it," she said softly.

Ridge gently pulled her down beside him and took her face in his hands. "Suzanne's nothing to me. I don't think of her, dream of her, or wish for a life with her." He let out a gruff bark of laughter. "It's you I want."

Addie threaded her fingers through his. "Are you happy, Ridge? With our life, that is?"

"Very happy. You were the one I was meant to marry, not Suzanne Dickerson."

"I'm glad." She shot him a careful glance. "I confess I was jealous when I saw the tintype."

"You have no need for that. I'm not going anywhere." He kissed the tip of her nose. "Besides, she's married to another man now—a rich man with money to burn. And I wouldn't trade what I have for all the Suzannes in the world."

"I'm sorry I tested your patience. You must've gotten tired of waiting."

"No, sweetheart. I wanted to give you all the time you needed." The gentle tone of his voice, his touch, brought tears to her eyes.

How blessed she was to have found him.

Tenderness spilled over to the slow way he tugged the gown Addie had just put on over her head. "You'll have no need for this."

No, she wouldn't. "Roll over," she requested. It was her turn to take charge. Once he complied, she massaged his tight back muscles all the way down to his waist. Then she worked on his nicely formed butt, kissing, stroking, loving every inch.

"Aww, you have magic hands, my love." Flipping over, Ridge pulled her down to him and began to explore her body once more. Soon Addie grew breathless and ached for him again, and the rapids of pleasure they were sure to ride.

&

Ridge rose before dawn and saddled the horses, taking care not to wake Bodie when he went into the barn. He stuffed leftover ham, cheese, and bread into the saddlebags, then went inside to make coffee. When it was boiled, he carried a tray up to their bedroom and set it on a small table. He stood looking down at his sleeping wife and the peaceful expression on her face. How truly fortunate his life had turned out. He couldn't have asked for a prettier or more caring wife, and now he had confidence they matched in every way, including the marriage bed.

The bounty he'd been given flooding over Ridge, he kissed Addie's tempting bare shoulder. "Want coffee first, then go for a ride?"

A smile slowly curved her mouth. "Give me five minutes."

"Whatever you need." He'd wait as long as it took.

She threw the bedcovers aside, and he followed her naked body with his gaze, admiring the heaviness of her breasts, flat stomach, and the curve of her fetching behind. He noticed something odd on the skin of her back, but before he could see clearly, her chemise dropped, covering it. Dragging his attention from her was quite a feat, but he managed, then poured the coffee, adding sugar and cream to hers.

"Where are we going?" She reached for the formfitting Levi's and dragged them slowly up her legs. To heaven, if things went according to plan. The thought made hot, aching hunger pool inside him, even though they'd made love all night.

Nineteen

OUTSIDE IN THE PREDAWN AIR, RIDGE REMOVED THE PINS FROM Addie's hair and watched the strands tumble down around her shoulders and back in a golden mass of silk. He plunged his hands into the wealth and kissed her with every ounce of emotion he possessed. Addie returned his attention with equal fervor.

Their passion sated for the moment, he helped her into the saddle, and they set the horses to a slow pace through the darkness. Dawn would arrive within the hour, bringing light and a new day.

"You never said where we're going," Addie reminded him.

"A place I know."

"Have I been there?"

"Not yet. You are a very curious woman, you know that?"

She laughed, the sound filling Ridge's heart. "You're not going to start the day complaining are you, husband of mine?"

"There's nothing about you that I would change." Ridge maneuvered his horse close so that their legs rubbed.

They left their property and rode toward a row of craggy mountains covered with mesquite, scrub oak, and a few junipers. Once they reached the foothills, Ridge wove through a faint trail into the interior until they came upon the oasis he'd found a year ago. They reined up in a little grassy area, dismounting just as the sun rose. The golden rays glimmered off the streaks of light and dark rock in the cliff walls.

Addie let out a soft gasp at sight of a small pool of glistening water at the base of some large boulders. "This is beautiful. Do a lot of people know about this spot?"

"I don't think so. Jack and Clay do. Not sure how many others." Ridge took two towels from his saddlebags and grinned. "Care to get in?"

"Does a dog have a crooked hind leg?" Addie already worked at the buttons of her blouse, popping them free.

Ridge chuckled, unbuckling his gun belt and removing his boots. She beat him into the water, dropping her shirt a second before diving in. If her cute butt hadn't distracted him, he'd have won the race.

"It's warm, Ridge." She splashed like a pup getting its first bath. "I expected cold water."

He dove in and swam up beside her. She wound her arms around his waist and pressed against his body, kissing him. The shy little bride who'd slept underneath the stairs had vanished. She was no longer afraid to take what she wanted.

He let his hands roam over her, touching, caressing, his lips nibbling the sensitive flesh behind her ear, down her neck, and across one shoulder. He stilled and flinched when he encountered thin scars in a crisscross pattern over her back.

A jolt, then understanding settled inside him. His thoughts returned to the previous night and how she'd never exposed her back to him, kept him from touching the raised flesh. Now he knew why. This had to be Ezekiel's work. Silent curses damned the man to a fiery hell.

"I want you, Ridge." Her husky voice held hunger, and her green eyes darkened. The thick, breathy words sent all thoughts of Ezekiel from his mind.

His hardness strained for her, and when her hand closed around him, moving along the length, he sucked in air through his teeth. "Careful, lady."

"It's your fault. You brought me here and tempted me with your body. The least you can do is play nice." She stuck her bottom lip out in a pout.

"I always play nice." Ridge's soft threat brought a laugh. He scooped her up and floated to a little ledge just beneath the water. He sat and pulled her in his lap. "I'll show you nice."

He reached for her breasts, cupping them, rolling the nipples between his thumb and forefinger. He put his face in the water and took one into his mouth, lightly raking his teeth across the swollen tip.

Breathing hard, her hands moved along his muscles, kneading, smoothing, working, responding in kind to his movements. Trembling with need, he kissed her deeply, thrusting his tongue into her mouth. Neither spoke, their heavy-lidded eyes and ragged breathing revealing the depth of mutual desire.

Hands around her waist, Ridge lifted her up and slowly lowered her onto him. The buoying water helped them set a frantic tempo, friction driving him forward toward the release he sought. His heart thundered from the intense pleasure.

Addie took hers first, as Ridge had intended. She gasped and threw back her head, tightening her hold around his neck. She clung to him with all her strength as though he would vanish if she let loose. Once reassured by her gasps of pleasure, Ridge gave himself free rein. The crashing, thundering, billowing ecstasy rushed from his belly and down his jerking body.

The water settled into a lazy swirl, little waves lapping around them as they rested. Addie lifted her head from his chest, and Ridge pushed back strands of wet hair from her face, staring into eyes as green as spring grass.

His words came out hoarse and raspy. "I'm not the best man for you. Lord knows I ain't, but no one will ever cherish you as much as I do. I promise you that."

Addie searched his gaze as though afraid to believe. "Are you sure?"

"Never more so about anything."

Addie sighed contentedly. "I've found the one place in all the world where I am meant to be. Right here. With you." She got off him and climbed from the pool, wrapping a towel around her. "I want to tell you about my past. I should've followed Eleanor's advice and done so long ago, but it took time to find the strength."

Ridge followed and picked up the other towel. "I'm a patient man and didn't want to press you. There's a lot I do wonder about, though."

"Do you remember what I told you about my father and

the town of New Zion?" She sat on the lush grass, and he joined her.

"Yes. You said he owned not only you, but everyone else."

"He never let us forget that. I never accepted his ways or that false religion of his, so I continually found myself at odds with him. I taught school and began privately teaching the girls about their bodies and having babies, including what herbs, bark, and roots could stop them from conceiving. Someone told my father what I was doing, and I'd never seen such anger burn inside anyone. I'd gone against him, and he couldn't let that go or he'd lose face. He whipped me in the public square and burned every schoolbook and pamphlet."

"The bastard!" Ridge put an arm around her and held her close to his side. He prayed to cross paths with the man one day. As God was his witness, he'd get justice for Addie or die trying.

"My father only had girl babies and blamed my mother for that. He called her inadequate and lazy—among worse things. He ranted like a madman that he needed a boy, a son, to carry on his life's work. He became obsessed for a son."

Her voice lowered to nearly a whisper. "I should've realized what ran through his demented mind, but I didn't know the depths to which even he would stoop. One night while I was finishing up my work alone in the classroom, one of my older students, Jane Ann, snuck in. She was in labor and begged for my help. That shocked me, of course. I had no idea of her pregnancy. Although she had begun to wear jackets and baggy dresses, so I guess that kept her growing belly hidden."

"And of course, you couldn't turn her away," Ridge murmured.

"I made her comfortable and ran to get the midwife. Zelda Law and I shared the same opinion about Ezekiel and his teachings. She taught me about herbs and roots. Together, we birthed the babe there in the schoolhouse. It was a boy. Jane Ann was weak and had lost so much blood. Nothing we did would stop the bleeding; she told us she wasn't going to make it and didn't want to carry her secret to the grave. She told me…" Addie's voice broke, and she cleared her throat. "She revealed the identity of her child's father."

"Who was he?" Ridge squeezed her cold hand.

"Ezekiel Jancy."

Twenty

SHOCK RACED THROUGH RIDGE. DAMMIT! HE THOUGHT HE'D despised Ezekiel Jancy enough before, but this cemented it. The man had to be beyond depraved to force himself on a girl. "Did Jane Ann's father know?"

Addie nodded. "She said he did, and that Ezekiel had threatened her father if he uttered a word to anyone, saying he knew how to make him disappear."

"So, Jane Ann's baby boy is…" His sentence trailed.

"My half brother," she supplied. "Zelda and I knew we couldn't let that baby fall into Ezekiel's hands, so Zelda wrapped him up warm and left town under cover of darkness." Addie shook as though chilled despite the early sunshine.

Ridge pulled her close and rubbed her arms. "Let's put our clothes back on."

"I need to tell you everything, and I might not be able to start again if I stop."

"Okay, love." He was still curious how this could've led to Addie being sent to prison. Confused, he shared his warmth, kept rubbing her arms and listening to her story.

"Zelda told me she'd go to her brother at Seven Mile Crossing. I held Jane Ann as she drew her last breath and folded her arms across her chest. Before I could move, Ezekiel burst in—along with Jane Ann's father and about half a dozen men from the town. Ezekiel was furious to find the babe gone. He accused me of murdering Jane Ann because I was jealous of the baby. I tried to lie and say she'd had a stillborn and Zelda had buried the babe. I later found out one of Ezekiel's spies had watched everything through the window. The man had seen Zelda escape into the night with the babe and tried to catch her, only she lost him somehow." Addie shuddered in the grip of the memories, reliving that horrible night.

"My—Ezekiel—became enraged. I'd never seen him out of control like that," Addie continued. "He grabbed me by the throat and choked me until everything went black. When I came to, he demanded to know where Zelda had taken the boy. I wouldn't tell him anything, and he ordered the men to take me to the whipping post. They tied me there to wait until morning for my punishment."

"Dammit!" Ridge tightened his arms around her, so in love with this brave woman he'd married. She'd suffered so deeply. "You don't have to say any more."

"You have questions, Ridge, and I want to answer them all. I expected the worst with the sunrise. Ezekiel ordered everyone to come watch. A good many wouldn't look at me. He told them that I killed Jane Ann and stole her baby. He said if I revealed where the baby boy was, he'd be merciful and let me go. I told him hell would freeze over first.

"He handed Pickens a whip and ordered him to give me the first ten. Pickens delivered a few, I'm not sure how many, and the fiery pain running through me was so intense, I could barely draw breath. I think I lost consciousness for a bit." Her voice was strangely flat, with no emotion. It sounded more like she was reciting a recipe from memory than a tragic story.

"Enough, Addie," he begged. Her gaze had clouded, and he knew she couldn't hear him.

"A circuit judge rode into town, and it turned out to be Judge Mabry from Waco. The judge made Pickens stop the flogging, then he and Ezekiel went behind closed doors to talk. After which they held a hastily arranged trial. One by one, five men stood and testified they watched me refuse to help Jane Ann, and while they ran for others to take charge of the childbirth, I killed her and got rid of the baby."

"Did Mabry let you speak and tell your side?"

"No. All I was allowed to do was sit. So I sat there and listened to the judge sentence me to ten years in prison. He lowered it to three after Ezekiel convinced him that I posed no further threat."

Ridge suppressed a chuckle. "He didn't want you locked

up and out of reach quite so long." Now, having men waiting outside the prison to grab her made sense.

"Absolutely. He's desperate to find the boy. No matter what they do to me, I'll never tell," Addie spat. "When all this came out, my mother was full of despair. She begged Judge Mabry to place me in solitary confinement, away from any guards who preyed on the women prisoners. She protected me the only way she could."

"At least she did that much." Pitiful little, in Ridge's opinion. "So now what?"

"I suppose we wait. I wrote to Zelda after our marriage and haven't gotten a reply, which worries me. I'd like to find out how she and the boy are faring."

Ridge moved her hair aside and kissed the back of her neck. "Say the word, and I'll take you to her." Her scars showed above the edge of the towel wrapped around her. He silently called Jancy every name but the Son of God. New Messiah, his ass!

"I know." Addie's words were soft. "I want to make sure it's safe first. Ridge, what are we going to do with Tiny and Pickens? We can't keep them locked up forever."

"Jack's going to load them up in a few days and take them to Lost Point. Sam Legend will do what he can under the law to hold them, but he'll probably have to turn them loose."

"Then we'll be in the same situation as before." Addie let out a sigh. "When will we be safe from those hunting us?"

"I wish I knew. We'll just have to stay on our toes. If it's within my power, I won't let anything happen to you. I promise."

"It's crazy, sitting around discussing this." Addie rose. "Let's do something fun. Want to watch King perform?"

"You're not going without me, and I'm getting hungry. We need to eat."

But Addie was already heading for a large cedar tree for a private moment.

By the time she threw on his shirt and he tugged on trousers, the sun was full strength overhead. A few clouds began to gather as they ate the ham he'd packed, and he hoped a storm wasn't brewing.

After they ate, Addie led King over, grinning wide. "Prepare to sit and be amazed."

He never ceased to be amazed where his lady was concerned. "I'm ready."

She pulled a red streamer from her saddlebag and took the bridle off King's head. The horse seemed to know what was coming. He pricked his ears and nickered, his tail raised high.

"Come, boy." Addie raised the streamer high and began to make a series of turns, laughing and calling him. King followed every movement exactly, intent on his mistress. Clothed in only his shirt, Addie stopped in front of the buckskin and lifted her arms high. King lowered his front legs, bent at the knees, his head dropping to only inches above the ground.

"Very good," Addie murmured. She lowered her arms, and when King stood tall, she ran, trailing the colorful streamer behind her.

Ridge clapped. He'd never seen anything like this. "You have an amazing friend," he called.

She laughed and used the ribbon to put the buckskin through a series of intricate turns and circles. The bond between woman and animal was so strong, Ridge got a lump in his throat watching them work together. Damn her father for refusing to let her have a horse. She was worth more than a thousand Ezekiels.

How Ridge loved her. She was his whole world, and he doubted she even knew it.

❧

After hours of swimming in the clear pool and making love in the grass, Addie's bones had turned to exhausted masses of quivering jelly. She could get used to being Ridge's wife. This had been a perfect day, despite the dark clouds building.

A weight had lifted from her shoulders to have her past out in the open. She had nothing more to hide. Her marriage seemed solid. Not perfect, but it now had a firm foundation of honesty on which to build.

She lay naked on her stomach, soaking up Ridge's soft touch and whispers of love. Groggy from the emotion-filled hours they'd passed together, she felt like a sleepy kitten and didn't want to move.

"We should head for home." Ridge kissed his way down the long curve of her back, then patted her behind. "We'll probably get drenched before we get there, from the looks of that sky."

"I don't care. This has been the best day of my entire life." Ridge had declared his love for her, loudly and clearly. She hadn't mistaken that. Addie stood, clutching the towel. "We're quite scandalous out here in the open, naked as jay-birds, me letting you do all manner of things."

"Do tell, Mrs. Steele." He gave her a threatening scowl and started toward her, teeth bared in pretend play.

Addie shrieked and ran, laughing and dodging his long reach until he finally caught her. Breathless, she stared into his face. It was a lot more fun being in his arms than playing a child's game. She caressed the lines around his mouth and those that slashed through each cheek, saw smoldering passion in his gray eyes. He'd had so little reason to be happy since going on the run, and she planned to change that.

Ridge studied her for a long moment, as though committing her face to memory, and traced the curve of her lips. "Addie, I hope you know how very happy I am to have you by my side. I want to make sure you understand the depth of my feelings for you. Not only now, but every minute of every day."

His solemn words touched her in ways nothing else in her life ever had. Although he still couldn't speak of love, this came awfully close. And if he never could, this would be enough. Shaken, she leaned toward him, and he claimed her lips. The kiss held promises of long nights in his arms and more days of carefree abandon. Ridge Steele was her anchor in the storms, her bright spot when things grew dim.

Addie blinked hard. She could face anything as long as he was beside her.

When he released her, she let her gaze sweep over their oasis. "I wish we could stay here. Build us a house and live in this bit of paradise."

"Me too. Maybe one day we will." Ridge gathered his clothes, glanced at the frightening clouds, and began to dress in a hurry.

Addie handed him his shirt, and in no time made herself presentable. They packed up, and as they rode away, she turned around to stare back at the oasis until the sandstone formations around it blocked her view.

Midafternoon found them at the little creek that ran across their property. Despite the cloud cover, it was a hot, stifling day with ripples of a strange current riding on the wind. They dismounted to water the horses and wade in the stream to cool off.

The angry clouds frightened Addie, but she knew they'd soon be home. Wrapped up in each other, they didn't notice the wind picking up speed until it was swirling around them.

"This is making me nervous, Ridge."

"We need to go."

A sudden gust hit them, nearly knocking Addie off her feet. She grabbed Ridge to steady herself. The horses were in a panic, running and pawing the ground, letting out loud screams of terror.

Ridge raised his arms to try to calm them, and Addie ran to help. She'd never seen King in such a state. The wind shrieked, whipping her hair, and black clouds flattened, dropping lower—almost forming some kind of shelf. She'd never seen a storm this fierce or a sky so utterly terrifying.

Like Cob, King refused to settle. His eyes rolled back in his head, and he ran each time she came near.

"What's wrong with them?" she yelled over the wind.

"They sense the weather change."

Before they made any headway in calming the animals, the horses broke away and galloped toward home.

A sense of doom filled Addie. They were stranded at the creek with a storm swallowing them up.

Ridge put his arm around her. "We have to find shelter."

"Where?" No cave was in sight—the ground around them was flat as a table, with nothing in which to ride out the storm. "Home isn't that far away. We can walk."

"No time to make it. The storm will catch us in the open." The wind snatched Ridge's hat away and tore at his and Addie's clothes. The loud rumble of a steam engine came from behind them, even though the nearest tracks were hundreds of miles away.

The temperature suddenly plunged, and Addie's ears popped.

Ridge turned to face the wind and froze. "Run, Addie! Run!"

She followed his gaze and could only stare at the huge, twisting, whirling black snake that hung from the clouds, coming straight for them.

Twenty-one

THE HORRIBLE SOUND GREW LOUDER AND LOUDER AS THE tornado gobbled up the ground like an angry beast. Ridge grabbed Addie's hand, and they started running. Their only hope of survival rested in a ravine some distance to their right. Only one problem—the tornado was moving faster than they could run.

Sheer terror seized Ridge. He'd once seen the carnage left after a twister and on the people caught out in it—their clothes in tatters, hide stripped from them, and objects embedded in their flesh. One man even had a small sapling driven through his skull, as though the hard bone had been made of paper.

His legs pumped hard, and he gripped Addie's hand. "Faster! Faster!"

"I can't!"

The whirling wind grabbed them, trying to pull them back. He couldn't, wouldn't, let it win. A rock smacked into his back, jarring him. A whole scrub oak ripped from the ground, roots and all, hurtled past them.

The ravine lay about twenty yards away now. They had to make it.

The deafening roar vibrated his internal organs and sent a shock wave through him. Ridge kept his eyes glued to that bit of hope, lengthening his stride, pulling Addie along. Almost there, she stumbled and went down.

He cursed, set her back on her feet, and grabbed her hand again. He ran as fast as his legs would carry him, praying to reach the ravine in time. If they could make it to that, they might have a chance.

Had he found the life, the woman, the love he wanted, only to lose it all?

No, he couldn't let that happen.

The suction pulled them back, and at times he wondered if they were moving forward at all. The powerful wind tore at his clothes, sand stinging his eyes and filling his mouth until he could barely breathe.

The yawning edge of the ravine was now in sight. Just a little farther. *Run faster!* Ridge's chest burned from pure desperation. They had to make it. He would cheat this monster of its prize.

As they closed the gap to the last five yards, his body shuddered. The roar behind them magnified, the tornado nipping at their heels. Panting, his heart hammering, he missed a step and crashed down on one knee.

~~~~

Addie screamed when Ridge went down, but the wind gobbled up the sound. In that moment, she knew they weren't going to make it, and she had no time left to bargain with God for their lives. At least if they were going to die now, she was going to do it by Ridge's side.

Ridge recovered from the stumble and kept running. Addie clung to him with a grip of steel. She wouldn't be the weak link, the one to kill them both.

The vicious wind whirled, lashing and ripping at them. Helpless in its grasp, she could see nothing through the sandy, choking air.

She kept moving, praying for some kind of miracle.

In the bedlam, unable to hear anything, she glanced at Ridge. If he spoke, it was wasted breath—she couldn't hear or speak. He seemed to have something in mind, though, and she would follow him to the ends of the earth if it called for that. If it was to their deaths, so be it, as long as they left this world together.

She wished they'd had more time to be husband and wife, time to figure out these new roles. Maybe had a child of their own. She would've liked being a mother.

Her thoughts went to Bodie, and she prayed he was safe. Maybe he could take over the farm and live there. She'd like that.

Ridge's hand gripped hers harder, as though he was preparing for something.

Jump!

Addie didn't know where the word came from, but she pushed off into the air with her feet, and for a moment they were both airborne.

Then she was falling, falling, falling, the earth yawning big and swallowing them whole.

She landed hard, Ridge's arms around her, shielding her with his body. The shrieking, angry wind moved over them, the suction of the powerful vortex trying to yank them up and out of the crack in the land. Terrified, she gritted her teeth and clung to Ridge with both hands, shaking and cold, her hair whipping about her face. She wished she knew what the outcome would be. Having that knowledge would've help her bear whatever she must for as long as she had to.

Then mercifully, the tornado passed. The sound began to fade, and rain and hail pounded them.

"Are we alive?" Addie asked.

Ridge grinned, his face inches from hers. "We made it."

"It looks like we did." She kissed him, grateful to be alive and in one piece.

A hailstone larger than a silver dollar struck her arm, the pain sudden and sharp, the hit sure to leave a bruise. If that was the worst injury she got, fine and dandy with her. She moved back a little from Ridge and saw they had leaped into the ravine. She'd been lying flat on the bottom, with Ridge on top to weigh her down. Once more, he'd saved her life.

The hail and rain fell around them as he stood and pulled her to her feet. "Are you hurt anywhere?"

Addie followed a burning sensation to her arm and noticed blood trickling across her skin from scrapes and cuts. "I must've landed on a rock after we jumped. But other than that, I think I'm okay. How about you?"

"Nothing broken, but my back hurts. Something struck me when we were running."

"Turn around."

"Probably nothing." Ridge presented his back to her, and she gasped in horror at the sight through his ragged shirt.

A jagged piece of metal about two inches wide protruded from his right shoulder blade. Lord only knew how deep it went into the muscle. A mass of blood covered the wound. She described it to him. "It's bleeding pretty bad."

"Can you pull it out?"

"I don't know. Maybe. But I need to find something to use as a bandage first." For once, she regretted wearing trousers. A dress and petticoats would've provided oodles of material.

"What's left of my shirt will do. I can go without one. The house isn't that far."

"Do you think the tornado got Bodie? Or the house?" Her stomach clenching, Addie grabbed hold of the metal, gave it a quick yank, and flung it. Ridge let out a yell and doubled over in pain. More blood flowed, but at least it wasn't gushing. The metal obviously hadn't gone too deep after all. She wadded the shirt into a ball and pressed it hard to the wound.

When Ridge could speak, the words came through clenched teeth. "I guess we'll find out about Bodie and the house when we get there. The boy's smart. He'd know to hide until the tornado passed." Ridge winced at the pain. "I'm not worried about the town. Set in that canyon like it is, the high walls will protect it. Not sure about the Lassiters and the McClains though, out here with us."

"I hope they were spared." She refused to think about anyone else having to endure that devastating wind.

"How bad?" Ridge craned his neck, trying to see.

"I've seen worse."

"Wrap it and let's go. I need to get back and see what's left of our place."

"Not yet." Addie held the compress firmly against him for several minutes more. Finally, at Ridge's insistence, she lifted it and saw that the blood had slowed some. She bound the shirt tightly around him, her mind on King. Had the tornado gotten her beloved horse? When she finished, she took Ridge's hand and let him pull her from the six-foot-deep ravine. The hail had stopped, but a light rain was still in the air. Addie shivered in the cold.

A strange odor struck her, like the smell of something dead, but not a person or animal. It was the land that had died. Addie turned around slowly. The tornado had wiped the land clean of all vegetation as far as she could see. Her head stung and itched, and when she scratched it, she found dirt caked underneath her fingernails. Surprised, she released a little cry.

"It'll be all right, Addie." Ridge's voice was gentle. "Everything embedded in our skin will come out in time."

"At least we're alive. Everything else seems minor," she agreed.

They set out, and she matched her stride to Ridge's. An hour must've passed before the house came into view. Bodie saw them and came running. "I feared the worst when the horses came back alone."

"We're fine." Ridge turned his attention to the house.

Addie followed his gaze to the missing corner of the roof and wall. The spare room had been clipped and was now open to the sky. "Ridge is hurt, but nothing serious. Where did you hide, Bodie?"

The kid crossed his arms and stuck his hands in his armpits. "I rode it out in your little room under the stairs."

"Good." She swiveled to look at the barn and noticed not a board out of place. "The horses?"

"They're fine. So is the milk cow." Bodie gave her a quick grin that vanished as soon as it formed. "You might've lost a few chickens. The worst part is the Lassiter kids, Ely and Jenny, were up fishing in that creek that runs across your property and theirs. They've vanished. Don't rightly know if the tornado scooped them up or what. Everybody's out looking for them."

Concern crossed Ridge's face. "Get me doctored, Addie. I need to help search."

"Of course." Her thoughts in a tangled mess, Addie hurried to the house with him. How could a couple of kids have survived that storm? Ignoring the smashed dishes on the floor, she jerked out the box of medical supplies. Her fingers trembled as she washed Ridge's latest wound and swabbed it good with antiseptic.

The instant she secured the bandage, Ridge got to his feet and hollered out the back door. "Bodie, saddle my horse!" Then he raced upstairs for a clean shirt.

Addie stood at the kitchen door and handed him an old hat, since the storm had taken his new one. "Find them."

"I'll do my best." Ridge gave her a peck on the cheek and hurried out. A second later, he and Bodie galloped away from the house.

She stood in the eerie stillness, the strange odor of the storm engulfing her. The house carried the same horrible stench of something dead. The bent elm tree in the yard had been stripped of every inch of bark. She'd never seen anything like that, or the long pole speared clear through the tree's trunk, as though driven in with a giant hammer.

The magnitude of what they'd escaped overwhelmed her, and she sat at the table, her head in her hands. Her brush with death played over in her mind, and tears burned the back of her eyes. Rebel must be frantic to find her children. Those poor little dears.

First order of business was getting cleaned up, then she'd head over to the Lassiter house to see what she could do. She bustled upstairs to the bathing room and drew water. Her upper body was a mass of bruises, stinging cuts and scrapes that the tepid water soothed. After soaking for a few minutes, she tackled her hair, scrubbing her scalp with both hands. Two washings removed a portion of the dirt and something that resembled black tar, but a lot was still embedded. As Ridge had predicted, it would come out in time.

Her hair dried during the muddy ride, and she dismounted at the Lassiter home. It had been hit worse than theirs and was missing its entire roof.

Rebel stood in the yard holding little Rafe, surrounded by a half-dozen women from the town. The former saloon girl's red-rimmed eyes held worry. "Thank you for coming, Addie."

"I'm so sorry, Rebel. I came to see if there's anything I can do." Addie patted the baby's leg and got a slobbery smile in return. Now that she was there, she could see that Rebel needed far more than the piddly help she could offer. Everyone seemed in shock.

Tally strode over, red tendrils of hair blowing in the breeze. "You can help sort their belongings, Addie. We're putting them in two piles—one is immediate things the family will need while they're living at the hotel, and the other is for things to store until they rebuild their house."

"I'll be happy to. How did the town fare, Tally?"

"The tornado bypassed the town, thank heavens. It only hit out here where there's no protection. The McClain place is even worse than this. It pretty well reduced their home to matchsticks. Nora and some of the other women are working over there." Tally shielded her eyes with a hand. "I love the sound of your voice! How does it feel having it back?"

"There were so many things I had wished I could say, and now I can."

Tally's worried gaze wandered to Rebel. Clearly, her attention was on their friend even as she made other conversation. "I'm overjoyed for you. Ridge said you and he got caught out in the open during the twister. That must've been terrifying."

"I've never seen anything like that. I thought we were going to die. We probably would've without a ravine nearby to jump into. Even so, the wind embedded a two-inch piece of metal in Ridge's back."

Rebel gasped. "He didn't mention that."

"Of course not." Tally chuckled. "He's like Clay—thinks it so minor, it's not worth talking about."

"Exactly." Addie didn't ask about Ely and Jenny. She could tell by the long faces there'd been no word, and the last thing Rebel needed was a reminder that her children had vanished. Addie reached for a different topic. "Ladies, as a new member of your committee, I vote to postpone the Harvest Dance. We really have nothing much to celebrate right now."

Both women agreed, and Tally added, "Nora said the same thing earlier. Besides, Clay is working on a way to have the affair inside the barn, which will be a lot better."

"Wonderful!" At first, Addie had thought it odd that they had only one big barn to serve the entire town, but Ridge had told her the lack of space had made sharing necessary. A community barn. A community fire. A community dance.

A community of people helping people. And now they pulled together to find two lost kids.

Twenty-two

By nightfall, the men had returned from their search empty-handed. Jenny and Ely—assuming they were alive—would spend the night alone with no food. Probably no water either. Deep sadness enveloped Addie, and she went about her chores in a fog. Ridge and Bodie barely said a word during supper or afterward, while they hammered temporary boards over the damaged portion of the roof.

Addie kept to her thoughts, happy to have been able to do something, however small, to ease Rebel's burden. While they'd been cleaning up and sorting household goods, Tally had told Addie the horrifying story of how she and Clay had rescued Jenny and Ely from the same horrible asylum where Tally had been imprisoned. They'd been left there by their poor excuse for a father following the death of their mother. Rebel had taken them in, then Travis had adopted them. Now this. What more could happen to that family?

Lying in bed later, Addie snuggled next to Ridge, her head on his chest, and listened to his strong heartbeat. Gratitude welled inside her again that they'd been spared.

Ridge idly ran a hand down the arm she'd thrown across his stomach. "I wish I knew where to look next for those kids. Rebel and Travis are about to go out of their minds."

"We would too if they were ours," she answered.

"Do you want kids, Addie? We've never discussed it."

"Yes, I would. I'd love to feel a child of yours growing inside me." She raised her head and met his gaze. "What do you want?"

"The same. I think four is a good number—two boys and two girls. But I can't let myself consider it while I have these charges hanging over me. I don't want to bring a child into this world of danger. Riders could come and haul me out of here any day."

The possibility squeezed her heart as though an iron fist had reached into her chest. "You're safe here with Clay, Jack, and the others to help keep watch."

He ran light fingers across her face, his voice soft. "I'm not safe anywhere. Eventually I'll face another posse or bounty hunter. Or Tom Calder. He'll never give up on his desire for vengeance."

"Maybe he's dead by now."

"I doubt that. Hate like that keeps a man living. No, he'll come one day."

"Why aren't you fighting mad? You should be angry."

"I clung to anger and bitterness for a long time before I realized it accomplished nothing." He sighed. "I've accepted my fate. Now it's time for you to do it too."

How? She refused to consider the possibility of his capture. "No, Ridge. I'll never fold my hands in defeat. As long as I have breath, I have hope."

"My way eases the knots in my belly." He pulled her down for a long kiss and ran his palms over her body.

Addie forgot everything except this man with a slow touch of fire and a need rising for what he could give.

⌘

The morning dawned gray and dreary to match their moods, big puddles still standing from the storm the previous day. Ridge hurried to eat, then rode over to the Diamond Bessie Hotel to join the search party again. He'd left Bodie at home to do chores and repair the roof. Addie had wanted to come, but he'd talked her out of it this time.

A group of men stood silently in the light rain, their somber faces saying all he needed to know. His spurs jangled as he dismounted and strode to Travis, who was hunched over a map with Clay and Jack under the awning. "Morning all," Ridge said quietly. "I was going to make some suggestions, but I take it you've beat me to a plan."

Travis glanced up, his eyes hollow, his face gaunt. "Yeah. We have to find Jenny and Ely today. I promised Rebel I wouldn't come back without them. It's a promise I have to keep."

"We'll find them. Just keep believing." Ridge glanced at the map and stabbed a finger at a section of inhospitable terrain that was littered with caves—Devil Back Range. "I'll take this. That's about the general location where the tornado lifted back into the clouds. If the storm picked them up, it may have dropped them there."

"Exactly what I was thinking." Clay adjusted his hat on his head. "I'll take the area just in front of that and then help Ridge. It'll take a while to look in all the caves."

"Ely's a smart kid. If they were dropped there, he'd look for shelter." A measure of hope flitted across Travis's eyes before it faded. "That is, if he and Jenny are still together—and alive."

Jack laid a hand on Travis's back. "Don't go there. You have to hold fast to hope. It's the only way you and Rebel are going to get through this."

Travis lifted his chin. "You're right. We're going to find my kids." He called the men over and gave them their search assignments. Brother Paul was ready to ride with them, as was Todd Denver, the schoolmaster, and some of the older kids.

Tiny and Pickens showed a keen interest in their doings from the strap iron jail sitting in the square. They'd gotten a good drenching from the rain and hail yesterday, but they'd needed a bath anyway.

Brother Paul stood on the hotel steps and delivered a prayer, after which the men scattered to search.

Ridge galloped toward the unforgiving hardness of Devil Back Range, a bleak landscape that stretched for miles. If the kids had dropped anywhere in there, finding them would be like looking for a single kernel of corn in a hundred bushels of grain. Still, he'd do his best. But chances were high that if they did find the kids, they'd find them dead. The same thoughts had been in Travis's eyes that morning.

Ridge methodically scoured the caves and ravines, yelling their names every few yards. The sun bore down with a vengeance, and he had to stop and drink often from his canteen.

He thought of his Bible teachings and the comfort he'd often given parishioners when they were going through difficult times but found no comfort for himself now. Ridge dismounted and gazed at the sky that went on forever. Rage burned inside him.

"Why in the hell did you send that tornado? Why hurt two innocent little kids? You're supposed to be a loving God!" Shaking, Ridge kicked a clump of sage. "I see nothing but vengeance. You took Jenny and Ely. You took everything from me. You brought Addie so much misery. Bodie too. What more do you want? When will you be satisfied? Figured there would be no answer." Ridge snorted, calling himself a lunatic for arguing with someone who'd marked him off the list.

He finally got back in the saddle and had neared the middle of Devil Back when Clay joined him, having finished his designated section.

"I take it you found nothing." Ridge rested his arm on the pommel and took in his friend's worried eyes.

"Not exactly." Clay pulled a shoe from inside his shirt. It was the right size and style for a little girl.

Ridge swallowed hard. He wasn't surprised. "We don't know if it's Jenny's, but who else's could it be?"

"I agree. This will kill Travis and Rebel."

"Hey, I'm not ready to give up. They could still be alive." Maybe it was his former profession as a man of faith, or maybe it was plain old stubbornness, but something urged Ridge to keep looking. "Now that you're here, we can cover twice as much ground. I figure we have six more hours of daylight." He glanced up at the sun midway of the sky, and the spit dried in his mouth. A large flock of vultures were circling. "See that?"

Clay's face froze. "Yeah. We'd best go find out what died."

They worked their way toward the site, but navigating over the rocks took some time. Dread lodged in Ridge's chest. They needed to find the kids, but he prayed that this wasn't them. Not like this. Not dead.

At last they rounded some mesquite and juniper, and Ridge took his first full breath since seeing the vultures. One of the huge black birds perched on a dead antelope.

"Thank God." Clay reached for the tobacco and papers in his pocket.

The big man did have a sense of humor, Ridge would give him that.

"I sure didn't want to have to go back and tell Travis and Rebel." Ridge turned his horse around.

Jack and the oldest Truman boy joined them about an hour later, and Clay showed them the shoe. "This seems the most promising spot," Jack said.

For the next several hours, the men searched every cave and rocky ravine. The sun would go down soon and stop their search for the night. Dammit! How long could the kids survive out here alone? How much longer could Travis and Rebel cling to hope?

Ridge removed his hat and wiped his forehead. A sound alerted him. He stilled. "Everyone stay where they are and listen."

Nothing. Only the sound of the wind.

"What do you think you heard, Ridge?" Jack asked.

"A weak voice. I think I must've imagined it."

"Let's yell their names, then be quiet and see if we get a reply," Clay suggested.

They did, and a moment later, they heard it—a weak cry for help. Someone was there! Ridge raced over the boulders and sharp rocks, following the voice. They paused several times to call out, and the voice grew louder. The sound led to an open pit, a rock wall rising all around. He judged the hole to be a good fifteen feet deep.

A small child stood at the bottom, waving her arms. "Down here!" Someone else laid curled up at her feet.

Ridge breathed a sigh of relief. "Jenny? That you?"

"Yes. Ely's hurt. Hurry."

"Okay, honey. We're coming," Clay answered.

"We'll have to drop down and hoist them up." Ridge removed his coil of rope and tied one end to Cob's pommel.

"I'm coming too." Jack got his rope and did likewise to his mount. "That way we can bring them both up at once. Clay and Henry can work with the horses to keep the lines taut."

Fifteen-year-old Henry, oldest of ten brothers, grinned, anxious to prove himself to his heroes. "Sure, Mr. Bowdre. I'll keep inching your horse back a little at a time. I won't let you slip or nothing."

Jack winked. "You're a good man, Henry."

Ridge watched the exchange, seeing in them the boy he used to be with his father. His eyes burned. Kids needed to feel important.

At last, the rope secure about his waist, Ridge eased over the side and down the slick wall. Jenny threw her arms around him, sobbing. "It's all right now, honey. We found you."

"I was so scared, and Ely wouldn't stay awake."

Her feet were bare. Deep bruises discolored her dirty face, and a tattered dress hung from her small form. But all that and Ely's injuries aside, however serious those might be, they were alive. The kids were lucky.

"Okay. I'm going to get you out of here, then see about your brother." Ridge tied the rope around Jenny's small waist and hollered to Clay to back the horse and pull her up.

Once she'd begun the ascent, he hurried to Ely and squatted next to Jack. Blood still oozed from a deep gash on Ely's forehead where something must've struck him, and one leg was bent wrong and looked broken. Jack removed a canteen he'd slung around his neck and placed it to the boy's mouth. Ely groaned and opened his eyes.

He took a small sip and yelled. "It hurts! I want my papa."

"I'm sorry. Try to hold on. We're going to get back to town to the doctor." Ridge laid a gentle hand on Ely's shoulder. "Your mama and papa will be mighty glad to see you both."

"I thought we were dead."

"That was a bad storm." Ridge looked at Jack. "How are we going to do this? I don't know if he's in any shape to go up alone."

"I doubt it." Jack pinched the bridge of his nose in thought. "He'll have to go up with one of us holding him."

"Probably work best." The kid was slight and couldn't weigh much over fifty pounds. "I'll take him up with me."

Jack got the rope on them and called to Henry to back the horse. Slowly, Ridge and Ely inched toward the top where Clay hauled them over the lip. He carefully laid Ely down and spoke the question that had to be in Ridge's eyes. "How will we get him home?"

After Jack made it to the top, they agreed the boy would ride in Ridge's lap with his leg padded by a blanket Jack had thrown in that morning. Jenny rode in front of Clay. Purple twilight fell over them by the time they arrived at the hotel. Travis and Rebel sat on the wide porch, Rafe in Travis's arms.

Rebel screamed when she saw them and raced down the steps. "My babies!"

A crowd began to gather. It seemed as though the whole town had been holding vigil, and now they all ran to see the miracle.

Rebel clutched Jenny to her. Travis handed Rafe to Addie, then gently lifted Ely down and carried him toward Dr. Mary's small hospital.

Addie hurried to Ridge's side as he dismounted. "Thank God you found them. I knew if anyone could, it would be you."

"Oh, you did, did you?" He felt as though he sat atop a bucking bronc and was losing his grip. Blame it on the dancing light in her eyes and a smile that sent thoughts of soft sheets and bare skin whirling in his head.

Her sassy little grin said she must share similar thoughts. Her voice was husky. "I know things."

Ridge chuckled and slid an arm around her waist. "Darlin', I'm sure not about to argue with that."

Nora strode toward them with a knowing smile. "I have a feeling you need someone to take little Rafe off your hands. The way you're looking at each other, you're both about to combust."

"You're an angel, Nora." Anxious to be alone with his wife, Ridge quickly transferred the baby from Addie's arms to Nora's, then drew his wife closer. "Let's go home, Addie."

Twenty-three

LIFE RAMPED UP IN HOPE'S CROSSING OVER THE NEXT FEW
days, as Ely adjusted to his broken leg and Jenny found herself
at the center of lots of attention for the first time in her young
life. Men were working everywhere Addie looked, collecting
stockpiles of materials and hauling them out to the worksites.
She'd never heard so much hammering and sawing as rebuilding the two destroyed houses commenced.

As for the women, they carried on with their plans. Addie
invited Tally, Melanie, and Nora to her house for tea one day
and showed them all the decorations she'd made for the dance.

"These are so pretty." Melanie fingered the festive bunting,
a pensive expression on her face. "I can't wait until we have
everything back to normal."

"Me too." Tally held up a streamer. "I miss our dances, but
it's not right to celebrate when the Lassiters and McClains are
hurting."

Addie brought the teapot to the table. "But just think
of what a happy celebration we'll have when those families
are back in their homes. With the way the men are burning
daylight, I doubt it'll take too much longer."

"Jack says everything is going well." Nora cut slices of
pumpkin bread and arranged them on small plates. "I'm thankful the storm didn't destroy the town."

Melanie reached for her dessert plate. "It could've been a
lot worse, for sure."

The conversation wandered to children for a bit, then some
speculation about when the banker would arrive.

Tally leaned close. "Clay said a telegram came from Mr.
Wintersby yesterday, and the banker's decided to stay in San
Francisco. He's sending his daughter to oversee their holdings
here instead."

"A woman banker?" Nora arched an eyebrow. "I didn't know there were any."

"Me either." Addie wondered if the woman would have qualms about opening a bank in an outlaw town. That would take some gumption.

"My sister Ava had hoped to get a job there. It took them too long, though, and she's already gone. She left a few weeks ago with a rich English gentleman who's touring the West and doesn't know when she'll return." Melanie lifted a bite of pumpkin bread to her mouth. "She's excellent with numbers."

"So are you, dear." Tally gave her a knowing smile.

"That was a long time ago. I gave up playing cards for money. Now I chase after two ten-year-olds and a five-year-old." Melanie laughed.

The more Addie learned about these women, the more she realized that having a past didn't have to define you. Everyone had one, and it was simply something that happened on the way to becoming who you wanted to be.

"And soon to have a baby," Nora added.

A smile on her face and dimples showing, Melanie rested a hand on her round stomach.

"How does Tait feel, being an uncle and now soon to be a father?" Addie was curious about these outlaw men and how Ridge might react if, down the road, things turned out in their favor and they could start planning.

"I've never seen him so happy. You'd think those kids hung the moon and stars."

"Tait's going to make a fine father. You have my word on that. He's like Jack." Nora closed her mouth around her fork and groaned. "I've died and gone to heaven. Did you make this, Addie?"

"I tried to recreate an old recipe of my grandmother's from memory. I hoped it would turn out."

"It more than turned out." Tally reached for Addie's old notebook and pencil and slapped it down in front of her. "Write it down for me please."

Happy they found her attempt at making the pumpkin

bread more than satisfying, Addie wrote down the recipe, and the ladies left her house, chattering like magpies. The warm feeling of companionship, of being wanted and understood, stayed with her long after the ladies left. For the first time, she knew the full scope of what she'd been cheated out of. Like plants needed sun to grow, true friendship required laughter and sharing to nurture one's soul.

~❧~

A week flew by before Ridge knew it. He spent his days helping rebuild the damaged houses and his nights holding Addie close, whispering in her ear, touching her, and making sure she knew how much he loved her. He found it hard to put into words, so he mostly showed her.

Addie had become his truest friend, his forever wife, and he'd fallen totally and utterly in love.

Bodie's words came back. *You know, it's not so much what you say but how you say it. When you talk to her, your voice gets all gentle and melty like my pa's used to.*

The kid had been right all along. Ridge's idea that love was something big and noisy had been way off the mark. Instead, it had snuck in quietly while he had his back turned. Each time he thought of how goofy that sounded, he threw back his head and laughed.

Up to now he hadn't spoken of love. That was about to change. He meant to open his heart at the next opportunity.

He barely recognized Addie from the woman who'd first appeared in town. She had confidence now, had changed in front of his eyes from a caterpillar into a breathtaking butterfly, flitting around and touching people's lives for the better. He couldn't wait to get home at the end of the day and see her.

Ridge began packing up his tools at noon. Jack had left midmorning to get ready to take their prisoners to Sam Legend at Lost Point.

"Hey, you quitting?" Tait Trinity asked.

"Yeah. You know I have a business to run in addition to this."

"Not to mention a pretty new wife at home." Tait winked. "I know how it is."

"When's your baby set to arrive?" Ridge tossed his hammer, plane, and level into his box.

Tait grinned, the corners of his eyes wrinkling. "In the next three or four weeks. Joe and Jesse are coming up with all sorts of crazy names, like Mistletoe, Garland, or Rex. Our little Becky has her heart set on Angel or Belle. Could be a problem for a boy."

"Aren't those pretty much—"

"Christmas names? Yep, but try telling that to my bunch." Tait wagged his head.

Ridge laughed. "Good luck. Might be best to name the child yourself."

Leaving the worksite, Ridge stopped by the house for Addie, and they soon reined up next to Jack's wagon. Addie dismounted and went to Nora, who stood with the baby, ready to see her husband off. Two-year-old daughter Willow squatted in the dirt to play.

Ridge hurried to help Jack at the outdoor cell, snapping manacles to Tiny's and Pickens's wrists. "Need help?"

"I think I have it, but thanks." Jack turned his attention back to the prisoners. "March to the wagon and sit down in the bed. Do as I say, and we won't have a problem."

"I'll have a word with Adeline first," Pickens snarled.

"You'll go nowhere near my wife." Ridge fixed him with a hard stare. "I ought to kill you for whipping her."

Pickens shrugged. "I was only doing what her father paid me to do."

Jack gave the man a shove. "Get along. You have a lot of damn nerve."

The stage rumbled through the town's entrance. The dogs raced toward it, barking and raising a holy ruckus. A woman in a gigantic hat sat perched on top like a queen, looking from side to side and waving both arms and whooping.

"What the hell is that?" Ridge asked. "Are we having a parade and no one told me?"

Jack removed his hat and scratched his head. "Not exactly sure, but the crazy woman'll fall off if she's not careful."

The stage stopped in front of the hotel, and Clay emerged to see the cause of the ruckus.

Before Ridge could swing back to the job at hand, Pickens pulled a sharpened fork from his shirt and stabbed Jack in the neck. He wrenched the fork free, and flowing blood immediately soaked the collar of Jack's white shirt. He yelled in agony, clutching his throat, blood running through his fingers.

Rooted in shock and disbelief for a moment, Ridge jerked off his shirt and pressed it hard to the wound.

Addie and Nora screamed and tried to run to Jack.

Pickens held the fork out toward them, the tines sharpened to fine points. "Stay back or you're next."

"You won't get away with this," Nora spat. "Rot in hell."

"Watch me."

Tiny bounded into the hitched wagon with Pickens right behind and grabbed the reins. Addie made a dive for little Willow, playing in the dirt, and snatched her up just in time to avoid being trampled by the horses. Dodging bullets, the two prisoners headed directly for the stage. The strange woman climbed down from the top, and Tiny yanked her into the wagon.

Men ran toward them, firing and cursing.

Pickens held the homemade weapon against his hostage's neck and yelled, "Stop shooting or this woman dies."

"Better say your prayers 'cause you're gonna need 'em," hollered one of the men.

Without another word, the prisoners and their hostage raced away. Men ran to find their horses, and those already mounted took off after the wagon.

Ridge could only watch. His focus was on making sure Jack stayed alive. The loss of blood had already turned his friend's face ashen. "Get the doctor! Hurry!"

Nora knelt next to her husband, and her hands shook as she whipped off her shawl. She wadded it up tightly, and Ridge switched it out with his blood-soaked shirt.

"Where's Dr. Mary?" Ridge barked, then glanced up and breathed a sigh of relief to see the doctor hurrying toward them.

Jack gripped Ridge's hand. "Go after them."

"I will." Ridge stood to make room for the doctor. His gaze went to Addie, who had collected the Bowdre kids around her. She seemed rattled but fine.

One look, and Dr. Mary ordered, "Let's get Bowdre to my hospital. Thank God they missed the main artery, but he'll die if I don't get the bleeding stopped."

Ridge and others carefully picked Jack up and carried him to the hospital. Half the town was still standing in the square, talking about what had just happened. Everyone was asking about the strange woman from the stagecoach, but no one knew who she might be. Several people speculated that she came to help Tiny and Pickens escape.

Tossing around theories seemed a waste of time, in Ridge's opinion. He dealt in facts, and right now there weren't many.

He thought about praying that his good friend wouldn't die, but maybe God didn't need a joke today, and that's how Ridge felt about asking for favors. Best to stick to the man he now was. The one who'd learned the best luck was what you made for yourself.

Once Jack was in Dr. Mary's surgery, Ridge emerged from the hospital and went straight to Cob, still standing where he'd left him. Addie was nowhere in sight, and someone told him she'd gone to the Bowdre house with the children.

With that, Ridge swung into the saddle and galloped away, chasing the dust cloud left by the others who'd already lit out. How quickly the men of Hope's Crossing had stepped back into their old roles—outlaws thirsting for some justice. There were none better. Ridge urged Cob faster and soon passed the stragglers. He kept riding, pushing the horse harder. He'd made Jack a promise and would do his best to keep it.

Before long, he caught up with the lead riders, who'd reined up. "Why are you stopped?"

Dallas Hawk pushed back his hat. The large man's complexion seemed even redder than normal, anger probably playing a big part. "We lost 'em. They went around this stand of mesquites and just disappeared."

"What do you mean…disappeared?" That didn't make sense to Ridge. "How far back were you?"

"I mean they weren't here, or up the road, or anywhere." The breeze danced in Hawk's long, bushy beard. He blew out a frustrated breath. "Me and the boys were probably seventy-five yards back. No more than that. The mean one that stabbed Jack was still holding the woman in front of him, so we couldn't shoot. How's Jack?"

"The doc was looking after him, trying to get the bleeding stopped. It doesn't look good." Ridge scanned the brush. "I'm going to ride on and see what I can find."

"Mind if I come along?"

"Suit yourself." Ridge trotted away, keeping an eye out for anything out of the ordinary.

"That guy sure had a sharp fork," Hawk remarked.

"He'd filed the tines down to knife points."

"Next time we get a prisoner, we oughta make him eat with his damn fingers."

Ridge agreed. "Or hang him on the spot."

They rode for about two miles, then turned around. Near the stand of mesquites where the escapees had disappeared, Ridge cut off to the left and went down into a gully that was invisible from the road. There lay the wagon on its side, the horses gone. Guns drawn, he and Hawk dismounted. Not a soul was in sight.

A piece of paper fluttered in the breeze, stuck to the wood of the wagon by the sharpened fork. Ridge pulled the note off and read the words. *Better luck next time.*

Dallas snorted and clenched a meaty fist tight. "I hope I meet up with them again."

"So do I." Ridge scoured the area and found what he was looking for at the other end of the gully. He squatted in the sand next to a lot of tracks—both human and animal. "Horses were waiting here for Tiny, Pickens, and the woman to make the transfer. They abandoned the wagon and rode off."

"Wonder what they did with Jack's horses from the wagon." The big fiddle player scanned the area. "Did they take them along?"

"Either that or turned them loose." Ridge let out a string of cusswords. They'd lose more time having to look for them. Dammit!

"Awful strange about that goldarned sassy woman. Did they take her with them?"

Ridge bit back deep irritation. He'd never known Dallas to be so full of questions. "It does appear that way."

"Why? They didn't need her anymore."

"I wouldn't be surprised to learn she was in on the whole plan." Ridge strode to Cob and stuck his foot in the stirrup. "We need to look for Jack's horses and get back to town. I'm interested in what the stage driver has to say."

"If he hasn't gone out on his run. But ain't this Friday?"

"Yep."

"That's good luck for us. He always has a layover on Friday and won't head out until tomorrow."

Ridge spurred his gelding. They needed some answers, so they could be ready in case Tiny and Pickens returned.

After spending a couple of hours looking for the wagon team and coming up empty, they gave up and headed back to town. If the horses were loose, they'd eventually find their way to grass and water.

Ridge and Dallas aimed straight for the stage line office only to learn the driver, George Finch, had made tracks for the local watering hole. Being in the shank of the afternoon, the Wild Rose Saloon business seemed to be picking up. Piano music met Ridge's ears as he pushed through the batwing doors. George sat a table with a cold, frothy beer in front of him, enjoying his short layover.

Ridge's spurs clinked as he strode toward his quarry and pulled out a chair. "A good day to have a drink, I reckon, George."

The driver looked up with a long face. "Never in all my born days have I seen the like."

George Finch was about Ridge's age, best he could figure, although his black hair and mustache sported a few silver streaks. The man was built like a bull, stout and tall.

"It's been an odd one, that's for sure." The beer looked inviting, but Ridge had no time for relaxing. "You up to answering some questions?"

"Steele, I had nothing to do with that breakout."

"I'm not accusing you, George. I need to know about the woman on your coach."

"She flagged me down a couple of miles outside of town and gave me a dollar to ride on in and an extra two bits to let her sit up on top."

"Any idea why on top?"

George took a big gulp of beer and wiped the foam from his thick mustache. "She said she wanted a good view of the town when she rode in. That's all I know. If I'd have thought she was mixed up with those prisoners, I wouldn't even have stopped for her."

"We don't know that for a fact." Although it certainly appeared that way. "Did she give you a name?"

"Nope, but then I didn't ask either."

"How about any baggage with her?"

"Nope. Just her by herself. To me, it looked like she'd been hurrying, because of the way she was perspiring."

"Like how?"

"Sweat stains under her arms and trickling down her neck into her...uh...you know."

"Bosom?" Ridge tried not to laugh.

"Yeah, that. I tried not to look, but I couldn't help it. She had real big ones, and the material of her dress was some filmy, see-through kind. Her lips were bright red and shiny."

"What did the rest of her look like? You did lift your eyes up to her face, didn't you?"

George flushed bright red. "I tried. Really, I did. But she kept fiddling with her buttons, and before I knew it, she... uh...she spilled out. I'm no pervert. I just couldn't get my eyes to focus on anything else."

Which meant he'd never know her to see her again. Everything became clear. She was definitely in cahoots with Pickens and Tiny. She could've dressed normal and entered town beforehand to look everything over, maybe even talked to the prisoners to make plans under cover of night where she wouldn't have been seen. As far as knowing where to come? It would have been simple enough for one of the men to have told her they were coming to Hope's Crossing, and if they didn't return by a certain time, to come hunting them.

"Anything else, George?"

"That's it in a nutshell, Steele. Glad you caught me early." George's smile came and disappeared fast. "I plan to be good and drunk by sundown."

"Do me a favor and take it easy. There's more to life than this." Ridge stood and put his hat on.

"Not for me. I got money to spend and no one waiting."

Ridge moved to the doors and turned around, his gaze on the lonely man. Until Addie came into his life, he used to be in George's shoes. In fact, so were each of his best friends. Thanks to Luke Legend, they were all married now and far more satisfied than they'd ever been riding the outlaw trail, dodging the law and digging out bullets.

His thoughts turned to Dr. Mary and her all-out battle to save Jack. They'd been lucky until today. The whole lot of them had gotten too comfortable, too lax. Danger still lurked thick around them, only now it was hidden behind heavy-lidded eyes and fake smiles.

Dammit! If Ridge didn't watch it, he'd be planted in some hole, and Addie would be wearing widow's weeds.

Twenty-four

BEFORE RIDGE HEADED HOME, HE AND ADDIE VISITED JACK IN the town's two-bed hospital that was empty save for him. Jack lay with his throat wrapped and eyes closed. At the sound of Ridge's spurs, his eyes flew open. "About damn time," he croaked. "Did you catch them?"

"Sorry." Ridge gave him a full accounting. "I can't prove it, but the woman had to be in on the escape."

"Yeah. The bastards."

"They'd best stay far away from here is all I got to say." Ridge pulled two chairs next to the bed, and he and Addie sat down.

Addie folded her hands in her lap. "I'm sorry about the turn of events, Jack. I've never watched anything more horrifying."

"I hear I have you to thank for saving Willow. If anything had happened to that little girl, I'd never have forgiven myself."

"I'm just glad I could get to her in time. Sawyer's upset. He hasn't eaten anything all day."

"That's because he's been in here pestering me and Dr. Mary flat to death with a million questions." Jack put an arm across his forehead. "He did the same thing when I got rattle-snake bit a while back. I keep telling him I'm too mean to die, but that boy doesn't listen."

Ridge barked a laugh. "You're full of hot air, Jack. Are you sure you should be talking?"

"If I shouldn't be, do you think I would?"

"Absolutely yes." All kidding aside, Ridge was relieved to see Jack sounding something like his old self. For a moment, when he was trying to stop the gushing blood, it appeared all Ridge's efforts might be in vain. Losing Jack would be like losing a brother.

They talked until Dr. Mary came in and told them to let her patient get some rest. Ridge pulled to his feet and put his old Stetson on. "Is there anything we can get you before we go?"

"Nope." Jack's smile pulled up on one side. "Check back tomorrow though. I'll probably need my bedpan emptied."

"In that case, I'll send Bodie."

"You would too." Jack reached for Ridge's hand and shook it. "Thank you for saving my life. Doc here said it's a good thing you were there."

"Anytime. We're brothers in every sense that matters."

"Amen."

Ridge stood outside the small building a long moment, staring up at the sky awash in swirling shades of blue. If a man was lucky enough, once or twice in a lifetime he might find true friends—ones who would be there when the chips were down as well as when things were rosy. Jack, Clay, and Travis would stand with him at the Alamo if a situation called for it. That much he was certain of.

Addie seemed to sense his mood and slipped an arm around his waist. "He'll be all right."

"For now. But what about the next time, or the next? We've all cheated death over and over. There has to be a reckoning at some point."

"That's true for all of us, dear. But one thing I know, Ridge Steele, that day is not now."

"Then I guess we'd best go home, love. We need to feed our boy."

"And continue with his lessons. Tonight, I think I'll start teaching him to cipher. A man always needs to be able to do basic sums."

She looped her arm around his elbow and leaned closer. Her fresh scent and the nearness of the soft rise and fall of her breasts sent his senses reeling. For a moment, he struggled to remember his name or where he was.

"You shouldn't do that, love." He shouldn't have glanced down into his wife's upturned face, her eyes double-dog-daring him, her lips lush and slightly parted.

"Do what?" she asked innocently.

Never one to let a dare stop him, he slid his big hands into her golden hair and kissed her right there, smack in the center of town, in front of God and everybody.

❧

A week passed, Jack continued to get stronger, and the excitement settled down. Ridge and Addie's roof had been a small job compared to the other houses, and it hadn't taken long to repair. The work continued on the others.

Addie spent her days working in the garden, helping Bodie with his lessons, and riding King. Wednesdays, she had tea with the ladies. But Thursdays she reserved for Eleanor, and they became very close, sharing things they'd never told anyone. She enjoyed all the warm and lively discussions she had with her friends, but mostly the teasing that went on among them that made her truly feel she was a real part of something good and lasting.

But for how long? Tiny and Pickens would've raced back to her father, so it was no stretch of her imagination to think that Ezekiel now knew where to find her.

The cold hand of vengeance seemed to be reaching for her.

She was stronger than she ever had been, though, and had Ridge beside her. They'd outraced a tornado, killed a stalker, and they'd handle Ezekiel together. Her father had no hold over her. None whatsoever.

Last night she'd lain in Ridge's arms after making love and shared her fears. "He's coming. I feel it so strong. The truth is I don't know what he'll do, and that's the part that terrifies me. He's so volatile, and that makes him difficult to predict."

"You have me now, and you've never seen the depth of rage of which I'm capable." His eyes had blazed in the low light of the room. "To get to you, he'll have to go through me, and I can assure you I will make that very hard." He'd softly caressed her cheek. "I love you, Addie. The depth of it goes bone deep and sometimes I lie awake watching you sleep and feel all this emotion bubbling inside until I nearly burst.

You're mine until the end of time, and I'll kill anyone who hurts you. That is a promise."

Addie didn't think she could ever love anyone as much as Ridge. The nights in his arms had made her even more aware of how deep her love went. He seemed to know exactly which places to flick, caress, and kiss to bring her to a shuddering climax. Each lovemaking session left her boneless, limp, and wanting more.

Propped on an elbow, she twisted a finger in his hair. "I love you, Ridge. I think I've known for a while, but I wanted to be sure Dr. Mary was right. I never knew even a parent's love, but when I snuck up to your bed and laid down beside you, my heart became so full of this longing to be whole. I knew then that I had to fix myself so I would be able to share the good times and bad."

"My dearest, no words exist to describe the depth of my love for you." His hands were shaking. The kiss shot heat into her core, and tears filled her eyes.

Whispers of hope curled against her spine that no one could ever steal this happiness.

After they stopped talking and he'd thought she was asleep, he stood at the window for ages, staring out at the darkness. What had he been thinking about? Likely about the upcoming confrontation. Perhaps he was planning exactly how he'd handle Ezekiel Jancy.

When she was with Ridge, it seemed as though nothing in the world could touch her, as though a protective shield was around her. But what if Ezekiel caught her on her own? What then? How courageous would she be?

How defiant?

Questions and doubts rushed over her, but by daylight, Addie worked to put her father out of her mind. No use buying trouble early.

On one day, she rode King into town to have lunch with Ridge as she often did.

Her husband emerged from his office, grinning. "You're right on time, Mrs. Steele, and looking prettier than one of those wild roses you love." He swung her down from the horse, desire shimmering in the depths of his eyes. "I wish I could freeze this moment forever."

"Compliments will get you whatever your heart desires, cowboy."

Jack Bowdre strode by on the boardwalk, his throat heavily bandaged. "Keep looking at each other like that, and you'll need to get a room at the hotel," he rasped.

Addie laughed. "Thanks, Jack. We always love your advice."

"You're welcome to stuff it under your hat next time," Ridge hollered.

"Glad to help." Jack kept walking and entered the newspaper office. He seemed fit enough, considering his brush with death, and Nora confirmed that he was recovering nicely. No one had seen hide nor hair of Tiny and Pickens or the mysterious woman who'd aided their escape.

They were evidently long gone.

Ely was recovering as well. The eleven-year-old hobbled everywhere on his crutches, playing with the other boys. Addie was happy to see him still enjoying most of what he wanted to do.

The stagecoach rumbled into town, and Addie turned to watch it pull up in front of the Diamond Bessie Hotel. The door opened, and a dapper gentleman in a tailored, three-piece suit stepped out, then turned to offer a hand to a young woman inside the coach. His close-cropped silver beard and mustache gave him a look of distinction that held her attention. He had an easy smile that crinkled the corners of his eyes, the kind that made you feel happy to be alive. Addie guessed him to be somewhere near fifty and itched to know who he was and why he'd come. No one dressed that fancy ever came to town unless he was a businessman—or a gambler. Yes, perhaps he was a gambler.

That bit of speculation made, Addie turned her attention to the other traveler.

Rather plain was the first description that came to mind for the young woman. She was in her early twenties and wore a fitted brown dress that matched her nut-brown hair. Only the dress was twisted and pulled in disarray. As if that wasn't bad enough, a large red bow perched at a curious angle on her head and was not the least becoming. The new arrival appeared rather…well, mousy. And yet she seemed like someone Addie would like to know. She didn't have that store-bought look Addie tended to mistrust.

The woman took a deep breath and gave the town a long, appraising glance before thanking the man for the courtesy.

"My pleasure, miss." He reached back inside the coach for a silver-knobbed black cane. "Perhaps we'll see each other around."

"I'm sure we will, Mr. O'Connor. It was a delight traveling with you."

"For me as well." He spoke in an Irish brogue, tipped his black Stetson, and turned to collect his bags.

Addie filed those little details away in her mind. "Ridge, do you know the man, O'Connor, who just got off the coach?"

"Afraid I don't. Maybe he's just passing through. Why?"

"No reason. I just find him a little unusual for our town."

Ridge chuckled. "I'll ask around, Miss Detective."

The woman traveler glanced left and right before peering at the hotel. With an unsure hand, she lifted her skirts to step onto the boardwalk. She almost seemed to expect someone to meet her.

Fascinated by her odd behavior, Addie leaned over. "Were we expecting someone, Ridge?"

"Only the banker, but I don't think that's her. I'll introduce myself."

They hurried over. Ridge stuck out his hand. "Welcome to Hope's Crossing, ma'am. I'm Mayor Ridge Steele, and this is my lovely wife, Addie."

A smile touched the new arrival's brown eyes as she grabbed his palm, relief showing in her face. The slender woman stood a head taller than Addie, and a smile transformed her plain features. "Pleased to meet you both. I take it my telegram didn't make it. I'm Charlotte Wintersby, the banker. Please call me Charlotte."

"How wonderful, Miss Wintersby...Charlotte. We've expected you for weeks." At first glance, Addie liked her. The second glance didn't change her opinion. Miss Wintersby wasn't stuffy or imperious like she'd imagined most bankers would be. Still, she also didn't fit the image of a professional who dealt with large sums of money. Who knew? Maybe Charlotte would surprise them all. "I'm curious about your traveling companion. I think you called him Mr. O'Connor."

"Yes. Angus O'Connor. He has the most delightful Irish brogue."

Now, Addie was even more curious about why the man was in Hope's Crossing.

Ridge took Charlotte's bag from the stage driver and arranged to return for the large trunk. "Let's get you settled in the hotel. I'm sure you're tired from the journey."

Addie's attention wandered back to the dapper man disappearing into the hotel. Curiosity pricked at her again. No one that well dressed would ever be connected to her father. Still, there was something about him that drew notice. No one had met him, so maybe he was passing through, like so many who arrived these days.

"Yes, I'm a little tired." Charlotte gave the town another stare. "I wasn't sure what to expect, but I love what I see here."

"And why *did* you want to come to a town formed by outlaws, Miss Wintersby?" Ridge held the door for her and Addie. "Didn't you consider that it might be a little...how shall I put this...dangerous?"

Addie wondered the same and moved closer so as not to miss the reply.

"Not really. Who is more naturally suited to protecting their own money and investments? I begged father to let me take this bank. San Francisco had become stifling." Charlotte straightened her shoulders, stepped inside, and headed straight to the registration desk.

The mysterious Mr. O'Connor strode toward the stairs, carrying his bags, evidently having already checked in.

Dragging her attention back to their new banker, Addie whispered to Ridge, "What do you think of Charlotte?"

"She's young. Inexperienced. But I suspect she has a good head on her shoulders."

"That's my impression too. I like her and can't wait to get acquainted. I'll make a nice welcome supper for her tomorrow night and invite the Colbys, Bowdres, and Lassiters."

"Sounds good, Addie. Thank you for stepping into the role of hostess." He threaded his fingers through hers, his gaze searching her face for something. "We never talked about dinners and entertaining you'd have to do."

She grinned and shrugged. "We're in this together, and I'm happy to do whatever you need, whether it's a dinner party or"—she lowered her voice—"be a lovestruck wife."

"Are you? Lovestruck, I mean."

"You have to ask?" Her voice came low and husky.

"Some things a man likes to hear spoken aloud."

"I am utterly lovestruck," she whispered in his ear. She rested a palm on his vest, met the dare in his eyes, and pressed a long kiss on his lips.

Soft laughter broke them apart. Charlotte stood nearby, smiling. "I take it you haven't been married long."

"A little more than a month," Ridge admitted. "I didn't think it showed."

"Mr. Steele, it's beautiful to see people in love." Charlotte tugged off her kid gloves, also brown, one long finger at a time. "Maybe one day, if I meet the right man, I'll know what it's like. Mother's about to lose all hope for me."

To say something of that nature to strangers struck Addie a bit odd, but she released a light laugh and, instead of breaking apart, wound her arm around Ridge. "It'll happen. Did you get a room, dear?"

"I did. It's Number 204."

"I'll collect your trunk and bring it up." Ridge kissed Addie's cheek. "I'll be right back."

Addie nodded and went upstairs with Charlotte. "I'm giving a dinner for you at our house tomorrow night. Nothing real fancy, as we're not fancy people, but I think you'll enjoy meeting some of us in a private setting. We'll introduce you to the town founders."

"That sounds like fun." Charlotte unlocked her door.

"I think you'll be happy here. Everyone is so friendly. I wasn't sure what to expect when I arrived to marry Ridge, but they made me feel really glad I came." Addie appraised the room and found it similar to the one she'd almost stayed in that first night. "One thing you'll discover is that we all have a past we're not that proud of and that it doesn't matter."

Charlotte turned, an odd expression on her face. "Then I should fit right in."

Addie didn't know how to reply. It sounded like Charlotte carried some sort of baggage, but she wasn't about to ask any questions. An awkward silence filled the room.

"The town is only about three years old, but we have almost everything you could want, and being on a stage route helps the isolation. Let's make ourselves comfortable." Addie motioned toward a seating area, and they sat down. "I'm sure you'll miss all the shops of a big city. We're going to have a harvest dance as soon as we can and introduce you to everyone."

"I don't know. I'm not much of a dancer." Charlotte laughed. "I have too many feet and can't keep any out of the way."

"I'm sure it's not that bad."

"Believe me, it is. What did you mean about having the dance as soon as you can?"

Addie told her about the damage the tornado did. "We were very lucky."

"It does appear so," Charlotte admitted. "I hope to escape all of those."

Ridge returned with the trunk, and once Charlotte was settled, the three headed toward the café for supper. Just as they neared the establishment, Addie spied Angus O'Connor entering Dr. Mary's hospital. A figure stood in the doorway, waiting. Then he was hugging...whom exactly? Addie strained for a better look. Dr. Mary? *Their Dr. Mary?* All too soon the door closed, blocking her view.

Stunned, Addie was set back on her heels. The good doctor appeared to have a secret of her own.

"Coming, love?" Ridge asked.

"I just saw something rather...odd." Or maybe her eyes, or the twilight, played tricks. Still thinking about the turn of events and the mystery man who'd come to town, she followed Ridge and Charlotte into the eatery spilling with scrumptious smells.

Twenty-five

THE DINNER PARTY WENT OFF WITHOUT A HITCH, DESPITE BEING Addie's first, and Ridge found the new banker very knowledgeable about a variety of subjects. Clearly, she'd been well educated—at least by their standards. Ridge thought they'd done well in getting her. The young woman had thankfully left her horrendous red bow at the hotel this time and had tidied her hair. She still wore all brown though, and this dress was the color of mud. First impressions aside, she was quick on her feet, her replies witty, and answered all their questions without stumble or pause.

"Why did you choose Hope's Crossing?" Clay asked. "Surely you had better opportunities."

Charlotte met Addie's gaze. "I always wanted to see the real West. When I was a little girl, I was fascinated with"—she glanced around the table—"outlaws. Men who weren't afraid to deliver justice themselves, who didn't back down from a fight, men like you who've seen the best and worst of times. I think I shall enjoy living here."

She ended with a wobbly smile, and Ridge led the clapping. He raised his glass. "To a long and fruitful stay, Miss Wintersby."

"Please, just Charlotte. I've found it good business to dispense with formality."

The woman sure seemed to want to fit in and was saying everything right, but what about matching those words with actions? That would be the true test.

Later, as Ridge and Addie stood at the door saying good night to their guests, Clay took him aside. "What do you think of her?"

Ridge considered it for a second. "She's holding something back, but frankly, that's her business. We all have a few things we'd rather not divulge. I think she'll be good for Hope's Crossing. Are you worried?"

"No, far from it. She's young, but I like her attitude." He glanced at the doorway where Tally was waving him over. "Sorry, we need to get back to the kids. Can we talk more tomorrow?"

"Sure."

Clay kissed Addie's cheek on the way out and congratulated her on the party's success. That was the mark of a true friend, and the moment he took to compliment Addie warmed Ridge's heart.

He came up behind his wife and kissed her bare shoulder. "You worried for nothing. I told you they'd love the meal you prepared."

Addie half turned and laid her hand along the side of his jaw. "I was a bundle of nerves."

"You were a very gracious hostess, and I'm not the only one who thinks so." He swept her up in his arms. The wagons trundled away outside, but the noise didn't distract him from the lovemaking on his mind.

"Where are you taking me? Put me down. I have a kitchen to clean."

"I'll help you in the morning. Right now, I plan to strip that dress off my wife and make her squeal with delight."

"In that case…" She sighed and slid a hand into his hair. "Take me to paradise, cowboy."

"Yes, ma'am." He nuzzled the sensitive flesh behind her ear.

Halfway up the stairs, a knock sounded on the door. Maybe one of their guests had left something. Though part of him knew it wasn't likely. On the other hand, the men hunting him and Addie wouldn't knock.

Ridge met the alarm in Addie's eyes. "I'm sure it's nothing. A slight delay."

The knock sounded again, this time more insistent. He set her down and drew a Colt from his holster, glad he'd worn one to dinner. But then, he rarely went without these days.

"Who is it?" he called.

He could barely hear the mumbled reply. Pistol raised, Ridge jerked the door open.

Startled, the woman on the porch stepped back. A dark scarf partially hiding her face made it difficult to make out any detail in the night.

"I apologize for scaring you, ma'am." Ridge lowered his pistol but didn't holster it. "Can I help you? Are you lost?"

"I'm looking for Ridge Steele, and I came a long way to find him."

"Who are you?"

The strange woman glanced down. "Shiloh."

The name was vaguely familiar, but not enough to help him understand. Who the hell was she? Why couldn't he place her? Something whispered he should.

Addie edged around him in the doorway and took the caller's hand. "Won't you come in?"

"One moment, ma'am." Ridge moved Addie back into the house and kept his voice low. "Don't invite her in without first knowing what she wants."

"We will be civil and charitable to anyone who comes to our door," she whispered furiously. "It's the polite thing to do. She appears to have come a long way to talk, *dear.*"

"Not if you're a wanted man—sweetheart," he grated back.

"Don't you think if she came to kill you, she'd have done so when you opened the door? Let her in, and let's discuss whatever she came for."

"Fine." He ignored the tempting urge to strangle his lovely but naive wife. Ridge strode back to Shiloh. "Please come in, ma'am, where we can talk in private."

Before the woman could take another step, she fainted dead away on the stoop. Ridge reached for her but was too late.

Addie scrambled outside and knelt beside her. "No fever. Ridge, carry her to the parlor, and I'll get the smelling salts."

While he did that, Addie hurried to the kitchen. By the time he laid Shiloh on the sofa and removed her scarf, Addie had returned. Most of the woman's face lay in shadows where the lamp didn't reach, but Ridge thought she seemed rather pale. He could see that she had coal-black hair, and no silver threaded through the strands. He guessed her to be young.

Addie waved the smelling salts under Shiloh's nose, and her eyes fluttered open.

Shiloh startled awake. "I'm sorry," she gasped.

When she tried to sit, Addie stopped her. "Give yourself a moment to recover. I'll get a glass of water."

The woman's piercing dark gaze swept to Ridge as Addie left the room. Her eyes were the key, jostling his memory. They'd looked the same on that night long ago when his faith in God and humanity was driven out of him.

"I know you. That's why you didn't give your last name."

"Duke. I'm Shiloh Duke." She sat up. "I was afraid if you knew, you wouldn't let me in."

He knew that family name all too well. Bitterness enveloped Ridge, and his voice turned to ice. "You're damn right. You and your lies ruined my life. Put a bounty on my head. Set the Calders on my tail."

Addie returned with the water and handed it to Shiloh. She stood silently, her earlier warmth gone.

Shiloh drained the glass and glanced down. "I wanted to find you and apologize. What I did was despicable, but believe me, I had no choice. My father would've killed me as soon as we got home if I'd gone against him. He was a mean drunk, and he'd already shot my mother."

"So you decided to frame an innocent man instead. How can I believe you?" Although her story smacked of the truth, Ridge was in no mood to let bygones be bygones just like that. She'd have to give him some proof of her sincerity first. "How can I trust anything you say now?"

Shiloh pulled herself to her feet with considerable effort, her faded cotton dress hanging limp on her scrawny form. "I... You... This was a mistake. I shouldn't have come."

"Damn right," Ridge managed through stiff lips. Her arrival had brought back all the painful memories he'd tried his best to lock away for years.

Addie stopped Shiloh before she took two shaky steps. "I can't let you go. You're obviously not well."

"Leave her be, Addie!" Ridge barked.

"I will not." Addie stuck out a mulish chin, determined to pick a fight, and of all times to do it. She would persist in trying to fix things that couldn't be fixed. "No matter what she's done, she's sick and needs our help. Settling the past can wait until morning. Meantime, I'm going to do whatever I can to make her better. It's what we do in this house."

"Fine." He stormed to the door and spoke with his back to her. "I'm going for a ride. Don't wait up."

"Ridge, please—"

He didn't wait to hear her plea. He needed air. What had brought that woman here? Now? If she could find him, Tom Calder was likely not too far behind.

Bodie woke while Ridge was saddling Cob and stuck his head out from his little room. "What's going on? Where are you going?"

"Just need to take a ride. Go back to bed, son."

Ridge led the horse from the barn, mounted, and rode toward town. He needed a stiff drink or three. But then, he doubted anything less than a full bottle would wash the sour taste from his mouth.

The stage driver, George Finch, was sitting at a table in the half-empty saloon and waved him over.

A stop by the barkeep for a bottle delayed Ridge's progress. Well-armed to stay awhile, he sat across from George. "I didn't realize this was your layover night." Was it already Friday again? Ridge opened the whiskey and poured a liberal amount into a glass, threw it back, and let the alcohol burn a path to his gut.

It felt damn good. Maybe it would burn away the pain and shame.

"These weeks go fast to some, but for me they drag." Judging from George's slurry voice, he'd been here awhile. "This is the only time I can unwind and think of anything but my job, the horses, the passengers, and the like. I sure get tired of being hollered at."

"I can imagine. What else do you know how to do?"

"I'm pretty much a jack-of-all-trades, but I used to be a gunsmith." George paused. "Before I fell in with the Ellis Gang and got sent to the penitentiary."

Damn, George Finch had a sadder story than his.

"How long have you been out?" Ridge tipped his glass and drained it.

"Three years. Lost everything I had, including a wife and son. I was so damned foolish."

"Aren't we all?" Ridge thought of Addie at home, possibly alone, wondering where he was right now. He oughta have his rear kicked.

George fixed his bleary eyes on him. "Say, don't you have a pretty, young wife?"

"That's correct." Maybe not too much longer, if he didn't apologize for walking out. In the heat of the moment, it'd seemed she was taking sides against him.

Amid the noise of the saloon, he thought about what Shiloh had said. It could be she was telling the truth. Her father had been a surly, mean-looking cuss, jerking her around by the hair. Her life couldn't have been pleasant. And she had been the one to come looking for him and apologize. It had seemed important that she got things off her chest.

Whoa, slow down. What if she was like the woman who'd helped Tiny and Pickens to escape? Maybe she was helping Tom Calder. He took off his hat and rubbed his face. He didn't know what to think.

In the next second, Addie's extension of hospitality crossed his mind. Of all people, she shouldn't have trusted Shiloh. But she had, and others as well. Maybe she should be his bellwether. Addie read people far better than he did.

And he'd left her at home to deal with their sudden guest.

Ridge slid his bottle over to George. "Enjoy. I've got a place I need to be."

"Thanks, Steele."

Standing, Ridge grabbed his hat and headed for the door.

Back at home, he noticed light in the windows. Addie was

still up. Unsaddling and putting Cob in his stall, Ridge stepped into the kitchen to see Addie and Shiloh sitting at the table. Addie's bright, forgiving smile at the sight of him swept away wrongs and lies.

She rose to kiss him, and he pulled her close, savoring the softness that he'd found too little of in his life.

Addie moved back, breathless, her cheeks pink. "Would you like something to eat, dear? Shiloh hadn't eaten for three days, which is why she fainted, so I fixed her some eggs and pork."

"I'm fine." He removed his hat and hung it on the nail by the door. "I'm sorry for losing my temper."

Shiloh lifted her face. Under the light, he saw her greenish black eye and the dark bruises along her jaw.

When she spoke, her words came out quiet and raspy. "You don't need to apologize, preacher. It's me who owes you. I shouldn't have come without word, especially not at this late hour, but I needed to talk to you. I wanted to tell you that I wish I could go back to that night and set things right. My life was already ruined, but I didn't need to let them ruin yours too."

Ridge pulled out a chair. "I see you haven't had it any easier than me. Who hit you?"

"My pa, but it was the last time I'll take a beating from him." She blinked hard. "A week ago, I killed him. I'm used to fists, but when he reached for the gun, I knew he was going to kill me this time. So I grabbed it. We struggled, and it went off. I took what money he had and ran."

Good riddance. Ridge doubted anyone would mourn the man.

Addie patted her hand. "We do whatever we must to survive."

"That night you came upon us, he'd given me to Beau Calder and his rowdy friends to pay off a gambling debt. You killing Beau was a pure accident, but Pa said I'd not live to see morning if I didn't say you struck Beau then attacked me."

"Why? I had no clear notion of what was happening. I

could've ridden on." Only he'd made the mistake of getting off his horse.

"No, preacher. They wouldn't have let you. No matter what you did or didn't see, they knew that you being a man of God, you'd've brought the law down on them. It was looking out for their own necks that made them accuse you." Shiloh finished her glass of milk. "This food is mighty good, ma'am. There's been little of that where I came from."

"I'm happy I could feed you. Would you like more?" Addie asked.

"No, ma'am. I've put you out enough. I'll just be going now that I've done what I came for."

Addie put a hand on the girl's shoulder. "Wait. I wonder if you'd do something for us."

"Anything I can."

"Would you be willing to write down everything you just told us and sign it? Maybe Ridge can get those charges dropped. You'd really help us out a great deal."

That Addie would think to do this before Shiloh disappeared into the wind amazed Ridge, but she was dead right. The girl's own words might get him a clear slate. Except he'd killed Tom Calder's son Wes. Still, Wes had come hunting him down, and returning fire was self-defense, long as the law saw it that way.

Shiloh smiled for the first time since she'd arrived. "I'll be more than happy to do whatever you need, if that will fix the wrong."

"It might and it might not, but it really will give me hope, Miss Duke. I have a friend who's studying to be a lawyer, and he'll know exactly what to do." Ridge stuck out his hand to her, and she shook it. "Thank you for coming. This means more than you know. Now, you're welcome to stay the night with us."

"I couldn't. I've been enough bother. I'll just make camp close by."

Addie put an arm around Ridge. "We have a perfectly good spare room that's never been slept in. We insist."

Shiloh stood for a moment, weighing everything. "How can I refuse? Thank you both."

"I'll see to your horses." Ridge started for the door.

"Actually, they're mules, and they're a mite cranky, I hate to say."

"They haven't met my husband yet." Addie smiled sweetly at Ridge. "Dear."

Laughter rose as he went out. The light from the kitchen window cut through the blackness, and Ridge felt real promise for the first time. He laughed so hard, tears rolled from his eyes. The mules stared like he'd eaten locoweed. Ridge couldn't remember feeling this hopeful, this *blessed*, in a very long time.

Twenty-six

RIDGE SNUCK OUT OF BED BEFORE DAWN, MADE COFFEE, AND sat on the back steps with the cats to watch the sunrise. This one was a beauty.

The creak of the screen door met his ears, and Addie sat next to him, clutching a shawl around her nightgown. "Isn't that a pretty sky, dear?"

"One of the best I've seen." He put an arm around her and kissed her temple. "It seems different somehow this morning—more special."

"It does to me too." She rested her head on his chest and petted Squeakers. "It's strange how fast life can turn on a person."

"You stole my thought, love. Thank you for not being mad when I got back last night. I'm sorry I stormed out. You should've kicked me to Fort Worth and back. I deserve it."

"You were hurting and had some thinking to do. I didn't take that personally. And you did come back," she pointed out.

"I hadn't intended to. But I got to talking with George Finch, and I imagined you sitting here alone, waiting for me, possibly with Shiloh Duke, and I couldn't dump all that in your lap. I had to make amends."

"It's exciting, isn't it, the thought of clearing your name?"

"All I can think about. I figure we'll go into town right after breakfast and find Jack. But I have to warn you, there's a complication."

"What kind?"

"I shot and killed the Calder boy, for one." He looked away. "There have been others since."

"How many?"

Her whispered question floated on the breeze, and for a

moment he wasn't sure that it hadn't been inside his head. Her expectant look told him he hadn't imagined it. "I'm not exactly sure. It never seemed like something I wanted to keep a tally of."

"In self-defense, I'm sure. You're not a cold-blooded killer." Her words hung in the air. Finally, she asked, "Are you charged for their deaths?"

"Not that I'm aware of." Ridge finished his coffee. An outlaw didn't really know what all he was accused of most of the time. Lawmen liked to pin crimes on wanted men, even if they couldn't possibly have committed them, just to clear the case and make themselves look better.

"Then they don't count. Or at least that's probably what Jack will tell you."

"We'll see." Ridge stood and pulled her up. "We have to get this day started. Our guest will be up soon, and she looked half-starved."

Addie squinted up at him, concern wrinkling her forehead. "I don't think she's eaten much in a quite a while, and when her sleeve fell away from her wrists last night, I noticed the marks of some of kind of restraint. I think her life has been a living hell for a long time. I wouldn't be surprised if her whole body wasn't a mass of bruises."

"I saw them too, and you're probably right." A noise in the kitchen got them moving. He went to do the milking and left Addie to dress and get breakfast on.

Soon, they sat down to a hearty meal. Shiloh appeared more rested, the shadows under her eyes less dark, though she was dressed in the same thin cotton dress dotted with multiple old patches. She dug in to the meal without any urging. Addie must've cooked everything she had on hand, making their table the fullest he'd ever seen. Bodie was at an age to eat a man out of house and home, and between him and Shiloh, they had no leftovers.

Ridge got up for a refill from the coffeepot. "Miss Duke, you mentioned you're passing through. Where are you headed?"

"Not sure. California, maybe. The West is large enough where a woman like me can get lost, and the nightmares won't be as strong." Shiloh glanced down at her plate, fighting back tears.

Bodie forked the last bite into his mouth. "The good thing about this big country is that you can be whatever you want to be. All you have to do is dream it, Miss Shiloh."

The kid's simple advice often startled Ridge, and this pronouncement certainly did.

"That's true." Ridge sat down to sip his coffee. "What would you be if you could be anything?"

Shiloh raised her battered face. "A singer. I'd like to sing, and folks say I have a beautiful voice."

Addie smiled. "Then a larger town is where you need to go—Denver or San Francisco. And the next time someone asks you what you are, say that you're a singer. Say it with fervor, and make them believe it. Pretty soon, you'll start to believe it yourself." Her gaze found Ridge's. "I wanted to be the wife to a good man, and it happened because I believed it could."

Bodie wiped his mouth and reached for a cup of coffee. "I wanted to be free, and now I am."

Ridge had always thought that a person's past was what determined their future, but he could see now that it didn't have to be that way. Strong desire to change could override all else, determine a new outcome of a life. He'd dreamed of being out from under the stain of his past, and maybe now he had a real shot.

He reached for Addie's hand where it rested on the table, and her smile blinded him. Years ago, his world had descended into hell. Now he had riches beyond compare.

❧

Ridge pulled up to the hotel, set the brake of the wagon, and helped Addie and Shiloh down. They went inside to the sheriff's office. Jack glanced up from his desk and stood, the bandage stark white around his tanned throat. His voice still carried that raspy sound it had picked up when he'd been stabbed. "To what do I owe the pleasure?"

"How's your wound?" Ridge asked.

"Doing better. I know you didn't come to talk about that, or you wouldn't have brought these lovely ladies."

Ridge introduced Shiloh and explained why they'd come. "Is it possible that you could use a sworn statement from Miss Duke to get my charges dropped?"

"Have a seat." Jack dusted off the chairs for the ladies. "It's really fortunate for you that she came, Ridge. This could go a long way to clearing your name." He riffled around in a drawer and pulled out a tablet of paper, handing it and a pencil to Shiloh. "Write down everything that you can remember about that night. Don't leave out a single detail, even if it seems too small to be important, and be sure to include the names of everyone there and what they said."

"Yes, sir." Shiloh took the pencil and tablet and began.

While she wrote, Jack, Ridge, and Addie talked about the dinner party and Charlotte Wintersby.

"I did some checking, and you won't believe what I found in the *San Francisco Chronicle*." Grinning, Jack leaned back and propped his feet on his cluttered desk.

Ridge ignored Addie's frown. "From the look on your face, it's a doozy."

Addie glared. "I swear, you two are worse than a couple of widow women. Leave Charlotte alone. I like her, and so what if her past isn't perfect? Whose is? That's why it's called a past. It's meant to be left behind—if certain people will let you."

Thoroughly chastised, Ridge turned the conversation to the prisoners' escape. "Have you had any useful information back from those telegraphs you sent out?"

"Not one word. They seem to have disappeared."

Addie reached for Ridge's hand. They couldn't go to Zelda Law yet. "I have no doubt they ran straight to my father. By now, he knows exactly where I am, and he'll be on his way."

"He'll find no welcome here." Jack's eyes hardened. "His kind can keep on riding."

"That's what I keep telling her." Ridge had made a promise and he meant to keep it. Ezekiel would never get his hands on her again. The biggest fear, one that often woke Ridge in a cold sweat, was that Jancy could snatch Addie when she was alone.

He'd just have to stay vigilant and trust that he'd be around to stop Jancy once he showed his face.

A short time later, Shiloh Duke finished writing her affidavit and signed the bottom. "What happens now?" Ridge combed his fingers through his hair as he stood.

"I'll attach this to the application to have the charges dropped, and file it at the courthouse in Mobeetie. The judge will review it and give his decision." Jack put the affidavit in a large envelope and stuck it in his desk drawer.

"By filing, do you mean to hand-carry it?" Addie put an arm around Shiloh's thin waist. Ridge had harbored hate for that woman for so long, but now that hate had faded. She'd begun to let hope in as well, and he saw it in her eyes.

"Yes, I'll leave tomorrow unless something comes up," Jack replied.

Ridge blew out a long, worried breath. "How long will this process take?"

Jack rested a hand on his shoulder. "Hard telling. It depends on how soon the documents land on the judge's desk, and there's no way to predict that. My best advice is put it out of your mind and go about your business. You have to be patient and let me do the fretting now."

Ridge didn't tell Jack that the matter of his pardon had never been far from his thoughts for the last five years and sure wouldn't be going away now. "Another thing. I've had blood on my hands since. Will I have to mention those other deaths?"

"Only what you're charged with. Besides, those others were done in self-defense." Jack shook Shiloh's hand. "Thank you for coming forward. This means a lot to Ridge and those of us who care about him."

"I got him in this mess, and I pray I can get him out. He was only trying to do the right thing." Shiloh's soft words had sprung straight from her heart.

Ridge still felt like a jackass for the way he'd first treated her. He ushered the women out to the wagon and drove to the farm, thinking of what he could do to repay her now.

What did you give someone who'd given your future back?

            ∽

Addie talked Shiloh into staying at least until morning, then they gathered her dirty clothes and washed them.

Shiloh stood at the tub of soapy water and Addie at the rinse tub. Her heart went out to this poor girl who'd had such a miserable life. "Shiloh, what happened to your mother? You mentioned something last night about her."

"Mama overheard Pa talking about using me to pay off his debt to Beau Calder and told him she was going to take me and run away. They argued. He was falling down drunk, and when he got that way, his horrible temper came out." Tears ran down Shiloh's face and into the wash water. "Ever since I can remember, he'd always treated Mama like a servant, beat her for the smallest thing."

Addie nodded. "I know the kind."

"That night she finally stood up to him."

Addie's stomach twisted. She could guess what happened.

"Pa told her to sit down and shut her mouth. Mama grabbed me, and we headed for the door. Never made it. He yanked out his gun and shot her." Sobbing, Shiloh scrubbed her threadbare dress until Addie thought she'd rub a hole right in it. "So much blood. He dragged her out into the yard and ordered me to clean up the mess. By the time I finished, Mama's body was gone."

"I'm sorry." Addie dried her hands on her apron and put her arms around Shiloh. The woman was all skin and bones. "You've had a worse life than me, and I thought mine was bad enough. What you've gone through since then, I can't imagine, but I know it must have been horrible."

"I thought a lot about killing myself and ending it. I wasn't brave enough."

"I'm glad you didn't. I wouldn't want to have missed

meeting you." Addie went back to rinsing and wringing out the clothes, mulling over an idea. "Shiloh, why don't you stay here in Hope's Crossing? This is a good place to start over. The people here would help you."

Shiloh's face softened. "That means more to me than you'll ever know, but I need to keep moving. The law is going to come looking for me, and I'll only bring you trouble."

"We're used to trouble. A little more won't make any difference."

"Thank you, but no."

Addie let out a worried sigh. "Promise to write me and let me know where you decide to stay."

"Of course. I know you care."

Addie cooked one of her best suppers for Shiloh's last night, and afterward they took a walk while Ridge and Bodie worked on lessons.

"Be careful, Shiloh. Some men are as handsome as sin and make your knees go weak. I used to think I wanted that type of man, but those generally don't stay long. Just be wary and don't let some fast talker break your heart. I hope you find someone like my Ridge. He's as steadfast and kind as any man you'll meet. Stubborn though. But he can't help it. He stood in the mule line instead of the people line when the good Lord called it out. Sometimes he can't hear all that well."

They stopped at the corral where the horses enjoyed what was left of the twilight.

"You've sure got yourself a special one, Addie. I hope I helped some in clearing his name." Shiloh rubbed her mules' heads when they came up to the fence. "I don't plan to ever marry. I've done too many bad things to deserve happiness."

Addie faced her. "Listen to me. You have to forgive yourself. That's the only way to make it through life. You and I have done the best we could."

"Yes, ma'am."

The next morning after breakfast, Addie and Ridge stood with Shiloh, her mules loaded down and ready.

"Thank you for not running me off." Shiloh's eyes glistened with tears.

Addie gave her a big hug. "We were happy to help you. Don't forget to write."

Ridge handed Shiloh a pouch. "I can't begin to tell you how much your statement meant to me and Addie. There's enough money there to get you to where you want to settle and give you a good start on a new life. If you get down on your luck, send a telegram."

Shiloh nodded, evidently not trusting herself to speak. Silently, she mounted and rode away from their lives.

Addie wiped her tears. "Do you think we'll ever hear from her again?"

"Yes, I think so." He folded his arms around her and kissed her cheek. "We're all the family she has."

The statement sounded odd at first, but when Addie thought about it, the more it seemed true. Shiloh had no one else, and everyone needed someone to stand in their corner.

"I'm glad she came here, and not just for what she could do for us." Addie tilted her face to look up at him. "I feel good inside that you gave her the stake. She needed that."

Pride in him rushed through her. Ridge Steele had more heart than anyone she'd ever known. It took a big man to forgive something like what Shiloh had done.

Twenty-seven

ADDIE WAITED UNTIL RIDGE LEFT TO GO FINISH UP THE REPAIRS on the McClain house, then she saddled King and went to pay Eleanor a visit.

The woman opened the door, pure joy on her face, so unlike the first time Addie'd visited. "Come in, my friend."

"We have a lot to catch up on." Addie gave her a hug. "So much has happened since I last saw you."

"I'll put the tea on."

While they waited for the kettle to whistle, they spoke of the prisoners' escape. Addie couldn't get it off her mind. The image of Jack with his throat stabbed open was something that refused to leave her thoughts. "I fully believe that crazy, wild woman was working in cahoots with them." Addie smoothed a little crocheted doily on the center of the small table. "It's the only thing that makes sense."

Eleanor set out the cups and perched on the other chair. "You're probably right, but we may never know the truth. There are lots of mysteries in this world."

"Yes, there are." Addie told her about getting caught in the tornado and the sheer terror of running for their lives. "I had accepted that Ridge and I were going to die. I had no doubt in my mind and knew it was far too late to try to bargain with God. Time for that had passed. So, I began to wonder what dying was like. Have you ever found your mind wandering there?"

The kettle whistled, and her friend went to pour the hot water over the leaves in the teapot and brought it to the table. "There've been times. Even now in the still of the night, I find myself thinking about making the crossing one day, seeing my Charley and the kids."

Addie gazed out the window at Eleanor's garden where

a rabbit hopped between the rows. "If you don't mind me asking, do you ever think about them?"

"Almost every day. I'd like to think my boy would've been a doctor or lawyer, but the truth is, he probably would've wound up like his father and been an outlaw. People like us don't have a lot of opportunity come our way."

Comfortable silence spun a golden web between them while Eleanor served the tea.

Addie wondered about that too. What chances would there be for any children she and Ridge might have one day? A remote town like Hope's Crossing was a strike against them. The best chances for education and gainful employment lay in populated areas. Sure, the town was growing, but not fast enough. She wanted better for her kids, and she knew Ridge would want that too. And if Jack was successful in getting the charges against Ridge dropped, they could go anywhere. But would she be able to bear leaving Hope's Crossing?

Waiting for word from the judge in Mobeetie would take every bit of her patience. For Ridge, it would be even worse. She hoped they would hear something soon.

She sipped her tea while their conversation wandered to her horse King, the town, and how close the McClains' and Lassiters' houses were to being finished.

"I'm sure we'll have the dance soon to celebrate. Eleanor, please come."

The woman's face registered interest, but before it took a good hold, sadness crept in. "Honey, it's been far too long. I don't dance anymore. I doubt I'd remember how anyway."

"That's foolish talk. I've only danced once in my life, and that was on my wedding day, but I'm sure going to try again." She pressed her friend harder. "There'll be many single men there wanting to take a spin around the floor. You'd have no shortage of partners. It would do you good."

"I don't know. Maybe I will."

"I'll hold you to that." Addie gave her a hug and left with a promise to call again soon.

As she made her way to Ridge's office, Nora caught her. "We're full speed ahead for the dance on Saturday."

"That's wonderful! I just came from Eleanor's and we were talking about that. I invited her to come."

"Good. We've tried for a year or more to get her to mingle with us and this will be an excellent opportunity."

"She seemed excited at first, then it faded. I'll keep trying." Addie's thoughts flew to what she might wear. Maybe her blue dress. No, the red one. Yes, Ridge hadn't seen her in that yet, and it would be perfect. She could picture his eyes lighting up, and a shiver raced up her spine. "How about we take Charlotte under our wing and spruce her up a bit?"

"Do you think it'll upset her?" Nora worried her lip. "With a little help, she could be pretty, but I wouldn't want to cause her to think she's not good enough."

"Let's go see."

They went straight to the hotel and knocked on her door.

Charlotte seemed happy to see them. She had piled her hair messily on top of her head with two pencils stuck through the heap holding it in place. "Come in, ladies."

Once seated, Addie took the lead. "Nora and I were wondering about something, and we hope we don't offend you by asking."

"Good heavens, I'm sure you won't."

Nora took the plunge. "We want to show you a few tricks to do with your hair and clothes."

"My hair and clothes? I've always been plain, and no one expected anything else." Charlotte glanced from Nora to Addie. "It used to hurt, and I always looked at beautiful girls with envy, but I've accepted who I am. My mother is fond of reminding me that beauty is only skin deep, but I know she only says that to make me feel better."

Addie's heart broke, and she could imagine how devastated Charlotte had been growing up. "You have such pretty features. You only need a little help with your hair."

Her thoughts went back to her release from prison and how Josie Legend had helped her feel pretty just by teaching her how to fix her hair and buying a few new dresses. But finding the beauty inside was something no one could help with. She'd had to search for that.

"If you can change me, I welcome it, but I warn you, my hair is as straight as a ramrod." Charlotte rose and sat on a stool in front of the large dresser mirror. Tears came in her eyes and she began to sob.

Addie drew a chair next to her. "What's wrong? Did we offend you by offering to help? I hope we didn't make you uncomfortable?"

"Nothing like that." Charlotte wiped her eyes. "Can I tell you something?"

"Of course," Addie murmured. Nora met her gaze and lifted her shoulders in question.

"I met someone last year. He was so handsome and said all the right things, except he never would take me anywhere, always insisting we stay far from people. I truly thought he cared for me until one night I overheard his conversation with a male friend in which he admitted that he was only after my money. The ugly little rich girl, he called me. They laughed." Charlotte's voice faltered. "All my life, the people I thought were friends were only after what I could do for them. Never just me. They never saw the person inside, yearning for someone to share things with."

"Oh, honey." Addie laid an arm across the banker's shoulders. "How devastating."

"By the time we get through, you'll show all of them the error of their ways," Nora declared.

Charlotte dabbed at her eyes, her chin trembling. At last she whispered, "I've failed miserably at everything I've tried. My father sent me here after my failures repeatedly became a source of embarrassment. He gave me a year to prove myself."

"And if you don't?" Nora asked.

Charlotte shrugged. "Then I suppose I'll stay permanently."

Addie patted her hand, her reply quiet. "I can think of worse places to spend a lifetime."

"Me too." Her voice held grit. "I don't think I shall miss San Francisco all that much."

Addie liked this woman with determined brown eyes and what looked like a great deal of courage to keep trying in the face of disappointment. "Let's get started on showing the world who you are and what you're made of."

Charlotte forced a laugh. "I'm all for that."

Addie and Nora pulled the pencils from Charlotte's hair and began the transformation. A short time later, they stepped back to view their handiwork. Addie was amazed at the difference.

Charlotte touched the hair falling around her shoulders in loose, shiny waves, then moved to the fringe of bangs they'd cut to soften her face. "I can't believe this. I'm…I'm—"

"Pretty," Addie supplied. "You're a pretty woman, and don't forget it."

"Now, your clothes." Nora went to where they hung, all in various shades of brown. "You need color, Charlotte. Lots of color. Greens, blues, reds, purples."

Addie linked her arm through Charlotte's. "You're going shopping. A new dressmaker has come to town, and you're sorely in need of her help."

"But—"

"No buts." Nora got on Charlotte's other side and tucked her arm through Charlotte's elbow. "It's time to step out of your shell."

They strolled down the street to Tara Quinn, Proprietress. Two hours later, they emerged with a stunned Charlotte. She faced Addie and Nora, tears in her eyes. "I can't believe the big difference little things can make. I owe you both so much."

Addie kissed her cheek. "It was all there. We just helped you find it."

"You're beautiful, Charlotte. Now step into life." Nora hugged her. "Take back your power."

Their paths separated, and Addie and Nora headed down the street. Nora went back to making plans. "We'll begin decorating the big community barn Saturday morning. The men will hang whatever we need and arrange hay bales. I'm sure Ridge will help."

"Bodie too. I think this will be good for him. He stays

out on the farm by himself too much, and I worry about him sometimes. You know?"

"He seems a well-mannered young man."

"I've never seen anyone so young with such a desire to help. All he needed was for someone to believe in him, and now he's flourishing."

"My Sawyer was that way. He seemed far older than his nine years. By the time we found him in an outlaw camp, he'd already been through hell and back." Nora searched the buildings and corral, her eyes softening when she spied the boy with Jack. "This unforgiving land makes old men of the young. I hope that changes one day."

Addie knew exactly what she was talking about. "Me too." Her thoughts sprang to her half brother, and she prayed he was all right. If only she would hear from Zelda.

Addie went home after they parted, daydreaming about waltzing in her red dress with Ridge.

❧

Ridge woke to clouds and rain on Saturday, and he watched Addie's spirits fall as she worried about getting the decorations safely into town without the weather ruining them. By midmorning, however, the clouds moved out, and sunshine instantly improved her mood and his.

Chatting over dinner, Addie told them about Charlotte's transformation. "Just wait until you see her."

"Bless you for helping her. I know you and Nora have worked wonders."

Bodie stared off into space. "I wonder if Violet can dance."

"Son, you needn't worry. Violet can do about anything anyone with sight can. She once walked a tightrope in a circus the kids put on and never fell."

"Really?" Addie gave him a sideways look of disbelief.

"A tightrope? I'd like to have seen that." Bodie urged him to tell more.

"Well, it was actually planks stretched between two sawhorses." Ridge grinned. "But it was still pretty incredible."

"She's brave." Bodie lapsed into silence, and Ridge imagined he was woolgathering about waltzing with a certain young lady.

Ridge did some dreaming of his own. He put an arm around Addie and prayed that one day he could be the kind of man he saw reflected in her eyes.

❧

Ridge dressed for the dance and waited for Addie in the parlor with Bodie. She'd bathed, then locked herself in the spare room with strict orders not to bother her.

As if he were that brave.

He grinned. He liked this bossy side of her. Once the sun went down and they crawled into bed, she was all kitten, and he could make her purr in short order.

"How long do you think she'll be?" Bodie fidgeted in the new shirt and pants he'd bought earlier in town. "I don't think I can stand this wait. Why do women have to take so long? We just throw on our clothes and comb our hair, and we're done."

"Son, you have a lot to learn about women. They have a lot more to do than you and me, and one day you're going to appreciate the pains they take. Sit down and quit pacing."

Bodie perched on the arm of the chair. "What time is it? Do you think we'll be late?"

"Stop. No, we won't be late." Ridge knocked cat hair off his black trousers and ran a finger between his neck and collar to loosen it. "One thing I have to warn you about. Violet will be dancing with Sawyer too, and maybe Henry Truman. She can dance with whoever she likes. There will be no fighting. None. I hear about any, and I'll have to hold back your pay. Understand?"

"I won't fight. I promise."

Footsteps sounded upstairs at last. Ridge pulled himself to his feet and went into the entry. He gazed up, and all of sudden his throat closed, and he couldn't speak.

Addie floated down the stairs in a red dress that whispered

like silk with each step. She'd left her hair down like he preferred, and the golden mass of curls cascaded over the tiny bit of fabric covering her shoulders and spilled down her back.

How was he going to get through this night? Talk about Bodie fighting for his girl, it was Ridge who'd have trouble. He'd probably knock out anyone who dared ask Addie to dance.

She slid her foot onto the bottom step. "Cat got your tongue?"

"Something sure did. You're beyond my wildest dreams." He kissed one delectable shoulder.

Bodie came from the parlor and whistled. "You're really pretty, Addie."

"Thanks, Bodie." Addie straightened the collar of his shirt. "You look very handsome."

The kid ducked his head. "Aww, I'm just my same old me."

Ridge reached for the new Stetson he'd bought to replace the one he'd lost in the tornado. "Ready?"

"Just a moment more. I want to get a good look at you. I do think I'll be the luckiest woman at the dance." She gazed up at him, her palms resting against his black frock coat. The fragrance of wild roses circled around him. "You're the only man for me, Ridge Steele. The only one who knows the way to my heart. The only husband I will ever need."

The shimmering in her eyes, the way the avowal slid off her tongue, weakened his knees.

His chest about to burst with deep longing for a bed, he lowered his head for a kiss instead. He'd meant to keep it short, but the moment his lips touched hers, they were like soldered steel, held together by a fire that burned within.

Behind them, Bodie mumbled and scuffed his feet, breaking them apart.

"Let's go before Bodie has a conniption." Ridge settled his black hat on his head and handed Addie her shawl.

The full September moon bathed everything in silver, a light breeze blowing. The darkness wrapped around them like a lover's arms, whispering secrets and hope.

People had already started arriving, and the musicians were warming up by the time Ridge maneuvered the wagon into a spot near the barn. Bodie leaped out before Ridge set the brake and went off looking for Violet. Ridge prayed the kid wouldn't get his heart broken, but his interest in Violet was all part of growing up. He'd have to discover for himself that life didn't play favorites, and both the good and the bad were for keeps.

Sometimes if a man got real lucky, he found a second chance.

He lifted Addie down from the wagon and held her against him for a long moment, savoring the feel of her body, her wild heartbeat, the way her breath fluttered against his face like angel wings.

She met his gaze. "Ridge, will we still have this sizzling connection when we're old and doddering?"

"I can't speak for you, but I'll feel the same way until I die." He brushed her cheek with the pad of his thumb. Lanterns hanging outside the barn made her eyes shimmer like green diamonds. His voice was husky. "I'm afraid to blink, or you'll disappear."

Addie cast a nervous glance around. "If I do vanish, will you come looking for me?"

He placed his mouth at her ear. "Better believe it, lady. No one had better try taking you away from me."

"I'm glad. I live with the fear that this will all end one day, that I'll wake up in a strange place. I'll look for you, but you won't be there." She shivered and forced a smile, linking her arm through his. "Let's forget all that and enjoy ourselves."

"Absolutely. Plus, I have to keep an eye on Bodie. The mood he's in, he might get into trouble either with Clay or the other boys."

"Oh dear, I sure hope not."

Heads turned when they walked in, and Ridge knew they weren't looking at him. Addie really was a vision in red. They'd barely taken three steps before people came over to chat and congratulate his beautiful wife on the decorations. He finally left her to the women and joined Clay, Jack, and Tait over by the wall.

"How's it going, hermanos?" Ridge glanced around for Bodie and relaxed when he saw him talking to Henry Truman and Tait's twin nephews.

Tait plucked a piece of straw from a hay bale and stuck it in his mouth. "Between keeping an eye on Melanie, making sure Joe and Jesse are staying out of trouble and Becky isn't into something, I'm as good as a man can hope for. Those twins can run a man ragged, and I'm doing double duty with Mel out of commission."

Jack laughed. "Stop griping. You've got no more than the rest of us. Just think, three years ago, we were all bachelors with no wives or kids. How times have changed."

"Then Tally showed up with Violet and started the ball rolling." Clay reached into a pocket for his cigarette makings and tapped a straight line of tobacco onto the paper. "The town is big enough now that we need to put up a population sign."

Tait pulled a flask of whiskey from inside his coat, took a swig, and passed it.

"Not a bad idea." Ridge took a sip from the flask and handed it to Jack. "We also need to open up the back entrance and soon."

"I've had that on my mind too and think it's something we need to address again." Clay rolled the cigarette, lit it, and took a drag. "It's past due."

"More and more folks arrive every day, and I'm selling land left and right. Business is booming." Nothing scared Ridge more than success, because with it eventually came failure. He was used to having nothing and doing without. That was safe. Comfortable. He wasn't cut out to be a rich man with all new problems.

The new banker strolled in wearing a deep-blue dress, and Ridge almost swallowed his teeth. Addie had been right about Charlotte's newfound confidence. Tonight she was drawing men's glances like honey drew flies and would have her pick of partners to dance with. She joined the women, and Addie immediately struck up a conversation with her.

"We'll have the time now that the house rebuilding is done. I'll call a town meeting Monday." Jack glanced around. Just then, Dallas Hawk and his three-piece band launched into the first waltz, and he wandered off to find Nora.

Ridge went to Addie and held out his hand. "Let's make a memory, Mrs. Steele."

"I've been as impatient as Bodie." Her face glowed with love and happiness. "One more memory added to the hundreds I already have won't hurt."

"Nope, not one bit." His arm encircled her as she moved against him, her body warm and face flushed. Her movements were sure and confident as he swung her out into the throng of dancers. "You've been practicing."

"Trying." She grinned up at him. "I've been doing some practicing when I go riding lately."

"Don't tell me King was your partner?"

She laughed. "He's not *that* good, but I bet he'd try if he could stand on two legs long enough." She got serious, and desire deepened the green of her eyes, giving her voice a throaty sound. "You changed my life, Ridge."

"No, I can't take credit for that. All I did was offer you a safe place to live while you got stronger. Everything was already in place inside you. You just had to find it."

They lapsed into silence, Ridge soaking up the feel of his beautiful wife and the way her body molded to his. Every dip and sway and swirl was like a match to dry tinder and a resulting flame.

With one hand on her waist and the fragrance of wild roses teasing him, he guided her around the floor in wide, sweeping circles. She lost step a time or two but quickly recovered.

Dancing, like life, was all about learning the steps, making sure to avoid any obstacles, and not stepping in a pile of manure. He was still a work in progress, but he hoped he was getting better at dodging manure.

Bodie went by with Violet and wore a dumb look on his face that was a mixture of sheer happiness and utter terror.

Ridge probably wore the same expression on more than one occasion. He did for sure when he glanced down at Addie as they danced and a gap in her bodice allowed him to see the rising swell of her lush breasts.

God in heaven! He'd be lucky to make it home before he lost every shred of sanity.

As soon as the music ended, he pulled her out of the lantern light for a long kiss, his hands splayed across her back. She returned the kiss with equal passion, her fingers tangling in his hair. The music, the laughter, the crowd forgotten for the moment.

When he let her up for air, he whispered in her ear, "You make me crazy with wanting."

She gazed up, her eyes staring into his, an arm around his neck. "I love you, my darling. There is no one else for me from now to eternity and even beyond, because my love is too large for just one life. You satisfy, thrill me, complete me in every way."

Twenty-eight

ADDIE LEANED CLOSE. "LET'S GO OUTSIDE FOR SOME FRESH AIR, dear."

"I'd follow you blindly through a pasture of giant red ant beds." He kissed her neck, took her hand, and went outside. He gazed up at the stars. "It's a beautiful night."

Now that Addie had him to herself, she didn't wish to talk about the stars, the fall air floating on the breeze, or the prospect of rain. She stared up at him and cupped his jaw. "I think I'll remember this moment for the rest of my life."

"Better believe it." His voice was husky.

She didn't know if he pulled her or she fell into his arms by herself. Before she knew it, her lips were on those of her sensitive gunfighter's, and the kiss was another scorcher. Addie's heart fluttered, an insatiable hunger curling along her spine and sweeping upward. His touch left a delicious heat that made her blood race hot through her veins.

Somehow, someway, Ridge had taken all her broken pieces and put her back together far better than she ever had been.

When they broke apart, a smoldering flame burned in his beautiful amber eyes. "I told myself it didn't matter that you hadn't spoken the words, but I lied. I wanted to hear you say them to really know for sure."

She chewed her bottom lip. "I was waiting for the perfect time, only it never came. Maybe there's no such thing as perfect."

"You're a smart lady."

"You are my forever love, Ridge," she whispered and closed the scant inches between their mouths. Trembling, she poured out all the love she felt for him.

He ran his hands down the sides of her body. Heat flared hotter with each touch, and Addie knew for certain the power of love. Their kind would never fade or dull with time.

The noisy dance filled the night behind them, but they were lost in each other.

When he raised his head, emotion darkened his eyes. He lifted her hand and pressed his lips gently to the delicate underside of her wrist. "I didn't know what I was getting when I told Luke Legend I'd marry you."

"Or me with you." Addie inhaled a deep breath of the fragrant night air and toyed with the ends of Ridge's hair. "I only prayed that you wouldn't be mean like Ezekiel."

"You don't have to worry there."

"I know. I saw your kindness and caring first thing. Even before I met you."

"Yes, that night in Fort Worth when you were beating the living daylights out of that drunk with your shoe." Ridge laughed. "I knew right then you'd be a feisty woman. I just didn't know you'd be mine." He nibbled on the curve of her neck.

Someone cleared his throat behind them. Addie's eyes flew open. "Bodie?"

Ridge kept her in the circle of his arms. "Do you need something, son?"

"I missed you and thought you might've left for home without me." The gangly kid's face flushed to have to admit his insecurity.

"We just came outside to get some air." Addie touched his shoulder, sudden anger at Bodie's kin rising. The way they mistreated him were the cause of this. "We wouldn't leave without telling you. How are you liking your first dance here?"

"I like it fine except for sharing Violet."

Ridge gave a soft snort. "I told you to expect that, but you didn't believe me."

"I ain't gonna cause a ruckus or anything. I like Violet too much to complain, being as how she has to depend on her hands to see. If she knew how ugly Henry Truman is, she might not take a turn with him." Bodie thought a moment. "That ain't exactly true. Violet is kind to everybody and cares about their feelings."

"That she is." Ridge draped his arm around Bodie's shoulders. "You know, there are a few other girls here about your age."

"Yeah, but they aren't as pretty."

"Do you know what? You haven't waltzed with me yet." Addie put her arm through Bodie's. "I know I'm far too old, but I promise I won't embarrass you. Might step on your feet though. I'm not very good."

"Shoot, Addie, I thought you were only allowed to dance with Ridge. Except that wasn't exactly what you were doing just now."

"Go on. I can live for a few minutes without my gorgeous wife." Ridge's mouth twitched. "I'll try to restrain myself from getting jealous and fighting you."

"Thanks, boss."

Addie gave Ridge a kiss and walked to the dance floor, glad she could help ease Bodie's loneliness. Once they started to dance, she found herself surprised at his skill. "Did your parents used to go to many dances?"

"All the time," he answered, sweeping her across the plank floor. "My papa played the fiddle, so we were always at a dance somewhere. I danced with my mama a lot because she never got to otherwise."

"She taught you very well. I think you're probably the best here."

"You mean it?"

"I do. I never attended a dance before I came here. It was a sin where I came from, so Ridge had to teach me what little I know."

"Everything was a sin when I lived with my aunt and uncle—even laughing." Sadness oozed from Bodie's eyes. "I walked on eggshells, afraid I'd break one of their rules and they'd kick me out. I miss my mama and papa."

"I'm sorry, Bodie. You got cheated." They both had. She'd make an effort to laugh with Bodie more.

"It's okay." He was silent a moment, and she watched his sensitive eyes, so full of despair. "Addie, do you think a girl could ever love me?"

Tears filled her eyes, her heart breaking for the insecure young man who'd lost so much. "Bodie honey, one of these days the right girl is going to come along, sweep you right off your feet, and you'll forget this conversation ever happened. You can count on that."

He broke into a wide grin. "You really think so?"

"I know so."

"I'm glad. Thanks, Addie."

"You're welcome. Just try not to get in a big hurry. You have your whole life ahead of you."

They waltzed to another song, then Bodie saw his chance to snag Violet, and Addie went for some punch. She was standing with Ridge when a stir raced through the crowd. The mysterious and very dapper Angus O'Connor entered the barn, and the woman on his arm gave Addie a start. *Dr. Mary?* Addie blinked and looked again.

She almost didn't recognize the lady doctor. Her brown hair hung in loose curls that tumbled around her shoulders, and the gorgeous dress of shimmering gold caught in the lantern light.

"See, Ridge? I told you. Believe me now?"

"Well, I'll be. It does appear our Dr. Mary has gotten her a fellow," Ridge murmured. "Good for her. She's been alone ever since I met her. I wonder why he stayed away?"

"You've never seen him once?"

"Nope."

O'Connor dropped his silver-knobbed cane on a hay bale and led the good doctor onto the dance floor. The two made quite a handsome couple—he with his silver hair and close-cropped beard, and her absolutely glowing with happiness. Addie admitted to herself that she'd never viewed Dr. Mary as anything other than a professional woman and doubted anyone else in the town had either. Her hair was always pulled into a severe knot, and she never seemed to care for things like dresses, homemaking, or prettying herself up.

They waltzed by, and Addie couldn't help but notice how Dr. Mary gazed into O'Connor's laughing eyes. Most of the couples stopped, open-mouthed, to watch their Dr. Mary looking young and carefree for the first time since they'd known her. There appeared to be a whole lot more to the woman than any of them had considered.

Addie was no expert by any stretch, but the gold dress looked expensive. Maybe O'Connor had brought it with him as a gift. Or did Dr. Mary have other surprises of her own?

"O'Connor looks like a fine gentleman," Ridge decided aloud. "Let's quit gawking like a bunch of folks fresh out of the sticks and let me get back to showing off my beautiful wife."

"You give the best compliments, dear."

They stepped on the dance floor, Ridge whispering all kinds of maddening, suggestive things in her ear. She floated on air, counting the minutes until they'd be home in their bed.

An hour later, Addie had an occasion to waltz with Angus O'Connor. In a thick Irish brogue that she found so romantic, he complimented her red dress.

"Thank you, sir. I love Dr. Mary's as well. I'll have to ask where she got it."

"I brought it with me. A gift for Margaret."

"Oh, you have excellent taste!"

Laughter sprang from O'Connor's lips. "Nothing brings me greater joy than making my woman happy." His gaze sought Dr. Mary, and a smile curved his lips when he spied her.

That was true love if she ever saw it. "Have you known each other very long?"

"Margaret is an old, very dear friend. We met while she was in medical school, then later when she came West. I hear you're a newlywed. How are you liking married life, Mrs. Steele?"

"It's been two months, and I find myself more in love with Ridge every day. I never knew men like him existed."

"I'm glad to hear you're so happy." O'Connor expertly swung her around. "That's how marriages should be."

"Are you a doctor as well?" Addie glanced up into a pair of the bluest eyes she'd ever seen and found herself unusually flustered.

O'Connor chuckled. "Far from it. She used to come into my saloon to play cards. I own a place in Kansas City."

Addie trampled his feet. "I'm so sorry. I still have a lot to learn about waltzing."

"Don't give it a thought. Everyone has to start somewhere."

"You're very kind. How long will you be in town, Mr. O'Connor?"

"That depends. I'm trying to buy Hope's Crossing's establishment. I want to turn it into a showcase like in San Francisco and Denver." A grin curved his mouth. "I like it here so far. And if things go well, I'll move my business here and open up an opera house next door."

"Oh my. You're a very ambitious man."

"So I've been told."

They lapsed into silence and swept across the floor to "The Blue Danube." Addie scanned the crowd, and her heart swelled to see Eleanor in a pretty dress. Not only that, her friend was dancing with the lonely stage driver, George Finch. This was truly a night for surprises. And miracles.

On the far wall, Bodie sat with Violet, talking and laughing. He'd finally gotten his chance, and it appeared he'd taken full advantage of the short time.

Ridge went by with the rounded Mrs. Truman and winked. After eleven children, she was still quite spry and having a lot of fun. Tait and Melanie were sitting on the sidelines, which wasn't surprising. Melanie would have her baby any day.

Angus O'Connor glanced down at Addie. "I've always wondered if outlaws had time for this sort of thing. I'm glad they do. I think I'll love it here. Everyone is so happy."

Addie smiled. "Mr. O'Connor, outlaws live normal lives. Home means everything."

"I see that, Mrs. Steele. My visit has been most enlightening."

The music ended, and he kissed the back of her hand. "This has been lovely."

"Good luck, Mr. O'Connor. I hope your plans work out. You can make a real difference here."

"I hope so."

Addie watched him head back to Dr. Mary, then turned to find Ridge striding toward her. She relayed what she'd learned.

"If the man does what he proposes, he'll put us on the map, and we'll have a boom town. It's even more crucial to open up the back entrance."

"I agree." Yet worry gnawed at her. Ezekiel was coming. He could waltz right in.

Before the music started, Todd Denver stood and got their attention, his dark red hair slicked straight back. The young man was quite dapper in a suit and his customary bow tie. "Sorry to interrupt, but this will only take a moment, then you can get back to the party. As you all know, I'm going to have to resign my teaching position in order to get married. What you don't know is that I'm leaving by dawn. I'm already packed and ready to ride out."

"We're sorry to see you go!" a voice in the back yelled.

Denver smiled. "I'm sorry also. I loved every minute here. You have a great bunch of kids and a special town in which to raise them. Good luck finding my replacement. I know you'll choose wisely." He stepped away from the musicians and was besieged, everyone wanting to wish him well.

The music, the laughter, all the new developments made the night truly magical. Addie felt as if everything was changing. But maybe it was she who'd changed—from an ugly duckling into a beautiful swan. She sighed and rested her head on Ridge's chest. All those terrible nights in prison seemed like a distant bad memory. She'd fit into Hope's Crossing like a foot into a slipper and had become one of them now.

Here on the high plains of Texas, in the last outlaw sanctuary, she'd found love and the man of her dreams. She gazed up into his eyes. "Thank you for giving me this life, Ridge Steele."

Twenty-nine

Ridge strolled toward the barn early the next morning, whistling as the sky turned from dark gray to pink. He felt unusually happy, considering his former moods. The days and nights with Addie had made him a changed man.

Yet he knew not to get too comfortable. Life could turn and bite a man.

The wait to hear the judge's decision on his reprieve was killing him. If this didn't work, he'd have to go on the run—now that the law officially knew where he was. As much as it would destroy him to do so, he'd have to leave Addie behind. He wouldn't drag her along and put her in danger.

Ridge didn't know how he'd live without her now. She'd saved him from utter despair and loneliness.

His mind on Addie, he didn't see the lurking figure until the man stepped away from the side of the house, a gun in his hand.

"I finally found you," Tom Calder grated out. The big rancher's eyes were sunken and glittered with hate. "I followed Shiloh Duke but lost her trail a week ago. She'd told me she was coming to find you."

Ridge's heart clenched, and he was glad he'd strapped on his gun belt. "You should know she gave a sworn statement about that night, and my lawyer has already taken it to a judge in Mobeetie. I didn't kill Beau, and now everyone knows that. I wouldn't have shot Wes either if you both hadn't come hunting me. His death is on you."

"You took my boys, and don't deny it," Calder yelled. "You ain't nothing but scum, pretended to be a big preacher, all the while nothing but the devil. You forced yourself on Shiloh and made out my son to be the violator."

Bodie stumbled from the barn with no shirt, barefoot, and tugging on his trousers.

"Go back inside, Bodie," Ridge barked. "This is between me and Calder."

"I'm finally going to get some justice for my boys!" Calder yelled. "And it's going to be mighty satisfying to see you lying on the ground like they're lying cold in their graves."

"You won't find me the inexperienced man I was back then." Ridge kept his voice as even as he could, but it dripped with sadness. It had been only a matter of time before the devil would demand his due. "I don't want to fight you, Tom."

"Too yellow?" the man snarled, obviously not in any mood to listen.

"I don't intend to draw unless you force me. But if you do, know that one of us is going to go down. I really don't want to die on such a fine morning, and I doubt you do either."

"You don't know anything about me. Don't pretend you do."

"Of course I don't. It's just that we have this special sunrise to enjoy. The birds are singing, and the air carries a hint of fall. I appreciate being able to see it."

Fury flashed in Calder's eyes. "I have nothing left. You took it all."

"You still have your land, that fine ranch. I hear you have the finest cattle in all of Texas." Ridge looked for some sign that the man heard anything he was saying but saw none.

Except Calder hadn't shot yet. What was he waiting on?

"Wes left a wife and child behind, a little son without a father, but I don't suppose that matters to you."

Behind him, Ridge heard Addie rattling around in the kitchen. He had to resolve this. She'd be out in a moment to feed her chickens that were scratching around in the dirt.

"You hungry, Calder? Let's go inside and eat. I already put coffee on. Smell it?"

"I know what you're doing. My business with you doesn't include food."

The moment Ridge had prayed he could avoid, came. Addie opened the back door. He felt a change in her and knew the minute she'd figured out what was happening, felt her indecision.

"Ridge?" Her voice trembled.

He kept his back to her and forced calm into his voice. "It's all right, love. Tom Calder and I have some things to work out. Why don't you get breakfast started, honey?"

"That sounds good. Mr. Calder, you'll be welcome to sit at our table, but you'll have to leave your gun outside." The words strangled in her throat.

The squeak of the screen door sounded, letting Ridge know she'd gone back inside.

"Does she know she married a killer, a man who forces himself on women?" Calder spat.

"I keep no secrets from my wife. She knows everything."

"Your version."

"The day's wasting, Calder. Whatever it is you have a mind to do, let's get it over with." The sun would be up in a moment and shining in his eyes, blinding him.

Tom Calder shifted his weight and stuck his gun into the holster at his hip. Ridge guessed the time for talking had ended. He mentally measured the twenty paces between them, the slight breeze, the face of the grief-stricken man facing him, his eyes so full of hate. It would devastate anyone to lose one son, much less two, and Ridge bore him no ill will. It just frustrated him that Calder refused to see the truth. Maybe it was easier to believe a lie.

Ridge straightened his shoulders and inhaled, flexing his hand. "I forgive you for what you're about to do, Tom Calder."

Rage blazed across the rancher's weathered face. He jerked his pistol from the leather and fired.

One second separated Ridge from death.

No time to think. To aim. To try reason one last time. Pure reflexes kicked in. He drew.

The bullet struck Calder's hand, the force ripping his gun away. Blood flew, splatters following it.

The acrid taste of gunpowder filled Ridge's mouth. Through the haze of smoke, he watched Calder clutch his bloody hand and drop to his knees, sobbing.

Bodie ran from the barn where he'd evidently been watching. He came full of purpose, but when he reached them, he stopped, crossed his arms, and stuck his hands in his armpits. He clearly wanted to help but didn't know what to do next.

Ridge knew little more than the kid. "It's all right, Bodie. It's over."

Addie flew from the house in a panic and ran to Ridge. "Are you hurt?"

"I'm fine." He walked to the rancher and knelt beside him, laid an arm across his shoulders. "This is done. Go home to your ranch and your grandson, Calder. It's not too late to put your life back together."

Calder scowled at him from under shaggy eyebrows. "With a useless hand?"

"Others have managed with much less. You still have one good one, and you're alive. That counts for a whole lot."

The breeze blew the hem of Addie's dress around her ankles. "Come into the house, Mr. Calder, and let me wrap your hand. Then we'll eat breakfast and you can tell me about that fine grandson of yours." She stood aside while Bodie and Ridge lifted the rancher to his feet. "What is his name?"

"Jacob Calder, ma'am. He's three."

"I'm sure he's a fine boy." Addie held the screen door while Ridge and Bodie helped the man inside and settled him at the table.

Ridge's hand trembled as he poured coffee, and Bodie plunked a cup down in front of Tom while Addie got out her medical supplies. Ridge watched the care with which she tended the wound and wrapped it. No anger, no harsh words. Just a heart full of forgiveness. His chest swelled with pride.

He'd waited five long years to resolve this part of his life, and to do it without more killing seemed a sweet miracle. He bowed his head for a moment of thanks.

❧

After Calder left to seek Dr. Mary's services before heading back to his ranch, Addie found herself alone with Ridge. She took his hands. They were so large, callus-lined from work. He could hold a child or an animal as easily as his Colt.

"You have so much power in these hands, but you also have great tenderness." She pressed a kiss on his palm. "What I love is that you know which one to use for different situations. I'm glad you forgave Calder. He was hurting and had let hate override his judgment." Her words were soft as she felt her way toward what she wanted to say. The smell of his soap brought a measure of peace. She breathed it in and traced the corded muscles in his forearms, the blue veins that carried his precious lifeblood. "Will you ever take up the pulpit again? You'd make a fine preacher."

"Hope's Crossing has the only minister it needs with Brother Paul. I'm done with preaching. All I want to do is to be your husband. Thank you for being kind to Calder."

"You teach me how every single day."

"I don't know about that." Ridge kissed her cheek. "I need to finish the chores and go into town. I have to help put the barn back together."

"I'd like to go with you if you don't mind." She watched a happy light fill his eyes.

"I was hoping you might."

The screen door opened, and Bodie stepped into the kitchen. "Hoped she might what?"

Addie laughed. The boy was getting comfortable with them and had lost his fear of Ridge—if he ever had much to start with. "We're going to town. Want to come?"

"I might. Sawyer, Henry, and me talked about going hunting today."

Addie and Ridge shared a raised-eyebrow look.

"You did, did you?" she asked.

Bodie shrugged. "Yeah, they're pretty fun to be with."

"So you're over wanting to fight them?" Ridge grabbed a cold biscuit and took a bite.

"Yep."

Addie patted his arm. "What about Violet?"

"She said she's writing Noah Legend. She's too young for

me anyway." Bodie took the last cold biscuit from the plate and went out the door.

"The love life of the young." Addie laughed.

Town was a hotbed of activity when they arrived an hour later for the town meeting. Angus O'Connor presented his plans, and Charlotte Wintersby talked about the bank. Then after various others spoke about it being time to quit hiding and walk in the sunshine, they took a vote. It was unanimous to open the back passage. Everyone scattered to begin the town's transformation. One group worked in the community barn, and others had already started to remove the large boulders that had been put in place years ago to block the back entrance when the town was little more than an outlaw hideout, the old Devil's Crossing.

Addie joined Tally, Nora, and Melanie, who'd gathered to watch Charlotte Wintersby organize the young men moving her into the new bank—and to add their two cents if asked.

"This is exciting, to have so much going on in one day." Addie scanned the town and smiled when she saw Ridge rolling up his shirtsleeves and moving to help the men loading sleds with the gigantic rocks.

"I think this is just the beginning." Nora brushed a strand of hair from her eyes. "Soon, our town will have everything the larger communities do."

Tally draped her arm around Addie and Nora and leaned in. "Clay said Dr. Mary is going to enlarge her hospital and add six more beds. That is, if she stays. I have a feeling that if that handsome Irishman heads back to Kansas City, she may go with him. I wouldn't blame her one bit."

Nora giggled. "Who knew she had him stashed away?"

Addie found an opening to give her predictions. "Personally, I think we'll see a wedding. If we're lucky, maybe two— Eleanor and George."

Peter Stone, Martha Truman's handsome brother, walked past carrying a beautiful oil painting of a seaside town. "Where would you like this hung, Miss Charlotte?"

Charlotte laid a finger to her chin in thought. The sunlight caught the brown of her twinkling eyes, and her features softened. "I should put it out where patrons could enjoy it, but I'm going to be selfish. Hang it in my office, facing my desk."

Peter smiled and winked. "Wise choice. Nothing wrong in being a little selfish."

After he went inside, Addie moved to the banker's side. "I don't like to pry, but I get the feeling that painting means something special to you."

"It holds very fond memories and is a place where I was happiest." Charlotte forced a laugh. "I fear I'm quite a sentimentalist."

"There's nothing wrong with that. We all cling to certain meaningful moments." Except for Addie, those moments had all seemed to come after she'd become Ridge's wife. She chose to erase everything that occurred before that.

"It's gone now, and I must move on. Love isn't meant to last. Not for me."

"You might be surprised. You can make new memories and be happy again."

"I will try, and who knows? Maybe you'll be right. Excuse me, I see I'm needed." Charlotte went to a worker motioning her over and instructed him where to place a long, oak cabinet.

Before long, Charlotte had completed the move into the bank, and everything was spic and span for business on Monday morning. While they stood around talking, Tait's twin nephews ran to tell them that Melanie had given birth to a daughter.

Addie hurried to the Trinity home to congratulate the happy mother and father. Her eyes filled with tears at the sight of Tait cradling his tiny baby girl in his large hands. She could easily picture Ridge doing the same with his son.

"One day soon," she murmured softly as she left the new family to rest.

The rest of the day passed pleasantly. Addie was on her way to find Ridge when she spied Dr. Mary emerging from the Trinity home, back in her practical dress, her bullet necklace glinting in the sun.

Addie hurried to fall into step with her. "Doctor, thanks to you, we have a new addition to the town. I'm very relieved everything turned out well."

Dr. Mary smiled. "It was an easy delivery. Not all are that way."

"Yes, I'm sure." Addie let a moment's silence drift between them before getting to the crux of the matter on her mind. "I was so happy to see you at the dance."

Dr. Mary stopped and scowled. "Is that all anyone can find to talk about?"

"You have to admit that you gave us quite a shock." Addie smiled and went on. "I'd never seen you with your hair down, and apparently no one else had either. For a moment, I thought you might be a new arrival. I found Mr. O'Connor quite an interesting man."

"One thing about that man, he likes to talk and flirt with the ladies. But I don't mind, because I understand it's part of his personality and make allowances." Dr. Mary laid a hand on Addie's arm. "When you get to be my age, you learn quite a bit about how men think. I suspect you're still trying to figure that out."

"Yes, ma'am, I am."

"It'll take a while, but Ridge isn't as complicated as some." Dr. Mary's voice was firm but soft. "I will say for sure and certain that I do not intend to leave Hope's Crossing, and everyone can put that in their pipe and smoke it. I've found the place I'd been searching for all my life."

There was that bliss that Nora had once spoken about. Angus or no Angus, Dr. Mary had found hers already.

"I think I have too." Addie stared at the high walls of the canyon around them, the last rays of sunshine creating a stunning mosaic pattern on the rocks.

A smile curved the doctor's lips. "I've known wealthy men who spent thousands of dollars looking for a place that satisfies their soul, and we have it right here. I have plans to enlarge my hospital, and to get the space might require me moving out where you and Ridge live."

"We'd be proud to have you for a neighbor." Who knew? At some point, maybe all the businesses would move out where there was room.

Dr. Mary's gaze pierced her. "Be sure to spread it around and save me from having to take out an ad in the newspaper alongside the prices of turnips and hogs."

"I will." Addie looked up at movement and saw Ridge and Angus heading toward them. "There come our men. Must be quitting time."

Addie went to meet Ridge and could've sworn his face reflected the bliss that filled her heart. Right here was where she'd stay, and she'd be buried here one day. Next to her one true love.

Thirty

Several days later, Addie forgot to stay alert when she built a fire out back, intending to do the wash. Fear that her skirts would get caught in the flames had led her to dress in her Levi's trousers. Ridge had eaten breakfast and headed out to resume work on the rubble blocking the back entrance to town, and Bodie had gone off with Sawyer and Henry, leaving her alone on the property.

Addie hadn't given that a second thought until a whisper of warning shot up her spine.

Something evil drifted on the breeze. She shivered and started toward the kitchen door. Two steps from safety, a black-clothed figure leaped from behind their rain barrel, cutting her off. She shrieked and ran, but she wasn't fast enough. The man closed his bony fingers about one wrist and yanked her around to face him.

She stared into the face of the devil, smelled alcohol on his breath. The blood in her veins froze, and memories of a dozen beatings raced through her head.

"You thought you could hide from me!" Ezekiel drew back a hand and slapped her face.

Addie's head whipped back, pain shooting through her.

"You disgust me, prancing around in those men's clothes like a jezebel, living with outlaws and killers. I taught you the Word of God, tried my best to beat the spite out of you, but you spurned the hand that fed and clothed you." Spittle flew from Ezekiel's mouth and left droplets on his brown goatee.

The vile stream of hate circled her head, his words a flock of vultures diving in to peck and maim her.

Still addled from the slap, Addie had trouble getting her wits about her. She had to think. Had to get away, had to get to Ridge. He wasn't here. She had to save herself. But

Ezekiel's grip was like a band of steel. She jerked hard against his strength, trying to break his hold, her efforts futile.

Ezekiel shook her. "Where's my boy? I want him now."

She took a deep breath and lifted her chin. "He's far from your clutches. I don't care what you do, I'll never breathe a word." She gathered up a wad of spit and let it fly. The glob landed square on his nose and across part of one sunken cheek, trickling down his skin.

Addie held her breath. What she saw in his eyes filled her with terror.

"The sight of you and your devil ways sickens me!" He jerked her around and tied her hands behind her, then took a black hood from inside his shirt and threw it over her head. Her world turned pitch-black and reeked of sweat. He dragged her along, tripping and stumbling, and when she sprawled on the hard ground, he picked her up and threw her over his shoulder and strode on.

To where?

The snuffle of horses reached her, and a second later he tossed her onto a wooden floor—no, the bed of a wagon. Her right elbow took the brunt of the hard landing, and pain stole her ability to breathe for several long moments.

"What are you doing, Ezekiel?" The timid voice belonged to Addie's mother.

"Whatever I have to in order to find my flesh and blood," Ezekiel snapped.

"*She's* your flesh and blood!" Ingrid Jancy cried.

"Silence, woman! This…this devil worshiper is no daughter of mine." The wagon shifted as Ezekiel climbed into the seat, then they were moving.

If her mother had been stronger, together they could've stood up to Ezekiel. But he'd beaten the fight out of Ingrid years ago. No, she would be no help.

Addie didn't know where Ezekiel meant to take her, but the black foreboding choking her said she would never walk away. He wouldn't let her live. The darkness in his own twisted, demented mind would demand he put an end to her.

The wagon jolted over the rough ground, taking her farther from the man she loved. A quiet sob rose. She'd never see Ridge again, ride to their hidden pool, or make love until dawn. Never again sit and read with Bodie or train with King. No more good times and bad to share with her friends in Hope's Crossing. Tears rolled down her face inside the hood.

Everything that made her life worth living was slipping away, and she couldn't stop it.

She worked feverishly at the rope binding her wrists. If she could get free, she had a chance. Only the knots wouldn't budge, and the painful slick wetness at her fingertips told her she'd ripped her fingernails down to the quick. She had to think of something else. She felt along the wooden bed for something, anything to use as a weapon.

Her situation was dire, but she wouldn't give up until the last shred of hope was gone and life had left her body. She'd survived beatings, three years in prison, survived a tornado, survived too many things for her life to end now. Like this.

Inch by inch, she ran her hands along the sides but encountered only some useless small scraps of wood and a bundle of paper. The only things that might be helpful were two large boxes wrapped in what felt like burlap. If her parents had been on the road awhile, the boxes probably held supplies for the trip.

At the end of her options, she sat back to think.

Ridge would come after her, that much she was sure of. He'd see the fire and the vat of water she'd set heating for the wash and follow the tracks. He was good at tracking animals— and men who behaved like them.

Then another thought made her freeze. Ezekiel would kill Ridge without a second thought.

Oh God, she couldn't let that happen.

If only she could see trouble coming, feel the breeze on her face. She lay down and tried to get the hood off by scooting along the wagon bed. Several times she managed to pull it up a little, but it always caught on her chin or fell back into place.

Discouraged, she lay there listening for anything that might tell her what was going on.

How far did he intend to drive before darkness fell?

To take her back to New Zion would require days of travel. No, he wouldn't wait that long to try to whip her into obedience. Or, failing that, kill her.

He'd also eventually figure out that his son wasn't that far away.

Addie gave up trying to apply logic. There was none inside the head of a madman. God help her.

⚬﹏⚬

The hot sun signaled the noon hour, and Ridge hadn't been able to shake a bad feeling in his gut. He laid down the sledge-hammer he'd been using to break up the boulders and wiped the sweat from his face. He couldn't think of anyone else who could have him in their sights.

Nothing but random lawmen and bounty hunters.

But Addie had her own danger. Maybe? Cold sweat drenched him.

Jack came toward him, waving an envelope. Ridge went to meet him. "What is it?"

"Heard from the judge's clerk. You have to appear in court in Mobeetie."

Ridge's knees tried to buckle under the startling news. Finally. "When?"

"Don't know. They haven't set a date yet."

Why wasn't Jack smiling? He should be happy. Shouldn't he? "What are you not telling me?"

Jack was silent for a moment. "If the judge throws out Shiloh Duke's statement, you'll be arrested on the spot. Then there's the matter of the judge. Ever hear of Horace Greely?"

Ridge's stomach twisted. "Hanging Horace? Every outlaw around here's heard of him. Dammit!" Just his luck to get Greely. Hellfire and damnation! The cards were already stacked against him.

"Are you willing to roll the dice?"

This was the reason for the gnawing in his belly and the sense of doom. His experience with dice was that they always came up snake eyes. Only Ridge's luck stood between hanging and freedom, and Hanging Horace sat smack in the middle. He didn't have a good feeling.

"I'll have to think about it and talk to Addie, of course."

"It's a big step with an unclear outcome." Jack laid a hand on Ridge's back. "Let me know what you decide."

"Thanks for all you're doing. You're a good friend, Jack." Ridge strode toward the corral and Cob, his thoughts whirling. He had to get home. Why hadn't he considered that this might not go his way? If Addie wasn't in the picture, he wouldn't hesitate to try. But she was there now, and he wouldn't trade her for any piece of paper proclaiming his innocence. All the way home, he worried over what he was going to say to Addie. He wouldn't worry her, but neither would he lie if she asked directly about his chances.

"I'll tell her the bare minimum," he mumbled to Cob. "No more than that."

Only the farm was too quiet when he rode up—eerily so. He rode around back and dismounted, his gaze on the vat of water sitting on cold ashes. The basket of dirty clothes sat nearby.

His heart hammered as he ran for the back door. "Addie! Addie, where are you?"

Miss Kitty gave him a scolding, but there was no other sound in the house. His mouth bone dry, he tore through the rooms, but she was nowhere to be found. The gnawing in his gut that morning hadn't been for him. It had been sending a warning about Addie.

Maybe she'd gone for a ride with Bodie. Only Bodie was with his friends. Riding on her own? Not with the laundry sitting out. He hurried to the barn to find King there in his stall. Where was she? Ridge jerked off his hat and fisted a handful of his hair, staring into the distance—hoping, praying to see movement.

Calm down and figure this out.

Minutes ticked by as he studied the ground, reading what it was telling him. A man's large boot prints stood clear in the dirt, along with Addie's small ones. There'd been a scuffle. From there, only one set of footprints—large ones—led away. What happened to Addie? Panic crawled up Ridge's throat. The assailant must've picked her up and carried her.

Jamming on his hat, he lifted Cob's reins and followed the footprints to where a wagon had sat. He mounted up and began the hunt. The ruts left gashes in the dirt that he could see from Cob's back. Hopefully, they'd lead him right to the kidnapper—and Addie.

Ezekiel Jancy. The man had found her. And now he'd exact his retribution. She'd sworn never to reveal the boy's whereabouts, but if she didn't, Ezekiel would torture her. Ridge was sure of that.

In that case, Ridge would have to kill her father. He'd never taken pleasure in snuffing out the light in a man's eyes, but when it came to someone hurting Addie, he'd take particular pleasure in sending them to hell. Jancy didn't deserve mercy, nor would he get any.

There would be no turning the other cheek.

The timing was deep irony. He'd just received what was likely to be his only chance to clear his name, and now he was riding toward a man who had no right to take up breathing room on this earth. What he meant to do when he caught up with Jancy would definitely end his chances for a clear slate. It would put Ridge back on the run.

Dammit! When would the killing stop? When would he be able to live in peace? Maybe a man like him was destined to always live with a target on his back and the law on his trail.

Ridge urged Cob into a gallop. He had to get there in time. She shouldn't suffer at Ezekiel's hands for one more second.

The miles flew by under Cob's hooves, and the memory of the welts on Addie's back hovered in the forefront of his thoughts. He struggled to draw air and urged the gelding faster. "Come on, boy. We've gotta find her. She's everything to me."

The ruts in the dirt were easy to follow for a while, but in areas where the ground had hardened too much and resisted any trace, Ridge had to dismount and search until he picked the trail up again.

All of it ate up the hours, time he didn't have to spare. And he was ever mindful of the sun slipping lower and lower. He should have caught up with them already. A lumbering wagon was forced to crawl, whereas Cob was fleet of foot. Yet he didn't overtake them. Was it possible he'd followed the wrong set of tracks?

Where was his quarry?

Ridge rode to the top of a high escarpment and stared down at the world below.

But he saw no wagon. No travelers. No Addie. Nothing but endless desolation and an empty horizon.

Thirty-one

"ARE THERE NO TALL TREES, NO WATER IN THIS GODFORSAKEN part of Texas?" Ezekiel hollered. The wagon stopped, and the springs protested as someone—Ezekiel, Addie supposed—climbed down from the seat. "What am I supposed to use?"

Short cedar trees and thorny mesquite from the rough terrain they'd just traversed had badly scratched her arms. Her skin stung, but she couldn't rub them or even see the damage. Relying on her ears to tell her what was happening had become difficult at times.

Her mother said nothing, as usual. Addie pictured her sitting impassive, staring straight ahead. Reduced to a beaten-down shell of a woman.

Would her mother ever find her voice, take charge, and step into life? A bit too late for that. A person had to have courage and determination, and if Ingrid had possessed any, it had been crushed years ago. This was Addie's situation to manage. And now she had yet one more pressing need. It could be to her benefit though—and possibly provide a chance of escape.

"May I please take care of some personal business?" Addie asked in a firm, clear voice. "I don't require long, but it is urgent."

"No." His voice came from quite near on her left side. He was probably leaning against the wagon, staring at her. The gurgle of liquid told her he was drinking, and a sinking feeling knotted in the pit of her stomach. "You don't get any favors."

"I can feel you staring. I know you're looking at me. Why?"

"Trying to figure out how God wills you to die. Your death has to be in accordance with how you've chosen to live. You shall suffer for your sins, and they are many," Ezekiel spat. "So too shall your punishments be many."

The silence stretched, and Addie heard a quiet sob. Her mother?

"The wicked shall burn in an everlasting fire!" Ezekiel shouted, startling her. "You're an abomination unto the Lord! God said, 'If thy right eye offend thee, pluck it out and cast it from thee!' I have been commanded to rid the world of an unclean soul. You, Adeline Jancy, will be cast away and burn in the deepest pit of hell for your sins."

Terror gripped her. What was he going to do? Torture her first? "If I'm to die, I request time to relieve myself first. Mother can take me. Or don't you trust her either?"

Again silence. Had he walked away? At last he spoke, and the sound revealed he hadn't moved. "Very well."

"And I wish to see. Remove my hood, please."

"You're in no position to make demands or requests. Wives must submit themselves unto their husbands, children to their fathers. For I am the holy one." Someone grabbed Addie around the arms, and she found herself yanked from the wagon onto the ground. "Ingrid, you may get out of the wagon now. Take Adeline to the bushes for decency's sake, but cross me, and you'll share her fate."

Lighter footsteps came toward Addie, and the bindings were removed from her hands. As she sat and rubbed her wrists, she heard Ezekiel mutter to himself, "Why aren't there any rivers? I should've crossed one at some point. I must make Adeline obey my commands as the Almighty ordained."

Gentler hands taking charge of her belonged to her mother, and they silently moved away from the wagon. A mesquite branch caught Addie's face, the thorns delivering a stinging scratch to her cheek through the fabric. Tears sprang to her eyes, but after blinking several times, she discovered a tear in the black hood that let in light and allowed her a limited view.

"This is good." Her mother stopped her and pushed her down.

Addie obeyed. For now. Her brain was whirling. She would try to get a clear picture of where they were before she escaped. Until then, she had no idea which way to run.

"Mother, please remove this hood. We can both leave, and you can be free of this miserable life. You can't be happy with him. He treats you worse than an animal."

Her mother stayed silent. Ever dutiful. A caricature of the person she used to be.

"In fact, he cares more for a nasty cockroach than he does you." Addie finished and stood. Angling her head, she was able to see her mother through the hole in the hood, and what she saw made her blood boil.

Ingrid Jancy's battered face and black eye told the story of her latest beating at the hands of a man who'd once sworn to love her. But then, he'd never loved anyone other than himself.

"I'm sorry for you, Mother," Addie said softly. "I wish I could've saved you, but I could barely save myself. You've taken the brunt of his anger far too long and it's time to end this. You can if you want to. For years, he's convinced you that you're weak, but you're not. Be strong and stand up to him. It's the only way we can survive."

Her mother's expression didn't change from the impassive blankness. If she heard, she chose not to listen.

They turned to head back to the wagon, and Addie picked her way across the rocky ground, grateful to be able to see out of the small hole. The wagon sat near a crumbling one-room shack sitting in the dusky light. Ezekiel had picked up some boards and was nailing them together. What was he doing? Something said it involved her and his plans to end her life.

"Hold your tongue," her mother whispered. "And don't sleep tonight."

The quiet warning surprised Addie. Maybe there was hope for Ingrid, hope for them both, after all.

"Thank you, Mother."

They went the rest of the way in silence. Then, in a move that Addie hoped was for Ezekiel's benefit, Ingrid shoved Addie to the dirt at his feet. She cried out and rolled to escape a kick. Her mother resumed her silent place on the wagon seat. Slowly, Addie stood.

Ezekiel's lips curled into a sinister smile as he whipped her around. In a flash, he bound her hands again, so tightly it sent sharp needles of pain through her arms.

When she could get her breath, she spat, "I'm not afraid of you. You rule over everyone through fear, but even as a child I saw your weakness. You can't take what's truly mine. That's what you hate in me. I won't let you tell me what to think, or how to feel."

"Shut up!"

"You'll never take control of my thoughts. You make people believe you're God, but you're nothing but Satan. I see it, and so did Jane Ann. That's why I will never ever let you have your son."

A jarring slap forced her head to the side, and her teeth sank into her lip. Shards of pain crawled along her body, stealing her ability to breathe.

"I said shut up." Ezekiel picked up a hammer and brandished it.

While she hated letting him think he'd won, she acknowledged the danger in continuing. She sat down to watch him, and soon fear crawled up her throat, strangling her.

He was fashioning a large cross out of the scavenged boards from the shack.

❧

Ridge retraced his path to the last clear set of prints and squatted to study them as the last of the daylight fell around him. He'd failed. He tore off his Stetson and held his head in his hands. Where was the woman he loved more than life itself? He'd sworn to keep her safe. What good was a promise if he couldn't keep it?

The light breeze bore the scent of wild roses, the flowers that she loved best. Or maybe that was his imagination, a fantasy caused by his incessant longing to see her. Hold her. Kiss her.

He straightened and jammed his hat back on. A cry tore from his lips, followed by an agonizing yell. "I don't know what to do! Addie!"

Silence answered back.

Cob nuzzled his shoulder as though offering sympathy. The sorrel kept it up until Ridge stroked Cob's neck. "I know. You miss her too."

Finally, Ridge wearily wiped his eyes and painstakingly followed the wagon ruts back the way he'd come, only to discover he'd taken the wrong fork in the road at first. He'd wasted precious time that Addie didn't have. The left fork took him down into a cedar brake and he found a trail left by a wagon breaking through the overgrown thicket. The person driving the wagon would've found it very difficult going, yet somehow by the looks of it, they'd persevered.

Darkness fell, and he kept riding through the night, driven by the horrors of what Addie was having to endure.

One time he let his eyes drift shut and almost slid from the saddle, catching himself at the last moment. Fear set in that he'd missed another turnoff on the trail, and he'd had to backtrack to make sure. After that, each time he felt his eyelids start to close, he slapped himself awake. He couldn't afford any mistakes.

Coyotes howled nearby, a reminder of the constant danger of night predators. They sharpened Ridge's senses and he moved with caution, driven on by one thought.

Addie needed him. She was depending on him to rescue her, and he wouldn't let her down. The conversation they'd had the night of the dance haunted him now. "If I do vanish, will you come looking for me?" Addie had asked.

Ridge repeated his answer to her aloud, "Better believe it, lady. No one had better try taking you away from me. No one. I *will* find you, Addie."

He meant that more than anything he'd ever uttered.

But when would he make good on the promise? Would he be too late?

Thirty-two

No MOON TRAVELED THE SKY THAT NIGHT AND IT SEEMED fitting. Ezekiel hammered the last board onto the makeshift cross, and Addie shivered at the cold hardness of his stone features. Fear, stronger than anything she'd experienced before, slid over her like the bony fingers of doom. Fear that was amplified by the liquor he'd consumed as he worked.

He stalked to her through the darkness, his black frock coat flapping like a crow's wings. "This can all be avoided if you tell me where my boy is. I'll give you one last chance."

She moved slightly to look at her mother through the hole in the hood covering her head. Ingrid Jancy remained motionless on the wagon seat where she'd sat for hours. Every bit of life inside her mother had shriveled and died. It appeared she awaited her own death now. It was impossible to think this was the same woman who had warned her a few hours ago.

Addie curled her mouth. "I'll tell you nothing, so whatever it is you mean to happen now, let's get it over with." She desperately worked at the ropes binding her hands, as she had been doing all along. But they still refused to loosen even slightly.

"And the fire of God came down from heaven!" Ezekiel yanked her violently to her feet and dragged her to the homemade cross, the width of which could support her. "Lay down on it," he snarled.

"No."

His fingernails dug into the tender flesh of her arm. "I. Said. Lay. Down."

Before she could form a reply, he shoved her backward onto the rough boards and sat his full weight on her. She couldn't breathe, couldn't move, couldn't see.

"Call me Messiah," he ordered, his nose touching hers, his

breath foul, and the hate emanating from him rolling over her in waves. "Say it!"

"You haven't the power to make me lie. You will never be the most holy. Not even close."

Ezekiel whipped the hood from her head and she stared into the face of a man who'd clearly gone mad. The rage pouring off him terrified her.

Where was Ridge? He'd vowed to come after her if she got taken. He always kept his promises. Though Addie's mouth was parched, she worked her tongue. "I hate you more than I thought I could ever hate anyone. You're evil."

His rage exploded. He landed a right fist to her jaw, followed by the left to her throat. Excruciating pain shattered inside her and spread through her body. She couldn't breathe. Her lungs refused to take in air. For several long moments, she gasped and struggled to keep the stars twinkling at the edge of her vision from closing into utter blackness.

When she was able to drag in air and blink away the darkness, she realized she was being stretched, her joints crying in agony. Ezekiel had untied her wrists only to lash her hands, arms, and legs tightly to the cross. Her shoulders were on fire, and she wondered if he'd pulled them from their sockets. Immense pain blinded her. She couldn't move when he dragged her, bumping over the uneven ground, to the wagon bed and propped the symbol of Christianity against the wooden gate. Now that her full weight rested on her ankles, Addie screamed with the unbearable pain.

Through it all, her mother never moved a muscle, never seemed to blink.

Maybe Ingrid Jancy had gone as mad as Ezekiel. His cross erected, he calmly reached for a second full bottle of whiskey and guzzled it.

Oh God, where was Ridge?

A few minutes later, Ezekiel staggered to the dilapidated shack, ripped off more boards, and built a fire, after which he must've remembered Ingrid. "You may get down from the wagon now, Wife!" he yelled, raising the bottle again to his lips.

Silently, her mother climbed down and moved stiffly to the fire as though she were a puppet carved from wood. After a while, with no mention of food, both Addie's parents laid down on opposite sides of the fire.

Don't sleep tonight, her mother had whispered.

Addie didn't know what that meant, but she had no intention of closing her eyes. A prayer on her lips, she went to work on the ropes binding her. The night progressed as quiet as a monastery, but despite all her efforts, the ropes held firm with little to show for her work except blood growing slick over her wrists. Her whole body was a raw mess, from Ezekiel's rough treatment, the battering from the wagon ride, and the splintered wood she lay on. The largest pain came from her jaw and throat, and only time would tell if she'd bear permanent damage.

It scared her to death that she might lose her voice again, that even if she ever saw Ridge again, she might not be able to tell him that she loved him. To never have the chance to tell him again would be her greatest regret.

The campfire sank to ash and went out, plunging her into thick gloom. Not long after that, the rustle of clothing alerted her to someone's approach in the moonless night. Her father? She prayed it wasn't Ezekiel but tried to ready herself for more torture.

The form stealing toward her materialized from the darkness, and Addie breathed easier. Though her mother jumped at the slightest noise, she kept coming. What was Ingrid's plan?

She pulled out a knife and climbed into the wagon. In moments, she began sawing through the ropes. Her voice was quiet and resigned. "I'll have you free soon. Run as far and fast as you can, Adeline. I won't be able to hold him back once he wakes."

"He'll kill you, Mother. You know that." This was the first time she'd spoken since Ezekiel had punched her in the throat, and she was relieved to still have her voice.

Ingrid's dirty hair fell over her face and her eyes were dull. "I'm already dead. Have been for a very long while. This way someone can put me in the ground. Please forgive my failings and try to think of me with kindness."

Ezekiel muttered something and made a gravelly sound. Both women froze.

Please don't let him wake up now.

He coughed once, then rolled over. Every nerve and muscle taut, Addie couldn't bring herself to relax.

Finally, the last of the ropes fell away. Addie stood and kissed her mother's cheek. "Come with me. We can both escape him. I don't want to leave you behind."

"It's too late for me. Now go." Ingrid slipped the knife in her pocket. "Go."

Addie glanced around. She didn't know where she was or what direction to run. She only knew she had to pick one. She grabbed her mother's hand. "Run away with me."

"I can't. I'll hold you back. Go."

Wasting precious seconds arguing was crazy. Addie turned her mother loose, made out the wagon ruts, and began to retrace the path toward home as fast as she could. Her heart pounding, she'd taken only a few long strides into the brush when Ezekiel roared awake. "Where is she? You stupid, stupid woman!" he hollered.

Three loud cracks echoed through the night, telling her Ingrid's torture had begun anew. For a moment, Addie almost turned back to help the woman who'd risked her life to save her. But now Ezekiel was tearing through the brush after Addie, hate in his heart, blood on his hands—and killing on his mind.

❧

Worry crawled up Ridge's neck like a big, black tarantula. Every second counted, and yet he had to keep backtracking because he wasn't paying close enough attention or had caught himself dozing off.

With no moon, the night was one of the darkest in recent memory. The clouds hid the stars, so not even a sliver of light dotted the sky.

"Whoa." Ridge reined to a stop. "We can't keep going, Cob. I don't want to kill you." He wearily dismounted beside a large scrub oak and built a fire. A few winks while he waited for dawn would refresh him. Until he could read signs, pressing on blind wouldn't do Addie any good. Hopefully, Ezekiel would sleep too and leave her safe for a few hours.

Feeling more alone than he'd been in his entire life, Ridge put his head in his hands. He whispered into the night, "Wherever you are, Addie, know this. Love for you spills from the deepest part of my soul. You're worth more than all the gold on earth, and I will bring you home. Mark my words."

Thirty-three

RUN FASTER! OH GOD, HE WAS COMING! ADDIE GASPED FOR AIR, her heart pounding against her ribs.

She turned to look behind her and ran into a mesquite tree. It knocked her backward, the thorny branches scratching her face and arms. Stinging pain ricocheted through her, taking her breath. A sob burst from her mouth. If only she could see! But the thick blackness of the night was as impenetrable as that hateful hood.

The thrashing in the branches told her the devil was closing in. She had to keep going.

Her legs burning from the mad dash, she struggled to her feet, wiping her nose. She squinted through the darkness for a place to hide but saw nothing nearby other than mesquite and cactus. Maybe she'd find a ravine or gully up ahead, somewhere to hunker down out of sight.

"Where are you, girl?" Ezekiel bellowed. "I'm gonna find you one way or another." Voices carried a great distance at night on the prairie; still, he sounded very close.

A loud squawk on her right startled her. She must've leaped a foot high. Just an animal of some sort. She tried to calm her trembles, her heart racing.

A twig snapped behind her. Addie swung around, her fists clenched tight, but no one stood there. Maybe that noise was an animal as well.

She began to gather her confidence. She could escape. Ezekiel was behind her, and if she kept running, she could stay ahead. Three long strides carried her to the shadow of a thick group of saplings and a creek that wound through the plains.

Had they passed the creek earlier? Ezekiel had been muttering about not finding water. Had she somehow left the trail?

Addie stopped and strained to see through the heavy gloom. A rustle came from the right. She whipped around that way.

An arm shot from the night. Bony fingers curled around her shoulder in an unbreakable grip.

A mouth lowered to her face. "You thought you'd get away from me," Ezekiel snarled. "You can't escape the hand of God! You shall be punished for your sins!" The smell of liquor gagged her and made her stomach roil.

The spit dried in Addie's mouth, and her tongue worked to speak, to say something, anything. Finally, she managed words. "My husband is looking for me, and when he finds us, he'll make you wish you'd never come to outlaw country. If you want to live, you'll turn me loose. Now."

"You'll be struck down for your arrogance. You'll beg God to save you, but it's far too late for that." He grabbed a handful of her hair and dragged her. Where? Back to the camp?

Fiery pain filled her head and throbbed in her temples. She tried to twist her body around to kick him but found it impossible. She opened her mouth and let out the loudest scream she could, yelling until her throat ached. "Ridge! Ridge! Help! Help me! Over here! I need you!"

If Ridge was anywhere close, he'd hear and come running. But they made it back to the wagon with Addie's prayers unanswered.

Her mother had crawled underneath the wagon. She didn't move as they approached, so Addie didn't know if she was alive or dead. All she knew was that her one, and probably last, chance to escape had met with failure.

It was over. Ridge was not coming. Tears bubbled in her eyes but she refused to let them fall. She'd show no weakness.

And now she was entirely at the mercy of New Zion's madman.

❧

Ridge awoke with a start, someone calling him in his dream. Addie. The dream seemed so real. He scrambled to his feet. "Addie! I'm coming!"

He kicked dirt on the fire and leaped into the saddle, straining to listen. "Let's go, Cob. Let's go find her. She's alive, and she needs us."

The bit of shut-eye he'd gotten had helped, and the sky had begun to lighten. It would be dawn soon.

Then God help the man who'd taken his wife.

Ridge pulled one of his Colts from the holster and checked the cylinder. Full. He then checked his twin Colt and found it the same. Now he was ready for whatever he encountered. Someone was going to die. God willing it wouldn't be him, but if it was Ridge's time to go, he was taking Ezekiel with him.

The screams came again. Surely, he hadn't imagined the pure terror. But wait a minute. Red foxes could sound like a woman screaming. Was it only that? Dammit! He clutched his head.

Minute by minute, the sky was changing from dark to gray. He had no trouble seeing the trail. Steadily, he rode across the unyielding terrain that at times stopped him cold, praying, willing that Addie be all right. If he found her dead…

He drew in a shuddering breath and blinked hard. "I won't. She'll be alive," he ground out into the wind. Addie was a tough woman, and she was calling for him.

He would not disappoint her.

❧

Addie's chin quivered as she sat waiting for whatever came next. Ezekiel had bound her hands again, then tied a rope around her neck. He gripped the end of it in one fist and held a loaded gun in the other.

He'd dozed off and on through the last of the night but never slept for very long. Her mother still had not moved under the wagon.

The sky lightened to a shade like silver pearl, and fear lodged in Addie's heart for what the morning would bring. Whatever new trials loomed on the horizon, she prayed for the strength to meet them with grace and courage.

This was her Armageddon. If she had to battle Ezekiel by herself, so be it.

Her raw, bloody wrists stung, and she could scarcely breathe with the rope so tight around her throat. She closed her eyes and pictured the face of the man she loved. Memories of their time together washed over her, calming her nerves. Lying in his arms, his lips on hers, she'd found great peace and happiness.

He'd taught her to forget the past, to focus on the things she could change and keep her eyes on the future. She knew she had a reason and a purpose for being in the world. That she had an obligation to leave things in better shape than she'd found them. She hoped she'd left something good and lasting in the short time she'd had.

The cool morning air made her shiver. She wished for a fire instead of the gray ashes. Squawking overhead drew her gaze toward the dawn, and there in formation were three or four dozen geese flying south for the winter. As she stared, they made a design, a loose heart in the sky above.

Ha! Now she was seeing things. Maybe pain and hunger had messed with her head.

As though he'd read her mind, Ezekiel got up and yelled toward his wife. "Woman, cook me something! Have it ready when I get back." Then he swung his attention to Addie. "We'll get to the Lord's business now."

Panic gripped Addie. Her heart beat so hard it tried to jump out of her chest.

Her mother roused and climbed out from under her shelter. Addie winced at her black eye and new bruises. Ingrid didn't meet her stare but kept her eyes down as she'd been taught. The man of the house was always superior and must be obeyed with no questions.

Silently, Ingrid lugged a box from the wagon, pulled out a skillet, some potatoes and onions, and a can of lard. Ezekiel kicked her, but not all the blows landed. Ingrid had gotten pretty good at dodging his feet.

She needed to relieve herself but knew not to ask. No, he'd show her no favors. She was an outcast, a sinner of the worst sort, and doomed to die by his hand any moment.

Ezekiel stared at her, picking his teeth. "I found me some water last night while I was chasing after you, girl. The Lord's commanded me to baptize you, make you clean before we get to the rest. You're a filthy heathen!" He stood and towered over her with a raised fist. "Living with a bunch of murdering, thieving outlaws. Laying up in bed with one. Letting him touch you and more. Do you carry his whelp?"

"I'd be happy to have his child. Ridge Steele is my husband by anyone's law, and I love him—" A brutal kick cut her words short. She took the pain inward, swallowing a cry. She stared up at him, her chin raised. "Get it over with. Whatever you have planned, just do it."

Taunting him might not've been the wisest thing to do. He yanked her up by the rope around her neck. The violent wrenching strangled her for a long moment before he loosened the taut hemp cord.

Her mother never spared them a glance, but kept her head down, slicing and stirring.

"It's time!" he yelled, pulling her along behind him. "God has willed you to die, and die you will. I am His right arm, a light in the wilderness, a brother."

"You're crazy!" Addie screamed back. "You're a crazy, vengeful lunatic!"

She struggled with all her might to stay on her feet. He'd not stop if she fell. Her frantic heartbeat and rapid breathing sent her body into shock. Her head swam, and the ground whirled around her. Where was Ridge? Didn't he care about her? Was she just someone he'd whiled away time with?

No, he loved her. He'd said so many times. Ridge Steele loved her.

Don't descend into Ezekiel's madness.

They reached a pool of water fed by the creek she'd seen the night before. Ezekiel didn't stop. He walked straight into the pool, pulling her after him. The water only reached his chest by the time he got to the center. If she could stay on her feet, she'd be all right.

But the water inched higher and higher up her chest, and fear held her in its grip.

"Adeline Jancy, I, the New Messiah, cast out this devil that's inside you." With that, Ezekiel put his hands on her head and pushed her under.

Addie held her breath, twisted and turned to escape his clutches, but found it impossible to break his hold. Her starved lungs exploded, sending pain through her body. She put her shoulder against his chest and pushed but couldn't get a grip or budge him.

She worked her wrists with feverish desperation, trying to free them. Her strength was fading. Her air had almost run out.

This watery grave held her bound as sure as quicksand.

She had been born Adeline Jancy, daughter of New Zion's false messiah. Here she would die. The wife and equal partner of Ridge Steele.

Thirty-four

THE SUN'S FIRST RAYS GLISTENED ON A WAGON UP AHEAD, THE horses still hitched to it. Gun drawn, Ridge raced into the clearing, his glance collecting the dying fire, a half-empty box of supplies, and a decaying shack that someone had once called a home.

Then his gaze fastened on something else that sent horrifying alarm whirling inside his head. He dismounted hoping, praying that his eyes were playing tricks on him.

A crude cross rested on the ground. Lengths of rope. A clump of golden hair. Blood.

He picked up the hair and tested the satiny texture between his thumb and forefinger, then held it to his lips. Roses. Addie.

A low cry rose in his heart, and Ridge sank to his knees. He was too late. He'd arrived too late to save his beloved Addie.

Slowly, his thoughts settled enough to allow logic. If she was dead, where was her body? There should at least be a grave, even a shallow one. Making sure he hadn't overlooked loose dirt, he took a long moment to listen to what the land, the birds, were telling him.

Evil, dark and deadly, permeated the air and the soil. But not death itself.

Strange that no one was around. A noise alerted him. Someone or something was scurrying through the brush. From the way they were moving, a person, not an animal. Maybe they had Addie. He wanted to call out to her, but he had to remain silent and it cost him dearly.

His heart hammered in his chest and sweat dotted his forehead.

Gripping his Colt, he kept low and rushed toward the sound as quickly and quietly as he could. He knew this place, a watering hole fed by a stream. He'd been here before.

Loud voices reached him. A woman's voice—and a man's. Angry, threatening yells. Curses.

Breathing hard, Ridge burst through a ring of saplings that rimmed one side of the pool, his eyes on a thin woman standing on the bank. She was battered and bruised; her straggly hair and slovenly appearance made her look like a vagabond of some sort.

"Did I give you permission to leave the campfire? Get the hell back to the wagon!" thundered a man in the middle of the water. "You know the rules!"

What was the shouter doing? Ridge strained to look and finally realized he was holding someone under the water. He was drowning someone.

It had to be Addie! Gripping his Colt, he stepped into the water. No one noticed him.

Before he could go deeper, the woman raised a rifle that had been hidden by the fabric of her skirt. "Rules be damned! God knows I've suffered long enough and remained silent while you hurt my children. Then that innocent girl and her child…that was the end of you and me."

Was that Addie's mother? It seemed so.

Ridge stared, frozen as the woman put the man in her sights. Fear strangled him. She could miss and hit Addie. "No! Wait!" Ridge ran toward her, waving his arms.

"I hate you with every bone in my body, Ezekiel Jancy! Say hello to the devil! If *he'll* even have you" With those words, she pulled the trigger.

Ridge watched in horror as Ezekiel's head exploded. Slinging his Colt aside, Ridge dove into the water and took long, sweeping strokes toward the center of the pond. *Addie!*

She hadn't floated to the top. She should have if she was alive.

No! She couldn't be dead.

He dove deep but the murky water blinded him. Desperate, he felt his way through the muck, searching for any sign of Addie. His lungs hurt with the need to fill them and he finally had to rise to the surface to gulp in more air before going back down. She hadn't given up on him, and he would never give up on her.

Frantic fear gripped him. She'd been down so long—who knew how long before he'd even arrived on the scene. He'd seen no thrashing or movement of any kind, but Ridge refused to listen to reason.

She might still be alive—if he could only find her.

It seemed like an eternity had passed by the time his fingers brushed fabric on the bottom of the pond. With a firm arm around her, he pulled her up and swam for shore.

"I have her." Mrs. Jancy helped get Addie onto the bank where Ridge untied her hands. The sight of the deep lacerations around both her wrists sickened him. Her white face terrified him, froth thick around her mouth. She lay deathly still.

Everything had been in vain.

Ridge let out an ear-piercing scream and pounded the ground. This wasn't supposed to happen. She couldn't leave him. They'd barely begun to love.

Tears rolling down his face, he began to say the long-forgotten words of a prayer.

A reply sounded in his ear. "And I will lay sinews upon you, and will bring up flesh upon you, and cover you with skin, and put breath in you, and ye shall live; and ye shall know that I am the LORD."

The same God that put breath in each person could make Addie live.

Something he'd once seen penetrated the horror, and a voice inside told him what to do.

Ridge rolled her onto her side and pounded her back. "Come on. Breathe, Addie." Nothing. Though he knew it might be too late, he clung to hope for a miracle.

Just one miracle. Please.

Panic rose and swamped him. Time worked against them, ticking off each second.

Tears rolled down Mrs. Jancy's face. She squatted and vigorously rubbed Addie's arm and patted her hand.

Returning Addie to her back, Ridge gently opened her

mouth, pinched her nose, and placed his lips to hers, creating a seal of sorts. He softly blew into her mouth. Her chest rose. He gave her three puffs.

Then three more.

Again and again, he repeated the process.

He was about to give up in despair when she suddenly coughed. Ridge rolled her to her side so she wouldn't choke, and water gushed from her mouth. When it stopped, he laid her back.

Her eyes fluttered and opened. She stared up at him for long seconds before she spoke. "You came."

"I got a late start, but I rode as hard as I could." He smoothed back wet strands of hair from her face. "I didn't know if I'd get here soon enough. You scared me."

"I'm sorry. I tried so hard to live."

"Thank God for your stubborn determination."

Addie gripped his arm, her eyes clouding with raw fear. "Ezekiel?"

"Dead. He can't hurt you anymore."

Addie put a weak hand on his jaw. "Oh, Ridge. You were trying so hard to get the charges dropped, and now this."

"I wasn't the one to pull the trigger this time."

Mrs. Jancy moved to sit beside Ridge. "It was me. I killed him. He had to be stopped, so I did it."

"Mama, I'm sorry."

"Don't be. You were right. No one was safe with him alive."

Ridge finally got a good look at Mrs. Jancy. Her black eye, battered face and hands told a story of horrible abuse. No one would blame her for putting a bullet in the man who'd done all that.

"Help me up, dear. I can't lay here all day when we have to get ready to leave." Addie glanced at her mother. "Where will you go, Mama?"

"I'll go get your sisters, then I don't know. We can't stay in New Zion."

Addie sat up with Ridge's help. "Live in Hope's Crossing

with us. It's a good, decent place where you can start over fresh, no questions asked."

"We'll see." Her mother rose and trudged toward their camp.

Ridge lifted Addie. She let out a sigh and snuggled against his chest. He tightened his arms around her, his heart over-flowing with gratitude. They'd been granted another chance.

While Addie helped her mother prepare a quick meal from the limited supply of food, Ridge unhitched the poor horses from the wagon and led them to the stream to drink. He fished Ezekiel Jancy's body from the pool so it wouldn't taint the water and covered the despicable man with rocks. Two hours later, they were on their way home.

Ridge tied Cob to the back of the wagon and everyone rode together. Addie and her mother had quite a lot to say to each other, and Ridge stayed quiet, happy they could repair their relationship.

It was late afternoon when they reached the farm. Bodie ran out, worry on his face, throwing his arms around like they belonged to a floppy doll. "What happened? I came back an' everyone was gone!"

"A long story." Ridge set the brake and climbed down. "Addie's father took her, and I went after them. Say hello to Mrs. Jancy, Addie's mother. She'll stay with us as long she wants."

"Welcome, ma'am. Do you know how to cook? I'm starv-ing flat to death."

Ridge died laughing. Trust Bodie to get right to the heart of the matter in two seconds flat. But laughter was welcome after the harrowing ordeal. He would never again take anything for granted—especially Addie. By all rights, she should be lying in a grave. They'd cheated death by such a slim margin and that reality brought a chill up his spine.

Bodie helped him unhitch the wagon. "Is Addie okay? She's bruised and cut up bad and looks horrible. Her ma too."

"It'll take some time, but I think she'll be as good as new."

"She didn't say anything to me. Has she lost her voice again?"

"No. She's just had a rough time. Give her a little extra help until she's recovered. All right?"

"Sure."

In hindsight, Ridge wished he hadn't said anything to the kid, as Bodie immediately made a pest out of himself, insisting on doing everything, and just getting in everyone's way.

Ridge's gaze never left Addie. She seemed hollow inside, her eyes haunted. Without a word, she staggered up the stairs and lay on their bed, staring into nothingness.

Mrs. Jancy wiped her eyes, then pulled herself together and set about cooking supper. Addie had always said her mother was weak, but without Ezekiel, she appeared to get much stronger and surer of herself. Maybe it was being away from her husband that'd done it.

Finally getting tired of tripping over Bodie, Mrs. Jancy took him aside. "Thank you for being so kind and helpful. I wonder if you could fetch me some onions and turnips from that garden over there. I can't bend over that well, and my old knees are pretty creaky. Then when you get back, you can sit at the kitchen table and cut up the turnips for me. I'd dearly like to hear all about your parents that you miss so much."

"Yes, ma'am. I can surely do that."

"Bless you, boy. You're a godsend."

Right then, Ridge knew that Mrs. Jancy—Ingrid—was a saint. Though she had no sons, she seemed to know exactly how to care for a half-grown man who grieved for his parents and home.

❧

Addie lay low for a week. Ridge didn't know how to help her recover except to give her some space and time to heal, but it killed him to feel so helpless. He held her in his arms at night and let her cry, then watched her during the days, careful not to hover like a brood hen.

Friday came, and Ridge saddled the horses. King would give her the comfort he couldn't.

Addie was sitting in the parlor, Squeakers in her lap, staring out the window when Ridge entered. "How about a ride with me? The horses are champing at the bit for exercise, and I can't stand much more of King's moping around. Those sad eyes are getting to me and I think you could cheer him up."

"I suppose." She sighed and rose. "I'm sorry I haven't been much good lately. I don't know why I can't get on with life. I'm scared."

Ridge folded her in an embrace. "What happened to you was beyond understanding. You endured torture and pain that few others could. Your brain has to heal as much as your poor body. It's something you can't rush. But you'll get there."

She leaned back to look up at him. "I don't deserve you. You're so patient."

"Don't make me out to be a saint, because I'm not." He covered her bruised lips with his and let the tender kiss do his talking.

Addie broke the kiss. "I thought the whole ordeal was a test of faith—faith that you'd arrive to save me. Faith that God wouldn't let evil win. Faith that good would triumph over hate. But I discovered it was a test of strength. I had to be stronger than him, keep looking for a way to escape, never giving up even when it seemed impossible. Does that make sense?"

"Perfect sense." Ridge breathed easier and his worry lifted. She'd started to examine what had happened and put everything in compartments. She wasn't back to herself yet, but she was getting closer. "You're the strongest lady I know."

"Thank you for letting me work through this. I have to do it by myself."

"I know."

They walked through the house arm in arm and out the kitchen door. Addie went to King and laid her face against his neck, taking deep breaths. Ridge kept silent, unmoving, watching the blankness fade and love paint itself across her features. Long moments passed until she lifted her head. She rubbed the space between King's dark eyes, caressing, massaging. "Hello, boy," she crooned softly. "I've missed you."

King snuffled and nuzzled her shoulder. It appeared to Ridge that the bond between horse and woman was healing both.

When she was ready, he lifted Addie into the saddle. Together, they rode toward their secret place.

The green oasis seemed even more beautiful and serene than ever. No swimming this time. Instead, they rested and soaked up the peace it offered. Addie sat with her back against Ridge, her fingers making unseen designs on his wrist. With the blue sky arcing overhead and the horses nibbling on the grass, it seemed almost perfect. Ridge moved her hair aside and kissed the sensitive skin of her neck.

"I never thought I could love anyone as much as I do you, Addie. But I'm finding that feeling grows stronger each day." He chuckled softly. "I can't imagine what it will be like when I'm old and gray. Hopefully, I won't explode into a huge bonfire."

"You won't."

"And what makes you so sure, pretty lady?"

"Because I'll hold you so close, it'll keep everything all inside."

He smiled. "You'd do that for me?"

"I'd change the world for you." She swiveled to face him. "There is nothing on this earth I wouldn't do for you. We're a matched set, Ridge Steele, and you've already given me more happiness than my heart can hold."

"I owe you an apology." Emotion roughened his voice. "I was trying so hard to get to you, and everything worked against me—the black night, losing the trail, dozing off and almost falling from the saddle. Good Lord! I could've spared you so much torment had I found you sooner." He kissed the healing wound around her wrist. "I failed to keep my promise."

"Shush! Stop. You got there in time, Ridge. That's what counts. You pulled me from the bottom of that water and blew life back into me. Don't look back. We have to move forward."

"You're a wise lady." He stretched out in the grass and Addie laid her head on his stomach.

He told her about the voice in his ear as he worked feverishly to save her. "I can't explain fully what that was, but I trusted in the scripture and prayer, knowing how God leads us. Sometimes, at the end of the day, trust is all we have left."

Addie propped herself on an elbow, studying him. "Do you want to resume your ministry?"

"No." He wound a strand of her hair around his finger. "Nothing like that. But I do feel called to help the youth so they won't make the same mistakes I did."

"That's wonderful, Ridge." She lay back on his stomach. "I'm glad."

They lay like that for a good while, and he even dozed a little, but it soon came time to head back. Ridge helped her onto King's back and mounted Cob.

"Thank you for making me ride, Ridge. I needed this to clear my head."

He winked. "I thought you might."

"I won't say anything to Dr. Mary, or she'll think you tried to horn in on her business."

Ridge threw back his head in hoots of laughter. His joy wasn't about what Addie had said, but that she felt up to teasing him at all. She joined in, and the sound of her happiness swelled up inside him.

Maybe soon she'd want to do more at night than be held. He missed running his hands over her body, kissing every inch of her.

"Well, Mrs. Steele, I'm pleased to see you up to teasing."

"Me too."

"Do you know what your mother's plans are? Her bruises are healing, and she seems to be feeling better."

"She doesn't know what to do, Ridge. Mama isn't up to traveling back home by herself, and she wants to stay here, but she also needs to get my sisters. Any suggestions?"

"Sending money for them to ride the stagecoach would be best and I'll be happy to arrange that. Or I suppose I could go after them. That would mean I'd have to leave you for two weeks or longer. Depending on what I'd have to do once I got there, it could be closer to a month. I prefer to send funds, but I'll do whatever you wish."

"No, I don't want to be separated. I think sending for them would be best. Let's do that tomorrow. I'd like to see them settled before winter sets in."

"Then we'll do that in the morning. Anything else? I still see worry lines on your face."

"I'm really concerned that I haven't heard from Zelda Law. Something's happened. The arrangement was supposed to be that she'd bring the boy to me when I got released from prison."

"We'll send a telegram to her brother at Seven Mile Crossing while we're in town in the morning. Anything else bothering you? I'll be glad to fix all your problems."

"No, that's about it."

Her beautiful smile blinded Ridge. Without that dark cloud of her past hanging over her, he would bet that things were going to be even better than before.

Thirty-five

ADDIE HUMMED AS SHE RODE BESIDE RIDGE IN THE WAGON THE next morning. Her mother had stayed behind at the property, unable to face people. Addie's face was also a mass of bruises and cuts, but it didn't bother her now. She saw her wounds as a badge of survival.

She smoothed the green dress she'd worn at her wedding. It seemed fitting to wear this one today. This was a new beginning as well, one free of her mad father. The slight breeze ruffled her hair, left down in curls the way Ridge liked it.

He leaned back and propped one boot on the high, wooden wagon box. "I'd better stay close by, or someone might make off with my pretty wife. You look especially beautiful."

"Thank you for saying so, but I don't think you have to worry."

"No?"

She waved her ring finger. The morning sun's rays caught on the silver band. "I'm spoken for."

"Indeed you are, Mrs. Steele, and everyone had best take heed."

Addie inched closer, and he put his arm across the back of the seat. She never tired of this game they played. Teasing and flirting had been sins all her life, and she'd never known why or the pleasure it gave. This man she'd married had taught her a lot about life and love and happily-ever-afters.

Although the day was just getting started, plenty of folks milled about the town. Addie and Ridge went straight to the telegraph office, sending a wire first to Addie's sisters, telling them to get packed and ready to come. Then another to Zelda Law's brother, inquiring about her and the boy. Addie prayed they'd get a reply soon.

"While we wait for the bank to open, why don't we get some coffee?" Ridge suggested.

Addie laughed and wagged her finger. "You don't fool me. You know if there's any gossip, you'll find it there."

Ridge gripped his chest in mock horror. "I'm hurt. I just want to keep my finger on the pulse of the town. As mayor."

When they opened the door, the racket inside the Blue Goose Café almost knocked Addie down. Everyone in town seemed to be at the eatery and excited about something. All the tables were filled, and they had turned to leave when Angus O'Connor waved them over. "Come and join us."

Addie led the way, and they took the last two seats at the table for eight, greeting Dr. Mary, Jack, Clay, and the other two men. "What's going on?"

O'Connor grinned from ear to ear. "We're celebrating my purchase of the Wild Rose Saloon. But most importantly"—he took Dr. Mary's hand—"our upcoming wedding. My Margaret agreed to marry me after all these years."

"I had to wait until you got through sowing your wild oats, you old fool." The doctor kissed his cheek. "And to settle down. I'm too old to follow you from pillar to post."

"Congratulations to you both. I'm so happy for you." Addie found tears in her eyes. Nothing reaffirmed life better than two people in love.

The waiter came and took their order, and Addie listened to the chatter going on, not only at their table, but around the entire café. These were the best of friends, many of whom had fought side by side to make a town from nothing.

Though everyone shot Addie curious glances, only Jack spoke, quietly enough for only them to hear. "You seem to have tangled with a wild animal, Miss Addie. Anything you and Ridge want to tell us?"

Ridge took her hand and told the story, after which everyone murmured that it was a good thing Ezekiel Jancy was already dead, or they'd string him up by his heels.

Dr. Mary leaned across the table to speak to Addie. "Are you all right? Maybe I should check you out."

"Thank you for your concern, Doctor. I'll be fine in a week or two."

"If not, you come to see me."

"I will."

"Miss Addie, I hear you used to teach school. How about taking the position of schoolmistress?" Clay asked from across the table.

She shot Ridge a glance. "I don't know. Can I think about it?"

"Sure. You can get back to me."

The tea she'd ordered arrived, along with Ridge's coffee. As she sipped, she realized that she'd never been happier than she was at that moment in the Blue Goose Café, with friends who cared and wonderful rays of silver light streaming in the windows.

Outside the café, Ridge put a hand on Addie's waist, and they strolled toward the bank. The shades on the windows were raised, which meant Charlotte had opened for the day.

Just then, two gunshots rent the air in the direction of the new Capital Bank and Trust.

"Get down low, Addie!" Ridge pushed her into a doorway, drew his Colt, and raced toward danger. Jack ran from the hotel to join him and Clay wasn't far behind.

Breathing hard, Ridge pressed to one side of the bank door, Jack the other. Nodding to his friend, Ridge slowly turned the knob and burst into the building, keeping low and rolling. He stopped and came face-to-face with the jail escapee Pickens, lying dead on the floor.

A thin ribbon of smoke still curled from the gun Charlotte Wintersby gripped. Her ashen face, wide brown eyes, and heaving chest told the rest of the story.

Ridge got to his feet while Jack gently took the gun from her. Movement in the corner behind Ridge alerted him, and he swung around, his Colt pointed at a woman slowly raising her hands. She was wearing a long duster over a plain dress. She squeaked, "Don't shoot."

"Who are you?" Ridge barked.

"Texanna Starr."

He'd bet a shiny gold piece the name was a fake one. In fact, the only thing that was probably real about her was the color of her gray eyes. "Weren't you the one riding on top of the stagecoach and helped Pickens and Tiny get away?"

"Well, sort of."

Clay stepped over Pickens and the large pool of blood seeping from his cooling body. "Well, what is it, lady? You either were or you weren't!"

"I was."

"Why in God's name did you help them?" Clay asked.

"Pickens and I were married last month. He was my husband. I had to help him."

Clay checked her for weapons and found none, and Ridge put his Colt away.

Jack tied her hands. "You're under arrest."

"What the hell for?"

"Helping your husband and his friend Tiny get away, for starters. Secondly, I take it you were trying to help him rob this bank, but we'll get to that in a minute." Jack pulled a chair over. "Sit here and don't move."

A little color had returned to Charlotte's face. "I couldn't let them take the money."

"You risked your life. It's safer to turn it over." Ridge pulled a chair out for her, and she thanked him. "Tell us what happened."

"I had just opened up, and they burst through the front door. The man on the floor had a gun and told me to hand over all the money. The lady there gave me a burlap sack, and I went behind the teller's cage. I keep a handgun there for protection." Charlotte lifted a shaky hand to her forehead. "I pretended to fill the bag, then I came back around, pulled the gun from behind the sack, and fired. I didn't want to miss."

Texanna Starr groaned. "I don't know why I ever got mixed up with that man. He was rotten to the core. He said he'd watched the sheriff from the outdoor cell and saw the weak security. He thought robbing this green banker would be like taking candy from a two-year-old."

"Where's the other one—Tiny? Did he come along?" Jack prodded.

"He didn't want any part of this, so we went our separate ways. Pickens and me came back for the money. I'm such a fool." Texanna shook her head sadly. "He was going to take me to Denver and buy me pretty dresses."

Greed caught many a person. Ridge turned to Charlotte. "You're something, Miss Wintersby. I don't think we have to worry one bit about our money with you on the job."

"I have a spot open for a deputy, if you want it." Jack grinned. "You have a dead aim."

"Thank you for trying to make me feel better, but I just killed a man. I took his life. He was breathing one minute, and the next his blood was leaking all over my floor."

"He would've killed you if you hadn't, Charlotte." Addie stepped from the door and went straight to her friend. "If you're through, gentlemen, I'll take her to the café for a cup of hot tea. Her nerves need bracing."

"Good idea, sweetheart." Ridge glanced at Clay and Jack. "If we have any more questions, we can ask them later. And don't worry, Miss Wintersby, we'll have Pickens out of here and the mess cleaned up by the time you return."

"Thank you, Mr. Steele. It's been a most trying morning." Charlotte disappeared out the door with Addie.

"What happens to me?" Texanna asked.

"Good news." Jack grinned. "You get to sit in our jail for a while and enjoy the fresh air."

"For how long? I said I'm sorry. You can't put me out there in the open. A lady needs privacy."

"You should've thought about that, Mrs. Pickens." Jack pulled her up. "Lucky for you, we have a vacancy, but don't expect eating utensils to come with meals. You're eating with your hands."

Texanna tried to jerk away. "You're nothing but a…a…barbarian."

"I wonder what I'll find when I start looking? Will I learn you're wanted for other crimes? Let's go." Jack waded through the crowd that had gathered. "It's all over, folks. Your money's secure. Go about your business."

Ridge stared through the window and noticed a wagon lumbering into town, an old man and a kid on the front seat. He wondered what their story was and how they'd found their way to Hope's Crossing. Their town was changing in tune with the world outside their doors, and if he didn't change with it, he'd get left behind.

"Clay, have you ever thought about hanging up your gun?" Ridge asked.

"Almost every day. You?"

"Me too. Do you think we'll ever get the chance?"

"Maybe one day far off, if we're lucky."

"Yeah." Ridge shook himself and asked for some volunteers to cart Pickens to the cemetery. Then a couple to clean up Charlotte's floor. He'd made a promise.

Damn, he was tired.

Thirty-six

Addie cooked breakfast with her mother the following morning and made plans for her sisters' arrival. They'd be there in two weeks, as per the return telegram. "You're welcome to stay here until you find something more permanent."

Ridge filled his coffee cup and moved to the table. "I think I might have a solution."

"What do you have in mind?" Addie turned the sausage.

"Todd Denver's place. I don't know what the rent will be, but I'm sure Clay will keep it low." Ridge raised his cup to his mouth. "Of course, it's kind of small, but it has a nice loft and a little bedroom below. Denver used the loft for his book collection."

"That sounds perfect!" Addie beamed. "And yesterday, Martha Truman told me that Miss Quinn is looking for help in the dress shop."

Ingrid set the basket of fresh eggs next to the stove. "I haven't worked for many years."

The change in her mother had taken everyone by surprise. With her injuries healing, her hair combed, and clean clothes, Ingrid bore little resemblance to the woman who'd sat in the wagon staring through dead eyes. She now appeared years younger, and full of dignity and hope. Addie had sat for hours, talking with her mother and rekindling their relationship, something that she'd worried had ended so horribly wrong three years ago. She forgave her for not doing more, truly understanding now how much Ingrid had been a victim too.

"But you know how to sew, Mama. Everyone has always complimented your fine stitches." Addie gave her a hug. "You just have to get your confidence back. No one is ever going to beat you or yell when you do something wrong. Not again."

"My bruises—"

"They're healing and fading fast. Besides, no one in this town will stare at you. I look a lot worse than you do, and I did just fine yesterday. You're still a pretty woman, Mama."

Now that vibrant life had replaced the haunted, vacant look, her mother was beginning to find more self-esteem. It would just take time to complete the metamorphosis.

"You really think so?"

"Absolutely." Addie removed the cooked sausages and added more to the skillet.

"I agree with my wife." Ridge ran his finger idly around the rim of his cup. "You're exactly what that dress lady is looking for. You have experience, and you'll soon have the women in this town raving about your needlework as well."

Ingrid allowed a small smile. "You've convinced me. After we clean up from breakfast, I'd like to go into town and talk to the dress-shop owner. What was her name?"

"Miss Tara Quinn." Addie kissed her mother's cheek. "And while we're there, we might look in on the house."

Ridge propped his elbows on the table. "Before I speak to Clay, I really do need to know if it'll suit your needs. Like I said, it's a little small."

"Thea and Tola will soon be marrying and making their own lives. That'll just leave thirteen-year-old Remy at home." Ingrid's mind seemed to be whirling with all the possibilities. Addie loved seeing her mother's excitement build, like a child's at Christmas.

Ridge chuckled softly. "If your other daughters are as pretty and as capable as Addie, I can vouch that the men in this town will beat a path to your door, Mrs. Jancy."

"Please, just call me Ingrid."

"All right, Ingrid. If Denver's old house doesn't work, I'll build one. That'll take a while longer, of course." He stood and took her hand. "We're family now. It's really good having you here, and I'll help get you settled any way I can."

Tears filled Ingrid's brown eyes. She squeezed Ridge's fingers and whispered, "I had forgotten there are good men left. I'm very happy Adeline found you."

Addie swallowed the lump in her throat. "Me too, Mama."

With that settled, Addie turned her thoughts to the other telegram they'd sent—the one to Ben Halsey. They'd gotten no reply yesterday, but perhaps one had come this morning.

The screen opened and Bodie strode in. "Breakfast smells good." He went straight to the coffee. "Is it about ready? I'm starving."

Addie watched a grin spread on Ridge's face. The bond between him and Bodie grew stronger each day, and they were more like a real father and son than either knew.

"You're always as ravenous as a bear after hibernation, son." Ridge's eyes sparkled with amusement. "Pour me another cup while you're at it."

"Yes, sir." Bodie brought the pot to the table, along with his cup, and sat down. "I got up early and did the chores. Do you need anything else done? Sawyer and Henry want me to go fishing."

The respect Bodie always showed Ridge never failed to warm Addie's heart. She turned back to her cooking, a mist in her eyes. Through watching these two men form a relationship, the trust grow between them, she'd learned to trust as well. She'd opened her heart and let love inside. Addie had kept it locked for so long. Self-preservation made a person do strange things.

"You go and have fun," Ridge urged. "I can't think of anything else I need doing. You'll have to ride three miles over to the Washita River to find water deep enough to sink a hook."

"I reckon so."

"I've always wanted to dig out the little creek that runs through our land, widen and deepen it, but haven't found time."

Interest showed in Bodie's eyes. "Let's do it—you and me. Maybe Sawyer and Henry would help too."

Addie couldn't miss the excitement in the kid's eyes. He asked for so little.

"I 'spect we could. We'll tackle that once we're through with the work in town." Ridge caught Addie's stare and winked.

Warmth stole over her, and she came near to dropping an egg. He made her feel like a schoolgirl making eyes at the teacher. She hurried to finish breakfast. She had two hungry men waiting, and she loved them both with every fiber of her being.

⌘

Hope's Crossing had never looked more welcoming when Addie rode in, sitting between Ridge and her mother. The sun's rays cast a golden glow over the town she'd grown to love.

She glanced toward the back entrance where only a few large boulders remained. "Ridge, I didn't notice how much you'd gotten done yesterday. I guess the excitement over the bank holdup took my attention."

"We should finish today." He parked the wagon in front of his land office. "Then we'll begin to clear a road."

"It makes such a big difference. Amazing." Her glance fell on the outdoor strap-iron jail. Texanna Starr stood at the locked door, gripping the bars and staring. Addie felt a little sorry for her, although Texanna had gotten what she deserved. "Ridge, what is Jack going to do with that woman? She looks so forlorn."

"He'll take her to Mobeetie as soon as he's able." He lifted her down from the seat and went around to help Ingrid. "She deserves to pay for the poor choices she made."

"I know, but it just seems a little harsh to put her outside where everyone can jeer at her."

"I love your soft heart. We can't lose our compassion for one another. That's what separates us from wild animals." He kissed her temple. "I'll get the key to Denver's vacant house."

In short order, they walked over to the church. The building also served as a school, the schoolmaster's house tucked in behind. Addie had never seen it before this, but she was impressed with how nice Denver had kept his yard, planting flowers and saplings. The care he'd taken spoke of the kind of man he'd been. She was sorry to have missed making his acquaintance.

"What do you think, Mama? You're awfully quiet." Addie took Ingrid's arm, not surprised at the hopeful smile. Ingrid was coming alive again, experiencing happiness that she'd had too little of in her life.

"It's so pretty. I can see myself living here, being in charge of my own affairs for once. The girls will love it. Let's go inside."

"Yes, ma'am." Ridge unlocked the door. "After you, ladies."

The rooms were small, like Ridge had said, but the walls were freshly painted, and the whole house was clean. Addie climbed the ladder to the loft. "There's room for two beds up here. It's very spacious."

"Oh good," her mother said. "I like the space down here too. More than enough for my meager belongings." Ingrid turned in a circle as though picturing in her mind where everything would go. "Yes, this will be perfect for our needs."

Clay strolled through the door. "Glad you like it, Mrs. Jancy. Now, here's the deal. The house is yours free for as long as you want it, but there's a catch." His gaze shifted to Addie. "Not a catch, so much as a trade-off. Addie has to teach school. I built this place for the schoolteacher, and if I have to hire someone from outside, the house will be theirs."

Addie laughed, and she shook her finger. "You're full of tricks and hoodwinking."

"Will you teach?" Clay asked.

That was what she'd loved doing and had dreamed of going back to, except she hadn't seen a way. Teaching kids to read, write, and cipher gave her so much joy.

Ridge put an arm around her. "Take it. That's what fulfilled you before."

She looked up into the urging in his eyes. "Yes. Yes, I will take it."

"Excellent!" Clay handed her mother the keys to the house. "Welcome to your new home, Mrs. Jancy."

"You don't know what this means." Ingrid wiped away a tear. "Thank you so much. Me and my girls will be very happy here."

"I'm counting on that. Now if you'll excuse me, I have to meet my wife." Clay turned and went out the door.

Addie kissed Ingrid's cheek. "See what I mean about this town? No one looks down on you here or whispers behind your back. And the best part is that there's no whipping post. We're free."

"That's the hardest part to imagine," Ingrid whispered. "Free."

Ridge stood, hat in hand. "You can live life however you wish, Ingrid. You can move in anytime."

"How about today? Even if I have to sleep on the floor."

"Yes, ma'am. I'll put the word out for some furniture and see who's got some things to spare. Before night, you'll find you have what you need."

"I used to know people like that, a long time ago," Ingrid murmured.

"Let's go check on that dressmaking job, Mama." Addie kissed Ridge. "We'll come to your office once we're done, dear."

"Sounds good." Ridge put his hat on and left whistling.

The music was the sweetest Addie had ever heard. It meant he was happy and satisfied with life. She felt bad about putting off making love with him since her ordeal, although he'd never once pressured her. Ridge was giving her time to heal, as much inside as out. But she had this block that wouldn't let her past kissing just yet. Maybe soon.

❦

After Tara Quinn finished showing Ingrid around, the three women sat talking.

"Please don't judge me based on the bruises." Full of nerves, Ingrid smoothed her skirt. "My husband went into a rage. But don't worry about him coming around. He's dead. I'll be a good hand for you."

Addie took her mother's hand. "Everyone admires Mama's fine stitch, and she's fast. Loyal to a fault too. You'll have no reason to complain. I think your business will thrive if you take her on."

Tara patted her rich auburn hair, artfully swept back today into a low knot on her neck. Addie stared at all the jewelry that adorned her hands, neck, and ears. Four long strands of beads hung from her neck, and she wore long, dangly earrings. Rings flashed from almost every finger. She was certainly unlike anyone Addie had ever met, but she liked the warmth and humor in the dressmaker's blue-green eyes.

Why had the woman never married? She was pretty and about Addie's age. Surely she'd had suitors.

After several long minutes, Tara spoke. "I'll hire you on a trial basis to start off and give you four dollars a week. After you prove yourself, I'll give you a raise. It's the best I can do."

Relief shot through Addie, and she watched a happy smile form on her mother's lips.

"That's only fair. I can start work tomorrow if you wish." Ingrid stared out the window. "The sooner the better."

Tara reached for Ingrid's hands, surprising Addie. "We all have things that haunt us. Work will help fix that, but you need to move in and get settled first. How about starting Monday morning? I like to start new things on a Monday."

Ingrid nodded. "That will do fine. Thank you."

"We're going to make some beautiful creations together, Mrs. Jancy." Tara's necklaces tinkled as she showed them to the door.

Outside, Addie turned to her mother. "Is your head swimming yet?"

"I can't believe my turn of fortune. A place to live and a job, all in one morning. And you, Daughter, can teach school again. I remember how you loved your students." Sadness filled Ingrid's eyes. "I apologize for leaving you in that impossible situation and not taking you and your sisters somewhere safe. I was too scared of your father."

"I know. Let's not speak of this ever again. I want to forget those horrible years—and him. I've wiped his name from my memory. You should do the same."

"I loved him once, in the beginning, and he gave me you girls."

"I have no good memories, and I won't let the bad ones ruin our day." Addie forced cheer into her voice. "Let's go tell Ridge the news."

Thirty-seven

A LITTLE OVER A WEEK LATER, ADDIE AND RIDGE DROVE INTO the small community of Seven Mile Crossing. A couple in another wagon directed them to Ben Halsey's farmhouse.

A tall, thin man wearing suspenders, crushing a floppy hat in his hands, answered the door and let them inside. "Zelda's in here, Miss Addie. I haven't left her side to send you a telegram."

"I've been very worried and knew something must be horribly wrong."

"Yes, ma'am. She's in a bad way. She might not be able to hear you."

Supported by Ridge, Addie followed Ben into a bedroom and found Zelda on a bed. Ben waved her to a straight-backed chair next to her old friend. Addie took the blue-veined hand with its papery skin. "Zelda, I'm here. It's me, Addie."

The old midwife's eyes opened; her voice was weak. "Addie, child. It's good to see you."

Addie barely knew when the men left her alone with Zelda. "I made it through prison and married a wonderful man, Ridge Steele. He's an outlaw but a good man, and we love each other."

Zelda tried to talk, but her mouth was so dry. Addie spied a glass of water and wet the corner of a washcloth, then dabbed it on Zelda's cracked lips.

"Ezekiel?" Zelda asked.

"He's where he can't hurt anyone ever again. Mama shot him."

Surprise filled Zelda's eyes.

"Mama finally had enough and put an end to it. She's safe with me, living in Hope's Crossing. She's sent for my sisters and they should arrive any day."

"Good."

A scurry of little feet sounded, followed by a moment's silence outside the room. The door creaked open and she saw the three-year-old boy she'd protected for the first time since he was an infant. He was blond-haired, blue-eyed like his mother, and Addie's heart melted. Images of that long-ago night in the schoolhouse flitted through her head, despite her attempts to push them away. All the blood. The horror. How shaky her hands had been as she'd tried to help Jane Ann. Then, unable to save her, she'd watched the girl's eyes close for good.

Zelda smiled. "This is Nico, short for Nicolas."

"I'm so happy to finally meet you, Nico." Addie lifted him into her lap. "You're such a handsome little man."

He nodded and silently held up three fingers.

"I see. You're three years old. What a big boy."

Nico nodded.

"Zelda, thank you so much for keeping him safe. When you left with him that night, I didn't exactly know what I was asking of you." Tears filled Addie's eyes. "I'm sure it wasn't easy raising him."

"Ben helped."

"Thank goodness for that. I'll be sure to show my appreciation." Addie kissed the top of Nico's head. "I'll take him home now."

"We d—did it, Addie." A tear eased from the corner of Zelda's eye.

"Yes, we did."

"P—prison?"

"It was hard. I won't lie. But I made it. I would've done anything for Nico."

Hearing his name, he looked up with a grin. "Nico." His face serious, he pointed to himself.

"My sisters are going to love spoiling him." Addie wasn't sure how her mother would take the boy though. Time would show that. "I'm going to let you rest a bit, dear friend. I'll be back."

"Don't cry...for me. Live your l—life."

Zelda had fallen back asleep before Addie and Nico left the room. Some bit of knowing inside her said the passing was measured in breaths. Tears ran down her cheeks. Ridge rose from the kitchen table where he sat with Ben and took her in his arms. They needed no words, just strength, which they took from each other.

They laid Zelda to rest under a large oak tree two days later. Ridge read a few words from the Bible, then they loaded up and left for home, Nico never far from Ridge.

A week later, they pulled up to the house. Bodie ran to meet them. "I'm glad you're back. It's still here."

"I had hoped, for your sake, it would be." Ridge climbed down, then reached up for Nico and made the introductions.

It didn't take but a second for Bodie to take the boy under his wing and show him around the place. Addie grinned and took Ridge's hand. "Well, it looks like we have us a babysitter."

"Yes, it does."

The kitchen screen door slammed, and her mother came from the house, followed by Addie's three sisters. "I thought I heard voices."

"We're back." Addie hugged her mother, then called Bodie over. "Mama, this is Jane Ann's son, Nico, short for Nicolas. He's the one I went to prison for, and I'd do it again."

Ingrid seemed to struggle for words as she smoothed Nico's fine blond hair. "He's such a sweet boy." Her mother tried to smile in what appeared an attempt to hide her warring emotions, probably very unsure of her role in this child's life. "What are your plans for him?"

Nico climbed into Ingrid's arms to show her the rock in his palm.

"Ridge and I will raise him, of course. He's my flesh and blood."

"I always wanted my own little boy, but I missed out on that." Ingrid lifted tear-filled eyes. "I loved his mother. She was like a daughter to me." Addie's sisters crowded around, touching Nico and making a fuss over him.

"Mama?" Nico asked.

Ingrid was visibly shaken. "Yes, honey. She would've loved you and cherished every minute raising you." Ingrid swung to Addie. "Could we talk in private for a moment?"

"Sure, Mama." They transferred Nico to Ridge and found privacy. Addie put a bolstering arm around her mother. "What is it?"

Ingrid's chin quivered, and she bit her lip. "What if...what if I take him?"

"Would you want to take on that responsibility?" Ingrid was just starting life over in a new place, with a job that was by no means secure. But Addie could see what it meant to her mother, and she and Ridge would be near to help.

"It'll be my way of making amends for what Ezekiel did. I already love Nico. He's such a precious boy."

Addie glanced at Nico in Ridge's arms. "That he is."

"Then it's settled?"

"Sure. The girls are going to spoil him rotten." Addie could already see it now. Remy would carry him around like her personal rag doll. Between her—*their*—three sisters, Nico would forget what his feet were for. "I think your life is about to get upended."

They returned to announce the decision, and Nico smiled for the first time that day. It was as if he knew that he'd found his place to belong.

Addie turned her attention to her sisters and sniffed back tears. "I'm so happy we can be together again. Come here." She enveloped each in a big hug. "We're going to have a great time."

Thirteen-year-old Remy clung to her. "I missed you, Addie. I was so scared."

"That makes two of us." Addie tucked Remy's reddish-brown hair behind her ear. "From now on, no more fear. Only happy smiles." Ridge slid his hand in hers, and she turned with a loving glance.

"Are you okay with Ingrid taking Nico?" Ridge drew his fingertips across the underside of her wrist. "It must've been hard seeing the child you were ready to give your life for."

She inhaled a shaky breath. "I keep picturing Jane Ann's face as it was that night. Her panic when she realized she was going to die. But I'll be all right. It's just going to take me a little while. I'm so glad Nico didn't come while Ezekiel was running loose."

"I believe things work out the way they're supposed to." Ridge tucked a loose hair behind her ear. "I think I love you more every day."

"Ridge, I'm sorry I haven't been able to make love, but I promise it won't always be this way."

"I can wait. We have our whole lives in front of us." He glanced at Nico, and his features grew wistful. "I'm disappointed that he won't live with us, but one day we'll have our own son. I'm sure of that."

Addie met the love in his eyes and threaded her fingers through his. "Me too."

Thirty-eight

"RIDGE, COULD THIS DAY HAVE GOTTEN ANY BETTER?" ADDIE sat next to him on the sofa after the supper dishes were washed, and he handed her the bag of knitting.

Bodie ambled in and stretched out on the floor. Ridge loved this time of the evening, when work was done, eating over, and his little family was together and safe.

"It was sure one of surprises." He couldn't have made it turn out any finer if he'd tried. "I'm glad to see your mother happy and little Nico with a home."

"Me too. Life is strange, and so often it makes you wait for what you really want." Addie's knitting needles clicked as she worked.

Bodie sat up. "That's the way it was today with me when I went fishing. We couldn't even catch bad breath—everything went wrong. Sawyer and Henry wanted to leave, but I said I was staying. We kept fishing and began to get nibbles. After a while, we were pulling 'em out faster than we could bait the hook. Never saw anything like it."

"Things like that don't come around often." Ridge toyed with the ends of Addie's hair. He'd come so close to losing her, the only thing in his life that gave it meaning.

His thoughts drifted to Shiloh and her confession, wondering if she'd found what she was looking for on her trip west. Wondering what the Mobeetie judge would do once he read the papers. His future happiness hung in the balance.

"You seem quiet, Ridge," Addie murmured.

"Have a lot on my mind, I guess. Nothing to worry you about."

They lapsed into silence, and in the quiet, the ticking of the clock on the mantel sounded like a hammer striking a nail.

Addie laid her knitting in her lap. "Dear, would you read

some more of *Oliver Twist* to us? We should be close to the end."

"Just a few chapters. Son, would you hand it to me?"

Bodie reached for the book, and Ridge opened to the marked page. As he started reading, Addie resumed her knitting, and a comfortable feeling settled over him. Like wearing an old pair of boots that conformed to the shape of his feet. The three of them had adjusted to life as a family and had nowhere else to be.

An unexpected knock on the door jarred Ridge. He laid the book aside.

Addie's knitting needles froze. "I wonder who'd be out this time of night?"

"I guess we'll soon find out." Ridge stood, his twin Colts within easy reach, and went to the entryway. He opened the door to find Jack on the porch.

"Sorry to call so late." Jack pulled a letter from the inside of his vest. "The late stage brought this, and I thought you'd want to see it."

"Come in." Ridge noted Judge Horace Greely's name on the left corner of the envelope. Uneasiness twisted in his stomach. Hanging Horace. Folks claimed he had no heart.

"Thank you. I would like to know what it says." Jack removed his hat and stepped inside.

Addie came from the parlor. "What is it, Ridge?"

"A letter. Jack, come on in here while I read it."

"Evening, Addie." Jack gave her a nod and followed, holding his hat.

"Have a seat." Addie picked up her knitting and moved her bag to the floor. "Nora and the kids all right?"

"Yes, ma'am. They're doing real good." Jack dropped onto the sofa.

Addie, Jack, and Bodie talked about the events of the day while Ridge opened the envelope and silently read. Worry twisted a path through him. This was his chance. But not without risk.

He glanced up to find three sets of eyes staring back. "I have to appear before Judge Greely in Mobeetie in four days. He'll deliver his verdict then."

"That's good, isn't it?" Addie asked.

"Not entirely."

"What do you mean, Ridge?"

Jack got to his feet. "If Greely throws out Shiloh's statement or doesn't like what Ridge has to say, Ridge can be arrested on the spot."

"But…that's not fair," Addie sputtered. "He's innocent of the charges."

"Greely is known as Hanging Horace. There's that too," Jack added.

"Why didn't you keep that to yourself, Jack?" Ridge growled.

"She's your wife and deserves to know…that's why."

Bodie jumped to his feet. "Don't go, Ridge. Make 'em come after you, and you can hide before they get here. You can't let 'em arrest you without a fight."

Ridge folded the letter. "Settle down. I'm not running and not hiding. Not anymore. This is a chance to clear my name, and I have to go."

"I'm not letting you go alone. I'm the best thing to an attorney you have." Jack squeezed Ridge's shoulder. "We've faced the flaming gates of hell together many times; we might as well face the roll of the dice the same way. Besides, I need to take Texanna Starr to Mobeetie anyway."

Ridge nodded. "Thank you, Jack. It would be a comfort."

"Then I'll say good night and be on my way." Jack put on his hat and left.

Addie's face had gone white. "I'm frightened, Ridge. How can you risk this? How?"

He brushed a finger across her cheek, his voice gentle. "I'm tired of looking over my shoulder, waiting for a bullet in the back. Tired of putting you in danger too. They could miss me and hit you, and I can't live with that. And when we have children, they'll be at risk too. Look at Eleanor's husband and kids, killed by a posse. Do you want that? I sure don't. Or what if I bring the law to Bodie? He's still wanted too. Clearing my name is the only way to keep you safe."

"I'm going with you, and I won't come back without you," she declared.

"Me too." Bodie stood at Addie's side, his face set in stubborn lines.

Ridge put an arm around each of them. "Thank you for your moral support, but I think you both should stay here and carry on."

Addie released an oath that shocked Ridge. He'd never heard her utter a word like that. "You know better than to even suggest that! I *will* be at your side whether you like it or not." She jerked away, her chest heaving. "Hanging Horace? Ridge!"

"You can't go by the man's reputation, Addie. Others call him a fair man."

She stared at him like he'd just proclaimed that eating mice was healthy. "I'm sure you believe you know what's best for me, but you don't. I make my own decisions now. After facing death at my father's hands, I think I've earned the right."

"That's not what I—"

Bodie looked just as mutinous. "We're going! I'll quit working for you if I have to, so you won't be the boss of me anymore."

"Settle down. Both of you." Ridge stepped away and ran his fingers through his hair, trying to curb his temper and not being very successful. "We'll make a damn picnic out of it, then! Bring our best tablecloth and plenty of fried chicken. And don't forget the lemonade, pickles, and toothpicks."

"Don't be ridiculous." Sparks shot from Addie's eyes. "You could die."

Ridge whirled. "So could you. Can't you get that through your head? It's dangerous being away from here with me. Hope's Crossing offers safety of sorts."

"I'll take my chances." Addie jerked up her knitting and stuffed it in the bag. "I'm going to bed."

"Me too!" Bodie disappeared toward the back door, and a second later, a slam shook the house.

Great. Now he had both of them as mad as drowned cats.

"Addie—"

Almost at the parlor door, she turned to meet his gaze and retraced her steps. "You once said that you won't ever own me. Don't become my father." Her voice softened. "I will consider you in all things, but in the end, I'll make my own decisions. You need me."

"That I do." Ridge released a resigned breath and pulled her against him. "I need you like I need air. I don't want to fight."

"Me either. I'm just so scared of losing you." She stood on tiptoe and pressed a kiss to his lips. His deep love for her shook him down to the core. He deepened the kiss and ran his hands down her sides, tracing every curve, swell, and valley before returning to cup her breasts.

"I can't live without you," he murmured against her mouth. "You're part of me."

Addie stepped back and took his hand. They turned down the lamps as they moved to the stairs, the cats following them up. In moments, Ridge had shut the felines out of the bedroom and frantically stripped off both their clothes.

"I've missed you. Make love to me, Ridge," Addie whispered, placing his hand on her chest.

Desire licked up his spine like a searing flame. His heart hammering, he laid her on the bed and covered her with his body, his swollen hardness seeking her. Unlike their other times, this would be hot and fast. Slow had its place, but not now.

"Now, Ridge. I can't wait." Addie's fingernails gently raked his back, trying to pull him inside. Her plea wasn't wasted. One thrust took him inside the center of her being, and he set a pace to match their rapid breathing.

Her muscles clenched around him, creating delicious friction that drove him to heights he'd never known. "Addie!"

She lightly nipped her teeth across his chest, and desire raced through him like a wild rainstorm across prairieland. He wanted everything she had to give. Had to have her or he'd lose his damn mind.

Luckily for his sanity, the climb was swift, and the peak was one so intense it took his breath.

"Now!" she cried, shuddering beneath him, her muscles gripping and releasing around him.

His heart exploding, he spasmed and pulsed inside her. Mindless release shot him into a white space void of sound. He hung there, drifting through a quiet haze, relaxed and peaceful. In this beautiful place, no one hunted him or threatened to hang him.

Then he dropped back to reality, conscious of the weight of his body.

Gasping for air, his skin sweat slickened, he rolled off to the side and lay panting. He glanced over at Addie. She lay on her back, arms at her sides, eyes closed, breathing hard.

Ridge fumbled for her limp hand and squeezed. "I love you, Addie."

The sheet rustled as she rolled to face him. "You complete me. I needed that desperately."

"Happy to oblige. Anything for my lady."

Addie traced the lines of his face, tears in her eyes. "There will come a time when I will never hear your voice, feel your touch, breathe your scent." She took a shuddering breath. "And I cannot imagine the pain of what that might be like. That scares the bejesus out of me."

"Pray God that's a long time from now." He lifted her hand to his lips.

"Ridge, I'm going to work hard at storing away memories for such a day. I'm going to love you full-out with every fiber of my being. I don't know how this trip to Mobeetie will end, but I'm not ready to lose you yet. I'm not. I'm so scared."

"Please try to let me do the worrying." He toyed with her hair. "I never thought I'd meet a woman like you, as fine and pretty and smart. I never imagined you were out there waiting for me. The happiest day of my life was when I married you and we started a journey together." He swallowed hard. "I want to tell you these things now in case…"

He couldn't finish the sentence for the emotion clogging

his throat. Panic rose for a moment, blocking out reason. Maybe she was right. They could run. This could be a trap, the judge's way to lure him into the open.

All his reasons for going vanished. What the hell was he doing?

Struggling to breathe, Ridge pushed off the bed and went to the window to stare out at the blackness. But all he saw was a large blood moon hanging in the sky.

An omen. But an omen of what?

Thirty-nine

BY MORNING, RIDGE HAD PUT THE BLOOD MOON OUT OF HIS mind. Lovemaking had been an excellent distraction, and they'd spent the better part of the night satisfying and loving each other. Now it was time to get back to taking care of his family. And the best way to do that was facing Judge Horace Greely.

The back door opened. "Morning," Bodie mumbled, his wet hair slicked back.

Addie took the eggs from the skillet. "That's great timing. Breakfast is served."

"I ain't very hungry." He took a cup from the shelf and poured coffee.

Ridge did a double take. "Addie, check him for a fever."

"There ain't nothing wrong. I feel fine." Bodie took a sip. "Fine as frog hair, as a matter of fact."

Addie sat down. "I wish I'd have known that before I cooked all these eggs."

"Sorry. Maybe I'll eat 'em later." He took his coffee and went back outside.

"Ridge, what's wrong with him?"

"I'll find out after I eat." But Ridge already knew what it was—worry. Bodie couldn't face losing another good person from his life. "The kid is trying to sort through all this."

"Let's take him into town with us. He might like to see Sawyer and Henry."

For someone just getting their day started, Addie presented quite a picture. Her hair lay in a wealth of golden curls and waves, and her eyes seemed greener than usual. There was a flush to her skin as well. He'd like to capture her likeness and hang it on the wall.

Ridge laid down his fork, a husky tone in his voice. "I have to say that lovemaking certainly agrees with you. I've never seen you lovelier than you are right now."

She sat quietly for a moment, blinking back tears. "Thank you, dear. You look rather handsome yourself."

They would only have one more morning like this. Then this fairy-tale marriage might come to an end. Suddenly, he wasn't hungry either.

❧

Later that morning, they rode into town, and Addie stopped in at the mercantile for a few things.

"Got a letter for you, Mrs. Steele." Owen Vaughn reached into a mail slot and handed her an envelope.

"Oh my goodness, I wonder who wrote it." Addie scanned it for a return address but found none. She carefully tore the envelope open, her attention flying to the signature at the end. Shiloh Duke. Her heart lifted. She went to sit on a bench outside to read in the sunlight.

> *Dear Addie,*
>
> *I pray this finds you and Mr. Steele well and in good spirits. I'm in a Colorado mining town, singing in a real fancy place. Folks flock every night to listen to me. They call me their songbird and I like that. I'm very careful in making acquaintances, so don't worry. I sure ain't looking for love. Anyhow, the miners here only have one thing on their minds and I'm staying clear of them. Don't need what they're selling. I make enough to live on with something left over and am finding that I enjoy my life. Tell Bodie that I believe in the power of dreams. Nightmares can't find me here. I'll write more soon.*
>
> *Yours truly,*
> *Shiloh*

Addie folded the letter, digesting the news. How wonderful

to know that Shiloh was alive and well. The young woman sounded very satisfied with her lot now. Addie wished she could write back to her, but evidently Shiloh wasn't ready to reveal her location. Addie hoped she would one day though. She didn't want to lose touch with the girl and had a sudden yearning to tell her about the school-teaching position and the kids that would be starting school in two weeks.

Addie rose and went to visit her mother. Little Nico met her at the door. "Add!"

Smiling, Ingrid came from the small kitchen, her hair in a loose arrangement on top of her head that was very becoming. "Addie, you don't have to knock. This is your home too." She studied Addie's face. "What's wrong?"

"Oh, Mama. I'm afraid for Ridge." Addie sank into her mother's embrace. God, how she'd missed her mama's soft shoulder. She needed the comfort.

"Let's sit down and you can tell me what this is about." Ingrid picked up Nico and they sat at the table. Nico laid his head on Ingrid's chest and stared at Addie.

She told her mother about Judge Greely and her worst fears. "Bodie says as long as Ridge is determined to go, he's coming too. Ridge stood thinking at the window a long time last night, and I suspect a part of him doesn't want to go through with this. Mama, I don't know if I can stand it if the judge throws out Shiloh's confession and arrests him. They might put him in prison"—she tried to steady herself—"or hang him."

If that happened, she didn't know how she could possibly teach school. It would be impossible to focus.

"Child, you have to be brave. Support his decision and try not to let him see your worry." Ingrid handed her a handkerchief and Addie blew her nose. "I've never seen a man love anyone like he does you. Don't expect the worst. This may very well be a godsend, everything Ridge has wanted."

"I know, and I'm trying. It's impossible to see hope when the risk is this great." But she'd do anything for him, even wear a smile when her heart was breaking.

❧

Two days later, Ridge walked from the hotel in Mobeetie to the courthouse with Addie, flanked by Bodie and Jack. He felt naked without his Colts and holster he'd left behind in the room. He paused on the courthouse steps and took Bodie aside. "I'm not good with saying how I feel, but our time together has been some of the best I've ever spent. I've loved teaching you and watching you grow into a fine man." Ridge drew him into a hug, fighting the break in his voice. "You've been like a son."

Bodie sobbed silently, tears wetting his cheeks. "Thank you for taking me in and seeing that I have worth."

Damn! Ridge blinked hard. "Wasn't that hard to see. If the judge doesn't grant my petition—" His voice broke. "In case he doesn't, go home with Addie and stay in Hope's Crossing. There'll be lots of men willing to give you work."

"Yes, sir. I'll take care of Addie too."

"Thanks. Now go on inside with Jack. I need a private word with Addie." Ridge waited until they moved away. Then, with the clouds threatening to spill rain, he took her hands and cleared his throat. "If this doesn't turn out right, promise me you'll go on and live your life the best you can without me. The house and land are yours. Don't keep your heart closed. Find someone else to give you children, to protect you from the darkness."

Tears spilled down Addie's face. She clung to him. "I'll never love anyone else. You can't make me promise that!"

"You're right, I can't." He reached into his vest for a handkerchief and handed it to her. "All I can do is hope you will listen and let your heart heal."

Her fingers tightened around his arm. "This isn't over yet. Stop talking like it is."

"I just want you to be prepared." How could he tell her to do that when he hadn't prepared himself? He stood to lose everything he'd ever wanted. How could he take a chance he'd leave here in shackles?

Part of him yearned to grab Addie and Bodie and run as far

and fast as he could. Yet the glimmer of hope shining through the cloud of doubt kept him rooted. He couldn't pass up a chance to be free.

Free. The word echoed inside his head and sent an anguished cry through his heart. Ridge took a deep breath, pulled his shoulders back. It was time to roll the dice.

He led Addie inside to a seat at the front of the half-empty courtroom and sat next to Jack and Bodie. The sheriff and two deputies standing at the door to the judge's chambers drew his attention, and his heart clenched in momentary panic. Judging by the way Addie gripped his hand, she must've also seen the stern-faced sheriff.

"I hope this won't take long," Bodie murmured. "My heart can't take the wait."

Ridge wanted to say his couldn't either, but he wouldn't let the boy see his nerves. "It'll be over soon, son. Hang in there."

Jack leaned close. "Don't pay any mind to Greely's reputation. Trust that this will end right."

The words had barely left his mouth before the door to the judge's chambers opened and a black-robed older man stepped out. He looked around with dark, piercing eyes. Someone said, "All rise."

It had begun.

"Court's in session." The gray-haired judge heard two cases before Ridge's. One man got five years in prison for horse stealing and was taken away by the sheriff. The other was a prostitute and she got time served for fighting. With a black eye, scratches all over her face, and copper hair that looked like wire, she was the roughest-looking woman Ridge had ever seen. He'd rather tangle with a bobcat. For a moment, he wondered what the other party looked like and if they'd fared any better.

Bodie squirmed, and Ridge felt the same impatience.

Finally, Judge Greely glanced over his round spectacles. "Ridge Steele."

"Good luck," Addie whispered.

Jack stood, explaining who he was. The judge motioned

him and Ridge forward. "Thank you for hearing our petition, Judge Greely."

The judge scowled at Ridge. "I read Miss Shiloh Duke's statement and found the events of the night on July 22, 1877 in need of some clarifying. Did you coerce that young woman into proclaiming your innocence?"

"Absolutely not." Shock that the judge would ask such a thing raced up his spine. Dammit, Greely was going to throw out the testimony. He should've listened to Bodie.

Jack cleared his throat. "Sir, the lady wrote that statement in my office in front of me, and I guarantee you that no one made her do it. She wasn't in fear for her life. In fact, she was very relaxed and happy to undo the lie she'd told years previous. Her conscience had bothered her."

"Is that opinion or fact, Mr. Bowdre?"

A tinge of anger showed in Jack's answer. "Both. Your Honor, I have two witnesses here in the courtroom right now who'll vouch for that and be more than happy to testify how Miss Duke came to be at the Steele house."

"Where is Miss Duke now? Why isn't she here?"

Ridge's heart sank even further.

"We don't know her whereabouts at present," Jack answered. "She came through Hope's Crossing on her way west. She's starting a new life. Her father forced her to do horrible things and used her to settle gambling debts. Now she's free to live as she wants."

"I would like to have spoken to her." Greely swatted a fly that landed on his desk. "Steele, what was your former profession, and what were you doing in the woods that night?"

Jack whispered, "Relax, don't let him intimidate you." Ridge had news for Jack. Greely already scared him into the middle of next week.

"A preacher, sir. I had a church in a nearby town and was on my way home after visiting a parishioner's sick child." Ridge didn't flinch from the judge's sharp, dark eyes. "I heard Shiloh—Miss Duke—cry out in what sounded like pain and went to see if I could help."

"How long did you preach?"

"Two years, sir."

"Quite a few outlaws claim to be preachers to get their crimes erased. Is that what you're doing?"

"No, absolutely not."

"Are you preaching the Good Book now?"

Ridge forced himself to remain still under Greely's skeptical stare. The sheriff took a step toward him from his post. "I lost my faith in God, Your Honor. I gave up the pulpit and haven't preached a word since that night. I couldn't see how the good Lord would let someone frame me for such unspeakable crimes. I was just riding by, minding my own business, stopped to help someone in need, and found myself with a noose around my neck and a hostile crowd wanting me dead. I am not using religion to get the slate cleared." Ridge inhaled a quick breath. "No, Your Honor."

Jack seized a moment of quiet. "Ridge Steele has committed no crimes since coming to live in Hope's Crossing." His voice rang out with clear conviction. "I don't know a finer man to ride with, and I consider him head and shoulders above the best."

"I'll take that into consideration, Bowdre. Steele, tell me about the rancher, Calder. The father of that dead boy. It says here he and an older son came after you."

Ridge winced, wishing he didn't have to answer. "Yes, they did."

"What was that? I didn't hear you."

"I said yes, Your Honor. They came hunting me with a vengeance."

"What happened?"

"I shot and killed his older boy after they attacked me. I defended myself."

"Did you kill the father?"

"No, he gathered his dead son and went home to bury him."

Greely grunted and swatted another fly. Ridge gave Jack a sideways glance, wondering what it all meant. Jack shrugged

helplessly. Great. Ridge inhaled a worried breath. He wanted
to turn to Addie and bolster her with a smile at least, but he
stared straight ahead, his shoulders squared, spine stiff. Hanging
Horace probably didn't like slouchers.

The silence dragged on. Someone coughed. A bead of
sweat trickled down one side of Ridge's face. He wiped it
away and let his arms fall to his sides.

Greely motioned for the sheriff to step to the bench, and
the two conferred in whispers. The sheriff stepped away, and
the judge spoke again. "I reviewed everything, and we con-
tacted the sheriff's office and others in Silver Valley who gave
you glowing recommendations. The law in the neighboring
town has been newly elected, but he was well versed on the
case. He spoke of unprecedented corruption of his predecessor
at every level."

He reached for a piece of paper and stamped it. "Therefore,
I will wipe out your conviction and give you a clear name.
However, I don't want to ever see you back in a prisoner's
dock. Break the law, and I'll throw the book at you."

Ridge's legs tried to buckle. They did it. He was no longer
wanted.

Addie's happy cry and Bodie's shrill whistle sounded behind
him.

"Order!" The judge banged the gavel. He signed a paper
and handed it to the bailiff. "Here's proof of the proceedings
today, Steele. Better keep it handy until word gets out that you
no longer have a bounty on your head."

Ridge stepped forward and took the envelope in a trembling hand. "Thank you, Your Honor."

"Court's adjourned." Greely banged the gavel again.

Ridge turned, and Addie flew into his arms. "We did it,
Ridge. You're free."

The kiss was long and deep. They could go home now and
live their lives without fear of the price hanging over Ridge's
head.

When he released her, she placed her mouth to his ear. "I
have a secret."

"Do you mind telling me?"

Her smile stretched from ear to ear. "You're going to be a father."

The shock seemed to have stolen every word from his head. He couldn't get his mouth to work for several long heartbeats. Finally, he managed, "Me? A father?"

She nodded. "Probably next June. Are you ready for this?"

"More than ready, my love." He could already picture their house brimming with kids of all ages and sizes. This was a dream come true. He blinked back the tears and kissed the little mama again.

Gradually, he became aware of others waiting to congratulate him, and they broke apart.

Bodie shook his hand, grinning. "I think that judge liked you."

"What makes you say that, son?"

Bodie raised his shoulders. "He didn't put you in jail."

"Nope, he didn't." Ridge turned to Jack. "Thanks doesn't seem a strong enough word for giving me back my life. I owe you. Anytime you need anything, I'll be there."

"I know. That's the mark of a true friend." Jack laughed. "Better get ready, though. Nora's going to throw you a big shindig when we get back."

"We can always stand to have a party." Ridge drew Addie close, and she slid an arm around his waist in turn. "Are you ready to go home, Mrs. Steele?"

"I can't wait to sleep in our own bed." Her hand dropped to his butt and squeezed. The twinkle in her pretty green eyes told Ridge that he'd be getting very little shut-eye. But then, he figured sleep was overrated anyway.

He was surprised he didn't float from the courtroom, as light as he felt with the weight lifted from his shoulders. He was a free man, had good friends, a kid to finish raising, a babe on the way, and the prettiest wife in the whole state of Texas to love.

The dice he'd rolled had come up double sixes, and a man couldn't beat that.

Epilogue

THE NOVEMBER AIR BROUGHT THE KIND OF COOL DAY THAT warned of a blue norther perched on their doorstep. Clay Colby buttoned his coat, pulled the collar up around his ears, and tugged his Stetson low on his forehead. He turned to his two best friends, the men who'd been there with him from the beginning. "Let's take a walk."

Ridge glanced at Jack and lifted an eyebrow. "Reckon we have time to spare."

Dodging children on their way to school, they climbed the bluff overlooking Hope's Crossing and stared down at the folks milling about the busy main street. A month ago, they'd blasted away the narrow entrance to town, which, combined with the open back road, threw aside what now felt like a thick, black curtain. They were respectable, law-abiding people and took pride in announcing that to the world.

Now, with the obstructions gone, the growing community had spilled out from its confines in the canyon. Angus O'Connor was constructing a second fancy saloon that he'd already named the Midnight Star and an opera house mere yards from where the narrow entrance once stood. The man's big dreams were going to put them on the map one day.

Wet paint still glistened on a population sign—their first— that read 95. Damn, it looked real nice from up here.

Clay took a big gulp of air into his lungs. All this had sprung from three wanted men with a vision of what could happen if they worked their fingers to the bone and kept looking to the future.

"What's on your mind, Clay?" Jack rubbed his hands together and blew on them.

"I guess you might say I'm getting a bit maudlin and want to take stock as I do from time to time." Clay fought back a thick wave of emotion that settled in his throat, choking him. "Only four short years ago, I stood up here, looked down at a dusty, dingy outlaw hideout, and saw a town. A dream formed." He blinked hard, and his voice got raspy. "Now, look at that. What do you see?"

"A thriving group of misfits banding together to eke out a living," Ridge answered. "When you told me your plans for this place, I immediately wanted in but had doubts it would work."

Jack shifted, nodding. "We were all tired of running and hiding, and you offered us hope."

"Brother, you gave us a reason to live." Ridge touched Clay's back. "And we're indebted. We needed a leader to follow, and you gave us that. You made us believe anything was possible. And I knew deep down it was a whole lot better than what we had."

"Shoot, I was no leader," Clay protested. "I didn't know the first thing about building a town, but I wanted to try. It nearly destroyed me when Montana Black torched our first two buildings."

Jack shook his head. "I tell you, if it hadn't been for your Violet befriending Montana and softening that worm-ridden heart of his, he would have kept burning us out until we gave up."

"Or killed him. That little girl sure is something. Only she's not that little anymore." Ridge chuckled. "I don't know who Violet will end up marrying, but whoever steals her heart will get one smart lady."

Clay scanned the street below for his daughter and spotted her confidently walking along, holding Dillon's hand, her "seeing stick" in front of her to warn of holes or obstructions. He'd loved teaching her how to get around without sight. She'd gotten a raw deal being born blind, but she'd never complained.

A few yards away, Addie's three sisters strolled into the

mercantile, laughing and talking. The two oldest had immediately found work and wouldn't be single for long, judging by the line of suitors outside their door.

A spate of weddings seemed to be on the horizon. Dr. Mary and Angus O'Connor had started them off by tying the knot soon after Ridge became a free man. Charlotte Wintersby and Peter might not be far behind, and Eleanor Crump had been keeping time with George, the stage driver.

Marriages, babies, and newly arrived couples were going to keep the town growing.

"It was a brilliant plan to populate by bringing in mail-order brides, Clay. I might never have found anyone to have me otherwise." Jack laughed. "My Nora sure is a special woman. Loyal to a fault and pretty as springtime, but she sure gets some crazy ideas sometimes. Still, I wouldn't trade her for all the gold in California."

"Or my Addie either," Ridge declared. "Clay, thanks for kicking us off with Tally."

"Well, I figured I'd better show you how it's done." Clay's thoughts went back to the day Tally had arrived to find the town burned down around them. He thought for sure she'd head back where she came from, but she'd stayed and worked at his side. She was the most beautiful woman he'd ever seen but broken inside, and he'd loved every step of putting her back together.

"Did you ever think we'd have all this?" Jack waved his arm across the bustling scene.

"No." Clay cleared his throat again. Dammit, why couldn't he say what we wanted without choking up like some old man? "I thought maybe a handful of people would join us. Never this." His gaze moved from one business to another— all fifteen. Damn, they'd done all right.

"I plan on sticking around to see what this place will look like in ten or twenty years." Ridge's voice seemed strained as well. "I wonder if it'll still be here. If we will."

They lapsed into silence, each immersed in his own thoughts. For a moment, Clay thought he could hear the laughter of their childrens' children a generation from now drifting on the breeze. One thing about it, life went on despite the highs and lows of the day-to-day.

Jack's low voice cracked the fragile quiet. "Who knows? We did our damnedest to give it the best start we could. Now, it's up to others to carry on and improve on what we gave 'em."

"Don't forget. We still have wanted men in town. Dallas Hawk for one. What happens to them?" Ridge asked.

"We'll have to help them try to get right with the law." Jack rubbed the back of his neck. "I'll be their attorney if they want, help them write letters and fill out applications."

"And if they still can't?" Ridge persisted.

"Then we hide 'em. They can blend in, and we'll protect them." Clay pulled his Colt from the holster and stared at the cold steel. "I'm so tired of killing I could puke. When will it all stop? When will we be able to live in peace? I never want our sons to have to wear one of these."

"We're a dying breed, Clay. Face it. Our days are numbered." Ridge bent over for a small pebble and rubbed it between his fingers. "This country is big enough for everyone. Greed should have no place here."

"I agree, but greed will always raise its ugly head no matter how much land there is or people on it. At least for now." Clay squatted to pick up a handful of dirt and let it sift through his fingers. "The clear fact is, some men want it all. I think there will always be a need for men like us, in some capacity, to make sure a few don't take everything."

Jack let out a resigned sigh. "I don't like it one bit, but you're probably right. We're the defenders of the weak and poor. We're the best ones to seek justice for them until the law can catch up with the westward expansion."

Clay pondered that for a moment, and damn if Jack hadn't arrived at the bald truth. They hadn't outlived their usefulness. Not yet. Great change wasn't far off, but it just might take a while. Until then, he'd best keep his gun handy, bedroll tied on, and his horse saddled.

They were still on guard awhile longer.
Sam Colt and his watchmen.
Still doing their best for God, country, and Texas.

A Cowboy of
Legend

One

Fort Worth Texas

Spring 1899

"DESTROYER OF MEN'S SOULS! BEWARE THE PITFALLS OF THE
devil's brew!" Grace Legend held up her sign and directed her
loud yells into the murky interior of the Three Deuces saloon.

A gust of wind delivered the stench of the nearby stock-
yards up her nose and a swirl of dirt to her eyes. She blinked
several times to clear the grit as the two dozen Temperance
women behind her took up the chant, banging drums and
shaking tambourines. They sounded impressive.

A surly individual went around her and reached for the

batwing doors. Grace swatted him with her sign. "Get back! Back, I say. This den of iniquity is closed to the likes of you."

Built like a bull and smelling like the south end of a north-bound steer, the man narrowed his gaze and raised a meaty fist. "This here's a free country and I can go anywhere I like."

Gunfire rang out down the street and a woman screamed. Grace was glad she'd stuck a derringer in her pocket. This section of town saw killings every day, even though the citizens cried for someone to clean it up and make it safe.

She wanted to take a step back from the surly man worse than anything. She really did. He had meanness rolling off him like rancid snake oil. But giving ground wasn't in her makeup. Not today and not as long as she was alive. She had a job to do.

Grace sucked in a quick breath, shot him a piercing glare, and parked herself across the doorway. "I bet your wife would like to know where you spend your time when you should be working. Shame on you wasting your money on whiskey."

"I earn it and I'll spend it however I see fit. Now step aside," he snarled and raised a fist.

"Or else what?" A voice in Grace's head warned that this course of action could be dangerous, but she never listened to that boring bit of reason. No, she saw it her right and duty to make a difference in the world, and make it she would. She couldn't do that sitting on her hands like some timid toad afraid to utter a sound.

At least a half dozen gunshots rent the air and people ducked.

A crowd had begun to gather and pressed close as though sensing a free show. Some of the men got into a heated shouting match with her ladies.

Before she could move, the quarrelsome fellow barreled into her, knocking her sideways. Grace launched onto his back and began whopping him with the sign. However, the handle was too long for close fighting and none of her blows landed. Hell and damnation!

She released a frustrated cry and wrapped both arms around his head.

"Get off me!" he roared.

"When hell freezes over, fool." She heard a door bang and the footsteps of someone new.

Masculine hands yanked the two of them apart.

"Hey, what's the meaning of this?" The voice belonged to a man she assumed to be the saloon owner.

Breathing hard, she jerked at the bodice of her favorite royal blue dress, straightening it before grabbing the immense hat that barely clung to one side of her head. She blew back a blond curl that fell across one eye, blocking her view. Only then did she get a glimpse of the gentleman whose livelihood she meant to destroy, and the sight glued her tongue to the roof of her mouth.

That he presented a handsome picture with coal-black hair and a lean form was indisputable, but it was more than that. There was confidence about him, but no arrogance. A Stetson sat low on his forehead—a cowboy? Grace did a double take. Saloon owners wore bowlers, not Stetsons. She was unable to move her gaze from piercing eyes that reminded her of smoke, shadowed by the brim of the hat. The stormy gray depths warned of the danger of crossing him.

And more. Oh my!

Aware that her friends were watching, Grace took in his appearance—the silk vest of dark green belonged to a gambler. Combined with tailored black trousers, he appeared a profitable businessman, the hat aside. Until she looked at his worn white cuffs and boots in desperate need of repair. Had he spent everything on the window dressing with no thought of footwear?

Her gaze rested on a well-used gun belt slung low on his hip, complete with what appeared a long Peacemaker. By now, most men left their firearms at home. However, having grown up with weapons of all kinds on the Lone Star Ranch, she understood the need to sometimes keep a gun handy. Although crime in the rough area had begun to decline some, running a saloon at the edge of Hell's Half Ace was still a risky business and called for protection of some sort.

She patted the small derringer in her pocket to make sure it hadn't fallen out.

"I asked what's going on here," the owner repeated.

Smelly glared, wiping blood from his forehead. So, she did get a lick in. "This churlish fishwife assaulted me when I tried to enter, and I demand that you do something."

"Churlish fishwife? Why you!" Grace swung her sign again—only it caught the tall saloon owner instead, knocking him back a step.

Towering head and shoulders above her, the man snatched the sign from her hand, broke it over his knee, and pitched the pieces aside. His eyes had darkened to a shade she'd never seen before and had no words to describe.

"Care to explain why you're running off my business, lady?"

The question came out silky and wrapped in velvet like her father's did when he wanted to put the fear of God into someone. That frightened her far more than yelling. This cowboy saloon owner was someone to reckon with.

Although quaking inside, Grace drew herself up and thrust out her chin, praying her group of women were behind her. Although the quiet failed to reassure her. "I'm asserting my God-given right to free speech."

"You tell him, Grace!" one of the women yelled.

"Free speech about?" he snapped.

"The evils of drink. It's destroying the fabric of our society and wrecking homes."

"And it's your duty to straighten us men out?" he barked.

His dark glower shot a shiver of alarm up her spine, especially when he edged closer. Why couldn't she have been born taller? She felt like a bug he was about to step on. He was every bit or more the height of her six-foot three-inch father.

How come she didn't hear a peep from her ladies? If they'd left her…

She inhaled a deep breath to steady herself. "As much as I'm able. I cannot turn a blind eye to hungry kids and wives bearing the scars of abuse. It's a sin and disgrace. I'm their voice." She clasped her hands together to hide the tremble. Her parents—and many others—had warned that she'd go too far one day. Dance to the music and eventually she'd have to pay the fiddler. Anger flashing from his eyes said this might be the time when she'd have to pay up.

The belligerent clod inserted himself between them. "You gonna stand here and jaw with her all day, Brannock? Send for the sheriff. She's breaking the damn law."

Brannock shifted his attention to the ill-humored patron, the tense set of his shoulders reminding her of a rattler coiled to strike. "You telling me my business now, Cyril? Go home. I have this under control."

"I came for my afternoon beer. You know I come every afternoon."

Brannock flicked his annoyed gaze to Grace, a noise rumbling in his throat. "The saloon is temporarily closed. You'll have to come back."

"Just wait until the others hear about this. We'll ruin you." Cyril stomped away.

"You'll have to get in line!" the saloon owner shouted, then bit back a low curse and swung his icy grays on her. "I don't want to throw you in jail, but you'll leave me no choice if you continue down this dangerous path, Miss—"

"Grace Legend." She smiled sweetly. "I have a—"

"God-given right to free speech," he finished for her. "I heard the first time. Didn't anyone warn you about the danger of coming here?"

"I don't listen to things of that nature."

"You may regret that one day." His deep voice vibrated across her skin. "I have a business to run and I intend to make money at it. Do I make myself clear?"

"Perfectly." She glanced up into those dangerous eyes the color of an angry sky, and before she could release a scathing retort, someone latched onto her arm.

"There you are, sis. In trouble again, I see."

Irritated, she glanced up into her brother Crockett's face. "Yes, here I am. I haven't turned to a pillar of salt, landed in jail, or shot anyone." She glanced around to find that her group of women had by this time indeed disappeared, left her to face the owner by herself. She realized then that if she was going to do this, she'd have to do it on her own. Just as she'd usually had to.

"The day's young." Crockett's grin faded when his gaze went from her sign lying in splinters to Brannock. "I'm sorry about the mess. I'm Crockett Legend, Gracie's brother. I hope there's no hard feelings."

The air spewing from Brannock's mouth said there was plenty of ill will to go around. "Keep your sister away from my saloon or I won't be so forgiving next time." The cowboy bit the words out like they soured on his tongue then whirled and went inside his establishment, slamming the wooden doors behind the batwing swinging ones and sliding a bolt just as a woman's scream sounded a few doors down.

One of those newfangled automobiles drove by and backfired loudly. The disappointed crowd began to disperse, grumbling at the lack of bloodshed.

Grace jerked her arm from her brother. "Not until I get my sign."

He bent to help. "Watch out for the sharp pieces. I don't know why you keep getting into these scrapes. Pa's ready to throw up his hands and Mama's wondering where she went wrong. Gracie, you don't have to get on everyone's bad side. Just do the right thing."

It irritated her that he kept referring to her babyish name. She'd long adopted the more adult Grace, yet her family refused to abide by her decision.

"I am doing the right thing. I'm living my life my way, on my own terms." She suppressed a yelp when a jagged piece of wood slid under her nail. She wouldn't cry out. Remaining calm, she juggled what she'd picked up and pulled the fragment out then wrapped her bleeding finger in a handkerchief Crockett quickly supplied.

"Give those to me." He took the mangled sticks from her. "What happened?"

"I was marching peaceably when a man tried to prove he was boss." As they moved down the street, she told him about the fight with Cyril and how Brannock had snapped the sign over his knee. "The nerve of him. He's very ill-mannered."

Still, she grudgingly had to admit that he was also a little intriguing. He was different from the men she was used to seeing in the lower end of town. Though he was angry, he didn't brush her aside like a bothersome fly and had sent the drunk on his way.

"Stay away from him, sis. Deacon Brannock has a reputation for showing no mercy."

"What does that even mean?" Was he a cruel man? She didn't feel that from him.

"Do I have to spell it out? He's ruthless. He crushes people. If a man doesn't pay his tab, Brannock takes him into the alley and they settle up one way or another."

"How would you know?"

"I hear talk."

Grace cut a glance at her brother who at age twenty so strongly resembled their father, Houston. They shared not only the same dark hair and eyes but muscular build and toughness. Houston once drove two thousand head of longhorns up the Great Western Trail, battling cattle rustlers and bad weather the entire way. Though she'd been just a babe, Grace had gone along with her mother. The harrowing stories of near-death situations were ingrained in her.

She'd survived for a reason. Wasting her life in foolish endeavor like needlepoint and cooking wasn't her idea of living a meaningful life. No, she had a purpose to fulfill, doing important work that changed lives.

Grace could see Crockett doing something like that too. And succeeding. By all accounts, he made a good living as a cattle buyer and kept a home in Fort Worth as well as on the Lone Star Ranch. Her brother seemed to have a forty-year-old mind in a young body. His life was set, and Grace envied that. She moved from one thing to another, never satisfied.

Crockett laid the mangled sign down and opened the door

of his home. "Sis, you have to stop getting in these fights that you can't win. You're worrying the family, especially Mama."

Her parents called her their crusader, always fighting against injustice of some sort. First it was saving her baby pig from slaughter. She'd made signs and sat in its pen until her father relented. That graduated to armadillos, the favorite tree where she sat to read, children's rights, and protesting the sale of wild horses and burros. You name it, she'd been involved. But this was different. Images of the battered women and children she'd tried to help over the past year flitted through her mind. Ava, Hilda, Beth Ann, and May. Beaten bloody and crying, but in the end staying with the only life they knew and preserving their marriage at such a great cost to them and their children.

The silent face of Libby Daniels frozen in death followed the endless line of those beaten. Grace stilled, recalling her best friend who'd married a charming man with a violent side and a taste for whiskey. She and Libby had gone to the ranch school together from age six. Libby had been the daughter of one of Grace's father's hands and had fallen in love with a drifter Houston hired to ride fence.

Less than six months after the wedding, Grace found Libby lying dead in the snow a few steps from headquarters.

Her vacant eyes staring heavenward still haunted Grace's sleep.

Grace blinked hard and whispered, "I can't stop. Lord, I wish I could, but I can't."

Her brother put his arms around her. "I don't understand what drives you. Go home and accept one of the dozens of marriage proposals you've gotten."

Not on a bet. Grace rolled her eyes. Her family was constantly trying to marry her off. On Sundays, she'd never known which cowboy would be sitting at their table, so she stayed away from the ranch as much as possible. She just couldn't take the cowboys' hound-dog eyes.

She laid her head on her brother's shoulder. "There's more for me than marriage and kids, Crockett. I have things I have to do."

He was silent for a long moment. Finally, he let out a long sigh. "Please be careful. Promise me."

She'd finally found the one cause that lodged in her gut, unable to shake. She was done with burying friends and acquaintances due to abuse. Shutting down these saloons and the flowing liquor would help save so many lives, marriages, and families. This would be her life's calling. This would settle the restlessness in her bones and bring calm and much peace to her soul. This would define her life.

"I'll do my best." She pulled away from Crockett and glanced through the window in the direction of the Three Deuces Saloon.

Deacon Brannock didn't scare her...that much.

About the Author

Linda Broday resides in the panhandle of Texas on the Llano Estacado. At a young age, she discovered a love for storytelling, history, and anything pertaining to the Old West. Cowboys fascinate her. There's something about Stetsons, boots, and tall, rugged cowboys that gets her fired up! A *New York Times* and *USA Today* bestselling author, Linda has won many awards, including the prestigious National Readers' Choice Award and the Texas Gold Award. Visit her at LindaBroday.com.

CHRISTMAS IN A COWBOY'S ARMS

Stay toasty this holiday season with heartwarming tales from bestselling authors Leigh Greenwood, Rosanne Bittner, Linda Broday, Margaret Brownley, Anna Schmidt, and Amy Sandas.

Whether it's a lonely spinster finding passion, an infamous outlaw-turned-lawman reaffirming the love that keeps him whole, a broken drifter discovering family in unlikely places, a Texas Ranger risking it all for one remarkable woman, two lovers bringing together a family ripped apart by prejudice, or reunited lovers given a second chance, a Christmas spent in a cowboy's arms is full of hope, laughter, and, most of all, love.

Everyone will be uplifted and believe in the joy and wonder of the season through these wonderful novellas.

—*RT Book Reviews*

For more from these authors, visit:

sourcebooks.com

Also by Linda Broday

Bachelors of Battle Creek
Texas Mail Order Bride
Twice a Texas Bride
Forever His Texas Bride

Men of Legend
To Love a Texas Ranger
The Heart of a Texas Cowboy
To Marry a Texas Outlaw

Texas Heroes
Knight on the Texas Plains
The Cowboy Who Came Calling
To Catch a Texas Star

Outlaw Mail Order Brides
The Outlaw's Mail Order Bride
Saving the Mail Order Bride
The Mail Order Bride's Secret
Once Upon a Mail Order Bride

Texas Redemption
Christmas in a Cowboy's Arms anthology
Longing for a Cowboy Christmas anthology